ALL MINE ENEMIES

THE COLIN BUXTON SERIES

BOOK 1

CC GILMARTIN

WWW.CCGILMARTIN.COM

COPYRIGHT

To all our family and friends for their support.

CONTENTS

Day 1

Autumn 1992

1

C olin smiled, tucking a shiny pebble picked up from the beach into his jeans pocket. He offered Lee a hand to help him off the motorboat, which bobbed awkwardly in the swelling sea. 'Careful,' he called out, as Lee wobbled on the short plank connecting the boat to the jetty. Grabbing his wrist, the touch of his skin was warm, reassuring.

Lee landed with a squeal of delight. 'Made it!' he said, clutching Colin and kissing him on the lips.

'Welcome to paradise.' Colin pulled him close; the two days spent apart had felt far longer.

With four large thuds, a flurry of suitcases came to rest beside them. Lee sneered at the squat, bearded skipper who'd sailed him across from the mainland. 'Thank you,' he snapped, before mouthing to Colin, 'for nothing.'

Lee's attitude said it all: the trip over had not gone well. Unsurprising. Outside the confines of London's theatre scene, he often appeared frazzled. Yet here he was – stylish suit, expensive Italian loafers, waxed leather case – being deposited on a Scottish island miles from anywhere. It occurred to Colin that secluded, Hebridean life might prove to be a challenge for Lee.

He'd arrived the day before with the rest of Lee's company. Pursued on their journey north by gathering storm clouds, it felt as though someone was intent on shrouding them in a large, black cloth. He looked up; if anything, the sky had grown even darker since yesterday. The island was little more than a glorified rock, half-a-mile long, quarter of a mile wide. With one house, no other inhabitants besides their group, and little in the way of walking, it was going to be intense.

'Why'd that megalomaniac insist on bringing us here?' Lee asked, his voice rising. 'I mean, we could have booked rehearsal space anywhere. There was this amazing space in Chelsea, close to fantastic restaurants, great transport links. But no, it had to be on an island in the middle of the freezing Atlantic.'

'I see you've come prepared,' Colin quipped, picking up the two largest bags.

'Watch that one.' Lee pointed to a maroon suitcase. 'The final appendices to the contracts are in it. Weeks of work,' he added, 'and I only finished them last night.'

Colin was already making his way to the line of Scots pine trees that began where the shore ended. 'We're up ahead. A few hundred yards. There's only a rudimentary pathway at the start, so you'll need to watch where you're stepping.' He nodded at the remaining bags. 'You'd better grab those.'

As the boat manoeuvred off, he watched Lee give a cursory wave, then discretely raise his middle finger.

'Now, now, Mr Murphy. Manners.'

'Ignorant twat,' Lee seethed, his mouth locked in a wide grin. 'He barely acknowledged me, yet he was giving me these side glances the whole way over. You know the type. It took all my patience not to blow a kiss at his ugly mug.'

'Enjoy your stay, boys,' he shouted in a thick Scottish accent. 'And watch out for the storm. There's a big one coming.' The skipper sniggered as he pointed the boat into the approaching waves, the in-joke very much his and his alone.

Lee rolled his eyes. 'I take it he's not referring to Lawrence?' Wiping the bottom of a suitcase clean, he held up his sand-covered hands. 'Really?'

'There's no sign of him yet.' Colin had half-expected him to arrive with Lee. 'We're this way.' He motioned to a clearing through the trees.

'No doubt he'll want to make a grand entrance,' Lee groaned, watching his step, sticking to the soft cushion of leaves rather than the earthy patches of mud. 'His agent didn't have a clue where he was. Said something about a drunken night out at *Annabel's* with some actress. Boring! I stopped listening.'

'Did you hear that?' Colin took hold of Lee's hand and felt his pulse racing.

Together, they took in their surroundings: above, the thick canopy of trees swayed, offering only glimpses of sky; all around them, the soft sound of birdsong mingled with the sea lapping against the shore. Heaven.

'We really are in the middle of nowhere, aren't we?' Lee's eyes widened, half in awe, the other half fearful of the unknown. 'Christ!'

'Accessible by private boat only. Nearest town's on the mainland, about sixty miles north of the slip you set off from. Or so the others were telling me. And the house. Wow! One of those big baronial things – turrets and stuff. But you'll be pleased to learn it's fully modernised; the rooms are comfy, loads of space, enormous beds, all en suite, open fireplaces. Superb views front and back. But the pièce de la résistance is the rehearsal space out in the barn.'

'Maybe Lawrence chose well after all,' Lee said, outwardly enjoying the picture Colin was painting. 'Though he did say it was pretty special – owned by some mega-wealthy acquaintance.' He stressed *acquaintance* like it was a dirty word.

'Jim and Georgie say the acoustics are incredible; you can literally hear someone whisper from one end of the space to the other. Oh, and there are mirrors all around the walls. Which will suit you.' He laughed, catching Lee's raised eyebrow. 'And if you all get fed up with each other, there's a huge partition you can pull over to create a cosy sitting area.'

'But they seem happy with everything so far?'

'Yes.' Lee's job was to know every little detail and Colin had become used to his exacting ways. 'Though it's odd. The father and son barely speak to each other.' He gave Lee a questioning look. 'There must be a story?'

'I've enough on my plate without worrying about their family squabbles.' Lee bumped playfully against Colin. 'Honestly, thank you so much for being here,' he said. 'I'd go mad if I had to stay here for two weeks with them all on my lonesome.'

'I wasn't doing anything else.' The truth was a little different. He'd almost committed to going on a package holiday to Majorca with two of his buddies from police college, but the prospect of being drunk from the moment they stepped off the plane till the moment they left held little attraction. When they'd both become single within a fortnight of each other, Colin had been looking for any excuse to bow out. Besides, after a minor bump in the road with Lee, spending time together seemed like the better option. 'Well, I am the new unofficial housekeeper, aren't I?'

'That local woman must be used to Hollywood types. Who gets paid five hundred a week for cooking and cleaning?' Lee pinched Colin's bum and skipped ahead. 'You were way cheaper.'

'Is that how I'll be getting paid?' Colin shouted after him, wishing his hands weren't so full. 'If so, we might need to renegotiate. Add in a few extra wee favours.'

Lee tripped on a fallen branch. 'Oops, nearly came a cropper there,' he yelped, standing up straight. 'You know, it could get ugly. Not everyone jumped at the chance. The mother, Georgie, dragged her heels. And Kath too. Lawrence does come with a reputation. In the end, we had to up their fees.'

'What? All of them?' This surprised Colin, as they seemed a genial lot.

'Strangely, Jim, the father was fine. Peter too. I hadn't heard that much about Jim, to be honest, but apparently he's one of the greatest actors of his generation. Who knew? His career never took off. But that's showbiz for you. I'm guessing there'll be a fair amount of neuroses lurking around there somewhere.'

'I spent last night playing cards with him; he seems sound. Pick any subject and he knows something about it. He's not like the rest. Actually listens. Doesn't complain either. You should have heard the others when they found out there was only one phone.'

'Well, it all needs to gel,' Lee said. 'Lawrence wouldn't budge on the cast. If they hadn't agreed, he swore he'd walk away. Made it very clear.'

'I suppose Hollywood royalty always gets what it wants.'

'Hollywood royalty can go take a running jump. Right, where's this house? Please tell me it's not far.'

'It's right in front of you.' Colin raised his arm and pointed through the trees.

A vast red sandstone house emerged before them. Castellated, with Gothic spires and lancet windows, it shimmered from the top of a slope. A labyrinth of pathways led to it, criss-crossing through elegantly laid out lawns and low hedges. The manicured garden sat incongruously against the backdrop of the rugged island.

'Bloody hell – this is amazing. And we're supposed to get work done here?' Lee asked, gazing at the central tower, which was crowned by a blue and white saltire.

'Afraid so,' Colin answered. 'Meanwhile, I'll be kicking

back and working my way through the pile of books I've brought.'

'Not on my watch.' Lee snorted, swinging one of the lighter cases at Colin, who dived out the way. As Lee pursued him towards the house, he shouted, 'You'll be washing pots from dawn till dusk, if I have my way.'

2

Kath watched Peter as he dozed on the bed. She gently circled his nipple, entranced by every slight movement of his smooth, toned body, freely bestowed on him whilst other mortals – saggy folds and ill proportioned – fought for the scraps. Though it had been a year since they first got together, sex still felt as exciting as ever. It was all the other stuff that remained a bit iffy.

He opened his eyes. 'You awake already?' he asked, brushing his fingers through his hair.

'Sounds like everyone's up and about.' She thrust her hand between his legs. 'Well, someone's definitely up.' She smiled. 'What would people think?'

Peter rolled over and grabbed his script. 'Not a word. You promised. It's our secret.' He looked at her sideways. 'Go on. Out you get. Before anyone sees.'

'We've lines to learn, Peter Selby.' She winked at him. 'It's why we came up here. Remember?' Kath tugged at his script, but he refused to let go.

Turning to a page where every second line had been highlighted in bright yellow, he muttered, 'We've got loads of time. Two weeks of no distractions.' He continued flicking through the pages, back and forth, studying them intently.

Kath got up and stared out of the window. 'I think Lee's arrived. I heard his boyfriend leaving about half an hour ago to go to meet him.' Not that she was spying, but Colin intrigued her. She couldn't put her finger on it, but he seemed contained, sorted, unlike most people in her daily life, who carried huge amounts of baggage. It was a relief to chat with someone who didn't mention their agent or their next job within the first five minutes.

Peter screwed up his face. 'Why's he even here? I mean, it's so unprofessional.'

'I think he seems nice. Made us dinner last night, didn't he? Told a few jokes. He seems fun.'

'A copper? With the Met?'

Kath didn't want to pigeonhole him. She'd definitely felt a connection. When Lawrence's name had been mentioned, and she'd made it clear she didn't want to speak about him, he had seamlessly changed the subject. Despite knowing nothing about her past or her career, it felt comforting, unlike Peter, who barely noticed the obvious contempt she had for Lawrence.

'How did those two worlds collide? Lee's a bit out there if you ask me – even for a theatre queen, he's camp. And Colin – well, PC Plod seems as dull as they come. Do you think the whole macho thing's a put on? Not what I was expecting from a *bent* copper.'

'Don't be mean. Opposites attract.' Kath folded back the curtains and caught Peter glancing at her naked body. She dashed over and slipped back beneath the covers. 'Look at us.'

'No, Kitty, I've too much to learn.' He winced as she tickled him. 'Stop it!' He wrestled her arm onto the mattress and held it there.

'Ouch! That hurts,' she screeched, pulling away and massaging her wrist.

'I bet you haven't even read the script.'

Pressing her body against his, she felt him respond. 'Once.' She pulled him closer. 'I prefer to learn it in rehearsals. But I've got the gist of the plot, everyone's motivations.'

'Mind, you're in, what, about two scenes or something? Hardly that difficult,' he said, before adding, 'for you.'

She pulled away from him, got out of bed, and began to dress. In the mirror, she watched his face contort as he returned to the script and mouthed his lines, each an exertion of Sisyphean proportions. His dyslexia meant he took ages learning lines, but instead of admitting it, he made excuses that the words got in the way of understanding the part.

'When's *he* arriving?' she asked.

Peter put down the script. 'This evening, I guess. Bizarre, isn't it? Exciting!'

'Lawrence Delaney is an actor like the rest of us.' She pulled up her knickers and grabbed her dress.

'One who's got awards flying out his arse,' Peter stressed, eyeing Kath's breasts. 'Let's face it, he's *not* like the rest of us.' He patted down the bedsheets, fiddling with his crotch, which was still semi-hard. 'And now, he's a friend.' He paused. 'Well, sort of.'

Having put on her dress, she slipped into her shoes. 'Right, that's me.'

'What was he like to act against?' Peter asked, his face serious, as though it was essential to know before Lawrence arrived.

'What are you talking about? You had scenes with him too.' Kath bent over to kiss him. 'Christ, you spent six weeks filming with him! I was only there for three.'

'Yeah, but it was just me in the background, not like you,' he said, pulling her onto the bed. 'One on one – all down and dirty.' He cupped her breasts, releasing one from her dress, and sucked her nipple. He stopped to look up at her. '*And* I had to share him with three others.'

She snuggled into him, relishing his smell. He used a particular aftershave that struck every chord with her. One sniff and that was it. Game over. As he placed his hand between her legs, she let it nestle there, before asking, 'Your mum and dad knew him, didn't they?'

Peter wriggled away, picked up his script, and studied it. 'Years ago. So?'

She peered at him; his body tilted from her. Suddenly, it felt like he was a million miles away. From hot to cold, in the blink of an eye, his natural disposition these days. Though, if she was being honest, he'd been like this since day one. She wasn't sure how much more she could put up with. Each day, trying to maintain his attention, his interest, felt exhausting.

'It's not like we spoke about anything meaningful,' he mumbled, still engrossed in his script, sipping the lukewarm coffee that had been lying on the bedside table. 'Just guy stuff. You know. Instantly forgettable.'

Kath stood and straightened her clothes. 'He chose you for this, didn't he?' she said, checking herself in the mirror. 'And your parents. So, you must have done something right.'

Peter peered over the top of the script and waited till she was facing him. 'Kath, maybe you can help me.' His warmth returned: he wanted something. 'There's this tricky scene I've got with Lawrence's character. I mean, I've read it a few times, and I think there's something a bit odd.'

Grabbing it, she scanned the page. Her eyes widened. 'Peter Selby, you're not five years old, are you? He wants to fuck you.' She threw the script back at him.

'Seriously?' Peter's face blushed, like she'd slapped him.

'How much of it have you read?' she asked, searching for her bag under the bed.

'The whole thing.'

'You mean, you've skipped to the parts where you've got lines?' She moved towards the door.

Peter stared at the pages. 'You think there's something sexual there?'

Holding onto the door handle, she spelt it out. 'The stage direction says: *He kisses you on the cheek, stops, waits, takes your hand, pulls away.* Grow up, Peter. It's the 1990s.'

Peter paused as he processed Kath's words. 'I'm not sure how I feel about that. I mean, he's so much older. Will people buy it? Me? Him?'

'You're unbelievable.' He was still leafing through the script as Kath cracked open the door. Whispering back the coast was clear, she saw him underline the aforementioned stage direction. 'See you downstairs.' She blew a kiss, but he didn't notice.

3

'$\bigcirc$ ome here, this isn't like you,' Jim said, wrapping his arms around her.

Georgie gave in to the comfort of his body. 'I don't get this woman. One moment she says one thing, the next another.' She threw the script aside. 'I hate the part. There, I've said it.' Sitting on the edge of the bed, she wiped the tears from her cheeks.

Jim plucked a tissue from the box on the bedside table. 'Why've you not said?'

'She's completely disagreeable. There's nothing redeeming about her at all.' Georgie fidgeted with her ring, twisting it around her finger, careful not to let it slip off. 'But I'm fine. Honestly, I'll find something to like about her.'

He pulled her closer. 'Nerves, love. Think about it, it'll be the first time in years we've worked together. And with Peter too. We'll help each other out. You know that.'

Georgie had spent a lifetime playing the greats – Shakespeare, Ibsen, Beckett, Pinter. She'd toured to every corner of the British Isles: seasons in Manchester, Glasgow, Edinburgh, Belfast. In her thirties and forties she'd focused more on new writing, at The Royal Court, the Bush, tiny little venues that sat sixty, the average age of the audience twenty. Throughout her professional career, work had always kept her busy. But aged fifty, when decent parts dried up, she decided to write and direct her own one-woman show, which she was still touring: a bit of chat, some singing, a few monologues from the classics. Audiences loved her. Performing came easily. Life, less so.

She looked at Jim, who was picking at the bedsheet, no doubt thinking the usual: *She does this every time, freaks out at the start of rehearsals, doubts herself.* 'Don't mind me, I'll be fine.'

'It's me who should be worried. I've not acted in over two years.' He took her hand and linked his fingers with hers, their wedding rings clinking against each other. 'I'm surprised I've not hit my stash of whisky yet.' He laughed. 'A bit of Dutch courage.'

'What are you on about?' she said. 'It's us dullards who find it difficult.' She lit a cigarette, picked up a glass ashtray and rested it on her knee, flicking the ash twice in quick succession. 'It's Peter I'm concerned about.'

Jim took the cigarette from her, placed it between his lips, and took a drag. 'Seriously?' He took another puff. 'He's twenty-five, got a few years' experience now, done commercials, films, that Godawful play we had to sit through in Chiswick. Who did he play? A priest training for a marathon?' He shook his head in disbelief. 'Peter's a big boy, love. He needs to find his own way.'

Georgie brushed away some ash that had landed on her trousers. 'This is going to be huge. His biggest role on stage by far.' She took back the cigarette and stubbed it out. 'Promise me you'll look out for him? In case, you know, he stumbles.'

'I'm his dad. Of course I will.' Jim handed her another tissue.

Georgie wiped her eyes. 'I still don't think I'm right for the part. And I'm not sure why he wanted me to play it.'

Lawrence had made it clear he wanted her and only her. Having stalled as the offer crept up and up, she finally agreed when it became impossible not to.

'Who are we to argue? He had carte blanche to choose any actors he wanted and he chose us. It's kismet. He'd worked with Peter, and it must have reminded him of the good times we had.'

Georgie interrupted Jim's trip down memory lane. 'It was six weeks of filming according to Peter. He told me they barely spoke. And the three of us was a lifetime ago.'

'Best buddies, I overheard him say on the phone. This business is about chance. Nepotism rules. So, why can't you accept that this time our luck was in?'

'And that's how you see it? So simply?' She waited for a response. 'That Lawrence suddenly remembered us and thought, *Hey, I'd love to work with those two again.*'

'Look, I see a decent part alongside an enormous star in a brilliant play that's going to the West End. Plus, I get paid each month and I get to spend time with my family.' He kissed her on the forehead. 'It's a no-brainer.'

'You know, Lawrence could walk away at any point. He might not even appear today. Remember his mood swings? Flying off the handle at the least little thing. And people don't change that much.' She was gazing at him, waiting for him to remember. But in truth, she knew he probably didn't. Typical Jim. Let everything go by him as if in a perpetual daydream. 'Where would that leave us?'

'We'd go back home and continue as normal,' he said. 'You're overthinking things, love. OK, it's true we can't take a break from each other. We're all stuck here together.' He looked out the window, across the lawn and beyond the trees towards the sea in the distance. 'But it's a beautiful place to be stranded. Things could be a lot worse. And the cherry on the cake: everyone's lovely.'

'So far,' Georgie added, grabbing her make-up bag. 'Until *he* arrives.'

'*His* name's above the title, so what he says goes,' Jim said. 'There's always a pecking order. That's how it works.'

Georgie sat at the dressing-table and applied new mascara. 'We've dinner soon, haven't we?'

'A couple of hours yet,' Jim said, stretching his back.

'Well, I'm going for a walk. Blow the cobwebs from this head of mine. See if that helps.'

'Want me to come with you?' Jim asked, grabbing his coat.

'No need. I won't be long.' Georgie got up and kissed him, the light catching the soft creases on his face. Kissing him again, he smiled faintly, bending his head to meet her hands. She stroked his hair and pulled away, leaving his head hanging. 'I'll be fine. I just need to get started, that's all.'

4

$\overline{\qquad\qquad}$

L ee entered the kitchen to unload the extra groceries Colin had requested. Marvelling at the sweet smell of the meat roasting in the oven and resisting a temptation to poke his head inside, he spotted Richard on a bench outside. He crossed over and tapped on the window, but saw he was lost in thought. *Best leave him.*

Placing the bags on the counter, he pulled off his coat and threw it over the first available chair. A large, imposing table sat in the centre of the space. Eight chairs were spaced around it, but it could comfortably sit another four. The kitchen was well-designed with modern, wooden cabinets set along three of the walls, providing drawers and plentiful storage. Plus, there was a small pantry: extra pots and pans, crockery, cutlery, fresh towels, kitchen gadgets, all neatly organised for any eventuality. Two huge sash windows looked out onto the surrounding trees, and to the side a heavy, glass-panelled door gave a clear view of the barn where they'd be rehearsing.

'Cost is not an issue,' Lawrence had insisted, refusing to even glance at Lee's budget projections. 'It's settled. I asked about the house and he said yes immediately. My friend wants us to be happy, that's all.'

'And you're sure we can have it for the full two weeks before we get into the theatre?' Lee had queried. He'd seen promises from supposed friends of Lawrence's fade to nothing before.

'Of course,' Lawrence replied, 'and the bill will be sent to me. My treat.'

'Are you sure?' Usually, rehearsal space would absorb a sizeable part of his budget. And although Lawrence's offer was very generous, Lee worried he'd pay for it in other ways.

'We go back a long way. Plus, he owes me a favour,' he'd added, rifling through sketches the designer had dropped off that morning. 'You can spend the extra money on the set. These designs are dreadful.'

The deal was done. Lee was remembering that whatever Lawrence wanted, he got.

'I can finish unpacking,' Colin announced as he entered, opening cupboard doors and checking where things went. 'Did you get the mozzarella?'

'Of course.' Lee held one up. 'Plus, extra lasagne sheets, full-fat milk, basil.' He was reciting Colin's instructions to the letter. 'Was that everything, Sir?' he said, giving a bow.

'Wait! I should give you a tip.' Colin kissed him on the lips. 'Now, back to the stables, boy.'

They both collapsed in laughter.

'You wish,' Lee said, 'though I do have a very fetching pair of breeches and a cloth cap that Sir might like.'

Colin continued unpacking. 'Why don't you go take a nap? I'll see to this.' He checked on the beef brisket and pork shoulder and reduced the oven temperature.

Grabbing his satchel, Lee sat. 'We're still short of a few thousand for the redesign; I need to get creative with the budget. I won't relax till it's sorted.'

'Can't it wait?' Colin placed his hand over the folder Lee

had taken out. 'Go on. You're knackered. Everyone arrived safely. What more is there to worry about?' He searched for a sharp knife.

'Everyone's arrived but the star turn. And you've not yet had the Lawrence experience, have you? Huge Hollywood smile, charms the socks off you, ends up a full-on tornado, before leaving you battered and bruised.'

'Pass me those onions.' Colin motioned to a bowl on the counter. 'Then, get ye to bed, laddie.'

'Catch!' Lee threw the bag over.

Colin ripped it open and began peeling.

'But it's *him* I'm most worried about.' Lee stared out the window at Richard, who remained sitting on the bench, gazing to the horizon.

'Who's that?' Colin asked, starting to chop.

Lee nudged his head to outside. 'Don't look! He'll think we're talking about him.'

'You mean Richard?' Colin oiled the pan and threw in the diced onion. 'He kept to his room last night. I mean, he had dinner with us, but didn't say much.'

'Exactly. And he's the one directing all of this.' Lee tapped the window again, this time receiving a smile and a wave. 'You know Lawrence phoned him from the States at two in the morning last week and went off on one? More last minute changes to the script. The poor writer was doing the best she could to get the new draft done on time, changing every little thing Lawrence wanted. Even then he went apeshit. Said he wanted him off the production, that if he couldn't control the writer, he'd no chance with the cast.'

'They'll sort it out. Shall I do another onion?'

Lee nodded. 'There're seven of us, aren't there?' He crossed to where Colin was standing, softened his voice to a hush and kept an eye out in case Richard entered. 'There's shady history there if you ask me. Richard tells me everything

– such a leaky sieve – but he's kept schtum about what's gone on between the two of them in the past.'

'You can't know everything, Mr Producer Control Freak.' Colin wiped the blade of extra bits of onion. 'Christ, that one was strong. Look, real tears.'

'Here.' Lee tore off a piece of kitchen roll and dabbed Colin's eyes. 'Better?'

'Right,' Colin said, waving him away with a wooden spoon. 'Out of my way, otherwise we'll be eating at midnight.'

'I'll get to the bottom of it.' Lee gave him a conspiratorial look. 'Wait and see; I have my ways.'

'I'm sure you will, but scamper.' Colin continued stirring. 'We're eating in a couple of hours and I've still loads to do.' He grabbed a handful of mushrooms and washed them.

Lee edged closer. 'And I take it he didn't have a drink?' he asked, lowering his voice further.

Colin had been asked in advance to keep an eye on Richard's drinking habits. 'Sober as a judge,' he whispered back. 'Unlike the rest of us,' he added, recalling the four shots of whisky he'd had at the end of the night.

'Long may that last. Right, I'd better go see him. Shout if you need any help.'

5

Steps from the kitchen led down into a small, cobbled courtyard, partly enclosed by a series of low outbuildings. Above it, trees swayed in the rising breeze, and beyond that, the silhouette of the barn roof loomed. Set against an ivy-draped wall, the wooden bench had been perfectly positioned to take advantage of the sea view. Despite the dark cloud hanging above the island, Lee hoped to catch the dying embers of the setting sun.

Richard was chewing at his fingers but stopped as Lee approached, stuffing his hands inside his pockets. 'That sky doesn't bode well,' he pointed out, half-standing to give Lee a tight hug.

'It was the same coming over.' Lee joined him on the bench. 'It looked as though the heavens might open. And the water was so still and dark. Eerie. I've never seen anything like it.' He took out his cigarettes and offered Richard one.

'I've given up,' he stated, eyeing the packet.

'Same here, but not for these two weeks. Stuff that!' Lee lit one. 'I need something.' They sat for a few minutes looking through the trees, to the sea beyond. He loved spending time with Richard; they'd such an easygoing way of interacting –

unusual in the theatre, where people often bristled from the fierce competition.

'Your man makes a fantastic roast chicken.'

'Perfect roast potatoes too.' Lee loved how Colin would spend hours preparing a Sunday lunch, only for them to devour it in minutes. 'I'm sorry I missed it.'

Richard nudged him. 'Bit of a catch, I'd say. His own teeth too.'

'The top half, at least.'

They both laughed.

'Oh, go on.' Richard put his hand out. 'Give us one. It won't kill me.'

Lee lit another cigarette and passed it over.

Richard clamped his lips around it and inhaled deeply, like it was pure oxygen. 'Four weeks since I last had a ciggie and it tastes bloody amazing. Well, it tastes awful, but you know what I mean.'

Lee's gaze followed the smoke as it rose from Richard's mouth, a lingering corkscrew floating off into the evening air. He had a look of a man condemned, waiting for his last meal to be delivered. 'Look, I know you've some concerns, but I'm handling Lawrence.'

Richard stared; his expression inscrutable. 'Really?' He gave a short laugh. 'You'd be the first.'

'His ego enters the room before he does,' Lee said, 'but once it's stroked a few times, it disappears.'

'Did I ever tell you that our paths crossed years ago?' Richard checked to see they weren't being overheard. 'The stories about that man would make your hair curl.'

And there it was. The Richard he knew and loved. Forgot nothing. Forgave even less. Spilling the beans way sooner than he anticipated. 'So our meeting at the Corinthian bar wasn't the first time you'd met?' Lee casually flicked his ash to the ground. 'I mean, I knew you'd a couple of friends in common, but not that you hung about in the same circles.'

'One friend,' Richard stressed. He took a puff of his cigarette, discarded it, and helped himself to another. 'One very deceased friend.'

'You knew each other well then?' Lee edged nearer as Richard settled himself.

'Lawrence was, shall we say, very close with this friend of mine.' He paused, as though waiting to be asked to continue. He then lowered his voice. 'Screwed my friend over, in every sense.'

My friend? If Lee wanted more, he'd need to press him. 'Richard, it's not 1952.'

'Apologies, he…' Emphasising each word, Richard clearly spelt out what he'd been trying to say. 'Lawrence Delaney screwed my friend Bernard over well and truly. Destroyed him.'

'I didn't know Lawrence was bi.' Lee had heard some gossip but that was the case for most actors. He hadn't set much store by it.

'In those days he was … what's the expression? Gay for pay, is it?'

'Honestly?'

'This was decades ago, of course. But with those looks, men were lining up to make him offers.'

'He and your friend – Bernard – they were in a relationship?'

Richard took another puff of his cigarette and threw it down before grinding it out with his foot. 'Bernard O'Neill. And yes, they most certainly were.'

'That name's familiar.' Lee thought for a second. He looked at Richard. 'You don't mean the West End producer?'

'Got it in one.'

'Bloody hell. Mr Theatre himself.' Lee wondered how he hadn't heard this before.

'Had four plays on in the West End in one year. Two on Broadway.'

'Didn't he...?'

'Hang himself?' Richard nodded. 'Oh yes. Backstage at the Corinthian. Somewhat over the top, even for my tastes. The story goes, and I can verify it, that Lawrence ditched him to shack up with some Hollywood producer. Proper big time. Instrumental in kick-starting Lawrence's career out there. But the sad thing is, Bernard, the silly old queen, had fallen for him. Hook, line and sinker.'

'This business. I dunno. It messes with your head.'

'And as luck would have it, Lawrence was the main benefactor of his will. Half a million. Or close to. And in those days, that was a lot. Still is. Though not for him. Pin money now.'

'Wow! That's what I call a career move.'

Richard sat back and stared him straight in the eye, before stating, 'Bernard's family got next to nothing, you know. It devastated them.'

Lee noticed the tears well up. 'Sorry, I was being flippant.' He offered Richard another cigarette, but he refused. 'So, Lawrence Delaney has always been a bit of a bastard?'

'Didn't even make the funeral. Which I can just about understand. But when we met for that drink a few months ago, you won't remember me saying, but it was at The Corinthian: the same theatre where Bernard hung himself. You won't remember, but I made some pointed comments.'

'I noticed something.'

'I mentioned Bernard's name twice. Deliberately. Bernard died here, I said. Do you remember Lawrence? Bernard O'Neill? He didn't move a muscle. Sat with that look on his face, like butter wouldn't melt. The least he could have said was, *Oh yes, poor Bernard. Terrible, wasn't it*? I wanted to say, *Do you remember him at all? How he pleaded with you — said he loved you*? What sort of person forgets a thing like that?'

'Sorry, Richard, I don't know what to say. When I put your name forward, he said he'd seen the Albee double bill you did with Glenda, plus the Rattigan with whatshisname?'

'Trevor fuckwit,' he deadpanned.

'He thought they were great, and he'd follow my lead. I knew nothing about this. I promise.'

Richard shivered and pulled his coat tight around his shoulders. 'I need this job. That fucker's gone away and put two and two together, decided I know too much and is finding any excuse to make that five.'

Lee gave him a hug. 'Well, I've got your back.'

'You're a wonderful man,' Richard replied, pulling away first. 'But watch, that one can turn on you in an instant.' He snapped his fingers. 'Be warned.' He got up.

Lee noticed how much weight he'd lost since they'd last met. 'We can look out for each other,' he said. 'If he crosses the line, let me know.'

Richard wrapped his scarf around his neck. 'It's freezing out here. Remember,' he emphasised, 'don't trust a word he says.'

'Me? Trust an actor?' Lee smirked. 'I wouldn't wipe my arse with one.'

Richard laughed as he sauntered off through the garden, towards the sea, shouting in a low, theatrical voice, 'I'll be back for dinner. Tell your gorgeous hunk of a man I wouldn't miss his lasagne for anything.' And with a little wave, he was gone.

6

Occasionally glancing at Lee and Richard chatting away like old friends, Colin combined the shredded beef brisket and pork shoulder with the sautéed onions and mushrooms in the tomato sauce.

Despite the moans and groans, this was Lee in his element; surrounded by creative types and providing a space for talent to flourish. As well as the exhausting task of raising the finance, being a producer meant listening, giving advice when asked, seeking the best solutions. It also meant mopping up tears when required. And that seemed to happen a lot – way more than Colin thought possible from professionals.

He saw how people respected Lee, were even a little scared of him. He had a way of fixing you with that penetrating stare – framed by Armani glasses of course – and picking away at every detail till it satisfied him you both agreed. It wasn't ruthlessness, Lee protested, just good business. Only the previous week, he'd overheard him refusing to give in to Lawrence's ever-changing list of demands, this time about his dressing-room in the theatre being redecorated to his exacting standards. Lee had stood his ground, pointing out that the other investors would not indulge Lawrence's whims, but if he was willing to provide the £10,000 himself, he'd be happy to oversee the work. All this from a thirty-year-old with no formal training, just a huge dream and razor-sharp instincts.

Colin hadn't heard Kath enter the kitchen. When she opened the fridge door, he jumped.

'Sorry, I didn't mean to startle you,' she said.

Colin smiled. 'You didn't. I was miles away.'

She leaned over, taking in the aroma. 'Smells good.'

'My epic lasagne with a heap of garlic.' He offered her a taste.

She took the spoon. 'Mmm, that's intense. No kissing for us tonight.' She returned to poke about in the fridge, pushing aside the piles of food they'd filled it with the previous day. 'I was sure there was some fizz.'

'I stuck it in the pantry to make room,' Colin said, pointing her in the direction.

She pulled open the pantry door. 'Where?'

'There's a wee fridge at the back,' he said. 'Over to the right.'

He listened to her rummage around. 'Amazing!' she shouted back.

'They should be nice and cold by now.'

'Lifesaver. I thought someone had necked it already.'

He laughed. 'What? The entire case?'

'I love my fizz.' She came back with a bottle held aloft in celebration. 'Join me?'

'Is it after six?'

'Two minutes to. I can pour really slowly,' she said, finding two champagne flutes in the first cupboard she came to. 'Bingo!'

Colin smiled again. This girl was easy to like.

Ripping through the foil with her fingernails, she expertly popped the cork and decanted its contents into the glasses.

'Why the hell you agreed to come here with us lot, I'll never know.'

'Anything to get away from the grind of police work.' Coming at the end of a summer of recession-fuelled robberies and violent crime, the idea of two weeks in the wilderness seemed idyllic. Over the last few months, he'd seen enough blood and guts to last a lifetime.

'Oh, the thrill of a man in uniform,' Kath giggled, taking her first sip.

'Ill-fitting polyester more like,' Colin said, enjoying the cool bubbles drifting down his throat.

'I know some who'd pay good money for that frisson.'

'Not me.' He held out his glass. 'Cheers.'

'Cheers big ears.' She sipped too fast, and the bubbles rose in her mouth. Burping, the liquid squirted out from the corner of her mouth. 'Such a lady, eh?'

Colin went back to stirring, noticing Kath pour more champagne for them both. 'Shouldn't you be learning lines?' he asked. 'I take it that's what everyone else is doing?'

'Have you seen the script?' She threw back a mouthful of champagne.

'Lee gave me a copy. I only glanced at it, to be honest.'

She held up one hand. 'I've five brief scenes. It's hardly *Medea*.'

'Five brilliant scenes,' he interrupted. 'Plus, a killer monologue to close the first act.'

She gave him a quizzical look. 'Thought you'd just glanced at it?'

His face burned. 'I had some free time.'

She crossed to the fridge and pulled out a block of cheddar. Slicing a bit off, she devoured it while gulping down a few more mouthfuls of champagne. 'You see,' she started, her words mangled by the cheese, 'I don't know about you, but I learn by doing. Honestly, sometimes rehearsals bore me to death. People try to think too hard. If you feel it, do it. What can go wrong?'

He wasn't sure if she wanted him to agree with her. But he knew he was ill-equipped to respond. Manoeuvring around her, he found a huge lasagne dish. 'I've no idea how you remember all those lines. I can barely remember my pin number.'

'That can't be true. You thrashed most of them at poker last night.' She stood beside him. 'Here, let me help you.'

'Ah, but not you.' As Colin spooned the meaty sauce into the dish, Kath handed him the lasagne sheets.

She giggled. 'Taught by a grande dame of the theatre on my first job.' She nudged him. 'Tell me, how did you and Lee meet? He didn't commit a crime, did he?' she asked, her face eager for some juicy gossip.

'Now, that would be telling,' he said, his face expressionless. He took some sheets from her, whispering, 'It's confidential.'

She stood back, gawping at him.

His face cracked into a huge smile.

'Stop it!' she cried.

'It was far more mundane. I was out at *Heaven* – the gay club in Charing Cross?' Colin said, applying a top layer of béchamel sauce.

'I know it well.' She'd decided to grate the cheese for him. 'I've had some wild times there.' She looked up. 'Is that enough? I should do it all, shouldn't I?'

Colin nodded, leaning back against the worktop, allowing her to finish. 'I saw Lee come in with a bunch of friends. I totally clocked him, but he looked right through me. Then, he and his mates practically took over the dancefloor, each move perfectly synchronised to Madonna. It took me ages to pluck up the courage. My hands were sweating buckets, assuming I'd be given the once-over, spat out and sent packing. But I thought to myself, *Nothing ventured, nothing gained*. So, with my best attempt at *voguing*, I got up as close to him as possible, waited for that perfect moment when I could smile or make eye contact. That sort of thing. But suddenly, I felt this hand grabbing me. *His*. Pulled me right up to his chest, pushed his face right into mine, shouted, "You're gorgeous" at the top of his voice, and started snogging me. And that was that. Seven months later, he's still dancing loudly and outrageously to Madonna and I'm still sweating profusely.'

'Well done on making it work.' Kath clinked glasses with him.

'We have our moments.' He wondered whether to trust her. Her bright smile suggested she was eager to hear more. He took a breath. 'It's not perfect. After a couple of months, things weren't working, so we took a break.'

'Oh!'

'It lasted about a week though. I think the seriousness of it all freaked us out a bit.' He picked up his glass and took a sip. 'But we're good now. He's the best thing that's ever happened to me.' He blushed. 'Right, that's enough about me. What about you? Do you have anyone special?' he asked, setting the temperature on the Rayburn.

The sound of footsteps bounding downstairs interrupted them. Peter entered, wearing only his boxers and a vest, sniffing the air. 'Wow. Something smells fucking fantastic.' He picked up the bottle of champagne and guzzled down a mouthful. 'Ah, that's better.'

'Peter, you do realise we've got company? You know you're not in that tiny flat of yours surrounded by beer bottles? That you're with actual grown-ups?' She passed him a glass, which he filled to the brim. 'I was asking Colin how he met Lee.'

'Oh, right,' Peter replied, opening the fridge and taking out some leftover chicken, which he proceeded to stuff in his mouth. 'How?'

'Clubbing,' Kath added.

'Oh, right? Cool.' Detaching himself from the fridge, Peter was now scouting the room. 'Kitty, did you see where I put my shirt?'

'What? Am I your mother?' she said, 'And I'm Kath. Not Kitty.'

Standing in the middle of the room, his face screwed up, his lip petulantly sticking out, he waited. 'Tell me, Kitty. Sorry, Kath.' When she wouldn't, he turned to Colin. 'Can you ask her to tell me? She's doing it to annoy me now.'

Colin busied himself with cleaning down the surfaces. Meanwhile, Peter dived out the door.

'I think it's still on top of the suitcase in the hall,' she shouted after him, sticking out her tongue.

'I take it you two have worked together before?'

'We've known each other for ages. National Youth Theatre stuff, drama school.' She poured another drink. 'He hasn't changed. He's always been a prick.' She poured herself more champagne. 'I'd not seen him in a while, but last year we did a film together. *Cobalt Dawn*.' She held her nose, implying it was a stinker.

'The one with Lawrence?' Colin asked, intrigued to hear more. If the theatre world was outwith his experience, the movie world seemed like another planet.

'Yeah,' she said, scraping the residue of the sauce from the pot with her finger and licking it. 'But I only filmed for a few weeks. Peter did way more. It was all a bit crappy if truth be told. Huge budget. Shite script. Director who didn't know what he was doing. The usual.' She poked her head out the door, checking on Peter.

'And the two of you aren't a...?

She shrieked, 'Christ, no! That would be like incest or something.' She stepped back into the kitchen. 'He's coming back!'

Peter re-entered, holding a white shirt and a pair of trousers.

'I take it they were lying on top of the suitcase?' she asked. 'The same one you've not even bothered to take to your room?'

He made an exasperated face and began to dress. 'How the fuck they got there I don't know.'

'This morning you were pulling out stuff, looking for something to wear. Don't you remember?' She strolled towards him and fixed his collar.

Colin observed the bickering, wondering who they thought they were kidding; the glint in Kath's eye suggested she enjoyed the deception. Peter even had his own pet name for her.

'I need to look the part.' Peter was checking himself in the glass door of an antique dresser. He spun round. 'Is this OK?' In his pants and socks, he'd been like any other jock, but with the added flourish of a white shirt and some black trousers, he stood transformed – a matinee idol stepping out from the silver screen. He smiled, like he was reading both their minds. 'One button or two?'

'Just the one.' Kath stood facing him and buttoned up the second one.

Colin paid attention to them both: how Kath pressed against him, licking her finger to dampen a tuft of hair, how he squirmed and shied away. 'Look after the lasagne for me, will you?' he said. 'I've set it to low, so it shouldn't burn.'

'Sure,' Kath replied. 'I'll keep checking.' She went back to adjusting Peter's clothes.

Smiling awkwardly, Colin left the room.

7

Georgie stepped from the house and breathed in the fresh air. To be away from the smog and buzz of London was a treat. The only break she and Jim had managed in the last year had been a trip to Devon to visit her elderly parents. Small jobs were forever cropping up – voiceovers, development workshops, table readings of new work (her bread and butter) – so finding time to get away was a luxury. Yet, what started out as an opportunity for some well-earned fun in the sun ended with them playing endless hands of bridge in her parents' front room. Two days was all she could stand.

Now, with only the sea, the sky and the earth beneath her feet for company, Georgie imagined herself adrift from the rest of the world on this tiny island. Jim had mentioned there were walks across the rocks to the north, but she hadn't brought the footwear for that. She would explore the woodland instead. Taking in another breath of air, she scanned the horizon. There was no other land visible in any direction; it felt like she'd travelled to the edge of the earth. In different circumstances, sixteen hours of travel could have taken her to

India or Brazil. But instead, two weeks on a private Hebridean island would certainly do.

The journey north had propelled her into her favourite time of year – the end of summer – the trees still in full leaf, a slight nip in the air, the sense of autumn lurking around the corner. It reminded her of precious times when Peter was a baby and the hours she'd spent pushing his pram around Regent's Park. Bliss.

Taking off her cardigan, she strolled through the woods, listening to oystercatchers screech against the constant swish and crashing of the waves. As far as jobs went, things could be a lot worse. No freezing church hall, no household distractions on returning home. She could take her morning stroll right there on the beach, lay down her yoga mat, enjoy the gentle lap of the waves as she exercised. She had it all planned out.

Spreading her cardigan on the grass, where it stepped down to the beach, she sat amongst the tall, overhanging trees. Despite her reservations about working with Lawrence, she was grateful for the gig. At an age when the offer of major roles was few and far between, her agent Lisa had begged her to reconsider her initial refusal. But the very mention of his name had been triggering; her insides lurching at the memory.

'It's a four-month run,' Lisa had told her. 'Longer if it's a hit. And anyway, Lawrence won't hang around. He'll be replaced by someone lesser known as soon as.'

Used to seeing *Lawrence Delaney* emblazoned on billboards, his face staring out from magazines, her mind could trick itself and forget they'd once been close. But never for long.

'This is a big deal,' Lisa had pressed. 'He's specifically asked for you and Jim to play these parts. Meeting Peter on the set of the film was the catalyst – he felt it was meant to be

– he wants to rekindle the connection you had all those years ago.'

Each word stung. Of course, she could see through it; she knew Lawrence too well. There was always an ulterior motive. He hadn't got to where he was by being Mr Nice. But using Peter's career as bait – and Jim's for that matter – was tantamount to blackmail.

'I'll have to think about it,' Georgie had replied, her fingers coiled around the telephone cable.

'Speak it over with Jim. See what he says.'

'I know what he'll say already. He hasn't worked in the longest time.'

'The rehearsal period is four weeks of your life, Georgie,' Lisa had insisted, her voice rising.

'Plus a few hours seven times a week for at least four months,' Georgie pointed out.

But Lisa wasn't taking no for an answer. 'It could give you time to concentrate on your writing. Look at the offer, Georgie. The part's interesting, the money's astonishing. I think you should do this.'

Lisa was right. Most actresses would kill for the part. The writer had done a great job. A stab of guilt hit her – lying to Jim, pretending the part wasn't up to scratch. And he'd bought it. The play was excellent and deep down she was proud to be part of it. If only Lawrence wasn't behind it all.

She stretched out, her cheeks hot, her palms sweaty. Curling into a ball, she closed her eyes.

It was the sound of voices that forced them open; a burst of laughter cutting through the silence – two men chuckling, like old chums on a night out. She sat up, knowing what this meant. Lawrence. The last to arrive. Deliberate. No doubt his chat with the skipper would have been rehearsed: every look and gesture, every little wink and touch of the arm.

She remembered it all so well.

Scrambling back to the shelter of the woods, she hid

behind the nearest Scots pine. The green canopy shrouded her in darkness as she scanned the shoreline. 'Shit!' she hissed, catching her hand against a sharp branch.

Lawrence's outline, athletic and assured, shimmered in the distance as he gripped hands with the skipper: his fist crushing him with charm, the usual bullshit of grabbing a drink later that, for some reason, people lapped up. With a wave, Lawrence picked up his pile of suitcases and strode off towards the house. For a moment, she worried he might look her way. She lurched back, pressing herself against the trunk, hoping and praying he wouldn't notice her. The crunch of his footsteps on the shingle ebbed away as he reached the edge of the woodland, preferring to avoid the path and make his way across the lawn. A fading 'Cheerio!' echoed as the boat manoeuvred off.

Safe for now, she thought, observing how absurd the sight of a middle-aged woman hiding from a Hollywood film star on an island in the middle of the Atlantic Ocean might seem.

The air felt cooler, and she noticed the wind had picked up a little. She put on her cardigan and buttoned it, heading further into the wood, confident that Lawrence had disappeared from view and the coast was now clear.

8

Peter stood in front of the mirror, grinning. 'Lawrence, long time, no see,' he said to his reflection. He shook his head and undid the second button on his shirt. Stepping back, he pulled a more serious face, but his closed mouth made him look angry. In an instant, he reverted to a smile, which looked forced. A knock on the door interrupted his preparations and he debated whether to answer.

'Peter, it's me,' whispered Kath.

Opening the door, he grabbed her by the arm. As he pulled her inside, the champagne bottle and glasses she held clinked against each other. Froth dripping from her fingers, she looked at him wide-eyed, surprised everything was still intact. 'Peter! Fuck's sake!' she snapped. 'Careful!'

'What are you doing here?' he said in a hushed tone. 'Haven't we discussed this?'

Placing the bottle and glasses on the chest of drawers, Kath sat on the edge of his bed and rubbed her arm. 'You're too rough.'

'Sorry,' he said, taking her arm. 'Let me take a look.' He kissed it. 'You know it's not the best time.' He kissed her again. 'And we agreed, didn't we?' He stopped kissing and stared at her. 'Kitty?'

She pulled away and sat further up on the bed. 'Did we? We've so many rules it's hard to keep up.'

Peter filled a glass for himself and took a sip. 'They're not just *my* rules.'

'Don't I get any?' She stretched out her hand.

'Christ's sake.' He poured another glass and gave it to her. 'Haven't you had enough?'

'I've not even started,' she said, taking the glass. 'Cheers big ears.' She patted the bedspread. 'Come here.' She patted it again. 'And don't sulk!'

'Who's sulking?' he cried out. 'Christ!' He joined her and together, side-by-side, they sat in silence, facing the mirror.

'Sorry.'

'Stop it. You're not.' He pinged his finger against the flesh of her leg.

'If the wind changes, Peter Selby, your face will stay like that.' She took his lips and sculpted them into a smile. 'There. Much better.'

'Don't,' he snapped, and threw back the rest of the champagne.

'OK, if you don't want to play, Mr Sourpuss,' she said, 'I'm out of here.' Moving from the bed, she picked up the half-empty bottle of champagne. 'Oh, I meant to say.' She stood in the middle of the room, ensuring she could see his reaction. 'Your mate's arrived.'

Peter stared at her. 'And? What do you want me to say?'

'I thought he was your best friend. All kissy kissy, huggy huggy,' she teased.

'Why'd you keep saying that?'

Using her free hand, she rubbed her body. 'I'm so happy to see you, Lawrence. What can I do for you, Lawrence? Want to see my really fit body, Lawrence?' She rubbed so hard she pulled down part of her top.

'Check yourself in the mirror, Kitty.' He laughed. 'Your tit's slipping out.'

She popped it out. 'Ta da,' she sang.

Peter threw himself back on the mattress and groaned. Kath rushed towards the bed, getting on top, letting her dress envelop his face.

He pushed it aside. 'We only did it a few hours ago.'

'But it's the only thing that makes you smile these days.' She wrestled with her knickers.

Taking the full weight of her body, he massaged her buttocks and thighs. 'Wanna make me smile, do you?'

'Not bothered.' She pressed herself deeper into his body. 'Just minding my own business.' She took his hand and sucked his thumb. 'Going through my lines in my head.'

'No one can know yet, Kitty,' he said, meeting her eyes. 'Seriously. Not during rehearsals or the run,' he pleaded. 'Afterwards, we can tell everyone.'

'You ashamed of me or something, Peter Selby?' She pushed his head back, watching him stare at her.

He took her tongue fully in his mouth. As he grabbed for his zip, there was another knock on the door. 'Fuck,' he muttered, pulling out from under her.

'Peter, it's Dad.'

They jumped off the bed, fixing themselves and straightening the bedclothes.

'Kath, are you there too?' Jim shouted, knocking again. 'Maybe you can both help.'

'Yes Dad, we're going through lines. Give us a sec.'

As though they'd rehearsed it, Kath scattered a script on the bed as Peter made his way to the door, pulling it open. 'The champagne,' Kath warned him.

But it was too late. The door was already open. 'Hey Dad.'

'The two of you must know your lines by now.' Jim stepped into the room.

'You'd have thought, eh?' said Peter.

'They're not going in,' Kath added.

'Is that champagne?' Jim strolled over towards the bottle and picked it up. 'The good stuff, eh?'

'Want a glass?' Kath looked around for a spare. 'Here, have mine.' She filled it and handed it to him.

Peter sat on the bed. 'What's wrong, Dad?'

'Eh?'

'You said you needed to speak to us.'

'Nothing important.' He wandered over to the window, checking the view. 'Lawrence has arrived and he wants to take over the large sitting room downstairs. He wants to use it as his bedroom-cum-study. Perfectly good bedrooms up here, so don't know why. Says he'll take the downstairs loo. There's a shower, toilet, washbasin in there. Everything he needs. Apparently, he walked into the front room, fell in love at once, and asked if a bed could be moved in.' Jim turned to leave. 'Would either of you mind?'

'No,' said Peter, checking with Kath. 'It's fine with me.'

'Kath?' Jim asked.

'He can do as he wants.' She opened the door. 'Isn't he paying for all this?'

'I didn't want to say.' Jim hovered beside her. 'Didn't want to ... you know.'

'Reinforce the point we're his minions?' Spotting her knickers on the floor, she kicked them under the bed without Jim seeing. 'Right, I'm off. 'Thanks for helping me with my lines, Peter. Another session soon?'

'Yes, sure, of course ... whenever you want,' he stuttered, fixing her with a stare.

'By the way, how is Lawrence?' she asked. 'I mean, is he happy to be here? It's just that, on set, he was distracted the whole time. Remember, Peter?'

'He's raring to go. Knows the script inside out. Well, says he does,' Jim smiled. 'We'll see.'

'For my money, I thought he was amazing on set,' Peter

gushed. 'Treated us as equals.' Realising both were looking at him oddly, he picked up his script and sat on the bed.

'See you both at dinner,' said Kath, leaving.

Peter sensed his dad had something further to say but was reluctant to speak. Over the years, they'd developed a habit of allowing the moments to tick away until there was no time left for any familiarity.

'Would you mind helping with the bed?' Jim asked.

'What?' Peter grumbled, not looking up.

'Lawrence's bed,' Jim repeated, reminding him why he was there. 'We need to move it from upstairs to the sitting room.'

'Now?' Peter turned a page, scanning how many lines he had.

'Son...'

'Sure. Whatever,' he mumbled. 'Give me ten minutes. I need to finish this.'

'I can help, you know.' Jim moved towards him.

'What? You're not even in the scene.'

'It doesn't matter. I can play one of the other parts.' He reached out for the script. 'Here, let me see.'

Peter pulled the script close to his chest. 'It'll confuse me,' he said, avoiding his dad's eye contact.

'I've been where you are hundreds of times, son. Let me help you.'

'Not recently you haven't.' Peter glared at his dad. 'Anyway, I'm better doing it by myself.'

'OK.' Jim backed away. 'Suit yourself. But you know where I am if you need me.'

'Sure.' He forced a smile. It ached, like someone had taken a knife and slit both corners of his mouth.

9

From the dining room window, Lee took in the view. Pressing his face against the glass, he was certain he'd spotted a shadow moving amongst the trees. He continued to look, searching for anything untoward. Nothing. Probably a trick of the light. He hoped so, as Lawrence had been adamant he needed complete solitude. 'The company and no one else,' he'd emphasised. 'I want no outsiders intruding on the work,' he went on to stress, saying isolation would help rehearsals. 'It echoes the main theme of the play,' he mused. 'And who doesn't enjoy indulging in a bit of method acting?'

Once the accommodation and rehearsal space on the island had been booked, it took all Lee's courage to ask whether Colin could join them. 'He's very low maintenance,' he'd explained, 'and a super cook.' On a logistical level, it would make life far simpler for everyone if Colin handled the food, but from a personal point of view, it would help Lee retain his sanity. Lawrence's exhausting demands – everything from script rewrites to how he liked his coffee – were never-ending. Obsessed with detail, he'd go over the minutest of points again and again. Keeping up with him wasn't easy.

'I'm told he's a police officer,' Lawrence had stated.

'Yes. With the Met.'

His face lit up. 'I suppose the added protection wouldn't do any harm.'

He went on to recount a story about a woman who'd recently jumped into his car while he was sitting alone at traffic lights in LA. 'Some crazy. Shouting I was the devil. Fortunately, she was won over with a signed photo. Next time I might not be so lucky.'

Lee knew that Lawrence's team had upped security recently. His suspicion was, rather than to support the production, Lawrence's insistence on the secluded island was more about giving him a break from his more devoted fans and assorted stalkers. 'Fame's a bitch!' Lawrence had exclaimed. 'You become a target for every bastard's fucked-up shit.'

Lee had thought it an exaggeration, but barely five minutes after his star's arrival he was already jittery, imagining any slight movement was a potential maniac ready to pounce on Lawrence.

A voice bellowed down the hallway. 'Lee? A word?' Lawrence's demands were about to begin.

'Chrissake,' Lee muttered, caught off-guard by the booming voice. 'I'll be with you in a minute,' he called back.

Heavy footsteps marched towards the dining room; Lawrence popped his head around the door. 'My room. Now!' he roared, grabbing the phone in the hallway and dragging it along to his room, a master with his wayward dog.

'Yes, I'll be one minute.' Lee poured himself a glass of water, listening to Lawrence stomp back down the hall. He waited a full two minutes before moving, smoothing the curtains, adjusting the ornaments on the mantelpiece. *Remember Lee, you're not his servant.*

· · ·

'CLOSE THE DOOR,' Lawrence snapped as he entered the sitting room, slamming the receiver down.

'You OK?' Lee checked his watch, ensuring Lawrence saw him do it.

'You've been told I want this room for myself?'

Lee had already arranged for him to take the master suite upstairs. It had a spectacular view, an enormous en suite, everything Lawrence had asked for. The best room in the house by far. 'Yes, Jim mentioned it. If that's what you want, the bed can be brought down as soon as you like.'

'This is perfect. I can see whoever's approaching.' He stood in the bay window, surveying the view: the manicured lawn, the tall, swaying trees, the endless grey ocean beyond. 'No one minds?'

'Of course not.' His choice was perplexing, but if that's what Lawrence wanted, who was he to stand in his way?

'Good. I don't want to step on anyone's toes.' He poured himself a whisky. 'Or get off on the wrong foot.'

Nodding to the phone, Lee pointed out, 'But maybe don't hog that too much. It's the only one.'

Lawrence sat and rolled his whisky around in the glass, inhaling the aroma, before taking a sip. 'I'll be sure to keep calls to a minimum. Anyway, my agent's been told we've not to be disturbed. There.' He placed the telephone under a side-table, somehow imagining it had vanished.

Lee moved closer. Lawrence's aftershave was overpowering, a pungent combination of spices and tobacco. Following any meetings with him, it often lingered on his clothes for days. Two weeks of it would test his patience. 'How was the flight?'

'Hellish. Turbulence most of the way.' Fixated on the view, Lawrence barely glanced at him.

Lee checked his watch again. 'If you don't mind, I was hoping to catch up with Richard before dinner. Go over some scheduling details.'

Lawrence reached for his leather satchel and pulled out a Dictaphone. He switched it on and laid it on the side-table. Lee had seen him do this many times. His insurance, he called it. 'So, Richard's already here?' he asked.

'He arrived last night as planned. Before I left, I sent your agent a fax confirming everyone's arrival times. Like you asked.'

'Not his assistant?' He stared at Lee.

'No, directly to Simon.'

'Good, because his assistant's fucking useless,' Lawrence muttered, looking over Lee's shoulder to a mirror on the wall behind. 'I need to know exactly what's going on. You understand?'

'Was there anything else?' Lee watched as Lawrence inspected his reflection in the window, stroking his jawline, adjusting his collar. The man's vanity was legendary.

'And your friend?' Lawrence picked at the crease on his trousers. 'He's arrived too?'

Typical Lawrence. The question had nothing to do with whether or not Colin was there. It was simply a reminder that Lawrence had allowed him to come. That no matter what, he was the boss. 'Yes, Colin's here. He crossed with the others yesterday. They all seem to be getting on like a house on fire. He's fixing dinner as we speak.'

'I look forward to meeting him.' Lawrence stood, smoothing his clothes as he did so. An actor thing, constantly checking to ensure no continuity disasters. 'What rank is he? Sergeant? Inspector?'

'Constable.' Lee knew this wouldn't impress.

'A newbie?' Lawrence moved into the bay-window.

'He's been a police officer for six years,' Lee explained, 'so pretty experienced.' What he didn't explain was the institutional homophobia; every time Colin sought promotion, he'd been vetted, putting a stop to any career progression.

'I see.' Lawrence peered out the window, his head cocked

to one side. 'I hadn't noticed that before.' He pointed to a pathway leading round to the rear of the house. 'Where does it go?' He craned his neck to see more. 'Can anyone gain access from the back of the house?'

Simon had warned him that Lawrence's paranoia had escalated, but he hadn't expected this level of agitation. 'The island's extremely secure, Lawrence. There's no need to worry. That path leads to the barn where you'll be rehearsing.'

The explanation seemed to settle him. The more assured Lawrence re-emerged. 'I've two things I need to run by you.'

This was the real Lawrence. No small talk, straight to business. 'Fire away.' Lee sensed his own voice changing to something more business-like. It felt like a more natural meeting point between them.

'Take a seat.'

'Do I need a drink for this?' Lee asked. Lawrence's little chats could last for hours.

'It's still my position that Richard should not direct this – that there are better options.'

Lee sighed. This particular argument had continued for weeks. 'I thought we'd settled this. A contract's been signed. Richard is perfect. Reneging now would be bad on so many levels.' Lee needed to disguise his exasperation, tread carefully; there was a real risk Lawrence could not be persuaded. 'Please. Think this through. Richard's here now.'

Lawrence stood over him and raised his hand. 'I know your arguments but hear me out.'

Lee sat forward, staring directly at him.

'Simon's told me that Richard's had some problems recently.'

'He's a recovering alcoholic. That's hardly a secret.'

'Yes. But how recovered is he?'

Lawrence's athletic frame seemed to fill his field of vision. For a moment, Lee considered standing too, but he felt if he did, he might be pushed back down. 'Are you asking or is there something more to tell? Because if you've new information, I'd like to know.'

Lawrence withdrew and paced the room. It reminded Lee of one of his hammier performances in a guest appearance on *L.A. Law* where he played an attorney and kept shouting *"Objection!"* every five minutes. 'Three weeks ago, he fell off the wagon.'

'First, I was not aware of that. Had I been, I would have spoken with Richard immediately. One, to ask how he was. Two, to see if there was anything I could do to help. And three, to reassure him he has my support.'

'You honestly believe in him?' Lawrence's eyes widened.

'One hundred percent! Two London Theatre awards, a Broadway Theatre Desk nomination, three Theatre Angels. His staging of *The Tempest* is currently playing in four theatres around the world, twenty years after it was first staged. Christ, Richard Harris and Peter O'Toole are begging him to do *Waiting for Godot* in the West End with them starring. He's respected.'

'And yet he's still a drunk.' Lawrence smirked, provoking Lee to suggest otherwise.

'That's language I would never choose to use.'

'My apologies.' Lawrence raised his whisky and gulped down a mouthful. 'The man drinks. A lot. According to my sources, our esteemed director was on a monumental bender barely a month ago, which saw him disappear for four days. He missed two technical rehearsals in Manchester. If he'd not been arrested – for cottaging no less – he'd probably still be AWOL.'

'Again, I repeat, I did not know about this. So, I apologise, and I will speak to him.'

'Good.' Lawrence sat back down and kicked off his shoes. 'I need assurances. And if I don't get them, fuck the contract – I can buy him out.'

'Next point.'

'Sorry?

'You said you had two things to discuss.'

Lawrence picked up the phone and dialled. 'I do.' For Lee's benefit, Lawrence held the receiver towards him.

'Who are you calling?'

'Jackie Adamson. Our esteemed writer. You hear how it keeps ringing out? At my insistence, Simon's been calling her on the hour, every hour, for the past three days.'

Lee stood, fearing the rumours about Lawrence were all true. 'In any other business, that would be considered harassment.' Supposedly, a catalogue of complaints against him in recent years had been swept under the carpet – from co-stars to electricians. There was even a story circulating about a dog-handler, who'd complained that Lawrence had kicked his dog when it failed to bark on cue. However, nothing had ever stuck.

'My reputation rests on this.' Lawrence continued listening before slamming the receiver down. 'You understand?'

'There's no easy way to say this,' Lee said, 'but Jackie will not be taking your calls. She's in a spa in Switzerland and will not be changing another word. The draft we have is the final one. She's more than fulfilled her contract. As far as I'm concerned, she's delivered on every request we've made.'

'You've got to be joking,' Lawrence shouted. He poured himself another whisky and threw it back.

Unblinking, Lee dared Lawrence to challenge him. In reality, the truth was a little murkier. Jackie had intended on travelling to Switzerland but at the last minute changed her mind. No one knew where she was exactly, only that she wasn't contactable. Her agent had announced all of this down the phone to him that morning.

'You've treated her appallingly,' Lee stressed. 'Jackie went over and above what could reasonably be expected. Your incessant phone messages and faxes, the pestering of her agent, the uninvited appearance on her doorstep when she had a sick child to deal with – all out of order. And yet she rewrote scenes, added more dialogue, changed the ending how many times? And it's still a brilliant script. No, Lawrence. Face it, you've had your pound of flesh.'

Lawrence slid off his belt and threw it towards the window. The buckle slammed against the glass. Lee crossed, running his hand across the pane to check it hadn't cracked; it had, but the damage was barely visible.

'I need my bed down here. Now!' Lawrence barked. 'When I get back from my walk, I expect it to be sorted.'

'I've two things I'd like you to remember whilst we're here on this island,' Lee said. 'One, I represent the majority of the investors in this show. Therefore, I'm in charge. And two, you're here as an actor. Don't confuse your role. Now, can you switch off your fucking Dictaphone? We're finished here.' Lee waited for a reaction, needed for him to say something. *You're Dismissed* or *you're fired*. But there was only silence. Instead, Lawrence unzipped a holdall. Ignoring Lee, he unfurled some bubble-wrap and lifted an award from his bag – an abstract fusion of marble and gold wire. Smiling to himself, he placed it at the centre of the mantelpiece, as if to say, look what I've got that you haven't.

Only as Lee went to leave, grabbing the phone on his way out, did he hear the click of the Dictaphone being switched off.

10

'What the hell's going on here?' Windblown, Georgie stood in the front doorway. Behind her, as large raindrops fell, the treetops twisted in anticipation of the approaching storm.

Halfway up the stairs on the landing, Jim and Peter were angled awkwardly, balancing a bedframe. A few steps above, Colin gripped a mattress. Below, Kath stood in the hallway shouting instructions.

'It's Lawrence; he wants his bed set up in the sitting room,' Kath replied.

'I've asked people and they're all fine with it,' Jim added. 'What about you?'

She didn't reply, but instead strode over to join Kath at the bottom of the stairs. 'Fuck's sake,' she muttered to herself. 'You're never going to get that round the corner,' she shouted at them. 'You'll need to take it apart.'

'What if I step back?' Jim asked. 'Maybe Peter can lift it. That might work.' Without waiting for a response, he'd followed his own instructions, which only made matters worse. 'It's stuck.'

'Why does he want his bedroom downstairs? And why's

he not helping?' Georgie looked for Lawrence, as though he might be hiding around a corner.

Kath shrugged. 'He commandeered the sitting room as soon as he arrived. The door's been closed ever since.' She shouted up the stairs, 'What if you take off the headboard?'

'Screwdriver anyone?' Colin asked. The mattress was now propped against the wall. He leaned over the banister – a bored removal man – waiting for direction.

'I'll check if there's anything in the kitchen.' Kath headed off.

Silence ensued as they listened to her root through drawers. She shouted there wasn't anything suitable.

'There's a small tool shed out the back,' Jim called.

'The key is hanging by the door,' Colin bellowed. Catching a whiff of burning, he said, 'Georgie, you couldn't do me a favour and turn the oven off?'

'Sure.' She walked along the hallway, past the sitting room, with its door resolutely shut, and entered the kitchen. She adjusted the dial, found tinfoil to cover the lasagne, and placed it on the bottom shelf. Out the window, the rain was now falling in leaden sheets. She watched Kath struggling to force the shed door. As she was about to help, the lock burst open. 'Well done,' she shouted, sticking both thumbs up. It was only then she noticed Lawrence's reflection standing in the doorway. Dressed in a dark parka, he appeared taller and broader than she ever remembered him looking. 'Christ! You surprised me,' she stuttered. 'Going somewhere?'

'What's all the noise, Georgie?' he asked, looking past her and out the window. 'Up to no good as usual?'

She looked at his mouth as he spoke, his sculpted lips forming her name.

'We need to stop meeting like this.' Studying her, he eventually said, 'What a gorgeous

top. Such a pretty pattern.'

She crossed her arms. 'They're carrying your bed. You should go help them.'

'With this back?' He laughed, mimicking pain. 'And Kath?' He gestured outside. 'What's she doing?' Looming over her, he went to kiss her, but she stepped away.

'Getting a screwdriver. The bedframe's stuck. They need to take the headboard off.' She looked at him, smoothed down her top and stuck both hands in her pockets. 'I should go help them.'

He walked around her and pulled open the fridge. 'I'm starving. When's dinner?' he asked, taking out a bowl of olives and popping one in his mouth. He smiled, blowing her a kiss.

'Fuck you, Lawrence.' She lifted a packet of cigarettes from the table.

'Charming,' he replied, offering her an olive.

She grabbed it and threw it towards the sink. 'Before anyone comes in,' she hissed, 'I need to ask one question and I want an honest answer – what the hell is going on?' Her hand trembling, she struggled to light her cigarette.

'You didn't need to take the part.' He offered his lighter and took a cigarette himself. 'I wouldn't have been offended.'

'You think I wanted to?' She inhaled deeply, blowing the smoke in his direction.

'Frankly, I was surprised when you did. Light?'

She threw back the lighter. 'You left me no choice. 'Offering me the part last, after everyone else had accepted, I didn't imagine that was by chance. How could I say no?'

A cheer from the hallway coincided with a shout from Kath outside. 'Got it!'

'We can talk later,' Lawrence whispered, as Kath came through the door.

'Think this'll do?' As she held up a large screwdriver, she pulled her soaking hair away from her face.

'How lovely to see you again.' Lawrence stepped forward,

hugged Kath, then kissed her on both cheeks. Georgie noticed the intimacy was not reciprocated. In fact, she detected an echo of her own reproach as he closed in.

'I think they've managed to get it down.' Georgie flicked ash into the sink, washing it away with cold water.

'How?' Without waiting for a response, Kath bolted into the hallway.

Georgie went to follow, but Lawrence held out his hand, brushing against her arm. 'Always so well groomed.'

'Don't you dare.' She fixed him with a stare, causing him to step back, hands raised.

'Well, it's going to be an interesting two weeks if this is how you plan to play it.'

'You think we'll last that long?'

'We've four months together.' He threw an olive in the air and caught it in his mouth. 'You got other plans?'

'To get off this island with my husband and son and never see your face again. Very simple.'

He gripped onto her arm and squeezed it. 'Over my dead body.'

'If needs be.' She pulled away from him. 'Make yourself useful and sort out a salad. Think your back's up to that? We'll be eating in an hour.'

'Sorry my dear, but I need to clear my head. I'm sure you can handle it yourself.' He opened the back door, raised his hood, and stepped into the rain.

Only after he left did she become aware of how firmly she was gripping the back of a chair.

11

With the bed finally in place, Jim slipped out and made a beeline for the shore. He loved the sea; how hypnotic the play of restlessness and calm could be. One day, he imagined he and Georgie retiring to a small cottage by the coast; Northumberland would be great, with its long sandy beaches and open space. If only he could convince her, the perennial city girl. Perhaps two weeks on the island might change her mind.

Despite Lee telling him the island was miniscule with few opportunities for walking, he'd brought his hiking boots. He didn't mind scaling the rocks; they didn't look too treacherous, a bit jagged perhaps, but he'd cope.

Weekends would often see him drive south of the city, spending hours at a time exploring new coastal paths and discovering new beaches. Sheer bliss. For now, the only challenges were the fast, fading light, and the wind which had picked up. He'd spotted a little beach which, with a bit of effort, he was determined to reach. Totally secluded, with a patch of bright sand, he reckoned he could easily make it there and back in time for dinner.

He was excited at the prospect of rehearsals. Not only was

he sharing them with his wife and son, but it brought him back in touch with Lawrence. As young men, they'd been inseparable. Like brothers, others would say. Besides Georgie, Lawrence had been the one person who knew him best: what made him tick, his strengths, weaknesses. But that was almost years ago. Now, they were practically strangers. Perhaps spending time together could rekindle something of what they'd lost. At the very least, catching up would be revealing, their lives having taken such different paths.

Jim gripped a boulder and hauled himself up. It was flat enough for him to stand on top and get a good view of the beach ahead. With its white sands and emerald water, it was an oasis. However, getting there and back this evening might be tricky after all. The sea wasn't happy. It seemed to snarl, as if it didn't want him there. To him, the sea and the rocks weren't mere objects; they were as real as humans with their own characteristics and emotions, ones he could feel as much as when someone shouted or cried or erupted into howls of laughter. He smiled to himself. 'I hear you,' he whispered.

As he scrambled back down, he noticed a figure in the distance. Too dark to make out who it was, their hand was raised, waving in his direction. It could be Lawrence. Jim's eyesight wasn't the best, and even squinting, it was hard to say for sure. But before he could wave back, they'd disappeared into a thicket of trees.

12

Climbing to the top floor, Georgie wanted to scream. Bang a wall. Do something that might get Lawrence out her head. All these years, and she'd learned nothing.

The last flight of stairs was steeper than the rest, and she had to pause at the top to catch her breath; despite running half-marathons, the smoking undid all that good work. Note number one: stop smoking! She walked down the corridor, heading for the room at the end, furthest from everyone downstairs. Halfway along, she heard a muffled sound. At first, she thought it was a bird flapping about. However, the harder she listened, the more human it sounded. She pressed her ear against one of the last doors. Unmistakable. Someone behind it was crying.

She gently pushed the door open to reveal a tiny bathroom. Both she and Kath shrieked as they caught sight of each other. 'Kath? What the hell?'

'Thank God it's only you,' she said, grabbing a piece of toilet paper and wiping her tears.

Georgie closed the door behind her and locked it. 'What's wrong, love?'

Kath put down the toilet seat and sat. 'Ignore me. I always

get anxious before the start of a job,' she said, blowing her nose and stuffing the scrunched-up toilet paper into a pocket.

Georgie moved closer. 'You sure that's all it is?'

'I can never bring myself to learn my lines beforehand. It's become a sort of superstition I suppose – I worry I'll get found out – it's horrible.'

Georgie knelt and took Kath's hands. 'I saw you play Maggie in *Cat on a Hot Tin Roof* two years ago and I was spellbound. You have something few actors have. An extraordinary ability to make audiences care.' She swept a strand of Kath's hair behind her ear, took another piece of toilet paper and handed it to her.

Kath wiped her face. 'Thank you.'

'Now, tell me what's really going on. And I want the truth. No secrets.'

Kath shrugged. 'I enjoy having my things around me. That's all. Yes, it's beautiful here, but there's going to be no escape. Usually, after a day's rehearsal, I need to be on my own – just to breathe.'

'You still can,' Georgie said, smiling at her. 'And we'll be nice to you. At least, I will. Any of the others give you a hard time, come to me. Promise?'

Kath nodded and stood, pulling a mass of tissues from her pocket, flushing them down the loo. 'I'm such a massive fan of yours.'

'Don't be daft,' Georgie said, blushing. 'You're far too young to remember anything I ever did.'

Kath's eyes sparkled. 'A few years ago, you did a masterclass in Soho – *The Female Voice* – cost me a tenner.' She laughed. 'I had to borrow it. You did a speech about women's voices on stage, then performed scenes from Shakespeare, Moliere and Shelagh Delaney.'

'I remember,' said Georgie. 'Elmire from Tartuffe, Helen from A Taste of Honey,

Portia's brilliant speech:

The quality of mercy is not strained;
It droppeth as the gentle rain from heaven
Upon the place beneath.'

'The place was packed.'

'I was probably hawking my cabaret night.'

'You were. I came along to see that too.' Kath hugged her tightly. 'I'm so happy you're here. To be working with you, it's a dream come true.'

Georgie felt Kath's grip loosen and let her pull away in her own time. 'I hope you don't mind me saying something, but here goes.' She liked the girl too much to keep quiet. 'Earlier, I noticed you with Lawrence. I sensed some bad blood. Am I right?'

Kath gazed at the floor. 'Nothing I can't handle.'

'You think you can handle that one?' Georgie rested a hand on Kath's shoulder. 'Look at me.'

Kath lifted her head. 'I've come across a lot worse. Haven't you?'

From downstairs, Peter shouted, calling Kath's name.

'Promise, you'll come straight to me if he starts with his nonsense. Because it'll be me he answers to.'

'Georgie, I've dealt with it. He knows the score. I wouldn't be here otherwise.' Her name was called again. 'I'll be there in a minute,' she shouted. 'Look, I need to go.' She opened the door. 'Thanks. And seriously, don't worry about me. It's nerves. Once we start rehearsals, I'll be right as rain.' She pressed Georgie's hand and mouthed 'Thank you.'

As she went to leave, Georgie pulled her back. 'Fight for every line. Don't, whatever you do, let him lessen your part. Because he *will* try.'

'I won't.'

'You promise?' said Georgie, still clutching her hand.

'Promise,' replied Kath. 'He did something like that on the film. But I've got him sussed.' She smiled. 'We can gang up on him.' Before leaving, she blew a kiss.

Georgie closed the door and leaned against it. She knew from bitter experience that the chances of Lawrence being finished with Kath were nil. Lifting her sleeve, she ran her fingertips across the faded, red marks running down her arm. A permanent reminder. Scars she'd lived with for more than twenty-five years. A lifetime.

Before rehearsals began, she needed to set the record straight with him.

13

Colin was in the dining room laying the table when he heard a commotion in the hallway. He crossed to the door and peered out. Georgie was outside Lawrence's room, hammering her fists against his door. She gave it one final whack before recoiling in pain. As she nursed her hand, she muttered in agitation. Part of him considered calling to ask if everything was OK, but he thought better of it and stepped back inside. He listened as her footsteps receded, and she said a cheerful 'Hi!' to someone.

A few moments later, Lee appeared, slamming the door behind him. He mimed tearing his hair out and gave a V-sign to the door.

'What's going on?'

'I could kill him,' Lee said through gritted teeth. 'I think he may well be an actual psychopath.' He poured himself a glass of red wine and took two large mouthfuls. The vein on his left temple pulsed: never a good sign.

'Lawrence, I presume?' asked Colin, pulling napkins out from the dresser.

Beckoning Colin towards him, Lee whispered, 'You have no idea what that devious shit's been up to. Not only is he angling for Richard to be fired, but he's been treating our award-winning writer like some intern. She's left the country – done a complete vanishing act.' He poured more wine. 'Now, he's going ballistic because she won't take his calls.'

Colin set about placing the napkins. 'So, when did *you* know?'

Lee lowered his head. 'In my own defence, only this morning. Her agent called me as I was leaving. She was seething. I've tried phoning her now but she's not picking up. Guilty by association!'

Colin put his arm around Lee's waist and, pulling him close, let him flop into his chest. 'It'll be fine. You always find a way to make things right. Big smile, honey.'

Lee pulled away and took another gulp of wine. He sat and stared out the window. 'He makes my skin crawl. And believe me, I'm not alone in that. Do you know how much advice I ignored to get to this point? It's been like signing a pact with the devil.'

Colin had seen Lee stressed about work before, but this was different – he looked defeated. He rubbed his shoulders, massaging them to ease the tension. 'Don't worry. As soon as rehearsals start, he'll be too busy with other things, and he'll calm down. I mean, what can he do?' He pointed to outside. 'We're literally in the middle of nowhere.'

'Demand that I sack the lot of them. Bring in a new cast.'

'But I thought he insisted on this casting.'

'You think that matters?' Lee motioned for Colin to hand him his wine. He grabbed it and downed the lot. 'A top up, please?'

Out in the hallway, Colin could hear people gathering for dinner. It was almost eight. A shriek of laughter echoed – above them all, Kath's throaty, infectious laugh. 'Is Lawrence joining us?' He poured Lee another glass.

'God knows. I mentioned it to him earlier. But let's say we

didn't part on the best of terms. Besides, he said he was going for a walk. I don't think he's back yet.'

'Well, he can't go far.' Colin stared out the window. 'You can barely see a thing out there.' The sun had set, leaving the sky a brooding canopy of black, the lawn a dark mass.

'He's probably checking I've not stashed the writer somewhere in the grounds. You know, I don't think he trusts me one iota.' Lee stood and adjusted himself in the mirror. 'I'll go tell them dinner's ready.' He strode over to the door.

'Wait!' Colin straightened the napkin nearest to him. 'It might be nothing, but I just saw something a bit weird.'

'What?'

Colin quickly picked the napkins up again. 'Nah. It can wait. Go tell them to come through.' He placed a folded napkin by each plate.

Lee stared at him. 'If it can wait, why's your face got that look?'

Colin set the last of the napkins and grabbed a box of candles. 'I'll explain later. Honestly, it's nothing.'

'Someone's not made a complaint about him already?' Lee closed the door. 'It's not about the accommodation?' He waited. 'You know I'll keep guessing till you tell me.'

Colin stopped what he was doing. 'I hate interfering.'

'Christ, spit it out,' Lee said. 'Whatever it is, it sounds like I need to know.'

'I don't want you to get het up about it. But I saw Georgie outside Lawrence's door.'

'And?' Lee checked no one was about to enter.

'Banging on it. With her fists. And she looked angry. I mean totally fuming.'

'Was she pissed?'

'I don't think so.'

Lee took a sip of wine and leaned against the wall. 'But he's barely been here five minutes. Mind you, he's just set a rocket up my arse, so God knows who else he's rubbed up the wrong way.'

'She seemed pretty determined,' Colin said, placing the candles in the candlesticks.

'They did a play with him years ago – her and Jim. Before they were married.'

'So, there's a bit of baggage, potentially?'

'That's all I need.' Lee drained his glass. 'Please can you make them go away, Colin?'

'I maybe read too much into it. What do I know anyway? I'm just the eye candy round here after all.' He winked.

'I've just made you executive producer. As well as cooking our meals, you can handle all their emotional fallouts. Deal?'

'You've had it worse. Wasn't there that actor who refused to speak directly to the rest of the cast?'

'Yes, the bona fide psycho that is Tim fucking O'Donoghue. Now, there's a man who'd give Lawrence a run for his money. What a wanker.'

'Like I said, you've dealt with worse.'

'This is going to be a car crash. I can feel it. Promise you'll still love me in two weeks? Because after a couple of days with him I might turn into a monster.'

'So long as I don't have to sleep with it.' He struck a match. 'Now, go round them up, Mr Hyde, while I light these candles. They'll be starving.'

14

There was a round of applause as Colin placed the bubbling lasagne in the centre of the table. His cooking had never received such a fuss. 'You do know it's only a lasagne?' he said, sliding into his chair.

'Shall I be mother?' Kath jumped up from her seat, grabbing a knife and spatula. 'I'm making sure I get the biggest portion,' she giggled, cutting it into equal portions.

'And no one's seen Lawrence?' asked Peter, glancing at the door.

'A polite hello, a chat about the bed, that's all.' Jim held up his plate to be served. 'Thanks. Whoa, that's plenty.'

Richard waved Kath's offer away. 'I overate at lunch.'

Lee registered the refusal from the other end of the table. 'Why not have a small portion, Richard?' he urged, as he mixed the salad. 'Colin will be offended otherwise, won't you, darling?'

'I spent most of the afternoon making it. Blood, sweat and tears,' Colin said. 'And I hate leftovers.'

Richard relented. 'I'll take a fraction,' he said to Kath, who cut off a tiny corner for him.

'Georgie? How much?' Kath asked, moving to her side of the table.

'Just a little. One glass of champagne is enough to ruin my appetite these days.'

'It was two, Mum.'

Georgie scowled. 'Who's counting?'

'Two and a half, to be exact,' Jim added. 'You had a small one upstairs. Remember?'

'Let's make it three and a half, shall we?' she countered, holding out her glass to be filled.

Richard topped her up. 'Cheers,' he said, clinking glasses.

'Yours is empty,' Georgie shrieked, grabbing the bottle. 'Here, let me.'

'No need.' Richard poured himself some water. 'It's full now! Cheers.'

Kath finished serving and sat, taking, as promised, a healthy portion for herself. 'So tasty.'

'Delicious,' Jim said. 'It's hard to get the meat so tender.'

'Thanks,' Colin replied. 'Brisket, some pork shoulder and slow cooking. That's the secret.'

'What are you doing?' Georgie was staring at Peter as he fumbled with something in his mouth.

'Manners!' Kath cried, elbowing him.

'A piece of gristle,' he mumbled, shoving it to the side of his plate. 'Nasty!'

'Oops!' Colin said. 'Can I get you another slice?'

'Christ, no! I'll take some salad instead.' Peter piled some leaves onto his plate.

The sound of the front door slamming and Lawrence's shadow passing made everyone look up. Expecting him to join them, they exchanged confused looks as he went into his room. Without saying a word, they returned to eating. For the next five minutes, only the hum of polite conversation drifted back and forth the across the table.

Lee broke the quiet chat by tapping his glass. He stood.

'I'm going to keep this very brief. Welcome one and all. There's a lot of work to do, but happily, out here in the wilds of bonnie Scotland, we're free from the distractions of the modern world. The best team, I feel, has been chosen to make this great script sing. So, cheers to all of you. And please, I beg you, no falling out.'

They all raised their glasses. As Lee sat, Richard propelled himself up and gripped the table. In the candlelight, his skin looked blotchy, his hands visibly shaking: slightly hunched, it looked as though the slightest breeze might topple him over. 'I've something to say.'

Lee, constantly alert to potential disaster, went to stop him, but Colin rested a hand on his arm, and he sat back down.

Richard glanced around the table, meeting everyone's gaze. 'As you know, I've had a problem with alcohol for many years. An illness which I inherited from my father, who had inherited the same curse from *his* father – God rest their souls.'

'You poor baby,' gushed Kath, placing her glass on the table. 'I didn't know. I'm so sorry.'

Nudging her, Peter whispered, 'Kitty! No need to overdo it.'

'Three years ago, at my lowest ebb, I entered rehab. I was at rock bottom, having managed to piss my so-called "illustrious" career down the pan.'

Kath hiccupped, waving her hands in front of her. 'Sorry. Ignore me. I always hiccup when I'm sad.'

Richard paused and raised an eyebrow in Kath's direction before clasping her hand. 'Thank you, dear. But drunks don't need sympathy. What we do need is support. Lots of it.'

'Thank you for sharing this, Richard.' Lee was halfway up from his seat. 'But...'

'Lee!' Colin cut in, 'Let Richard speak.'

'I know you want to protect me, but there's more. I'm

sorry. Please, I need to say this, and I promise I won't be long.' He seemed to glaze over for a second, staring at the dark wallpaper and the framed hunting images – stags fleeing from braying dogs, riders brandishing their crops – that adorned every wall. The shaking of his hands had worsened, and a tear formed in his eye. It was Georgie who gently lowered him into his seat. He thanked her and cleared his throat. 'Five weeks ago, after more than a thousand days, I fell off the wagon. Following a heavy day at work, I stopped off at a wine bar. Christ knows why. I debated for over an hour whether to have a drink, but finally gave in. Several days later I was arrested in a public toilet, making a nuisance of myself.'

'There's no need to continue,' said Lee. 'We're all friends here. No one's judging you and each of us will do their best to be supportive. As the producer of this show, I'll ensure that.'

But Richard was in full flow. 'I felt so ashamed. I'd failed so many people, but most importantly, I'd let myself down and all those I'd promised I would never drink again.'

'Should we put the wine away?' asked Peter.

Richard sighed. 'No, that's fine, certainly not for my benefit. When I sobered up in that police cell, I swore I would never touch another drop so long as I live. And I'll keep to that. Tonight, I'm making a promise to each of you in this room. I will remain sober throughout these rehearsals and beyond. I will direct you, attend to your every need – and steer this ship home.'

The chat was broken by the sound of metal against glass. Lawrence's silhouette filled the doorway. Demanding the table's attention, he tapped his gold signet ring against a whisky tumbler. Dressed in a scarlet blazer and bright, white shirt, the candlelight softly lit him as he made his entrance.

'Impressive speech, Richard,' Lawrence said, without looking at him. He scanned the rest of the room, giving everyone the benefit of his beaming smile. 'My, what a beautiful bunch you all are. And can I say ladies, you've outdone yourselves. What beautiful dresses. You almost look like sisters.'

Kath adjusted the straps on her dress, ensuring she wasn't showing too much cleavage. 'Twenty quid from a charity shop in Camden. It might still have the price tag on it.' She stood to check, revealing a striking pattern of black and white lines that swept across on the diagonal. 'A bit of a find,' she whispered to Georgie. 'It's Versace!'

'I'll be stealing that, darling,' Georgie enthused. 'Breathtaking.'

'Hey Lawrence, we've missed you.' Peter stood, practically knocking the chair over in his rush to shake his hand.

'My boy,' Lawrence replied. 'How lovely to see your handsome face again.' He wrestled Peter into a firm bear hug and held him there. Twenty, thirty awkward seconds passed. 'It's been far too long.'

Fork held in mid-air, Colin looked to Lee and mouthed, 'What the hell?'

'Right,' said Lawrence, 'I hear there's some lasagne on offer. And if Richard's dried up all his tears, perhaps the party can begin?'

'Excuse me a moment.' Richard stood. 'I've a few things I need to do.' He left the room and banged the door behind him, causing the paintings on the wall to shake.

'He'll be OK, won't he?' Kath asked, her face a mixture of concern and confusion.

'Finish your meal,' said Georgie. 'He needs time alone. We can check in on him shortly.'

With Colin's help, Lee fixed Lawrence a place at the top of the table and dished up a portion of lasagne.

'How delightful to see you all gathered together,' Lawrence said. 'My cast!' He grinned as though it had taken years of his own hard work to assemble them. 'A warm hand for Lee.' He clapped, the others following his lead. 'Congratulations on all your Herculean efforts. I realise it hasn't been easy planning.'

'You know me Lawrence, I thrive on a challenge.'

'The guy barely sleeps.' Lawrence winked at Colin before guzzling down a large piece of lasagne. 'Delicious.'

'A couple of hours a night is plenty,' Lee said, 'though calls at three in the morning are never ideal.' He placed a piece of lasagne in his mouth and swallowed hard.

Lawrence gawped at him. 'Why didn't you say?' he yelled across the table. 'I've been on LA time for weeks.' He crossed over and kissed Lee on the forehead: a huge, cartoonish smacker. 'My apologies.' He held up his glass. 'To the most fabulous producer any company could wish for.'

Everyone raised their glass.

'It's good to see you, Lawrence,' Jim said. 'It's been what, twenty-five years?'

'Twenty-nine,' Georgie interrupted, taking a sip of wine. 'The last performance was in 1963. August. I remember it vividly.'

'Whatever, it's been way too long, Mr Selby.' Lawrence poured himself a glass of wine and sat. 'Maybe it's the candle-light, but you don't look a day older – as if time's stood still. You too, Georgie. You both look stunning.'

Georgie pushed her plate aside and stood. 'I'll go see if Richard's OK,' she said. 'I think the circumstances over-whelmed him a bit. Excuse me.'

Lawrence reached across the table to offer Colin his hand. 'I don't think we've met.'

'I'm Colin, Lee's partner.'

'He mentioned you're a police officer?' Lawrence angled his head to find his light, taking only a brief second to do so.

'The Met's finest.'

'We'd better all be on our best behaviour.'

'Got the handcuffs ready and waiting.' Colin smirked. 'The least sign of trouble, I'm your man.'

'You're telling us all your secrets,' Kath burst out, leaning towards him, hand over her mouth, to whisper, 'I may need to borrow those.'

'Weren't you cuffed in the movie, Kath?' Lawrence interrupted, pulling his chair closer to her.

Kath positioned her chair away from him, all joy draining from her face. 'For one scene only.'

'You were excellent.' Lawrence dragged his own chair nearer.

'Yes, you told me,' Kath replied. She stood and gathered the empty plates.

Lawrence folded his napkin and set it aside.

'Lawrence is right. You did such a good job,' Peter added. 'Though when it comes to gurning in the background, there's no contest – I take the award.'

'Don't put yourself down,' Jim said. 'You put in a great performance, too. All ten seconds of it.' He grinned at Peter, who turned away. 'I'm teasing, son. You were excellent.'

'Did you count?' Peter snapped. 'I bet you did.' He began helping Kath clear the table.

'Poor boy. You were underused. The director was an idiot,' said Lawrence. 'It was a lovely scene I thought. Didn't you divulge the location of Kath's character? What was her name?'

'Rosie.' Kath lifted Lawrence's plate.

'Are you sure? I could have sworn it was something like Penny or Sally. Something non-descript like that.'

'Definitely Rosie,' Kath stressed. 'I should know. It was on my call-sheet every morning.'

'I stand corrected. My apologies.' He pointed at Peter. 'There was genuine honesty to your ten seconds. Though I'm pretty certain it was closer to a minute. I asked the director to put the full scene back in, but he claimed it slowed the action. Maybe if he'd listened to my suggestions, it wouldn't have gone straight to video.'

'I hate to talk business,' Lee interrupted, 'but I thought it might be a nice idea to look at the rehearsal space after dinner. Christen it before the fun begins tomorrow.'

'If you don't mind, I'll take a rain check,' Lawrence said. 'I've a few calls to make.'

Colin noticed the merest scowl flicker across Lee's face for a millisecond before he composed himself.

'And did I say, I'd rather not start rehearsals first thing?' Like Lee had warned, Lawrence seemed in his element, calling the shots. 'Instead, I'd like to have a chat with people individually, talk about their characters, see where they're coming from. That'll be nice for us all,' he continued, 'won't it?'

Once again, Lawrence beamed beatifically and scanned the room with his infamous green eyes. As a teenager, Colin had been struck by them, shining laser-like from the big screen, sparkling and seductive: they danced in their sockets, tripping effortlessly between emotions as the light caught them. Hypnotic.

'Richard won't mind me taking the initiative, will he? It'll give him another morning of prep.'

'Maybe we should check with him first,' Lee suggested. 'Or perhaps you could ask him?'

'Face his wrath? No thank you.'

Lee took a breath. 'I'll pop in on him later.'

'Dessert anyone?' Colin asked. 'I've made a pavlova.'

'I'll take some,' Peter said, sitting back down. 'So long as there's no gristle in it,' he added.

'None for me,' Jim replied, getting up to leave. 'I think I'd like to read. I'll see you all later.' He crossed to Lawrence before leaving. 'We should catch up. Ponder how so many years have passed in the blink of an eye.'

Lawrence stood and hugged him. 'My best buddy,' he said, kissing him on both cheeks. 'It's been way too long.'

Jim stumbled his way to the door. 'Sure has.'

'Watch yourself,' Kath called from behind. 'You'll do yourself an injury.'

'I'm fine,' he replied. 'I'll be in the library if anyone needs me.'

'Peter, you promised we could finish going over lines.' Kath was propping open the door, her hands full with the salad bowls.

'We haven't chatted with Lawrence,' Peter called after her. But she was already halfway down the hallway.

'You'll still be here tomorrow, Lawrence, won't you?' Kath yelled back.

'I'm counting on it,' Lawrence shouted at full volume.

'OK. Maybe I'll leave dessert for now,' Peter concluded, following Kath out.

Lawrence glowered after them. He gulped the rest of his whisky down and rolled the ice-cubes around. 'Not together, those two, are they?'

'I wouldn't know,' Lee said. 'Excuse me, Lawrence; I'll take your wine-glass if it's empty.'

'On set, there wasn't a hint of anything like that.' He handed his glass over. 'Or did I miss something?'

'People hook up. Happens all the time. No big deal. Anyway, it's no concern of yours if they're fucking like rabbits, so long as they get the job done. Right?' Lee left the room.

Lawrence adjusted himself, moving the candlestick to the side, focusing on Colin. 'What do you make of this theatre lot?' he asked.

Colin cleared his throat. 'People seem lovely. I mean, I'm getting used to it. They're more open to their emotions, that's for sure. More honest, I suppose.'

'You think so? More honest than your policemen friends?' he asked, maintaining his stare. 'I wouldn't trust them with my life. Pay their wages, however, and they'll say anything to impress you. Turn your back – now, that's another thing entirely. Daggers flying.'

'I wouldn't know about that.'

'No?' Lawrence raised his arms and stretched his back, giving out a long sigh.

Colin noticed how, for a man of his age, he was still incredibly fit. Lean and muscular with barely a wrinkle. He'd an awareness of his physicality and how to use it to maximum effect. At that moment, he appeared vexed. Tense.

Lawrence leaned across the table. 'I know we've just met Colin, but I have a proposition.' His expression became softer, more appealing.

He was performing and Colin was his audience. 'What kind of proposition?'

'Come to my room. I'll explain.' He smiled. 'No need to look so scared. My whisky's through there, that's all.'

Lee had warned him in no uncertain terms – Lawrence would try and control you, whoever you were, that people were mere pawns to him. Nonetheless, Colin was intrigued by the invitation. What was there to lose? After all, he wasn't part of the cast, there were no ties. 'It all depends on the quality of the whisky.'

'The best. Single malt. Thirty years old.'

Colin glanced outside to see Kath and Peter heading down towards the trees. A stroll in this weather? Why deny they were lovers when every sign said otherwise?

'Shall we?' Lawrence got up and led Colin to his room.

15

The first thing Colin noticed was the gold statuette gleaming in the centre of the mantelpiece. It glistened against the room's dark wooden panelling, an emblem of glamour and success.

Lawrence caught him admiring it. 'Do you want a hold?'

'Can I?' he asked, surprised by the eagerness of his response.

'Be my guest.'

What struck him most was its heaviness. Mesmerised, he held it to his chest like the stars he'd seen on TV. 'Impressive.'

'A mere bauble. Some Broadway thing; Best Newcomer in 1963. I beat Albert Finney, you know. As it happens, it was for the play Jim, Georgie and I performed together.'

Colin returned it to the mantelpiece. 'Must mean a lot.'

'I carry it with me everywhere,' Lawrence said, searching through his bags.

Colin fidgeted, tucking the corner of his shirt into his jeans, as he waited for Lawrence. 'So,' he began, 'what can I do for you?'

'Where did I put that damned machine?' Lawrence was rooting about in his suitcase, throwing things onto the bed and floor. Unable to find what he was looking for, he rifled through some papers lying on the bedclothes, and pushed aside several pillows. Reassembled in the centre of the room, and facing the bay window, the bed dominated the space; the rest of the furniture had been pushed out of the way. 'Ah, here it is. I knew I'd taken it out.' He waved the Dictaphone in front of Colin. 'You don't mind, do you?'

'Sorry?' he replied, observing Lawrence fumble with the switches.

'My lawyer insists I record my conversations if I'm alone with anyone. I'm so busy these days and my mind's like a sieve.' He flicked a switch.

Colin pushed his hands into his pockets, scanning the room, noticing a small chip on one of the windowpanes. 'Every conversation?'

'I never listen to them again,' Lawrence stressed. 'For the archives only.'

Colin felt the sweat on his palms. 'Sure,' he said. 'I guess that's not a problem.'

'Right. Settled. I wanted to speak with you before rehearsals began.' He crossed over to a bottle of whisky sitting on the dresser – a single malt Glen Grant – and poured two large measures. 'I'm assuming as a Scotsman it's your tipple?' he said, handing it over.

Colin accepted the glass, savouring the rich smell and amber colour before taking a sip. 'Wow! The good stuff.'

'You're making me nervous standing there.' Lawrence swiped a white shirt from an armchair and sat, gesturing for Colin to do the same. 'Take a pew.'

'A habit, courtesy of my job.'

'Quite.' Lawrence pointed to a chair draped in ties. 'Throw those on the bed.'

'You sure?'

Lawrence nodded.

In his hands, the ties – silk, expensive, in a myriad of

jewel-like colours – felt alive, like exotic reptiles. 'Not from British Home Store, I presume?'

Lawrence smiled and waited for Colin to sit, then raised his glass. 'Cheers.' He took a sip, savouring it far longer than was necessary. 'What do you think? Special, isn't it?'

It was like nothing Colin had tasted before. Malty, with a hint of Christmas cake. 'Incredible.'

Lawrence gazed across and took another sip. 'What I'm about to say is in complete confidence,' he said. 'I take it I can count on your discretion?'

Colin shuffled in the seat, placing his drink on a side-table. 'I'll need more details before I answer that.'

Lawrence rolled the amber liquid around in his glass, brought it to his nose and inhaled deeply before knocking it back in one. 'I've had a few skirmishes of late. My life's been threatened – more than once – which is not that unusual. But recently, there've been a few occasions when the threats have seemed more real. A couple of times where I've felt in genuine danger.' He stood, placing his empty glass beside Colin's. 'I was wondering if you might act as my personal security over the next two weeks?'

Caught off-guard, Colin shifted in his seat, aware of the sound of the leather squeaking. 'You do realise I'm off duty?'

'I'm not asking for much – just an extra pair of eyes for you to be vigilant on my behalf.'

'We're on an island, a forty-five-minute boat ride from the mainland, with a storm coming. We couldn't be more remote. And you don't feel safe?'

'No, I don't. I know it sounds irrational, but do you honestly think a bit of bad weather will stop the British tabloids or my more zealous fans?' He stuck his face close to the pane of glass, checking outside. 'I take it Lee's mentioned Jackie Adamson, the playwright?'

Colin nodded, recalling his description of her as modest

and professional, and Lee's exasperation at the obstacles Lawrence had placed in her way.

'We've had, shall we say, a few run-ins.' Lawrence sat. 'Between you and me, the woman's not of sound mind – deranged – if not downright dangerous. And she's on the loose. Even her own agent doesn't have a clue where she is. She could easily be making her way here to wreak havoc.' He leaned forward. 'I'd much rather take preventative measures now than risk leaving it too late.'

Colin wasn't sure what Lawrence was proposing. If it was to be on the lookout, fine. But if he imagined Colin patrolling the island, fending off aggrieved colleagues and crazed fans, he'd not signed up for two weeks of that.

'I'll pay, of course.' Lawrence declared. 'Name your price.'

Colin's face burned at the suggestion. 'No, no. I couldn't – I can't – accept any payment. Besides, I'm already your guest.'

'It would be good to have someone looking out for me. That's all. And you never know, if this works out, and if you'd be up for the challenge, when I get back to LA, I'll be needing someone to head my security staff. A little more glamorous than the mean streets of London, don't you think?'

Colin finished his whisky, letting the heat rest in his mouth before swallowing. The lack of sincerity, or interest in his own circumstances, didn't merit a response. He'd keep to the here and now, rather than a sugar-coated offer delivered to impress. 'Just to keep a watch?' A residual heat burned in his chest as he met Lawrence's smile.

'As simple as that.' Before Colin could say anything else, Lawrence had pounced up, grabbing his empty glass and, almost skipping to the dresser, poured another two whiskies. 'We've a deal?'

'I suppose so,' Colin said.

'My very own bodyguard.' Towering over him, he took Colin's hand and pressed it. 'I've a good feeling about you,' he said, before adding, 'very soft hands for a copper.'

At that moment, there was a knock at the door. 'Come in,' barked Lawrence.

Lee's voice arrived before he did. 'Have you seen...?' He hovered for a split second as Colin extracted his hand from Lawrence's grip. 'I'm sorry, I didn't realise...'

Before Colin could explain, Lee had backed out of the room.

'I'll let you tell him, shall I?' Lawrence said.

16

A MONTH AGO

Colin had barely hung up the phone when Lee burst into the room, strode over to the wardrobe and began to pull clothes off hangers. Throwing jeans and a pile of shirts onto the bed, he yelled, 'A full hour you've been gabbing on that fucking thing.'

'Sorry, is dinner ruined?'

Lee refused to reply or even look at him. Instead, he sorted through a shelf of toiletries, shoving bottles of aftershave and moisturiser into a bag, while scanning the bedroom for anything else to grab.

Colin moved towards him but was met with a glare. The crossed arms and the pulsing vein on Lee's forehead were further warnings to stay clear. 'I'm sorry. I'd no idea he was going to call.'

His ex, Ben. They'd had a messy break-up two years before, leaving Colin totally devastated. Lately he'd been calling, keen to make amends, asking if they could be friends. But regardless of Colin dutifully detailing every phone call, every conversation they'd had, it wasn't enough for Lee.

'I take it you'd told him about the interview?' Lee snapped.

'Yes.'

'Is that why he called tonight?' Lee didn't wait for an answer. Instead, he dragged his suitcase from the top of the wardrobe and let it drop to the floor. 'So, you discussed it with him before me?' Hands on hips, Lee stood in the middle of the floor. 'What? Cat got your tongue?' He threw a rolled-up pair of socks in Colin's direction. 'Fuck you!'

Colin retreated to the living room; there was no reasoning with Lee when he was like this. The TV was on mute, evidence that Lee had been listening in on his conversation. He turned the volume back up. As he did so, Lee stormed out of the bedroom, snatched the remote from him and threw it against the wall.

'Do you still love him? Well, do you?'

Colin bent down to pick up the pieces of plastic. The batteries had spilled out onto the carpet but, besides a hairline crack, the outer case seemed relatively unscathed. He looked around for the back cover but couldn't see it.

'I asked, do you still love him?'

Switching off the TV, Colin placed the remote on the coffee-table, sat back on the sofa, and silently stared ahead. Whatever he said, Lee would take it the wrong way, but he knew he had to try. Where to start, though? 'Can we talk?'

'I think I have my answer.' Lee returned to the bedroom and continued to pack. Though he hadn't officially moved in, Colin knew it would take him a while; in the last five months, each time he stayed over, he brought something new with him. Usually clothes, or more often toiletries, but sometimes a potted plant or a vase, insisting the place needed brightened. He'd bought him furniture too – the coffee table had been a present, as had the TV – saying he was a weirdo for not having a telly. But Colin hadn't minded. Every small addition felt positive, like they were building a home together. A future.

Thirty minutes passed. In between dramatic sobs and the

occasional expletive aimed in Colin's direction, drawers were wrenched open and banged closed. Only the shriek of a zip being pulled over signalled the end of the commotion. Lee appeared in the doorway, suitcase in hand, his face red from crying, his hair standing on end, his glasses halfway down his nose.

'Come here.' Colin beckoned him over.

Lee remained where he was, his stare rock hard. 'What's he got that I haven't?' he screamed, causing the neighbour upstairs to thump on the floor.

'Give me five minutes. Sit down and I'll explain everything.'

Lee stood in the doorway, refusing to budge.

Through the open window, a group of boys playing football in the summer heat could be heard screeching with joy, the occasional 'Yes!' proclaiming another goal scored. It amplified the silence between them.

'If you don't like what I have to say, OK. But storming out of here won't get us anywhere. Plus, you're wearing my t-shirt.'

Lee wasn't ready to joke. He ripped it off and threw it to the ground, searching for another one in his suitcase.

'You didn't have to do that.'

'I fucking hate the thing.'

It was a Cocteau Twins t-shirt from when they'd played at the Brixton Academy a year before. The first time Lee had spotted it amongst his things, he'd pounced on it and took every opportunity to wear it, even though it was too big for him. Seeing him wear it thrilled Colin – he looked so sexy in it – and ever since, it had been exclusively Lee's to wear. Colin bent down and placed it on the arm of the sofa.

'I promise it won't take long.'

Lee banged the suitcase against the wall and sank into the sofa. Still refusing to look at him, Colin sensed the worst had passed and that he'd be taking in each syllable of what he had to say.

'Get on with it then,' Lee said.

Had this been a year earlier, this conversation wouldn't be happening; he would have let Lee go. But, after six months of intensive counselling, Colin had emerged with an appreciation of how compromised his feelings for Ben had been and how fragile their relationship was from the very start. Colin thought Ben was the love of his life: easy to be around, attentive, fiercely intelligent, independent. He had all the qualities Colin admired and sought. But Ben wasn't exclusive. Never claimed to be. They'd had their first threesome two weeks after they got together, and this continued as a pattern until it quickly became about Ben going off on his own with whoever he wanted, whenever he chose. Colin's needs hadn't mattered, only Ben's. And that meant anybody was up for grabs, including a mutual friend of theirs: someone he trusted, who he assumed would never be capable of betraying him like that.

Colin edged closer to Lee. 'I bumped into him at *The Prince Edward*. It was the day I got the letter confirming my interview; you know, the night I came to see your show in King's Cross?'

'That was weeks ago. Why would you keep it from me?' Lee went to stand, but Colin eased him back down.

'You were caught up in other stuff. And it didn't seem important.'

'Meeting with your ex? Not bothering to mention it? Nah, unforgivable.'

Colin explained that Ben had happened to remember the interview was today, that he was checking in, seeing how it went. 'Though in reality, it was a pretext for him to talk about himself,' he added. Lee remained silent. He was listening to every word, as Colin hoped he would. This was a blip. They'd get through it. 'I've told you loads of times before that Ben's an idiot. Why would I be interested in him when I've got you?' Colin watched as Lee took off his glasses.

'Why give him so much time if he's such an idiot?' Lee asked, wiping his eyes.

'Because he's not a bad person. Just someone who wants something different from me. From you. Us. That's not a crime.'

Lee put his glasses back on. Staring at Colin for what seemed like an eternity, he relented and threw himself back onto the sofa. 'So why do I constantly feel like he's trying to take you away from me?'

Colin took Lee's hand. This time there was no resistance. 'Trust me when I say I will never, ever go back to him.' He forced Lee to look at him. 'I promise you.'

THE FOLLOWING DAY, the expected rejection letter had been left in his pigeonhole at the station. *"Unfortunately, on this occasion you've been unsuccessful."* Colin called Lee from the pub, hoping he'd join him, but was told to get in a taxi and come straight home, that drowning his sorrows was pointless.

Back at the flat, Lee had already ordered a carry-out and was dishing it up as Colin came through the door. 'So, they've screwed you over again?' he asked.

Throwing his coat over a chair, Colin sat. 'They gave it to Wilson – bloody Darren Wilson – he's been on the beat, what? Two minutes and can barely string a sentence together.'

Lee handed him his curry. 'Here. Eat. I know you don't agree, but it's prejudice, pure and simple.'

Colin shovelled a forkful of chicken tikka into his mouth, the heat of the spices stinging his mouth. 'I need to stick it out, see if I can make a difference. You know that.'

'There are plenty of jobs where you could do that without

the daily harassment from homophobes. The shit you have to put up with is tantamount to bullying.'

'That's the culture, people get singled out for something one way or another. The profession's full of Neanderthals. I went into it with my eyes wide open.' Which was true. Towards the end of his time at Hendon, the derogatory remarks had started. Having never mentioned a girlfriend, or "bird", he was soon earmarked for being "a poof", "a shirt lifter" – words straight from the playground. Once, in the communal showers, he was goosed by the ringleader – who held up his fingers in triumph, proclaiming he'd found the proof, whilst others, friends of his included, howled with laughter.

Lee heaped more curry onto Colin's plate and brought a naan bread out of the oven. 'You know what? I've a suggestion.'

'Think I should reconsider joining the priesthood?'

Lee tore the naan in two. 'I seriously worry about you sometimes.'

'What then?'

'Why don't you come to Scotland with me? Fuck Majorca and what the lads want.'

'Si and Mac are counting on me. Besides, they're the good guys, the only ones keeping me sane.'

'I think a break from all things police – Si and Mac included – would do you good. Maybe give you time to think? Get some perspective on what matters? And it'd be no bad thing for you to spend some time with a bunch of gays – that is, with me.'

'Is it not just you and Richard who are gay?'

'Get real – they're actors. They've all dabbled! I'd need to run it by Lawrence, but he won't mind, I'm sure, if I phrase it the right way.' He tore off a bit of naan and dipped it in the sauce. 'Think about it?'

Colin considered the last few months and all they'd been through. Giving Lee that peace of mind would be no bad thing. And he was right, a complete change of scenery was maybe what he needed. 'Let me see what I can do.'

17

'What the hell was that?' Lee roared as Colin entered their bedroom. 'Holding hands with a Hollywood legend – is that your thing? Something I should know? Well, is there?'

He felt Lee's eyes bore into him. The look was familiar. 'Not this again? You promised we'd chat like grown-ups if you ever felt suspicious.'

But Lee wasn't listening, wrapped up in what he thought he saw. 'I couldn't cope,' he sobbed, collapsing on the bed.

Colin moved towards him, uncertain how close to get, fearing he might lash out. 'It's not what you think. He was asking me to be his, I suppose, bodyguard. I don't know. He seems pretty neurotic for someone who's in the middle of nowhere.' Easily explained, but would Lee see his mistake, agree he'd misjudged the situation?

'Why did it look like he was about to kiss you?'

'What, this ugly mug?' He pulled a face, making Lee smile. It meant the world to see this reaction. 'Who'd be daft enough to find this attractive?'

'You're beautiful.' Lee stroked Colin's cheek.

'He was shaking my hand, that's all. And that's not a

euphemism,' he added, nudging Lee twice. 'Though he does like to get in close; he's a bit too familiar for my liking.'

'Like he did with Peter?'

'You saw that too?' Colin said. 'All a bit weird.' He drew Lee closer, and they hugged. Intimacy was what they both craved – free from any jealousies or shame. 'You can trust me – you know that. I would never, ever do anything to hurt you.' He took Lee's face in his hands and kissed him again. Feeling his body relax into his meant everything. 'No secrets.'

'No secrets.'

From outside, a blast of wind pounded at the house, rattling the sash windows, followed by the rumble of thunder and several flashes of lightning.

'What the hell was that?' They rushed to look out. The sky was black with cloud, and a garden chair tumbled across the lawn, hurtling towards the trees. Another gust of wind pummelled the house; a huge hammer battering against the stone walls. 'I'll huff and I'll puff, till I blow your house down,' whispered Colin in Lee's ear.

'Christ, I didn't even look at the forecast before coming over.'

'We should go outside and check. Make sure everything's bolted down.' Colin walked towards the door. 'You coming?'

Out in the corridor, they could hear the others gathering downstairs. As they got to the foot of the stairs, Kath and Peter dashed through the front door, completely soaked. Like puppy dogs, they shook themselves free of water, shivering and giggling.

'You poor things,' said Georgie. 'Come here.' She helped Kath out of her jacket.

'It came out of nowhere,' Kath said. 'We were at the shore and the sky went black, like there'd been an eclipse or something.'

'Super scary,' Peter added, pulling his sodden shirt out

from his trousers. 'It was like someone turned on a tap. 'I need to change.' He pushed past Colin as he ran upstairs. 'Kath?'

'Coming,' she said, following him.

Lawrence poked his head out from his bedroom. 'Crazy weather, isn't it? Thank God I got here on time.' As Kath disappeared round the landing, he shouted, 'Any chance of a word, Kath?' But she didn't reply and continued climbing the stairs. 'Kath?' he called again, but she was out of sight.

'Tell me you're not working tonight.' Georgie said. 'We've only just got here.'

'It's more of a personal chat,' he snapped, slamming the door shut.

Jim emerged from the library. 'I'm going to check the windows, make sure they're all shut properly.'

'I can help,' Kath shouted down, as Jim made his way upstairs.

The entire house shuddered like an enormous beast in its final death throes, and the lights flickered off and on. The shadows crossing Lee and Georgie's features made them appear like characters in an old-fashioned melodrama, Colin thought.

'What happens if we lose the lights?' Georgie asked.

'The electricity runs from a generator,' Lee explained, 'so we should be fine.'

A crash of wind against the house, as if the roof was being ripped off, was interrupted by a scream.

'Sorry. That was me,' Kath yelled. 'Just a branch banging against my window.'

Giggles from Kath and Peter followed.

'Are they?' Colin asked.

'Put it this way, for an actor, my son's kidding no one,' Georgie replied, heading upstairs. 'And Kath is an open book.'

'They're fucking for sure.' Richard appeared from the

kitchen, holding a glass of clear liquid. 'Don't worry, it's only water.' He held it out. 'Smell it if you don't believe me.'

'Of course, we believe you,' Lee said. 'Why wouldn't we?' He shouted upstairs, 'Right, we're meeting in the library next to Lawrence's room in five minutes. We need to organise stuff for tomorrow.' A flurry of activity signalled his instructions had been heard. 'See. All I need to do is click my fingers. Amazing.' He hurried Colin along. 'You, too, now you've been given an official role.'

'Yes, Sir!' Colin responded, as he slapped Lee's backside.

18

———

The room next to Lawrence's was small and crammed floor to ceiling with books. Not the job lot of redundant hardbacks used as decor by interior designers to validate their client's intellect; instead there were countless modern paperbacks with coloured spines, arranged randomly. Different sized books were jammed on shelves next to each other, chunky ones lying horizontally with smaller ones lined up on top, and columns of books stacked precariously on the floor. A treasure trove for any reader.

As Colin followed Georgie in, Lawrence could be heard shouting random words from behind the connecting door: his voice pitched to fill an auditorium.

'Is everything OK with him?' Colin asked, pulling the heavy damask curtains closed.

Georgie pursed her lips and continued flicking the book she was holding. 'Nothing is ever OK with Lawrence Delaney.'

As the others filed in, Colin dimmed the lights and placed a candle on the mantelpiece and another on a low table. The room glowed, illuminating the crimson red of the walls.

'Cosy, isn't it?' he said. 'I lit the fire earlier. I thought it would be nice to relax here later.' He pulled over the last curtain.

There weren't enough seats for everybody: only two leather armchairs, one of which Jim had taken, a pouffe and a small sofa. Colin sat on the sofa and was joined by Kath and Peter. Apologising, he shuffled to one side, to make more room.

'It's fine.' Kath grabbed Colin's arm and pulled him back. 'I don't bite.' She smiled. 'Well, not before midnight.'

Deep in conversation, Lee and Richard hovered outside the door. Colin could only make out the occasional phrase. *He did what? No way!* Whatever they were chatting about, the tone sounded serious.

Lawrence threw open the adjoining door, almost knocking Georgie – who was still rifling through the bookshelves – to the ground. 'You realise the damned phone lines are down?' Without looking at anyone directly, he continued his tirade. 'I need *someone* to do something about it! And soon.'

Lee stepped into the room. 'You mean me?'

'Of course, I mean you! If I'm not mistaken, you *are* the producer.' Muttering to himself, Lawrence launched himself onto the free armchair, tossing an overstuffed cushion to the floor.

'I didn't know it wasn't working. Did anyone else?' Lee asked.

Jim looked up from his book. 'Haven't seen it since we got here.' He returned to reading.

'Who is it you need to call?' From behind Lee, Richard's voice cut through the chat. 'Bill Cosgrove by any chance?' He took two steps forward and bumped against the table, knocking over the candle. As it went out, everyone's faces were plunged into shadow.

'Steady!' Colin bent over and picked it up.

Lawrence straightened himself in the chair and locked his

eyes on Richard. 'I think we could benefit from his additional input.'

Colin noticed the vein on Lee's forehead vigorously pulsate.

Looking at the others, Lawrence put up his hands in surrender. 'Go on, shoot me for trying to save this production.'

Lee let out a hollow laugh. 'Bullshit! Richard's been filling me in. What you've done is totally unacceptable.'

Georgie, clinging to the bookshelf, butted in. 'Can someone tell me why Bill Cosgrove's coming here? We already have a director.'

'Because Lawrence asked him to.' Richard glowered at Lawrence. 'He mentioned you'd been trying to get hold of him last week when we met at *Swan Lake*. I spoke to him again, earlier on the phone, while you were all still having dinner. He confirmed you'd invited him here to replace me, not for "additional input".'

'I'm so sorry Richard,' Lee said.

'Don't be,' he interrupted. 'This is Lawrence's doing.'

'You're not really going to do this?' Lee asked Lawrence, who'd sat back in his armchair, seemingly amused at the unfolding commotion he'd caused.

'If Bill didn't think he could help, he'd have told me so.' Lawrence surveyed the room, satisfied he had the audience in the palm of his hands. 'Haven't you considered that?'

'I'll be leaving first thing in the morning.' The soft glow from the fire masked the lines of Richard's face and the bags under his eyes. 'Don't fall into his trap,' he said, imploring the others. 'Do your job, say nothing, and you never know, you may have the privilege of working with the twat again.' Plucking a paperback from a shelf, he left the room.

'This is complete breach of contract.' Lee was at Lawrence's side, one hand gripping the wing of his armchair. 'None of the other investors will agree.'

'Won't they?' snapped Lawrence. 'Let's see. Anyway, he's resigned, hasn't he?'

'Come on,' Colin interrupted. 'Before anything's said you might regret tomorrow.' He clambered up from the sofa and took Lee's arm, encouraging him to step back, but Lee shook him off.

'It's fine,' Lawrence said, standing. 'I'm not offended that my own producer would take the word of a drunken sex pest over mine.' He squeezed Lee's shoulder. 'Don't worry though, I won't hold it against you. Nor will my lawyers. Not this time.' He swung a hand around the room. 'See, we have witnesses. They can vouch that this has all been a huge misunderstanding.'

Lee wriggled from Lawrence's clutch and walked out.

'Lee!' cried Colin.

'Best let him cool off,' Kath said, beckoning him. 'Come on, sit between us.'

Noting Peter's frosty expression, he instead perched himself on the arm of the sofa.

'I make no apology. Richard's a lush,' said Lawrence. 'Did you know that he...?'

'He told us.' Georgie snapped a book shut and threw it down.

'I was going to say, he almost closed a production last month.' He shook his head in dismay. 'I couldn't take the chance, could I? Our professional reputations are at stake.' He relaxed on the armchair.

'It's an illness though, isn't it?' Kath pointed out, pulling a cushion across her front. 'Instead of sacking him, you could show compassion. I mean, he opened up to us, told us the truth. That counts, doesn't it?'

Peter kneeled to stoke the fire. 'I'm with Lawrence on this one. Like he said, it's our careers on the line.'

'You don't believe that son, do you?' Jim sat forward, his expression pained.

'Hardly anyone gets a chance like this. We're lucky. Lawrence sees something in us and has given us an opportunity.' Peter stood. 'He gets what it takes to succeed, so I say let's trust his judgment.' He sat back beside Kath, who immediately distanced herself from him.

'Thank you,' Lawrence said. 'You're a wise boy. Your parents should be very proud.' He looked to Jim and Georgie; neither met his gaze.

Kath fiddled with the trim of a curtain which Colin hadn't closed properly. She stood up to fix it. When she turned to face the others, the room had fallen silent. Taking a long breath, she grabbed the back of the sofa. 'Peter didn't want me to say anything,' she started, 'but this is as good a time as any.'

'Kath?' Peter's neck stiffened. 'What the hell are you playing at?'

'And it's all thanks to you, Lawrence.' Her body trembled as she took to the centre of the room. Eyes glistening, she continued, an actress finding the right inflection to maximise the meaning of each word. 'I hate secrets. They eat away at you, gnawing till they've devoured every ounce of your soul. I thought I could pretend, say nothing. But I'm sorry Peter, I can't.' She looked over at him, but he was staring at the floor, refusing to acknowledge what was about to happen. 'I think most of you have already guessed – it's pretty obvious – but we're a couple. Me and Peter, that is. Happened on the set of *Cobalt Dawn*.'

Everyone focused on Peter, as he glared at Kath, his face like thunder.

'Like you said, darling, we guessed ages ago,' Georgie said. 'We're not idiots. Every time he disappears for a few days, he comes back saying Kitty this and Kitty that.' Georgie kissed Peter on the top of his head. 'Silly boy.'

Kath smiled. 'Does he really?'

'We wanted to respect your privacy.' Jim gave her a hug. 'That's why we said nothing. We're so happy for you both.'

Kath's face flushed. 'Thank you.'

'Since the film?' Lawrence's head was cocked to one side.

'We wanted to take things slowly, keep it between ourselves, but it's silly when we spend so much time together. And now we're all here, it felt wrong not to say. I didn't want us to be sneaking around anymore. I hope you understand.'

Arms folded, Peter sat on the edge of the sofa.

'Congratulations. Bagged a winner there.' Lawrence slapped Peter's back. 'I hope you'll both be very happy.'

'It's not like we're engaged or anything,' he said.

'But we have spoken about it, haven't we?' Kath joined Peter on the sofa and kissed him.

'Once.' Peter scowled at Kath, who grinned back at him.

Lawrence ran his fingertip along the edge of a shelf and blew the dust from it. 'If you'll excuse me, I'm going to try the phone again.'

Peter rose and grabbed Lawrence by the arm. 'It was late into the shoot. We would have said. I don't know why we didn't.'

'I don't know either.' He left, banging the connecting door shut.

Kath caught Georgie's eye, who was shaking her head.

'What the hell just happened?' Colin asked.

'I think he's got the hots for you,' said Kath, leaning towards Peter.

'Shut up!' he roared. 'Why do you keep saying that? It's not funny.' He lay on the sofa and placed a cushion over his face. 'That was so embarrassing.'

'Touch a bone, did I?' Kath tickled his stomach.

'Don't, Kitty!' he yelled, twisting his body away from her.

'Lawrence is complex,' said Jim. 'Far more sensitive than you might imagine. 'He was always like that, wasn't he? Georgie!'

Georgie was kneeling in front of the fire, staring at the flames. 'I've no idea. I don't know the man,' she said.

'Lawrence is a sensitive soul,' he repeated.

Georgie picked herself up. 'Is he? Tough! Aren't we all?' she retorted. 'I'm going to check on Richard.'

On the sofa beside him, Peter and Kath were now giggling and nipping each other. 'Well,' Colin grinned, 'I should find Lee – don't fancy playing gooseberry here.'

'For Chrissake!' groaned Peter, looking up. 'Is everyone going?'

'Your mum's off to start knitting some bootees, I'll bet.'

'See what you've done, Kitty?' Peter threw a cushion at her.

'It's what we should have done from the start.'

'And on that note, I'm out of here too.' Jim followed Colin out.

The crackle of the fire could barely be heard above the roar of the wind. Peter and Kath sat staring at each other, waiting for the other to speak.

'I wish you hadn't,' Peter finally said, frowning. 'It's so much better when it's just us.'

'Coward!'

'I'm not,' he squealed, dodging yet another cushion.

Kath nudged him to sit up, pulling herself onto his knee. 'Well, it's done. Out the box now. We're legit.'

'Did you see his face? I'm worried he'll think we're unprofessional.'

'Who cares what Lawrence Delaney thinks?' She played with his hair, still damp from the rain. 'It's our lives. He can go fuck himself.'

Peter held onto Kath as he repositioned himself and drew her closer. 'What have you got against him?' he asked, lowering his voice to a whisper.

'Nothing in particular,' she replied. 'I don't like him. What do you want me to do, pretend?'

'Sometimes I don't understand why you took this job!'

'Peter Anthony Bartholomew Selby, you have such a lot of growing up to do.' She leapt up from his knee. 'And so's you know, I'm not wearing any knickers.' She raised one eyebrow, opened the door, then whipped up her skirt. 'Oops, the wind must have caught it.' She laughed and ran along the hall and up the stairs.

Peter threw himself back on the sofa and lay staring at the ceiling. After Kath called his name a third time, he eventually lifted himself up and followed her out.

19

'Is he allowed to do that?' Colin asked Lee, who was peering out into the blackness. 'I mean, Richard's signed his contract, hasn't he?'

The weather had deteriorated. With the rain and wind beating hard against their bedroom window, and three strikes of lightning in the last five minutes, it felt as if, at any moment, the entire building might be split in two. Even the sea roared, its fierceness competing with the wind for attention.

Lee sat on the bed, his face blank. 'As well as being the star, Lawrence is bankrolling a chunk of this production, so he can do what he likes. On paper I'm in charge, but the reality is, I've little power. What he says pretty much goes.'

Colin could see Lee's brain testing various scenarios: strategizing, weighing things up, rejecting most. 'What about Richard's agent? Maybe he could intervene.'

The lights flickered and buzzed, as though about to die.

'Perhaps. But I can't do anything till the phone line's back. I'll call later, see if we can come up with a solution.' Lee took off his glasses, rubbed his eyes, sighed. 'In the meantime, I'll chat to poor Dickie. Maybe something can be salvaged from this shit show.'

As a crash of wind thrashed against the house, a violent bolt of lightning was followed by utter dark as the bedside lamps went out.

'What the...?'

A murmur of alarmed voices signalled the lights were out everywhere. Colin felt his way towards the door. As it opened, he was met with a complete blackout.

A voice asked if the generator had failed. It was Jim, emerging from his room.

'I think so. But you'd expect there to be a backup,' Colin called back. 'Can you find some candles or torches?'

'Sure thing.'

Behind him, in the gloom, Colin heard Lee sniffle. 'Are you OK?'

'I'll be fine. Just worried. Richard's fragile – all this stress could send him back to where he was before.'

Colin hovered in front of Lee's outline, the darkness magnifying every creak of the building's structure. 'He seemed pretty adamant he wouldn't have another relapse.'

'Richard talks a good talk,' he sighed, 'but he's a shadow of himself. And if there's one thing this industry does well, it's gossip. I don't want his career ruined all over again.'

Colin took Lee's hand and held it firmly. 'If anyone can convince Lawrence, it's you. Maybe all he needs is a good night's sleep.'

'There's more,' Lee said, tightening his grip. 'Things I didn't know until today. History between them. Nasty stuff.'

Footsteps advanced along the corridor. Jim appeared, holding aloft a candle. 'There's a massive box of candles in the kitchen and a couple of decent torches. I've left them on the table.' As he lifted the candle to their faces, long shadows spread out across the walls and ceiling, making the space appear cavernous.

'Thanks,' Lee said. 'Right, with my producer's hat on, I guess I should go deal with the generator. There must be instructions somewhere.'

'I'm good with stuff like that.' Jim stepped further into the room. 'I'll come keep you company.'

'Make sure I don't blow the place up, you mean?' Lee grabbed his arm and moved out into the corridor with him.

'Now, that would be the icing on the cake.' Jim smiled. 'Basement, I take it?'

As they were going downstairs, Georgie rushed out of the dark. 'I think Richard's gone outside.'

Colin swung round. 'Is he crazy?' he asked, gobsmacked anyone could be so stupid. 'It's a full-blown gale out there.'

'I was with him fifteen minutes ago and he seemed fine,' Georgie explained.

'Has he a death wish?' Colin listened to the howl of the wind as it pushed more forcefully, threatening to tear the roof off. Conditions were going from bad to worse. 'Right, I need to search outside.'

'Kitty's already gone to find him.' It was Peter's voice, coming from above.

'Why'd she do that? It's wild out there,' Colin shouted up.

'Don't ask me, I was in the bathroom.'

'Does she have a torch?' Colin asked, fearful he might be dealing with a two-person rescue mission.

'Who do you think I am? Her keeper? She does what she wants. I'm going for a lie down.' Peter went back to his room.

Colin grabbed a cagoule from the hallway cupboard.

'I'll come too,' said Georgie.

'No. It's better if no one else leaves the house,' he said. 'It's far too dangerous. A storm like this could kill someone.'

'Will today never end?' Lee put his hands to the side of his head, mimicking Munch's *The Scream*. 'Right Jim, let's you and me get the power sorted.'

'I'll light more candles, shall I?' Georgie said. 'Make myself useful.'

20

That must be Richard by the shore, Kath thought. She peered ahead, holding onto a tree to steady herself, struggling to focus on the blurred outline. But the rain was like needles against her face, and by the time she'd wiped her eyes clear, the figure had disappeared.

Soaked, she struggled on, determined to find him, but the wind had other ideas. Staggering between trees, she was almost knocked over, forcing her to crouch until it subsided.

After a few moments, she stood and tried to drive on through the wind. It screeched at her ears – a terrifying sound – telling her who was boss. No matter what she did to fight back, she was losing. Exhausted, she called Richard's name, but her voice was lost in the commotion. Then again, how would she even hear him respond? All around, the howl was deafening.

The trees to her left swayed wildly; in their frenzied dance branches bent and snapped, before being tossed into the air like matchsticks. Gripping one of the thicker trunks, she caught her breath. The shoreline was visible, and what she imagined had been Richard was merely a rock jutting out of the sea. There was no sign of him.

Through the cacophony, she heard her name being called. Spinning round, she saw a figure in a bright yellow waterproof striding towards her. For a brief second, she panicked, imagining it was Lawrence. But, as the person got closer, she recognised Colin's walk; each step assured, as if the storm was a mere inconvenience.

'Any luck?' he shouted.

'He's not here,' she screamed back, cupping her hands around her mouth, in the hope of amplifying her voice.

He beckoned her forward. 'Come on,' he said, 'we need to head back. You'll catch pneumonia dressed like that.' To steady himself, he wrapped one arm around a tree as she struggled towards him.

A sudden crack drew their attention. Above, a thick branch, strained beyond its capabilities, tilted downward, groaned, and with an explosive crack, gave way, hurtling to the ground.

Colin sprinted the few feet separating them, pulling her out of its path. Holding onto each other, they fell to the ground.

Kath laughed. 'Fuck! It's exhilarating,' she shouted.

'What?'

'I said it's exhilarating.'

He shook his head in disbelief. 'You're crazy.'

'Only on a full moon.' She drew in close, until she was practically nose to nose with him. 'There's no point going any further in that direction,' she said. 'It's too rocky – Richard would break his neck. And I've searched the other way.'

'You're sure he wouldn't risk climbing onto the rocks?' he yelled, helping Kath to her feet.

Their eyes met, both understanding the awful possibility each was considering.

'What about the barn?' Colin asked. 'It might be the one safe place Richard would head for.'

'I assumed it would be locked.'

He grabbed hold of her. 'Let's go. And if he's not there, I'll come back and double-check out here.' He unbuttoned his waterproof to offer Kath protection, and together they pushed against the gusts of wind, making their way across the squelching mud of the lawn.

With the shutters and curtains closed, the windows of the house stared blankly out at them. The only exception was Lawrence's bay window, which glowed with candlelight. As they passed, they caught sight of his shadow moving across the room. From nowhere, his face appeared – a trick of the light – gazing out at the darkness. Colin raised a hand in recognition, but Lawrence disappeared from view without acknowledging him.

Following the path round, they soon arrived at a spot sheltered by large trees in front of the barn. On the other side of a long, low window, a candle flared. 'It must be him.' Colin grabbed the handle of the barn door and pushed it open. Of course, that's where he'd retreat to; he should have searched there first.

Eyes closed, whistling a tune, Richard was standing in the middle of the space. He jumped when he heard them. 'Where the hell did you two come from?'

'Thank God you're alright,' cried Kath, rushing towards him. 'We didn't know where you were.'

'Sorry. I was about to head back.' He looked at their concerned faces. 'Did you think I'd topped myself?'

'We didn't know what to think.'

'Kath, my dear, I've fought bigger beasts than him.'

'So, you're OK?' asked Colin, adopting his officious police officer's voice.

'I'm absolutely fine. Having a moment of contemplation. Here, join me.' He gestured Colin over. 'Now, take a deep breath.'

Colin took in the barn's smell: rich wood, new, untouched.

'Seeing as I'll never get the chance to rehearse in here,'

Richard explained, 'I thought I'd take a look.' He breathed it in again. 'Wonderful, isn't it?'

'It's magnificent.' Kath ran a hand along the mirrored walls, pressing the sprung floor with her toes. 'Whoever did the conversion knew what they were doing.' She stopped. 'My God, will you listen to those acoustics?'

'It's got a good feeling, hasn't it? And look.' Richard pressed on the mirror next to the kitchen area. 'There's even a secret door.' It sprang open to reveal the forest beyond, rolling like the sea. Leaves tumbled across the immaculate floor as Richard closed the door over. 'Maybe that's where I exit, pursued by a bear, never to be seen again,' he giggled.

'Lawrence was letting off steam. He'll change his mind in the morning.' Kath turned to look at Colin. 'You're neutral. What do you think?'

His face reddened, but before he could say a word, Richard intervened. 'He's one of the honest ones.' He grabbed onto Kath. 'Look at him,' he marvelled. 'The face of an angel and too honest for his own good.' He clung on to her. 'He knows my fate, don't you?' Slowly dragging his finger along his throat, he groaned, 'I'm for the chop, aren't I?'

Colin looked aside, but the walls reflected his expression, making it impossible to hide. 'Lawrence holds the power here,' he said, glancing at them. 'But Lee will do his utmost to persuade him. You know what he's like. Dog with a bone.'

'This time, I think he's been wrong-footed by dear Lawrence,' Richard pointed out. 'We all have.' He kissed Kath on the forehead. 'The industry's full of these awful men, isn't it my dear? No conscience, always an ulterior motive. Power grabbing; like the Wild West.'

'Damn him!' Kath shouted, trying out the acoustics.

'Oh yes Kath, damn him,' Richard's voice echoed. 'Damn any person who gives that man a free pass and makes his life easy. Because as you've seen, he'd sooner piss all over you than give you a second chance. He's one of the worst. Believe me.'

'Someone needs to stand up to him,' Kath said, catching her reflection. She gazed at it, moving closer to inspect herself further. 'Christ, have you seen how angry I look?'

'Who'd call him out?' Richard said. 'That's the dilemma. Most decide it's too big a risk.'

'Well, I don't give a shit about my career, so I'm up for the fight.' She changed her expression and pointed at her reflection. 'See, that thought makes me happy. I've a mind to have it out with him now.'

'I'm not sure Lee would appreciate that,' Colin said. 'Best leave it to him to sort out. Another confrontation tonight will only make matters worse.'

'Sweet, sweet Colin. I hear you, but when a monster roars, I've come to realise through bitter experience, that's the time you've got to roar back.'

21

Using a candle to light the way, Georgie snuck into the empty library, where embers of the fire were still burning. She wished she could lie down on the sofa and sleep, forget the nonsense of the last few hours. Since Lawrence's arrival, everyone had become stressed, tiptoeing around his ego. It had propelled her into the past, made her feel like nothing had changed. But what she'd come to do was too urgent. Having waited until Lawrence left his room – bathrobe on, carrying his toilet bag in one hand, a candle in the other – she had to assume he was heading for the bathroom. He'd be away ten minutes at most she reckoned. Opening the adjoining door, she took care not to make a sound.

A small corridor – a windowless box room with even more shelves of books filled from floor to ceiling – separated the library from Lawrence's bedroom. She crept the few steps to his door and entered, casting the candle left and right, double-checking he wasn't coming back. Her heart pounded, half-expecting him to emerge from the shadows. She whispered his name to make sure. No reply. Thank God, she thought.

Out the bay-window, a sliver of sea was visible, pounding against the rocks. It really was the finest view in the house. Nothing but the best for Lawrence.

A Louis Vuitton case lay unopened by the bed, as though he'd arrived and without stopping had rushed out to see the sights. She moved towards it. A matching leather satchel lay to one side, unbuckled, papers extracted and arranged in two bundles.

Her hands trembled as she picked up the nearest pile, candlelight rippling across the walls. Outside, the maelstrom continued unabated, lashing everything in its path. It was now or never. Distant chatter forced her to pause. The front door opened and closed. Standing still, she listened – it didn't sound like Lawrence. She breathed out. It was Kath and Colin returning, and Richard with them by the sound of it. She could clearly hear his excited cackle. The voices disappeared as they passed through the house, presumably into the kitchen.

Undeterred, she looked at the pile of papers. Lowering the candle, she flicked through them. Some contract stuff, a few fax messages, nothing that caught her attention. At the bottom of the pile however, a large brown envelope with Lawrence's name and address stuck out. Putting everything else aside, she reached inside and withdrew a single sheet of stiff, white paper: a letter from the playwright's lawyer, threatening him with a restraining order. *A leopard doesn't change its spots.* Inside the envelope was another letter: this time with the word *Confidential* handwritten on it and underlined. Without hesitating, she opened it. Before her was the information she'd hoped to find. There was no doubt; Lawrence had come here with an agenda.

Lawrence's voice, proclaiming *Don't mind me*, echoed down the hall towards the room. *Shit, shit, shit!* She dropped the letter on the bed, amidst the myriad of others. Blowing out the candle, she retreated to the library, closing the doors behind her.

22

'We're not connected to the mains here,' Jim explained to Lee, who hovered behind him, holding up a candle. 'The whole place runs off this generator normally. The lightning must have blown the main fuse, which tripped all the circuits.' He pointed to the fuse box. 'I replaced it. Do you want to do the honours and flick the switch?'

'Should I?' Lee reached for the lever. 'I'm not going to blow the place up?'

Jim adjusted his glasses and stepped forward, scrutinising a tiny diagram on the side of the generator. He looked at Lee. 'Think you'll be fine,' he said. 'Just a bit old and creaky. Much like myself.' He grinned. 'Go for it.'

'Here goes. One, two, three.' Lee winced. With one pull of the lever, the lights sprang on. A cheer sounded from upstairs. 'That was easy,' he said, blowing out the candle.

The generator puttered away, its breathing unsteady, like it had run a marathon and was about to crash over the finish line.

'That storm's going nowhere,' said Lee. They both listened to the howl of the wind above them. 'We should look for more torches in case this conks out again.' It was remiss of him not to have checked the weather; he hadn't bargained on this type of interruption. Added to the whole Richard fiasco, his troubleshooting list was getting longer.

'Storms can last for days out here.' Jim was inspecting a cardboard box lying in the corner. 'We're exposed to the full force of the Atlantic,' he continued, picking up a hammer and a knot of fairy-lights. He held them up. 'Might come in handy.'

'Give me those.' Lee pointed at the lights. 'I'll untangle them.' Mundane tasks helped him focus.

Jim threw them over. Despite being in his early fifties, there was nothing jaded about him. Everything was done with a smile and a can-do attitude. 'I'm glad you're here,' Lee said, as Jim made his way upstairs. 'That you took the part, I mean.'

Jim turned around. 'You realise this is my first acting job in over two years?'

'Seriously?' Lee was having trouble unravelling the lights. A neat-freak, he couldn't bear to see anything messy. 'I'm surprised. Your agent, Kim, has a reputation for – how do I say this politely? Doggedness. She certainly puts the work in for her clients.'

'The formidable Ms Mansell.' Jim smiled. 'Amazing woman. Gets me loads of auditions. Well, for adverts, that sort of stuff. Playing the dad, pulling "*Oh no*" faces. Problem is – *she* doesn't have to do them. *I* do. And at my age, the meaty theatre roles are thin on the ground. Though if I can last another decade or so and outlive some of my more talented peers, that could change!' He smiled. 'Plus, schmoozing bores me. Not that I ever did much of that. But it helps, I suppose, being in the loop.' He sat on the step, bringing him into line with Lee's face, who was focused on winding the fairy lights around his arm. 'I mostly teach these days; I'm on a supply list for Hammersmith and Fulham. So, any given day I can be North, South, East, West.'

Lee observed Jim's smile. No self-pity, no blame. Most actors did two or three jobs to keep them afloat. Hit a certain age and if things still hadn't worked out, they'd normally give up. 'And that's enough?'

'To get along, it's more than enough. And Georgie, she's done OK. Well, more than OK, you know that. Of course, you do. She's been the main breadwinner if truth be told.'

'But I mean,' Lee said, sitting, 'does it nourish you – the profession I mean – if there's so little opportunity?' He looked at his feet, unsure if he'd crossed the line. He wasn't used to such intimate conversations with actors. Usually, he was the one doing the hiring and firing. As the producer, it was often easier to detach oneself, pass it off as the vagaries of the business. Which it was. But behind every rejection was a personal story. He tried never to forget that.

Jim smiled as though he'd asked himself the same question countless times. 'I was a kid when I fell in love with acting. You should have seen me, the shyest in the class, but always the first to put up my hand to read a poem out loud or play a part in the school show. No one could believe it. My dad, he swore it was from his side – they were all very musical – but I couldn't even play the penny whistle. Maybe he was right though. It's all performing in the end. To me, acting feels like an out-of-body experience. Not everyone thinks that. But for me, I lose myself. I go ... somewhere else.' He was animated now. His favourite subject – not the business, not himself, but the craft of acting. 'Take this part. He's a regular guy, been working his whole career to get by, but he has this secret that he's told no one. Lived his entire life keeping it to himself. One day, he tells someone. A complete stranger.'

'It kills him, though.'

'True. Once he's told someone else, it's as if he's got no reason to live. The secret is him; it's become his identity.'

A voice shouted from upstairs, asking if they were OK.

'Is that you, Georgie, dear?'

'Not coming to join the party? We've opened another bottle of champagne,' she shouted down. 'You'll have to hurry or there'll be none left.'

The floorboards above them creaked and there was the sound of movement between rooms, followed by laughter and chatter. Jim groaned as he stood. 'This damned neck of mine. If I was a horse, they'd have shot me by now.' He continued climbing to the top of the stairs.

'Wait a second.' Lee looped the final strand of lights around his arm. 'Things will work out.' He winced at the banality of his platitude but couldn't help himself. Humanity and decency shone from the man. 'You're going to be amazing. And the offers will come flooding in. You'll see.'

Jim shrugged. 'If so, great. The thing is, I enjoy teaching, so I'm not losing out. The kids get used to you popping in every now and again. "Mr Selby!" they shout when they see me. Always a little cheer. And I'm giving something back.'

'But you need to do what you love. Not think so?'

'True, it should matter – mean something. That's the important thing. Which is why I accepted this. Because I love the role. It speaks to me. And OK, maybe I did need an ego boost, because it's been a while since anyone's been interested.'

Lee thought back to the initial casting discussion he'd had with Lawrence. Jim was at the top of his list and was non-negotiable. He told a story about the start of his career, of working alongside Jim and Georgie and learning so much from them. It was a side to Lawrence – a sweetness – Lee had never seen before. Or since. 'It must feel good to be back together again – the three of you. Like you've come full circle.'

Jim shook his head and laughed. 'That's all down to Peter. They got talking on the set of *Cobalt Dawn*, and Lawrence put two and two together and realised we were his parents. Funny how things turn out.' He stared at the wall; his expression distant. 'Anyway, Georgie will have finished that bottle if we don't hurry.'

Lee climbed the stairs to join him. 'You're the only one who doesn't have a bad word to say about Lawrence,' he said. 'How come?'

'Someone needs to give me a reason to dislike them. Lawrence never has. But that's not to say he won't.' Jim pushed open the basement door. 'Now, let's join the party!'

23

By the time Colin returned from drying himself, Kath, Peter and Richard had gravitated to the kitchen. Having changed into a t-shirt and jeans, he felt refreshed. He stood in the doorway, watching the three of them in hysterics, comparing dance moves. Before arriving, this was what he'd hoped for: a friendly bunch of performers showing off and having fun. A world apart from the grim drinking sessions down the pub he felt obliged to endure with his own colleagues.

Georgie brushed past, having changed the music in the next room. Kath squealed with delight and sang along to the cheesy pop song. Grabbing Peter, she pressed her body against his, breathlessly shouting, *'Nah, nah, nah.'* He happily joined in, a bottle of champagne swinging from his hand, howling back, *'Ooh baby, ooh baby.'*

Richard, arms swaying in the air, was attempting to harmonise with Kath on the chorus – an assortment of *oohs* and *aahs* – careering up and down the scales until they both ran out of breath.

'Colin, come on,' Kath shouted, but he shook his head, refusing to budge.

Lee and Jim appeared from the basement and immediately entered the mood of the party with a tongue-in-cheek conga.

'I see you found Dickie.' Lee disengaged himself from Jim. 'Where was he?' He wrapped his arms around Colin's waist and planted a kiss on his lips.

'In the barn.' Enjoying Lee's touch, he whispered into his ear, 'I think he's OK.'

'All of you, come and dance! That's an order!' Kath yelled, dragging chairs aside to make more room.

'Let's get this party going,' urged Jim, as Kath grabbed him. Swinging his hips and placing his hands on Georgie's shoulders, he blasted out the next verse word perfect.

Lee danced his way over and was greeted with a welcoming whoop. He winked back at Colin. 'If you can't beat them, join them.'

For the next hour, cheesy song followed cheesy song, the dancing interrupted only to pass around the next bottle of champagne.

Inevitably, there were casualties; Kath was first to take a tumble. She dropped to her knees, laughing. 'I'm not drunk,' she insisted, holding out her hands, gesturing to be lifted. In their attempt to raise her, the others lost their balance, collapsing together in hysterics.

'Look,' Georgie pointed out, reaching over to touch Kath's high heels, 'we've the same shoes. That's why I love you, Kath.' She hugged her. 'We're going to have so much fun.'

Colin was thinking about heading to bed when he caught sight of Lawrence behind him. Standing in the shadows in the hallway, had he not moved, Colin wondered if he'd have noticed him. 'I'm sorry, I didn't spot you there.' He stepped aside to allow him a better view of the party.

'No need,' Lawrence replied, joining him. He peered inside. 'I'm more of an observer. Like you.' He raised his glass. 'Cheers,' he said to the others, who barely acknowledged him. After a few minutes staring at their antics on the makeshift dancefloor, he sidled up to Colin. 'Has anyone been in my room?'

'Sorry?'

'You have been keeping an eye out?' Lawrence asked, continuing to watch everyone dance.

Here goes, thought Colin. *Day one and the paranoia's already escalated.* Above the noise of the music, he emphasised, 'We've all been in here.'

'I mean, earlier.'

Was Lawrence seriously expecting him to monitor everybody's movements? If so, he'd be disappointed. He'd been asked to look out for any suspicious activity, not spy on the cast. He pointed at the empty glass in his hand. 'Off duty, I'm afraid.'

'About an hour ago,' continued Lawrence.

Colin shook his head. 'Nope. Sorry. Everyone's accounted for.' He squeezed past him. 'Excuse me.' He headed further into the kitchen to grab another beer, sensing Lawrence's eyes burn into him as he took a slurp. When he turned, Lawrence gestured him back over.

Carefully avoiding being pulled into the group dance, Colin rejoined him. There was an entitlement about him Colin didn't care for. An assumption that following their conversation and their tacit agreement, he'd become his employee. It wasn't going to work. He'd have to set him straight. And if that meant leaving the island earlier, so be it.

'Some of my belongings have been moved,' Lawrence whispered, holding onto Colin's arm. 'When the party's over, could you check the windows, doors, that sort of thing?' He withdrew his hand and lit a cigarette. 'It would ease my mind.'

Colin took another swig of beer, stepping away from the smell of the smoke. 'Once I'm finished here, that's no problem.' He smiled. That he was prepared to do.

Peter came staggering over, a jumper tied round his waist.

Out of breath, he burped as he reached them. 'Excuse me, that's rude, isn't it?' He was flapping his arms, oblivious to the beer spilling from the bottle in his hand.

'Careful!' Colin grabbed hold of the bottle, gently adjusting it upright.

'I've not told you how much this means to me.' Swaying, Peter's focus was entirely on Lawrence. Despite the invasion of his space, Lawrence didn't seem to mind. In fact, his expression didn't change as Peter leaned in even further.

'It means a lot to me too,' he replied. 'It's a great part for a young actor. Like I said on the phone, it suits you to a tee: young man, struggling to be heard, eager to prove himself.'

A serious, quizzical look flickered over Peter's face. It was obvious he wanted to take the conversation further. But as he grabbed Lawrence's arm to steer him off into a corner, Kath came rushing over and nuzzled Peter on the neck. 'Oh no you don't. Come back and dance.'

'Not now, Kitty!' he said, before adding, 'I'll be one minute.' Pressing Lawrence's arm he muttered, 'Sorry. Honestly, she doesn't give me a moment's peace.'

Kath ignored his brusqueness and focused her attention on Colin instead. Pulling a mock sad face, and in her best Eartha Kitt impersonation, she said, 'And I'm very upset that you won't dance with me either, PC Buxton.'

'Later. I promise. I'm not drunk enough yet.'

'And what about me?' Lawrence stared at her, both hands in pocket. 'Maybe *I'd* like to dance.'

'You can go fuck yourself. Oops!' Wide-eyed, she stepped back, one hand over her mouth. Without blinking, she rejoined the group and applauded Jim and Lee, who were attempting a breakdance.

'My cue to leave, I think,' Lawrence said. 'Awful music anyway.' He smiled nervously. 'Could you check my room now, Colin?'

He held up his half-empty bottle and smiled as politely as

he could muster. 'Tell you what, I'll pop in when I'm finished this.'

Peter put a hand on Lawrence's shoulder. 'She doesn't mean it,' he slurred. 'She gets overexcited, that's all.' He was swaying side to side, as if he might throw up at any second. Thrusting his face into Lawrence's, he begged, 'Stay and chat, please. I'll explain everything.'

'Leave him alone, Peter!' Kath shouted, barging over. 'Can't you see he doesn't want to?' This time, instead of stopping, she strode out of the room, champagne bottle in hand, exclaiming she needed to pee.

'See you in the morning, Peter.' Lawrence hugged him, before saying to Colin, 'I'll leave the door ajar – but don't leave it too late.' To the rest of the room, he yelled, 'Good night!'

Ignoring him and the ongoing drama, the party continued. Richard shouted, telling them to change the music, that he wanted something louder, before he and Georgie headbanged along to Def Leppard's *Pour Some Sugar On Me*. At times, it seemed as if they were trying to outdo the gale, which still roared, pummelling the house relentlessly. Eventually however, the mood quietened, and Lee persuaded Colin to join him in a slow dance. While Jim ran out to change the music yet again, Georgie switched off the lights, leaving only a few candles and the newly reclaimed fairy lights to illuminate the room.

Though the storm raged, hammering doors and rattling windows, no one paid it much attention. Over the course of the evening, it had become background noise. Swaying to the music, cocooned in their own little world of champagne and silly pop songs, they were oblivious to it.

'I'm sorry.' Lee's eyes, tired and drunken, were trying to focus, but he gave in and closed them, resting his head against Colin's chest.

'For bringing me here?' He felt Lee nod twice. 'Don't worry, you can make it up to me.'

A wicked smile spread across Lee's face. 'Colin Buxton. Behave!'

'Mind you, the state you're in, it might have to wait.'

Wanting in on the action, Jim approached, arms outstretched. Georgie, who'd been dancing by herself, rushed over too. Together, they squeezed Colin and Lee tightly.

'Gorgeous – the two of you,' Georgie beamed.

'Me too. I want some loving.' Richard sprang from the chair where he'd been nodding off, joining in with the group hug.

As one, they sang along to the song – something about eagles and blue skies. Georgie held a note so long she looked like she was about to pass out, whilst Richard and Jim harmonised an octave lower, showing off their vocal abilities. Colin only knew half the words, so he and Lee competed to see who could come up with the rudest alternative. *Bum* for *drum*, and *penis* for *seen us* was the best they could come up with, but it made everyone laugh hysterically. However, it wasn't long before they ran out of steam and fell apart.

'An early start tomorrow,' Jim said. 'We all need a bit of shut eye,' he slurred. 'Though we have out-partied the young 'uns. He smiled at Georgie, picking her up by the waist and swinging her around, much to her delight. 'Still got it, haven't we?'

'I'll tidy up.' As real and airborne kisses were thrown in his direction, Colin pondered how this would never happen down the *The Crown,* the pub next door to the station.

'Thank you, sexy.' Lee gave him a huge smacker on the lips to a round of applause.

'Enough!' Colin shouted, shooing them out. 'Get to bed. Drunks, the whole damned lot of you!' One by one, they left, kissing and hugging him as they went. Richard even came back for a second. Then a third. At the fourth, Colin raised his eyebrow and he finally agreed to leave.

Once alone, Colin did a circuit of the downstairs rooms, ensuring all windows and outside doors were secured. Finding Peter asleep in the library, he shook him. 'C'mon pal, you'll be more comfortable in bed,' but he resisted, coiling himself tighter into a ball. Placing another couple of logs on the fire, Colin put the guard across and closed the door quietly.

Outside in the hallway, he was about to go upstairs when he remembered Lawrence. 'Shit!' He'd forgotten to check his room. He looked at his watch. It was after midnight and his door was closed. Lawrence would surely be asleep by now. He tried to remember when he'd last seen him; after Kath had thrown a strop, he'd hung around for a bit, said goodnight – he could remember that – but for how long he wasn't sure. Tomorrow would have to do. It would give him the opportunity to refine the small print of their agreement.

He headed upstairs. At the landing, he heard hushed voices downstairs and paused to listen. At first, he was unsure where they were coming from. But as he listened more intently, his focus fell on Lawrence's room. Suddenly, a voice was raised. A woman's; Kath's. He held his breath. Except for the storm, the rest of the house was silent. For a moment, even that seemed to fade, holding back, eager to hear what came next. Again, Kath's voice rose: she was angry or upset. Creeping back downstairs, he drew closer to the sitting room door. Beneath his foot, a floorboard creaked. He winced and paused, but the voices continued. The handle turned, and he scurried to the kitchen and closed the door over, leaving a small gap. He'd only just made it when Kath emerged from Lawrence's room and rushed upstairs, the door slamming shut behind her.

For sheer drama, the evening's shenanigans were giving quiz night at *The Prince of Wales* in Soho a run for its money.

Forget the drag queens against the bull-dykes or the twinks versus the daddies; Lawrence Delaney against the world was not to be missed.

Colin relit the candles and closed the kitchen door. The rush of adrenalin had cleared his head and he knew he wouldn't sleep. Instead, he opened a cupboard and pulled out a bottle of whisky. Sitting at the table, he switched on the radio, tuning it to Radio 3 – Mozart's *Requiem* was playing – sheer bliss. He poured himself a large one. *Slàinte,* he whispered to himself, holding the glass against the candlelight, before downing it in one.

24

With a start, Colin woke, his head rough from the beer and whisky – a lethal combination he normally avoided. He switched off the radio, which was now playing a soft and pleasing work by Satie and glanced at his watch. 1.10 AM. Outside, though the rain had stopped, the wind still circled the house, and waves crashed against the rocks in a continuous loop: a destructive smashing sound, blunt with a thunderous echo.

His back ached. Getting up, he poured himself a glass of water. The house was quiet, odd after the evening's events. With everyone asleep, no egos were clashing, no tempers flaring. He wondered how long that would last. A day? Two days? More likely a few hours. He poured himself another glass of water and immediately felt better. Time for bed. No doubt Lee would be splayed out, snoring and wheezing. Preferring not to chance his wrath in case he woke him by mistake, a better option would be to crash in one of the empty bedrooms. That way, they could both get a good night's sleep. He blew out the candles.

In the hallway, the library door lay open. As he walked the few steps towards it, he marvelled at the grandeur of the house. Even in the dim light, the luxurious wallpaper, the ornate cornicing, and the antique ornaments made their presence felt. The only time he'd stayed anywhere as fancy was at a friend's wedding in a huge baronial mansion on the shores of Loch Lomond. Coming from a council estate on the outskirts of Glasgow, he wasn't used to such opulence. His mother's taste was more aertex swirls and ceramic cherubs. And of course, crucifixes. Lots of them.

He popped his head into the library; it was empty and the fire had died. Peter must have woken and gone upstairs. The door to the box room was ajar. Peering inside, he noticed that Lawrence's bedroom door was also open. Complete silence. Apparently, Hollywood stars didn't snore. He switched off the lamp and closed the door as quietly as possible.

In the hallway, the wind rose with a sudden shriek and battered against the windows, like it was trying to force entry. Hopefully, the storm would pass overnight and it would be clearer in the morning. He could maybe get outside for some fresh air, put his walking boots on and discover the wildness of the surroundings. There were a couple of coves he wanted to explore. However, the strength of the wind lifted again, sweeping around the house and pounding the front door, suggesting any walks might not be an option.

An icy chill blew towards him, whistling through the cracks and crevices. For the first time since arriving, he felt cold, his body shivering as he switched off the downstairs lights and made his way upstairs.

At the top, he turned onto the main corridor where most of the bedrooms were. Unable to remember who slept where, he was positive no one had chosen a room on the attic floor above, so continued up the next flight. As soon as he reached the attic landing, he heard what he thought was retching. *Who the hell's that?* The noise was coming from behind a door at the far end of the corridor. He walked towards it, listening, trying hard to distinguish between the noises of the storm outside and those coming from the other side of the door.

He knocked gently. 'Is everything OK?' No one replied. 'Hello?' Colin waited a few seconds then gently tried the handle, but the door was locked. He continued to listen, but the sound had stopped. *Better leave whoever it is*, he thought. *Don't want to embarrass them.*

As he made his way back along the corridor, he decided on a random room and prayed it would be free. He prised open the door and switched on the light, relieved to find it empty. The room was more plainly furnished than those downstairs, with a small double-bed, twin bedside tables, and a little antique wardrobe. However, it did have an en suite. Though the room was stone-cold, he reasoned that once under the bedcovers, he'd be fine.

He crossed over to use the bathroom. As he stood, pondering how he'd managed to become embroiled in Lawrence's neurosis, he could have sworn someone opened and closed the bedroom door. He called out "Hello?" and twisted round to look, but no one was there.

Stepping back into the room, he undressed, thinking he could still hear sounds coming from the end of the corridor. Even after switching off the main light and getting into bed, as the blackness of sleep descended, he imagined someone groaning. But as he rolled onto his favoured side, pulling the sheets over his head, the thought quickly faded.

25

Lee sat up in bed, his head thumping. In the dark, his hands scrambled around the mattress searching for Colin, but his side was empty. He switched on the bedside lamp. Squinting at his watch, he could see it was 1.30 AM. Where the hell is he? Unable to recall coming to bed, or if Colin had been with him, his mind raced over the night's events. The last thing he could remember was slow dancing to a song. Nothing after that.

Pulling on his trousers and a hoodie, he ventured into the corridor. An icy draught immediately greeted him. He shoved his hands inside his pockets and walked to the top of the stairs. Perhaps the party was still going strong in the kitchen. Enough alcohol had been consumed to knock out a herd of rhinos, but knowing this bunch, he wouldn't be surprised. Though it *was* unusual for *him* not to be the last man standing. Colin would usually be first to bed.

It seemed as though everybody had taken to him. Except Peter. But he was in his own bubble; he had such a rigid idea of how an actor should behave, he was in danger of disappearing up his own arse. Hopefully, he'd relax once rehearsals began.

Downstairs, it was clear the party was over. Not a sound. However, Lee thought it strange that Lawrence's door was open. He considered closing it but instead wandered into the kitchen. A half-empty bottle of whisky sitting on the table indicated Colin had stayed up late; it was his only vice. The single glass suggested he'd been drinking alone. *So, that's your plan? Wait till everyone's gone to bed and only then get blind drunk?*

He took a seat and lifted the glass, taking in the aroma, imagining Colin's lips against it, the hint of caramel sweetness giving him fond memories of them sitting up late, chatting about anything and everything, sipping whisky till the early hours. It was how they fell in love, realised how much they respected each other, and eventually how much they wanted and needed to be together. He placed the glass back on the table.

Outside the window, the trees swayed violently. In silhouette, they were like a surging sea, a tsunami about to engulf the house. Standing too quickly, he had to sit back down. The evening was still a blur. He remembered Kath pulling him aside, whispering into his ear – something about someone harassing her – but she wasn't making sense. She'd made a complaint, she kept repeating, but the company had closed ranks. Whose company? Not his. It was all a jumble of words. The likelihood was he'd misunderstood.

However, whatever she'd said had sparked his own guilt. Mistakes he'd made in the past. Nothing too serious and all could be blamed on alcohol. Way back when he was starting out, he'd propositioned the leading actor at the opening night party. The next day, the actor had called him out on it, saying how unprofessional it was, that it verged on being manipulative. Lee had agreed. But, on another production not long after, he'd slept with the lighting designer early in rehearsals, who'd turned out to be a bit of a handful – sweet in a particular way, but stalkerish in others. Letting him down gently had been a challenge and a complete distraction. So, he learned his lesson early on: business and pleasure were not happy bedfellows. His reputation had only been slightly dented, and these days he was the epitome of discretion and professionalism. Moderating his drinking had undoubtedly made life easier.

But there were occasions – like tonight – when it slipped. He put it down to stress or more specifically Lawrence Delaney. Thinking back to their first meeting, he was shocked by how naïve he'd been to the likely pitfalls; dazzled as he was when Lawrence walked into his office. For all his experience, he'd not managed to see past the Hollywood charisma and Broadway pizzazz. His judgement had been clouded by the fact a Hollywood A-lister was pitching him – Lee Murphy from Bangor, North Wales – an idea for a show. He'd been flattered. Of all the producers Lawrence could have gone to, he'd been chosen. It took them fifteen minutes to shake hands and agree on the terms. He'd made many deals in his career, but nothing like that. 'We're all going to be a little richer by the end of this,' had been Lawrence's parting words.

Concerned that he might have said or done something inappropriate, Lee needed to find Colin and ask him to fill in the blanks. With the house feeling so empty, perhaps Colin and the rest of them were in the barn. The only sound in the house was the wind – a dull, constant pressure, pushing against the building, testing its tolerance. If the others could brave the storm, so could he.

He took the torch from the kitchen table and pulled on a snazzy red cagoule from the hallway cupboard. The full force of the weather struck his face as he opened the back door. It was savage. Leaning into the wind, navigating it sideways at one point, it took him several minutes to reach the barn. Out of breath from the exertion, he pushed against the door. As it sprang open, he was met with darkness. Searching for the light switch, his hand trailed along the wall, but for the life of him, he couldn't find it. Instead, he tracked the torch's beam around the cavernous space, its flicker weakly illuminating random ghostly objects.

He squinted, wishing he'd worn his glasses, letting his eyesight gradually adjust to the dim light. Even in the darkness, the space appeared magnificent, the solid timber floor and mirrored walls giving the space a grand opulence. Whatever Lawrence's failings, he'd secured an amazing setting for rehearsals. Tomorrow, the months of planning would start to pay off, and the rehearsal space would be filled with laughter and no doubt a few tears. Voices would be raised, bodies would be hugged, and together they'd breathe life into the words that up until that point only existed on sheets of paper. And if there was a theatre God, maybe Lawrence could be dissuaded from replacing Richard.

At the far end of the barn, he found a small area hidden from the main rehearsal space by a long partition. Half-expecting to discover Colin asleep, or the others waiting to jump out, he was disappointed to find it empty. They were in bed after all. Wonders would never cease. He switched off the torch and lay down, closing his eyes, feeling himself drift off, continuing to wonder where Colin had gone. It wasn't like him. But then again, since Lawrence arrived on the island, nothing had quite gone to plan.

Day 2

26

Morning brought no respite from the storm. If anything, it had worsened, the rolling sheets of rain emphasising how cut off they were from civilisation. Standing in front of the window, Colin did some stretches; he'd slept reasonably well despite the rock-hard mattress, but now he was on his feet, the back of his neck felt stiff and his whole left side ached. Outside, mist cloaked the island, making it impossible to see much beyond the trees. Gusts of wind continuing to swirl around the house, laying siege to it. From the shore, the percussive sound of waves thundered, battering against the rocks like gunfire. There'd be no hike along the cliffs today.

As he crept downstairs, the entire building shook as if the storm could, if it wanted, pick the house up and rip it to pieces. He snuck into the bedroom and threw open the curtains. 'Morning, sleeping beauty,' he cried, tearing the covers off the bed.

Lee sat up in alarm, instinctively grabbing for them. 'Where the hell have you been?' he asked. 'I came looking for you, but I couldn't find you anywhere.'

'You couldn't have looked very hard.'

'And where are my specs?'

Colin picked them off the floor. 'I could have stood on them. Then where would you be?'

'Give!' he snapped, grasping at them. 'Why didn't you come to bed?' He perched his glasses on the end of his nose, waiting for an explanation. 'Well?'

'I reckoned you'd be snoring like the proverbial. So, Lawrence and I bunked up together.'

Lee's face fell.

'Kidding! I took an empty room upstairs so's I wouldn't disturb you.'

Lee groaned and sank into his pillow, pulling the sheet up to his chin. 'You could've written a note, stuck it under the door. Woke me. Something.'

Colin raised his eyebrow. 'Wake you? Seriously?'

Lee reached over and lit a cigarette. 'Yes. Seriously. I was worried.' He held out his hand. 'Ashtray, please.' Leaning over to take it, he coughed. 'What time is it?'

'I thought you were only a social smoker these days,' Colin said, undressing.

'Don't be so judgemental.' Lee took a puff, blew out some smoke and wafted it towards him.

'It's eight o'clock.' Colin headed into the en suite for a shower, waving the offending fumes away.

Lee's hacking cough returned. 'Still no sun?' He dragged the bedding with him and peered outside at the wall of grey mist. 'No one's getting on or off this island today, are they?'

Over the roar of the shower, Colin shouted, 'Doesn't seem so. It's like we've sunk to the bottom of the Atlantic.' He yelped. 'Any idea how to work this? The water's freezing.'

Lee popped his head round the bathroom door. 'Turn the top dial more to the left.' He slumped back on the bed. 'Phone still not working, I take it?' He stubbed out his cigarette.

'Haven't tried.' Colin appeared in the doorway, towelling

himself dry. 'That shower isn't working. Either that or there's no hot water.'

'Christ! This place. Another thing for me to sort no doubt.' He eyed Colin up. 'Come here.' He held out his arms. 'Let me warm you up.'

With one leap, Colin jumped on the bed, landing face-to-face with Lee. 'Right stinky breath, fancy a shag?'

'What's made you so perky?'

'The sea air. The clear head. The smell of fresh coffee.' He snuggled into Lee. 'Not having to go to work.'

Suddenly animated, Lee asked, 'There's coffee?'

'Sorry, that was a bit of poetic licence. It's downstairs. In a jar.' Colin went to sit up. 'I can make you one if you want.'

Lee dragged him back. 'Don't you dare go anywhere,' he said. 'Coffee can wait.' They kissed for a moment before Lee pulled away. 'No one else is up and about, are they?'

Colin took off Lee's glasses, placing them on the bedside table. 'Worried they'll hear?'

'I'm more worried they're outside that door, listening.'

'Don't bother your pretty little head about them.' He straddled Lee. 'Dead to the world. Not surprised either – they can fair knock it back.' He rubbed Lee's nipples, watching them spring into life.

'It's gonna be hell, isn't it?' Lee's fingers ran along Colin's back.

'Oh yes.' He kissed the soft patch of Lee's armpit before making his way down to his waist. 'Come here,' he whispered.

'You don't care, do you?' Lee forced Colin to look at him.

'Not really,' he replied, a huge grin on his face. 'So long as I get my end away.'

Lee took a pillow and bashed Colin over the head with it. 'Anyway, aren't you his personal bodyguard now, or is it his Man Friday?

'Toy boy,' Colin corrected, his hands pressing between

Lee's legs. 'Lawrence likes to keep me on constant call. You're just my fluffer.' Without warning, he tickled Lee, who let out a scream.

'I knew you were going to do that,' he screeched, attempting to wriggle free. 'Stop! Play nice.'

'Not till you say Lawrence is the best boss ever.'

'Never!' Finally, Lee gave in and let Colin spoon with him. 'The way he's treating Richard is unforgivable. But you know, way at the start, his ideas of how the play could be staged were beautiful. It was he who suggested all the characters' voices should be heard offstage at the end. Such a stroke of brilliance, for them to disappear one by one off into the distance.' He took Colin's hand in his, locking their fingers together. 'Nothing prepared me for how awful he was going to be to people. Yet here we are, stuck in the middle of nowhere with a bunch of actors who despise him.'

'You're exaggerating. Jim doesn't. Neither does Peter.'

'True. *They* just hate each other. Did you see how Peter looks at him?'

He had. On the first night, Colin had watched as Peter picked a stupid fight with his father about how he couldn't deal cards properly. It ended with Peter storming off in a huff. 'He doesn't know how lucky he is to have parents like Jim and Georgie.'

'And poor Richard. I don't know what to do; I'm concerned about him.' Lee turned to face Colin.

Imagining them both adrift, the storm sighing and wailing around them, Colin took hold of Lee's erection and smiled. 'Yes. Feels like you're very concerned.'

Lee squinted. 'Don't forget, Colin Buxton, I'm not emotionally invested in this. As far as I'm concerned, it's simply a business arrangement.'

Colin shrugged. 'Fine with me. A perk of the job, I suppose.'

Lee fixed his gaze on him, as Colin's hands ran down his

spine and explored the flesh of his buttocks. 'Skin and bone bumping and grinding against each other. That's all.'

'We all have needs.' Stretching over to the bedside drawer, Colin asked, 'Now, where's the lube?'

As they were about to kiss, a scream from downstairs ripped through the house.

27

Georgie's screams echoed through the hallway. 'He's dead! He's dead!'

Colin leapt down the stairs with Lee not far behind. 'What's going on?' he shouted.

Ashen faced, she stood barefoot in a nightdress and cardigan, her finger pointing at Lawrence's room. 'Help him,' was all she could say.

A panic of footsteps sounded from upstairs.

As Colin threw open the door he whispered to Lee, 'Keep everyone out,' before disappearing inside.

'What's happening?' Kath asked, tripping down the final set of steps, Peter following. 'Who's dead?'

Lee went to speak but was interrupted by Georgie.

'It's Lawrence.' She held out her hand for Kath to take. 'He's on the bed. There's blood everywhere.' She stared at the others, her mouth trembling. 'So much blood.'

Colin came out of the bedroom, strode over to the kitchen, disappeared inside for ten seconds, before reappearing. 'You all need to step back. Lee, take everyone to the kitchen and stay there.'

'Is it true?' Kath asked. 'Is he really dead?' She folded her arms around Georgie and pressed her close.

'There's no pulse.' Colin took a mental note of their reactions: how Georgie's shoulders tensed, whilst Kath turned away to face Peter who stood shaking his head in disbelief. Unmoved, Jim stood apart, as if he were a passer-by. Wide-eyed, Lee clung to the banister. Only Richard was missing. 'It looks as if he's been dead for a few hours. I need to contain the crime scene.'

'Crime scene?' Peter's face twisted. 'Says who?'

'Are you suggesting someone did this?' Jim asked.

'Yes.' Again, Colin scanned their reactions. Jim placed an arm around Georgie as she wiped tears from her eyes. Kath, meanwhile, was holding onto Peter's who seemed ready to explode. Still in shock, Lee remained motionless.

'Please Lee,' Colin urged, 'take everyone into the kitchen and stay there. Make some coffee.' He crossed over to him and whispered in his ear, 'Lee?' he stressed, 'I need you to do this for me.'

Lee blinked, coming back into focus. 'Yes, of course. Whatever you need.'

'Try to keep them calm. But whatever you do, make sure no one leaves the house. And don't let anyone else in. Got it?'

Lee nodded.

28

The first major scene Colin ever attended had been called in as a domestic late one afternoon. A normal run-of-the-mill report: a neighbour had heard shouting and things being thrown against the wall. However, by the time he'd arrived with his partner, Foster, a copper with twenty years' experience, things had gone tragically wrong. The husband had plunged a kitchen knife into his wife's chest, killing her instantly.

The similarity to murder scenes from films and TV was superficial; there was far more blood than he could have ever imagined. And the smell – sweet, metallic – was like nothing he'd ever smelled before. It stayed with him for months after, a putrid stench constantly in the background. It got so bad that every time he passed a butcher's shop, he had the urge to vomit.

He only glimpsed the crime scene briefly before Foster ordered him outside to secure the property ready for the arrival of the forensics team. But what he'd seen was enough: the woman's blood spattered across lilac walls, the knife protruding from her striped shirt, her face calm, almost serene, the husband cowering in a corner weeping that she'd made him do it, their baby crying from a stroller parked by the kitchen table. How could such a thing happen? No amount of explanation could answer that.

Before the squad cars and ambulances came roaring down the street, before the throngs of onlookers multiplied, he'd taken a moment. The sheer relief as the fresh air filled his lungs was like breathing for the first time. He retched, like he'd been poisoned, and spat on the ground.

'You can get nicked for that, son,' a neighbour, cigarette dangling between her fingers, shouted from the other side of the fence. 'I take it he's done her in this time?' she went on, before flicking the ash to the ground and leaving, without waiting for his reply.

Back at the station, his team had been supportive. This was in the early days, before they'd got to know him, before their suspicions into his private life had developed into vicious gossip; innuendoes aimed at every word he uttered, every movement he made. Never directly to his face though. Yet always within earshot. That day, all had shared similar experiences, recalling their first time, slapping him on the back, proclaiming he'd seen nothing that a good bevvy couldn't sort. Their banter had stopped though when his sergeant stepped in – decent, sceptical, ran a tight ship – noting how brutal and complex the scene had been, pointing out that their own first experiences were kids' play next to Colin's.

'You'll be OK, lad. Past the first hurdle.' He gave the others a warning look, ensuring they all got back to work.

Colin nodded, avoided the others' stares, and returned to writing his report.

For the rest of that shift, as silence fell over the usual din of the squad room, glances of respect, perhaps a little envy, were aimed his way. Yet for some reason, he'd felt a fraud. Perhaps the realisation he'd be expected to witness similar scenes of horror in the future – that it would all become normal and simply something to compare notes on – felt overwhelming. If the others hadn't been around, he'd have rushed to the gents and thrown up. Typing, focusing on letters and words fill the page, kept him going until his shift ended.

AFTER TYING plastic bags to his feet and grabbing a pair of rubber gloves from the store cupboard in the hallway, Colin re-entered Lawrence's bedroom. Without proper forensic equipment, and conscious he might risk contaminating the scene, Colin stood on one spot and surveyed the room. The shutters were bolted from the inside, which seemed to rule out forced entry. So, access had likely been via one of the internal doors. He recalled seeing the door to the library open when he'd done his rounds at the end of the night. That had been after midnight.

Inspecting the room more closely, he saw the floor was littered with papers and clothes, and a suitcase was angled by the wall, as though it had been thrown. Lawrence's body lay face down across the bottom of the bed. From the trauma to his head, it was obvious he'd been hit with force. Shards of white skull and grey brain matter gleamed among the dark congealed blood, which had dripped down his neck and seeped across the bedclothes. Most macabre of all was his dislodged eye, staring up from the bedclothes. Scanning the room for a weapon, nothing fitted the bill. The Chinese porcelain table lamp was a possibility but appeared clean and would have smashed on impact. There seemed nothing close by heavy enough to cause such catastrophic injuries. He looked towards the centre of the mantelpiece – the statuette he'd held in his hands the night before was gone.

He took two steps forward to scrutinise the body more closely. The side of Lawrence's face had a purple, reddish colour like a bruise, most likely caused by an accumulation of blood, suggesting it had lain undisturbed. So, death more than likely took place within the room. The body was cold, and checking the stiffness of the neck and jaw, he reckoned Lawrence had been dead for several hours. That was only an educated guess; he was no expert. He'd have to question the others, ask when they'd last seen Lawrence alive, determine the likely time of death more accurately. The first person would have to be Kath, who he'd witnessed storming out of the room just after twelve, but also Peter, who'd been asleep in the library next door.

The light from the central chandelier was not the brightest, but he could see no visible traces of shoe prints on the carpet, no traces of blood going toward either exits. Could the murderer have had time to clean up? Maybe Lawrence's hunch was right, that someone was following him and had struck whilst they all slept. The thought that an outsider was secretly hiding on the island immediately concerned him.

He took a mental note of which items appeared disturbed: a briefcase lying open, the scattered papers, two cushions placed or thrown to the side of the sofa, the strangely angled suitcase. Apart from these, any of which Lawrence could have done himself, everything appeared to be in order. Everything apart from the body that lay sprawled on the blood-soaked sheets.

He scanned the room again, capturing every aspect of the space as best he could. First instincts were crucial. It was at that point he realised the Dictaphone was nowhere to be seen.

He went through a list in his head. First, he needed to check if the phone was working to call in back up, then the house had to be searched and secured. Of course, identifying and logging evidence for a crime scene was second nature, but doing so for a murder was a different matter. A thought popped into his head; he could ask if anyone had brought a camera; that would help with gathering evidence and could also prove critical later. A search of the grounds and wider area of the island would be needed too – a lot for one person. How much of the scene he could realistically cordon off was also questionable. Under the circumstances – the ferocity of the storm, the group staying where the crime took place – isolating the entire house wouldn't be practical. He'd have to think what best to do.

But his main concern was the thought of a murderer still at large. With the storm raging, it was doubtful anyone could get on or off the island – that might be good for the investigation, but extremely worrying in terms of everyone's safety. One thing he knew for certain though: he needed to act quickly.

Making his way from the room, he double-checked for any sign of blood on the walls or carpet. He knew there would be microscopic evidence invisible to the naked eye, but for now, a superficial inspection would have to do. 'Lee!' he shouted down the hall.

Lee came running from the kitchen, his face gaunt. Seeing Colin in his makeshift gear, dark matter on the bright yellow gloves, he stopped. 'My God!'

Colin had no time to explain. 'Is there a key to the sitting room?'

'I've not seen one,' Lee said. 'I don't think there's even one for the front door. It's a private island, miles from anywhere.' He walked towards Colin.

'Stay there!' Colin said, one hand stretched in front of him. 'I need to minimise contamination.'

Lee did as he was told. 'Sorry. But Colin, you have to tell me what's happening.' He gestured towards the kitchen. 'They're asking questions. And as soon as the newspapers hear about this, it's going to be chaos.'

'Lee,' Colin interrupted, 'I need to figure out how far the crime scene extends.' He looked him in the eye. 'Then I promise I'll tell you as much as I can.'

'But surely it all happened in there?' Lee tried to look through the open door, but Colin pulled it shut.

'Whoever murdered Lawrence probably escaped through the hallway or the library. I need to try and work it out.'

Lee wrapped his arms around himself. 'He's really been murdered? You're sure?'

Colin stared at Lee, aware he was saying too much, that he'd have to be more cautious. Anyone in the house could have killed Lawrence. Even Lee. Christ, they all seemed to have a motive. 'Where's the phone?'

'Over by the front door.'

Colin peeled off the rubber gloves and picked up the receiver.

'I've already tried. Nothing.'

'Can you keep trying?' Colin asked. 'And check with Jim. Isn't he good with electrics? See if he can get it fixed. We need to contact the mainland as soon as possible.'

He returned to Lawrence's room – this time via the library. It appeared exactly as he'd last seen it – sometime about 1.15 AM. With nothing obvious amiss, he opened the door to the adjoining box room. Scanning the floor, checking the shelves of books, concluding that nothing seemed out of place, he pushed open the door to Lawrence's room. Remaining at the threshold, he scanned from side to side, double-checking if he'd missed anything, recalling where things had been positioned the previous evening. The human stench hit him this time. Not only blood, but faeces, urine. The smell of vulnerability. In the hallway, Lee was speaking, but he couldn't register what he was saying.

'I think you need to speak with them,' Lee repeated, careful not to step into the library.

Colin closed the box room door and returned to the hallway, closing the library door behind him. 'What?'

'They're very distressed.'

Lee was right. People needed to be informed, reassured.

That was his duty, too. 'Sure. Of course.' He then remembered. 'What about Richard? I've not seen him. Do you know where he is?'

Lee pulled a face. 'He was on the stairs when you ordered us into the kitchen. I told him to come with us, but he refused.'

'Drunk?'

'Stinking. He disappeared upstairs to look for more drink.' Lee registered Colin's concern. 'Should I find him?'

'I'll help you.'

'Don't be daft. I can handle him. Convince him drink's not the answer,' he added, crossing

to the bottom of the stairs.

'Say nothing about Lawrence,' Colin whispered. 'I need to be the one who tells

him.'

Keeping one eye on Lee as he climbed the stairs, Colin pushed open the kitchen door and stood in the threshold. The room fell silent. He registered their body language, watching for even the smallest reaction that might offer a clue. 'Look, there's no easy way to say this,' he began, 'but Lawrence is dead. And there's no doubt in my mind he's been murdered.' Their heads collectively bowed. 'I need to secure the crime scene as much as possible until the police arrive from the mainland, so it goes without saying no one can enter Lawrence's room or the library.'

Peter raised his head. 'How the fuck did this happen?' His eyes were fixed on Colin. 'Is there some loony out there?'

Colin paused as he considered his answer. Jim was whispering in Georgie's ear, words of comfort perhaps, Kath was staring out the window, but he could see her reflection in the glass, blank and distant.

'Well?' Peter demanded, standing up.

'Please, sit down.' An intruder was only one theory. In his mind, he'd already placed each of them in Lawrence's room and had walked through possible scenarios: reassessing, recalculating, re-evaluating which of them could have committed the crime. Lawrence had been hit by someone who was able to overpower him. That was clear. But he needed more time and evidence to come to any firm conclusions. 'I can't discuss any details. Sorry. If you stay in here for now, I'll tell you more later.'

He shouted down the hall. 'Lee, everything OK?'

'Coming,' he replied. 'He's awake.'

'Mum says there's a lot of blood. Was he stabbed? Hit?' Peter's eyes blazed accusingly.

'I can't say.' Already, Colin was wondering how much of the scene Georgie had taken in. What could she have told them that might interfere with his questioning?

'Why the fuck not?' Peter looked at the others. 'It's ridiculous. We've got PC Plod here who's been a copper for all of two minutes trying to take charge.'

'Honey,' Kath said gently, 'you need to let Colin do his job.'

Peter jumped up, scraping the chair against the floorboards.

'I can't let anyone leave the kitchen for now.' Colin blocked Peter's way.

'This is bullshit!' he screamed. 'What authority does this guy have?' He squared up to Colin, pointing his finger at his chest. 'Eh? I mean, what's your boyfriend up to right this minute?'

'Shush!' hissed Georgie, immediately silencing him. As he sat, she squeezed his hand. 'We're all in shock.'

Colin, confident the most volatile of them was being dealt with, asked, 'Has anyone got a camera?'

Jim raised his arm. 'I brought mine.'

'Great. Can you tell me where it is?'

'Upstairs in our bedroom. Top drawer of the chest of drawers. There are a couple of extra spools of film, too.'

'I'll get it,' Georgie said. 'I don't want a stranger going

through my private belongings.' She turned to Colin. 'You do understand, I hope?'

'I'm sorry, Georgie, but you all have to stay here for the time being. I promise to be respectful.'

'I'm sure Colin's seen a pair of knickers before.' Jim's attempt to lighten the mood was met with disapproval.

'Not mine, he hasn't!' Georgie pulled out a packet of cigarettes and lit one.

'I could also do with some paper and a pen,' Colin added, going over in his head what else he might need.

'There are loads in my room,' Kath said. 'If you go into my suitcase, you'll find a notepad. I brought it for rehearsals.'

Colin's scanned the faces in front of him. They wouldn't like what he was about to say. 'I'll need to interview all of you separately.'

'Are we suspects?' Kath asked, not waiting for his answer. 'We are, aren't we?'

From the hallway, they could hear stumbling footsteps. Lee entered, holding a half-conscious Richard upright. 'We definitely have a situation,' he whispered to Colin.

'Excuse me.' Richard pulled away and barged past Colin, making a beeline for the fridge from which he plucked a bottle of vodka. 'No one minds, do they?' he said, without making eye contact. As he headed for the door, the weight of silence seemed to stop him in his tracks. He looked around, doing a double take as he realised everyone had gathered in the room. 'What's going on?' he asked. 'Christ, not an intervention!'

'Richard, you might need to sit,' said Colin. 'There's something I need to tell you.'

29

Still cradling the bottle of vodka, Richard had fallen asleep on the armchair in the corner. Perched on a stool, Lee held onto his hand, subduing him, as he whimpered in his sleep. The others, meanwhile, were scattered around the kitchen, saying little. Peter stood at the window, staring out at the back court, whilst Jim made more toast and coffee. The first batch of toast lay on a plate, cold and uneaten, but the coffee was almost finished. Kath sat with her head on the table, eyes closed, as Georgie stroked her hair.

'He must be dreaming,' Georgie said, referring to Richard.

'I wish *we* were,' Peter commented. He opened the fridge and surveyed its contents, before slamming the door shut and returning to gaze outside.

Though the mist had lifted, the wind had risen again, driving the rain horizontally against the window. Each lash against the glass was worse than the last, until it was almost impossible to see anything.

They listened as Colin dragged tables and chairs along the hallway, their legs screeching across floorboards. Every so often, Lee would poke his head out and return with a shrug of his shoulders.

'What's he doing?' Georgie asked.

'Building a barrier, I think. But who knows?'

Blinking herself awake, Kath sat up. 'What time is it?'

'After ten,' replied Georgie.

'That's been two hours, hasn't it?'

'Christ! Two hours locked up in here.' Peter banged the worktop. 'Is he not finished yet?' he shouted, more for Colin's benefit.

'Soon, I'm sure,' insisted Lee, but for all he knew, it could be hours before Colin would let them out. Peter's patience was already wearing thin, but it wouldn't be long before the others grew weary.

'Well, I need a piss.' Peter opened the door to the hall, but before he could leave, Jim pushed it closed again.

'There's a bucket under the sink,' he said, picking off the end of a piece of toast and popping it into his mouth. 'We'll look the other way.'

'How can you eat?' Peter joined Kath at the table. 'Weren't you two supposed to have been friends?'

'I'm sure Colin won't be long,' Lee interrupted. 'He'll let us know what we can and can't do.' He contemplated Richard, slumped to one side, his mouth hanging open. When told by Colin what had occurred, he'd not reacted, but carried on drinking instead. It took half an hour of persuasion for him to stay in the kitchen. His only proviso was that he be left alone with his bottle of vodka.

'You've got to be patient, my darling,' Georgie added.

'What are we going to do with him?' Kath asked, nodding in Richard's direction.

'Hopefully dry him out,' Lee said, tilting forward to whisper. 'Colin said he'll interview us all later. Including Richard.'

Peter, his face burning, turned to his mother. 'I mean, what's that about? Does he genuinely think one of us did it?'

'None of us knows the circumstances yet,' Lee said, attempting to ease Peter.

'I think you'll find your boyfriend said Lawrence was murdered – that he had no doubts.' He pulled at his fingers, cracking each knuckle. 'There's a dead body next door sitting in a sea of blood. That doesn't sound like an accident.' Suddenly aware of his nervous tic, Peter crossed his arms.

Lee didn't rise to the bait, and instead crossed to the hob. 'Would anyone like some tea? All this coffee's giving me the jitters.'

A few nods encouraged him to go ahead. As he filled the kettle, Peter started to cry.

'Darling, it's OK.' Kath pulled him to her chest. 'You let it out.'

'It's all my fault.' He rested his head against her, as deep, heartfelt sobs shook his body.

'Don't be stupid, Peter.' Kath pushed aside his hair. 'Why would you say that? Now, come on. Sit up.'

He wiped away his tears and adjusted himself, suddenly composed as if the moment of weakness had never happened.

Colin appeared in the doorway, his face drawn and haggard. 'I've tried the phone again, but there's still no tone.' He helped himself to a slice of toast. 'Jim, any ideas?' He took another bite and poured himself a glass of water. 'Does anyone?' Gulping down the water in one, he sensed all eyes on him.

'The line must be down,' Jim said. 'I can't promise anything, but I can take a look.'

'Thanks.' Colin surveyed the room, his brain still in forensic mode. 'I'm thinking there might be a boat somewhere.'

'No, Colin!' Lee cried, waking Richard momentarily. 'Get that thought right out of your head. It's blowing a hurricane out there.'

'Don't worry. I'm not proposing setting off right now,' Colin said. 'But it would be useful to know we have it as an option.'

'Coffee? Tea?' Jim asked.

'Tea, please.'

A mug was handed to him, and he blew on it gently before taking a sip. Placing it on the table, he took stock of everyone. Their expressions were identical: exhausted, agitated. The situation was taking its toll. But he also knew the time spent waiting would have given them the opportunity to rethink their movements from the night before, to build their alibis. Every detail of what happened after they'd gone to bed would have to be scrutinised. 'The crime scene's been secured now.'

'So, it *is* a crime scene?' Jim asked, moving to the far end of the table. 'You can tell us that?'

'That's my initial appraisal. The manner of Lawrence's death suggests foul play.'

'What do you mean?' Kath buttoned her cardigan, thrusting her hands into the pockets.

'I'm sorry, I can't go into details.'

'He means Lawrence died violently – that someone did him in.' Peter sat back. 'Someone's got onto the island, broken into the house and killed him under our noses. That about right?' His voice trembled as tears welled again.

'Did he suffer?' Kath asked.

Colin lifted his mug and took another sip. 'Again, I can't be sure. Sorry, I can't discuss this.'

'Are you even a bloody copper?' Peter's voice, quivering through the tears, demanded. He stared over at him. 'It's a reasonable question.'

Colin considered Peter. Out of all of them, he seemed the most affected – the least stable too. Whether the anger, tears and the challenge to his authority was more shock or guilt, Colin couldn't tell. It was going to be tough: he'd need to question him, see how much he knew, get past the bluster.

'This isn't helping, Peter,' Jim said.

'But is he?' He wiped his nose against his sleeve. 'Isn't he like the lowest rank or something?'

'Georgie, can you speak to him? He's making matters worse.' Jim patted Colin's arm. 'Apologies for my son.'

'I'm not a kid,' Peter said, locking eyes with his father.

'Well, stop acting like one!' Jim muttered under his breath.

Making a note of the tension – evident since they'd arrived – it was a line of questioning Colin would need to explore. 'I've six years' experience as a constable with the Met. As the first officer attending the scene and in the absence of anyone more senior who can carry out an effective murder investigation, I'm all you have. A crime has been committed, I'm certain of that, and until resources can be brought from the mainland, you'll have to make do with me. So, you can either choose to cooperate or not. But make no mistake: we're all potential murder suspects.'

'Even you?' asked Peter.

'Even me.' Colin drained his mug.

Peter grinned. 'So, *we* can interview *you*?'

'As a police officer, it's my duty to carry out as effective an investigation as I can. As soon as senior investigators access the island, I will defer, hand over my notes, and like you, will be interviewed as a suspect.' His palms were sweaty; he wiped them against his trouser legs. 'Any more questions?'

They all fell silent. Colin sensed a change in the room, a change in himself. It usually came with the uniform, the effect it had on people, on their reactions, on the way you saw yourself, held your own body. It was the mantle of authority, a costume that demanded a performance of the wearer. He'd never felt that power out of uniform before. Here, in a room full of actors, the irony wasn't lost on him.

'I'm sure we'll all do our best to help you.' Jim refilled the coffee pot for the umpteenth time.

'No one is under arrest. At this moment, all I need is for

you to cooperate with my investigation. Should that change at any point, you'll be the first to know. Are we done?' He waited, but everyone remained silent. 'Right, now let me tell you how this is going to work.'

30

Colin spent a good fifteen minutes detailing the situation. The crime scene, and yes, he emphasised once again that's what it was, had been contained. 'I've arranged furniture outside to block entry to Lawrence's room and the library. With no keys, it'll have to do. My next task is to search the house top to bottom.' He continued to explain how they were all free to go about their business, as he had no authority to detain them. 'But I'm seeking your help. Without it, I can't draw any initial conclusions. I'd like to speak to you all individually, but it's up to you whether you choose to speak to me or not. In the meantime, if you could all keep to your own rooms and the kitchen, I'd appreciate it.'

A disgruntled Peter left, followed by Kath, who made her way out behind him, saying if there was anything she could do, to come find her. Georgie and Jim exchanged pained expressions.

'What you're telling us is we still have rights? Am I correct?' Georgie stood, arms crossed, her cigarette ash dropping on the floor. 'It would be good if you were clearer, that's all.'

Colin's eyes stung, as if he were a child being reprimanded. The violence of the crime seemed impossible to square with the location and these people. 'Georgie, I'm so sorry. Of course, you do. I'm only trying to do what's right and what's best for Lawrence, for everyone, before the authorities arrive.'

'I'm sure we'll all be as supportive as we can.' Jim held onto Georgie. 'But surely the only explanation is that there's someone else on the island? Like Peter suggested? Someone we're not aware of?'

'It's definitely one possibility, 'Colin said. 'After I've searched the house, I'll search the immediate grounds for signs of an intruder. Then, I'll scour the rest of the island.'

'What a mess!' Georgie stubbed out her cigarette. 'We should get out of here, Jim. Freshen up. Do something. Anything. Can you help me with Richard?'

Together, they lifted a swaying, incoherent Richard. Fully standing, he flopped forwards into their arms, and they steered him towards the door.

'I'll have a look at the telephone line later. Hopefully there'll be a bit of a break in the weather.'

'Thanks, Jim.'

'I can help if you like,' Lee added with a smile.

As soon as they left, Lee guided Colin towards a seat and poured him some tea. 'Thank God you're here.' Colin leaned back in the chair, his body limp like a rag doll.

'They'll come round.' Lee squeezed his shoulder. 'People are still in shock.'

Colin gripped onto Lee's hands. 'I need back up. And soon.'

Lee wiped away a spot of blood on Colin's wrist. 'You've years of experience. Trust yourself.'

Colin watched the steam rise from his tea, dissipating as it cooled. Closing his eyes for a moment, he felt safe from the world, untouched by the horror that lay in the room next door. 'You do know…' he began, then stopped.

'What's wrong, babe?' Lee asked.

He couldn't fully look in Lee's direction, didn't want to see his reaction. 'That I'll need to treat you the same as the others.'

'Like a suspect, you mean?'

Colin nodded. 'You understand?'

Lee tried to stand but sat back down. Resting his elbows on the table, his eyes met Colin's. 'The truth? I can't remember much beyond a certain point. I was drunk. Properly drunk. But angry as I was, I'm certain I did nothing to hurt Lawrence.'

Colin held Lee's face, staring at it like that first time in the club when they met, sensing the same warmth and connection. 'Anything you remember, you have to tell me.'

'I will.'

'Because if the storm continues and the authorities can't get here, this could get a whole lot worse.' Colin knew this was an understatement. 'But remember – I love you. You know that, don't you?'

The roar of the wind and rain outside grew louder, its power seemingly endless. It felt like they were being spun around in the grip of a malevolent force, intent on toying with them, relishing the pain being inflicted.

'Of course I do,' Lee replied.

31

In the gloom of his bedroom, Richard opened his eyes. Recoiling from the glare of the bedside lamp, he felt like he'd gone ten rounds with Mike Tyson. Even switching off the light proved too much. A voice he couldn't locate whispered his name.

'Richard!'

Raising himself on an elbow, he could make out the shadow of someone sitting in a chair. The figure rose, moving towards him, repeating his name. He tried to reply, but his head hurt too much. As the figure continued to approach, his heart raced. All he wanted to do was run away, but he felt pinned to the bed.

'It's only me.'

A second passed before he recognised Kath's voice; her tones soothing, caring. She reached over to adjust his tangled bedclothes. 'How are you doing?'

What a dumb question. He rubbed his eyes – they felt like someone had ground shards of glass into his sockets. He hoped his expression would transmit as 'piss off', but when that failed, he croaked, 'I feel shit.'

Kath held up a glass of clear liquid. He prayed it was vodka.

'Here, drink this,' she said. 'It's only water, but it'll make you feel better.' She pushed it into his hand.

The thought disgusted him. In his head he was flicking through a three-dimensional map of the various places he'd hidden bottles since arriving, hoping she hadn't the foresight to search his room. Once she was gone, he'd check. 'Alright,' he said, playing the invalid. A sip wouldn't harm him. He reckoned if he smiled warmly, told her he was fine, she might leave him alone. 'I'll try.'

'Sit up. Come on, let me help you.'

Her hands were behind him, pulling at his body, dragging him higher up. He groaned at each stretch and clumsy tug, attempting to wriggle free as her fingers wrestled with his ribcage.

'Richard, you could make it a bit easier.'

He finally surrendered. She was far too strong for him. Putting the glass of water to his lips, he snapped, 'Thank you, Nurse Ratched.'

'You need to drink it all. Come on, I'll not take no for an answer.'

'I'm fine. I just want to sleep.' He handed her the glass and sank back into his pillow.

'That's not an option I'm afraid. You need to get up, shower.' She took hold of his arm. 'Let me help you.'

'But I'm sick! Can't you see?' His voice rose, accompanied by a spluttering cough that came from deep within his chest. 'I think I've got the flu.'

'Richard. You were drunk. You *are* a drunk. I found a half-empty bottle of vodka under your bed and two full bottles of wine in your wardrobe.'

'They're from the party. People must have continued drinking up here and I just tidied them away.'

She gave him a look suggesting he quit the bullshit and

handed the glass back to him. 'Take another sip.' She moved closer and sat on the edge of the mattress. 'We told you about Lawrence earlier. Can you remember?'

Richard closed his eyes and considered whether to open them again, to acknowledge what Kath was saying. He recalled snippets, hearing some commotion downstairs, getting up, making it to the top of the stairs before sitting. The next thing Lee was directing him towards the kitchen, and he somehow made it over to the fridge door, thinking how cool it was. Did he sit down? He must have. 'Someone helped me over to the armchair. I remember that.'

Kath nodded. 'After you nearly fell flat on your face.'

Richard's face cracked, but no tears came. Instead, he thought about the speech he'd given at dinner, how convinced he'd been by his own words and how Lawrence was determined to humiliate him in front of everybody. Having built himself up with such fine words, it seemed doubly unjust that Lawrence could bring him down with a couple of well-chosen ones of his own: words that persuaded him to take that first drink, then another. After closing his bedroom door, everything was hazy.

'You were told something important about Lawrence.' She took his hand, warming it through with her own.

Fragments of words emerged from the back of his mind. *Dead. Lawrence. Murdered.* 'Is he?' As she nodded, he pulled the covers around himself, to disguise his body shaking. 'I didn't?' he asked. 'I didn't kill the bastard?'

'We think there was an intruder,' she whispered. 'But Colin wants to speak to us all, find out our movements.'

'Can't you tell him I was flat on my back, out cold?'

'That's not going to work.'

'It'll have to – it's all a blank. Nothing. I can't remember a fucking thing. Ask me did I want to kill him – one hundred percent. The man was a grade-A shit. But did I?' Richard closed his eyes again and shook his head, the exertion of trying to piece things together proving too much.

Kath moved towards the window and edged open the curtains. 'It's hellish outside. There's still no phone, no way of getting off the island or anyone getting on.'

'Let the storm take us. Who cares anymore?' He pulled the covers over his head.

'These are coming with me.' She picked up the three bottles of alcohol. 'You don't need them.'

He poked his head out from beneath the covers. 'Leave one bottle? The red.'

'This is crazy. It'll kill you.'

He raised an eyebrow. 'To tide me over. Make today a little easier. Please?' Without a drink, he couldn't function.

Relenting, she placed the red on the dresser. 'Just one.' She opened the door.

'Is it a screwcap?'

'Richard. Seriously?'

'Is it?' he repeated, licking his dry lips. 'Because I don't know what I've done with my corkscrew.'

'Yes.'

'Good. Now you can go.' He sat up and kept his eye on the bottle to make sure she didn't change her mind.

As she was stepping into the corridor, he asked, 'Did the bastard die slowly?'

Kath paused. Gently closing the door, she said, 'It was Georgie who found him. But only Colin's spent any time in the room ... with the body,' she whispered. 'But he's sure Lawrence was murdered.'

Richard leaned forward, eager for the distraction, however macabre. 'And what's Colin said?' About how he died?'

'Well, no detail. He says he can't go into it.'

'What a killjoy,' Richard cried. 'A boring old policeman after all. How disappointing. Georgie must have said something though?'

'I feel weird saying.'

Richard sat up, his face glowing with excitement. 'Go on. Tell me!'

'Only that there was blood everywhere. The light wasn't good, so that's all Georgie could make out. But it must have been bad – brutal – for her to say that.'

Richard downed the glass of water in one. 'Do you know why he hated me so much? And how I came to hate him?'

Kath shook her head. 'Jealousy?'

'Come on, Kath, you've been round the block enough times to recognise it takes more than a bit of professional jealousy to truly hate someone.'

'I know he resented you.'

'More than that. He detested me. Because every time he looked at me, I reminded him of the past.' Suddenly animated, he pulled his legs towards himself and crossed them, as if they were having a pyjama party. 'I knew too much – who he really was – where he came from, how rotten to the core he really was.'

'I should go.'

'Spoilsport!' He looked past her, at the dresser, where the bottle still sat within eyeshot. 'Well, if you must, be a darling and hand me over the wine, will you?'

Kath crossed the room and picked it up. 'Catch,' she said, tossing the bottle towards him.

It came flying across the room, and he just managed to catch it. Startled, he gave her a death stare. 'That wasn't funny.'

'Don't drink it all at once.'

32

Before heading outside, Colin had searched the entire house top to bottom, checking doors and windows. Every nook and cranny had been investigated for signs of an intruder, of forced entry, of the murder weapon – any potential clue that might help build a picture.

He'd opened cupboards, looked under beds, behind shower curtains. But there was no knife-wielding maniac, merely empty bathtubs and dusty shelves.

In the basement, he'd searched every inch, double-checking for concealed doors or secret passages. If there had been an intruder, they were no longer in the house. Or else there *was* no intruder and the murderer was one of the others. It seemed unthinkable, but it was a real possibility. Lawrence's body, with its skull shattered, lay dead in the sitting room – a man, the epitome of glamour and desirability, callously reduced to nothing more than a slab of fresh meat displayed in a butcher's window.

Happy the house was secure, the rest of the island now needed to be searched. The murder weapon was still missing, as was the Dictaphone. That meant checking the woods, the shoreline, any feasible routes across the rocks to secluded inlets or caves. Any search outside on his own could only be cursory, but it was better than nothing.

Making his way across the sodden lawn, the skipper's last words rang in his ears – something about a massive storm. Why hadn't he paid more attention? Mentioned it to the others? All the signs were there – the black clouds hanging heavy since they arrived, the savage wind rushing in from the sea unexpectedly. He prayed it would be over with soon.

The woodland which surrounded the house on three sides, and protected it from the ferocious Atlantic winds, was dark and dense. As he peered into it, he counted half a dozen felled trees, their roots helplessly exposed, taken out by the wind's attack. Unless they'd come prepared, he doubted anyone could survive out there for long. For twenty minutes, he scoured the area, the wind pressing against him the entire time. But there was nothing of note. No hut, no den, no places to hide.

He came to the short, pebbled shoreline which led to the jetty – an inlet no more than thirty feet long. But again, there were no obvious hiding places. It was becoming clear – in all likelihood, the only people on the island were himself and the others confined to the house. As the wind and rain battered against his body, he crouched to protect himself and scanned the beach, looking for any hollow where a person might conceal themselves. There wasn't one.

The high-tech walking boots he'd brought were a godsend but glancing over to his left he contemplated a bank of uneven, razor-sharp rocks which stepped up towards the sheer cliffs; they appeared to take up most of the northern part of the island. Even an SAS assassin with top-spec gear would struggle to navigate those. Of course, he'd have to wait till the storm had passed to completely rule that out. For now, it seemed likely the rest of the island was empty, and only someone with a death wish would consider hiding out there in this weather.

Last on his list was the barn. Once he'd ticked that off, he'd head back to the house to interview the others. Well, those who'd agree. That might prove interesting if this morning's conversation was anything to go by. Hostile was the word that came to mind.

Pushing the barn door open, he stepped inside and marvelled at how quiet it was; with the door closed, the storm became a distant memory. He stood in the middle of the space and turned full circle, noticing handprints on the mirrors, some muddied footprints on the floor. Unsurprising, as he knew for certain Jim and Georgie had visited the barn the previous afternoon, as well as Richard, Kath and himself in the evening. However, with Jim's camera, he took a few photographs and noted positions, possible sizes of shoes, distinctive patterns of shoe sole, and the direction of movement across the floor. Otherwise, he couldn't see anything out of place in the main space.

Following the dramatic slope of the beautifully engineered roof beams, he made his way to the more enclosed social area behind the partition. Two generous leather sofas, four Eames chairs and a low, smoked-glass table were arranged symmetrically, as though in a showroom. Only a couple of dented cushions suggested someone might have recently been there. On the table, several photography books were strategically placed – *The Fondas, The Barrymores, the Redgraves* – classic Hollywood. On closer inspection, he wondered if anyone had ever touched them, as they were so pristine, their glossy spines unbroken. Lastly, he checked the floor and underneath the sofas. With no signs of disturbance or blood, he moved back into the main area.

Only the small kitchen and adjoining toilets were left to examine. He put his head round the door of each of the toilets. Both were spotless, as if the plumbers had finished installing them only hours before. He checked each surface.

There was no sign of anyone having been in either toilet recently – no smudges on the taps or watermarks in the sinks.

The kitchen was the final place to give the once over. After doing that, he'd head back.

As soon as he pushed the door open, the stench of blood made him gag. He was catapulted back to his first bloody crime scene – pools of dark liquid gleaming in the shadows, blood-spattered white tiles, a ruby stained tea-towel.

In the sink, standing upright and caked in dried blood, sat Lawrence's award. He'd held it in his hands only the night before. But here it was, abandoned, its smooth, shiny curves and edges transformed by fragments of skull and lumps of scalp. Now, it looked like any other grisly murder weapon.

Colin stepped closer. A scrubbing brush lay in the bottom of the sink, its white bristles stained pink, proving that someone had tried to erase the evidence. Had the perpetrator hoped to wash and return the award to the mantelpiece of Lawrence's room unnoticed? Why not complete the job? Perhaps they'd been disturbed by someone. If so, he needed to identify that person and what they might have seen. Or did the murderer want the award found? If so, why remove it from the crime scene, and could there be any significance to this specific location?

He stepped from the kitchen to check again for clues. From the centre of the main space, he scanned the room. The mirrored walls reflected him rotating, the sole guest at the bleakest of balls. Spinning round for a second time, he spotted a smear of blood on the handle of the mirrored door which led outside. Whoever had been so careful in the house had slipped up here. This supported his initial theory that the murderer had been spooked while attempting to wash the award clean. A person could easily exit from the kitchen and out through the mirrored door without being seen.

If he was right, why had the person who'd disturbed the

murderer not come forward? Didn't they realise they were a witness, or might they be complicit in some way?

Hearing footsteps approach the rear of the barn, Colin darted behind the partition and waited, listening as someone entered and opened the kitchen door. He discretely poked his head out, but the person was already inside the kitchen. Drawers and cupboards were being pulled open and banged shut. But there was no sound of running water. This person hadn't come back to clean up. And the bloody statuette hadn't shocked them either. His mind raced through the possibilities; if they weren't continuing to clean the award, their intention must be to dispose of it. Now was his chance to catch them red-handed.

Shooting out from behind the partition, he shouted, 'Police! Stop!' But as soon as the words left his mouth, he heard the mirrored door crash shut. He'd not acted swiftly enough.

Rushing to the exit, he threw the door open and stepped outside. As soon as he did, he felt a pain at the back of his head, followed by a second at his temple. Dropping to his knees, his body slumped in shock. Dazed, he ran a hand across his head and tried to focus, but a dark, sticky liquid filled his vision. Despite every fibre of muscle urging him to stand, he felt his eyelids droop and close. The last thing he remembered was toppling face first into the mud, the deep earthy smell filling his nostrils.

33

_____

Georgie and Jim were lying in bed staring at the ceiling. Naked beneath the covers, they'd spent the last hour making love. Usually, it was scheduled for the weekend, but recently, more pressing matters had overtaken: shopping, gardening, the accounts. So, at first, when Georgie had pulled at his belt and kissed him passionately, Jim had been unsure, but she'd been insistent, shaking her head when he resisted, whispering, 'Yes, let's do this' until he relented.

He rolled onto his side and looked at her. 'That was unexpected.'

'Death can do that, I suppose.' She picked up her book – a pulpy romance series she insisted helped her brain from over-thinking – and flicked to her place, marked with a folded corner.

Jim searched for his underpants, which were caught up in the tangled covers, and slipped them on. 'Think Peter's OK?'

Georgie continued reading, her glasses perched on the tip of her nose; her one concession to getting older. She nodded. 'I'll check on him later.'

Jim sat up, yawned and stretched his body, feeling like he'd been hit by a tornado. 'You need anything?'

'This rain to stop, a boat to appear, to be back home.' She smiled, slamming the book shut and lying back against the pillow. 'Failing that, a large gin.'

'I'm not sure that's a good idea. Will coffee do? I'm going to get some, see if it'll wake me.' He watched as Georgie closed her eyes, snuggling into the mattress. Under any other circumstances, this would have been a perfect moment: the rain beating against the window, the wind howling in the background, a stolen hour mid-afternoon. 'I'll take that as a no.'

'Sorry, darling,' she said. 'I'm tired.' She pulled the covers tightly against herself. 'You go ahead.'

Moving round to Georgie's side of the bed, he knelt to face her. She kept her eyes closed as he twisted a strand of her hair around his finger. 'It'll be over with soon enough. Once we've given statements, we'll get back to normal in no time. I promise you, love.'

Her eyes opened. 'I don't say it often enough, but I do love you.'

Kissing her on the cheek, he switched off the bedside light. 'I know. I love you too. Sleep well, darling.'

IT WASN'T COFFEE that Jim needed. Regardless of Colin's instructions, he had to get out of the house, clear his thoughts, and pretend for a moment that the events of the last few hours might all be a dream. The rain was so heavy it felt like stepping into a shower. Quickly drenched, he ran for the barn and stepped inside, pushing the excess water from his hair. Taking a deep breath, he screamed as loud as he could. The echo bounced back, and he screamed again, stretching to release the maximum noise he could exert. 'Fuck! Fuck! Fuck!'

Jim shook his body loose before heading to the breakout area and crashing out on a sofa. Knowing he'd have to confront reality at some point, a moment of peace and quiet was needed. Letting his body relax, emptying all thoughts from his mind, he heard a voice shout. He picked himself up and discovered Lee darting about the main space. 'Everything OK?'

'I saw you run in here,' said Lee. 'I'm looking for Colin. You haven't seen him?'

'He went out about an hour ago.' Up close, he could see how pale Lee's face was, nervously scanning the room, suggesting he didn't want to stop and talk.

'It was much longer than that. More like two hours.' Lee looked around. 'He isn't here, is he?'

Jim thought about his scream, which would have woken the dead. If anyone had overheard, they'd have soon appeared, wondering who the madman was. 'Well, we can take a look, but I don't think so.'

Lee crossed the room and searched behind the partition. He shook his head. 'He must be somewhere outside. What an idiot. I shouldn't have let him go on his own, but he insisted.'

Jim could see how distressed Lee was becoming. 'I'll help you. Don't worry. Colin knows how to take care of himself, I'm sure!' He attempted to open the barn door, but a huge gust of wind pushed him back, as if it had been lurking outside, waiting. 'Bloody hell, it's getting wilder. We should head back before it gets worse.'

'I didn't check the toilets.' Lee hurried off, throwing open the doors, then stuck his head inside the kitchen.

Jim, meanwhile, tried opening the barn door again. As he was pushing at it, Lee told him to be quiet.

'Listen!' he said. 'Did you hear that?'

Jim looked at him, unsure what he was supposed to be hearing. 'What?'

'Listen.' Lee moved towards the centre of the space. 'It sounds like moaning.' He caught the sound again. 'There.'

Jim listened. 'Isn't that the wind?'

'It's coming from outside,' Lee shouted, running towards the mirrored door and forcing it open.

Colin, his face caked in mud and blood, was on all fours, struggling to stand. 'Help,' he croaked.

'What the hell?' Groaning, Colin kept slipping and sliding on the sodden ground. Moving forward to take his weight, Jim said, 'You're OK, mate. Let's get you inside. Lee, go grab a seat, will you?'

Jim waited with Colin, feeling his body go limp. 'Come on buddy, stay with me!'

Arriving back with one of the Eames chairs, Lee helped Jim gently lower Colin onto it. His head lolled to one side; his face was deathly pale and his lips blue from the cold, as if he'd just been rescued from a trek across the Arctic. Jim took off his jacket and pulled it around him. 'There now, you're safe,' he whispered. 'Look at me, Colin,' he said, rubbing his frozen hands vigorously. 'We need you to stay awake.' He noticed a bruise on his forehead and a nasty gash at the back of his head; it probably required stitches.

'Come on, honey, stay focused,' Lee said, rubbing his back to both calm and keep him warm. 'Don't close your eyes.'

'We need to raise his temperature.' Jim removed his own jumper and draped it over Colin's shoulders.

'Here, take mine too.' Lee arranged his own on top.

'The award,' Colin muttered. Struggling to keep his eyes open, his head rose momentarily before dropping again. 'Lawrence's award,' he repeated.

'I'll get some hot water.' Lee rushed to the kitchen.

Jim stayed with Colin, holding onto his body. 'Don't speak.' With both hands, he rubbed his arms and upper body. 'You need to stay awake.'

'Someone hit me.' Saliva drooled from the corner of his mouth.

Jim kept rubbing his body, doing everything to warm him up. 'You'll be fine, mate, I promise.'

Lee returned with a cup of hot water. 'Here, drink this.' He pressed it against Colin's lips.

For five minutes, they watched in silence as Colin gradually revived, enough to gasp, 'Thank you.'

'Who did this to you?' Lee asked.

'I don't know. They came from behind.'

Lee squeezed his hand and glanced at Jim. 'Who the hell would do this?'

Jim shook his head. 'We'd better get him to the house. See to those cuts.' He crouched and put his hand under Colin's arm. 'Can you get the other side?'

As they moved towards the door, Colin took a breath. 'It's the award.' He'd briefly caught the glint of metal as it came crashing towards him. 'Someone came back for it.' He held onto Lee. 'That's what they hit me with. That's what killed Lawrence.'

34

Both Jim and Lee helped Colin to his bedroom, where they immediately dressed his wounds. The cut to the back of his head was not as deep as they'd feared, but had still left a nasty wound, making Colin flinch each time it was touched.

'Count to ten,' Lee said, applying a touch of antiseptic cream before attempting the delicate job of covering it with a variety of plasters.

'You took quite a beating,' Jim explained, trying to distract him from the discomfort. 'But you're safe now.' His hand took Colin's, gripping it tightly.

Lee stepped back, ensuring the wound was properly covered. 'There you go, all better.'

'You've done a good job there.' Jim went behind him, admiring Lee's handiwork. 'You're best getting some sleep,' he said to Colin, who'd already lain back on the pillow and closed his eyes. 'I'll leave you to it, shall I?' He closed the door gently behind him.

Watching over Colin as his face settled, Lee ran through the events of the previous night: Lawrence's appearance dramatically souring the mood, the power-games with

Richard, followed by the excitement of the impromptu party.

The rest of the night was still hazy in places. Since the discovery of Lawrence's body, he'd tried to remember details of his movements. He recalled waking without Colin in bed beside him. What followed remained sketchier: going out to check the barn, falling asleep on the sofa in the barn. All of a sudden, a memory came flooding back. He had to stop himself waking Colin up. How could he forget? He'd been woken by voices in the barn. Weird, looping voices. And one of them had been Lawrence's. Another memory, connected to the last, resurfaced – a very distinct one – of someone running from the barn.

He remembered a sensation too – of kicking something in the dark – a small, plastic object, not heavy. For the life of him, he couldn't work out what it was. He needed to go back and investigate.

LEE ENTERED the kitchen where the others were already gathered, seemingly going about their business as if nothing unusual had occurred. It was only Kath who stopped what she was doing to step forward and hug him. Sitting at opposite ends of the table were Jim and Georgie. Jim had torn a paper napkin to pieces, the debris now organised in a tiny heap in front of him. Georgie appeared to have devoured a plateful of biscuits and was wiping a crumb from the corner of her mouth. Peter, sitting in the armchair by the window, yawned and adjusted the cushions. Only Kath seemed to have any energy.

'How's Colin? He looked in a bad way,' she said.

'Thank God you heard him, Lee.' Jim set aside the confetti and poured himself a mug of coffee. 'He could have been killed.'

'But he'll live. The cuts aren't as bad now they've been

cleaned. He's fast asleep. And I found a set of keys, so he's locked in and secure.'

Kath clung to him. 'Let's make you some fresh coffee. That pot's been sitting there for ages. Or would you prefer something stronger?'

'Coffee's fine.' Lee watched as Kath rinsed out the cafetière, sensitive to the silence in the room, broken only by the humming of a tune from the previous night's party. 'I take it Richard's still in his room?' he asked.

Kath poured hot water into the pot. 'Has been all day. I checked in on him a few hours ago. Against my advice, he's got more wine, but he's a grown man and at least he's happy.' Resting the pot in the centre of the table, she then filled the sink with hot water, squirting in some washing-up liquid.

The body of a man they all knew was lying feet away and yet, there in the kitchen, it felt normal, as though rehearsals had been postponed whilst Lawrence popped back to the mainland for a few hours.

'Well, this is cosy.' Lee eyed them up. 'So, what do we all think? First Lawrence, then Colin.'

Kath picked up a pile of dirty plates and placed them in the water. 'Peter, come dry for me.'

Jim and Georgie, their expressions glazed, sat sipping their coffee.

'Of course, Colin survived.' The words had been burning on Lee's tongue. Perhaps a bit of honesty might jolt a reaction.

Georgie looked over, her glacial expression thawing. 'You don't think one of us did it?' She placed her mug on the table and stared at him. 'You don't, do you? We've all been here in the house.'

Lee had a lot of time for Georgie; she'd a knack of getting her way, which he admired, of disarming people with a show of vulnerability before going in for the kill. She'd secured one or two jobs with that tactic, most famously the role of Mrs Warren at the National; when Diana Rigg stepped back from the project, Georgie practically steamrolled the director into casting her. Colin had mentioned she'd beaten on Lawrence's door earlier in the evening. It now took on a whole new meaning. For the first time, he wondered if he could trust her.

'Yes, I do.' After the attack on Colin, the notion that there was an intruder on the island seemed less plausible. Surely only someone who knew he was investigating the murder would have the motive to attack him. What Georgie asked was exactly what Lee was now thinking. It *was* one of them. Lawrence's own belief, that the writer was out to get him, seemed far-fetched. The idea that Jackie – five-foot tall and stick thin – could take on Lawrence, let alone Colin, was absurd. That was even before considering the weather, which would have stopped the most enthusiastic of criminals in their tracks. 'Whoever murdered Lawrence is very likely in this room.'

'I don't think we should go down this route,' Kath interrupted, passing Peter a plate, before thrusting her hands back into the soap suds. 'This is a situation where we all need to stick together.'

'Do we?' Lee asked. Someone in that kitchen knew something and wasn't saying. He was convinced of it.

Peter slammed the plate on the counter, almost smashing it in two. 'Let's get this straight. You're suggesting that for no reason whatsoever, one of us crept down here last night, snuck into Lawrence's room and did him in?' He stood, repeatedly drying the next plate Kath handed to him until it squeaked. 'Are you serious?'

'Peter!' Jim said. 'Lee's upset.'

'Yes Peter, let's quieten down. There's a man lying dead along the hallway.' Georgie stood and placed the clean plates in a cupboard. 'Lee's only thinking aloud.'

'He's saying one of you – either you or dad or Kath – is a killer.' He sneered at Lee. 'You're out of order.'

Lee held Peter's gaze. 'Or you.'

'And why would *I* murder Lawrence?' He threw the dish-cloth over his shoulder. 'Eh?'

'Peter, rein it in,' Kath said. 'There are more dishes to dry.'

Lee stood. 'All I know is that Lawrence is dead, and that someone attacked Colin. You were there, Jim. You saw the state he was left in.'

Jim looked at the others and nodded. 'It was pretty grim.'

'Speak with your boyfriend,' Peter said. 'Maybe he actually saw who did it. And anyway,' he went on, 'what about you? You've as much motive for killing Lawrence as any of us. And we don't know what your home life's like. Maybe you wanted rid of Colin for some reason too.'

Furious, Lee considered them: Kath draining the sink, splashing cold water to force the excess soap suds down the plughole; Georgie returning to her coffee, gazing out at the dark shadows of the trees swaying in the wind; Peter neatly folding the dishtowel and placing it through the handle of the Rayburn. Only Jim remained looking his way.

'I'm going to check out the phone line. Want to join me?' he asked. 'It'll take your mind off things.'

'Sure.' Hard though it was to comprehend, one of them *had* to be responsible. Their happy family routine didn't convince him anymore and Colin wouldn't be swayed by it, either.

Georgie opened the fridge door. 'That's after 3.30. We need to eat something. Anyone hungry?'

'Not really, but I'll give you a hand.' Kath rummaged inside and brought out a lettuce, a cucumber and a bunch of spring onions. 'There's plenty for a salad. I'm thinking something light.'

'Colin will get to the bottom of this,' Lee said. 'It's what he's trained to do.'

Peter grunted and left the room, banging the door shut behind him. Kath went to follow, but Georgie intervened. 'Leave him, Kath. He'll come around. He doesn't cope well with stress.'

'He idolised Lawrence. You should have seen him on set,' she explained. 'Everywhere Lawrence went, he followed.' She took out a bowl and cut through the heart of the lettuce. 'Like his shadow.'

'Lee, shall we?' Jim asked, pointing towards the door. 'I should warn you, even if we do find something, I doubt I'll be able to fix it.'

'All we can do is try.' He looked around. 'Where are the torches?'

Georgie dived into a drawer and handed each of them one. 'Neither of you can stay out there for long. The storm's crazy. And even though you don't believe it, Lee, there could be someone else lurking on the island. Someone dangerous. So, stick together and, any sign of danger, get back here immediately.' She kissed Jim and placed her hand on Lee's arm. 'I'll check all the windows and doors are closed,' she said, leaving the kitchen.

'None of us have a clue what we're dealing with here,' Lee cautioned. 'But when Colin wakes, let's see if he's got any ideas.'

'A salad's not going to be enough, is it? You'll need something warm when you get back.' Kath found a huge pot in one of the cupboards. 'I'll do a soup. My mum's recipe.'

'Come on,' Jim said to Lee, 'before the storm gets any worse.'

35

'Give me two secs, I need to get my cagoule.' Jim lunged up the steps two at a time.

'But there's plenty here in the cloakroom,' Lee shouted, as he disappeared around the corner.

'I prefer my own,' Jim called back.

Lee waited at the bottom of the stairs, contemplating the barrier of stacked chairs Colin had created to block off the crime scene. It was still inconceivable that Lawrence's body lay behind the nearest door. Half-expecting him to appear, making one of his ludicrous demands, he smiled; whether that was out of fondness or because he wouldn't have to deal with any of his bullshit again, he wasn't sure.

Jim came bounding down the stairs, minus the cagoule.

'Can't you find it?'

Jim shook his head. 'I'll take one from the cupboard.' Pulling out a bright orange cagoule, he held it against himself.

'Is that yours?' Lee asked.

'Must be,' he shrugged, throwing it on. 'Exact same colour.' It was a perfect fit. 'Christ knows how it ended up there.'

They stared at each other, both dressed like trawlermen heading out onto the high seas. 'Ready?' Lee asked.

Jim nodded. 'If we follow the telephone line from the house, we should find any break in it.'

Outside, they gripped onto each other for support, as the full force of the biting wind rushed from the shore, instantly freezing their fingers. They tried moving crablike into it with sidesteps, but the wind changed direction and thrust them backwards.

'This is impossible,' Jim screamed, wiping a veil of rainwater from his face.

'We need to try.'

Jim signalled OK and pointed toward the woods. 'Let's head over there. It'll be more sheltered – we can try and pick the line up further down.'

Pummelled by the worst of the weather, the trudge across the muddy lawn seemed to take forever. There was relief and a moment of relative calmness as they arrived beneath the dark canopy of trees.

'What now?' Lee asked, bent over, catching his breath.

'I'll work my way along this edge. If you can go in a bit deeper, see if you can find anything there.' Jim pointed his torch at him. 'Give three short flashes for danger. Two long ones if you discover anything.' He held up his hands and spread his fingers. 'Ten minutes tops.' He squeezed Lee's arm. 'Is that OK?'

Lee put his thumbs up, and they both disappeared in opposite directions.

The ground was saturated. Each step sucked Lee's boots deeper into the thick mud. Around him, shrill whistles and cacophonous booms resounded, the effect disorientating. There had been no let-up all day, and the ominous sky above suggested there was no end in sight. Undeterred, he pushed on, looking out for a toppled pole or any dangling cables. If they could find a break, maybe they could fix it and telephone for help. Otherwise, who knew how long before assistance would arrive.

After only a matter of minutes, Lee thought he heard shouting. Fragments of words through the din. He peered back through the trees and could make out a flashing light. Unable to tell if Jim was signalling danger, he stumbled through the undergrowth towards him. As he drew closer, he saw an orange shape crouched on the ground beside a fallen telephone pole. Jim turned to Lee, his face despondent.

'What's wrong?'

Jim held up a severed cable. 'It's worse than I imagined.'

'Can you fix it?'

'Only an engineer could. It's totally destroyed.'

Lee stared at the shattered pole and spirals of wiring, hoping that by some miracle they could be meshed back together. 'And you're sure?'

Jim nodded. 'Maybe if the wire had just snapped, but it's been a lightning strike,' he said. 'Look, you can see where there's been a fire. The wires have completely melted. There's nothing I can do. Come on,' he urged, 'let's get back to the house.'

Lee stared up at the sky, at the boiling black clouds and needles of rain that pricked against his face. 'Fuck you!' he shouted at the top of his voice.

'A plague upon this howling,' Jim joined in.

They continued to rail at the storm as they hurried back to the house.

Arriving outside the front door, Lee stopped. 'You go ahead. I've got to check something in the barn.'

'You're not going there on your own?'

'Honestly, I'll be fine. It won't take a minute.' The object he'd kicked in the early hours of the morning was still playing on his mind. It had occurred to him that the voices he'd heard might have been a recording.

'I'm coming with you.'

'Jim, I'll be two seconds!'

'There's some madman out there who's already killed someone and tried to kill Colin. There's no way I'm leaving you. Anyway, what's so important it can't wait?'

He didn't know if he should say. He hadn't even told Colin yet. But he trusted Jim. 'Last night, after everyone had gone to bed, I got up and went to the barn. It's a long story, but I thought Colin might be there.'

'Was he?'

'No. But stupid me, I lay on the sofa and fell asleep. The next thing I knew, there were these sounds...' As he was about to tell him about the voices on a loop, the person fleeing the barn and the object he kicked, there was an almighty bang, as if a whale, lifted from the depths of the sea, had been dropped on the house. 'What the...?'

Instinctively, they knew where the noise had come from. Fighting against the wind, they made their way to the barn. Kath, Georgie and Peter were already there, staring at a section of the barn's roof lying tangled on the ground.

'What happened?' Lee shouted.

'I was looking out the kitchen window,' Kath said, 'and this huge gust of wind came out of nowhere and ripped it right off. Like a giant can-opener. I've never seen anything like it.' Kath held onto Georgie, both shivering as they clung together.

'This place is cursed,' Peter declared. Shoulders slumped, he walked back inside.

The others looked up at the barn's roof, now a dark, gaping wound of ripped metal and shredded timbers.

'That's rehearsals over for sure,' Georgie said pointedly, following Peter into the house.

36

A sudden crashing sound – of metal and wood being ripped apart – forced Colin's eyes open. Disorientated in the gloom, he touched the back of his head with his fingertips but pulled away. 'Shit!' The wound pulsed rhythmically as if it were engorged with blood. A sudden memory of rain beating against his back, clawing at the muddy ground, Jim and Lee dragging him indoors, chilled him. A vision of Lawrence's body sprawled across his bed froze him further, a hideous reminder of how things could have gone.

Colin had the eerie sensation of having woken in the middle of a dream – one he'd no desire to rush back to. Perhaps the crash had come from his subconscious, echoing the crack of Lawrence's award against his skull? Pulling himself onto the edge of the mattress, he placed his bare feet on the floor. The carpet felt soft, almost liquid, like it might swallow him. Overcome by dizziness, he staggered backwards onto the bed. A second attempt didn't fare any better: his arms felt weak as he tried pushing himself up. Covering his face with his hands, he took a few deep breaths to steady himself. He needed to take things more slowly.

Earlier, in the safety of the main house, the others had

gathered around voicing their shock. Before bringing him upstairs, Lee had sat him down to clean his cuts, while Jim babbled on about anything and everything in an attempt to keep him conscious. Throughout, he'd felt he might throw up. Not from the pain. It was more awful than that. He knew that the person who'd attacked him, who'd deliberately smashed a heavy object into his head – not once, but twice – was likely standing in the room with him, feigning concern.

He lay back, going over what he knew so far. He was convinced someone – the murderer – had returned to the barn intending to reclaim the weapon. But why abandon it in the sink in the first place? While it was possible they'd bargained on no one searching there, the more likely explanation was they'd been disturbed scrubbing it clean. Whatever had happened, the bloodstained award had lain untouched for several hours. At the first opportunity, someone had risked retrieving it – all without reckoning on him being there.

He took another deep breath. Feet firmly on the floor, this time he pushed hard, finally standing and hobbling to the window. Pulling aside the curtains, the fast-fading light revealed the devastation the storm had wreaked on the barn. Before he could make sense of it, Lee entered.

'Babe,' he cried. 'What the hell are you doing? I knew you couldn't be trusted on your own.' Taking Colin's arm, he steered him back to bed and tucked the covers around him. 'I take it you saw the damage?'

'What happened? No one's been hurt, have they?'

Lee shook his head. 'Everyone's fine. The wind tore a section of the barn roof right off. Oh, and me and Jim found one of the telephone poles, but it had been struck by lightning: there's no way it can be fixed.'

'So, we're stranded till this storm blows over?'

Lee examined Colin's dressing. 'If anything, it's getting worse. Just trying to open the front door takes two people. How's your head feeling?' he asked, ensuring the makeshift dressing – cottonwool, several plasters and some strategically placed duct-tape – was secure. 'Let's see.'

'Ouch!' Colin cried. 'Fine if people don't poke at it.'

Lee nudged Colin forward and sat on the bed beside him. 'You were lucky. You know that, don't you?'

They sat together a few minutes, hand in hand, listening to the soaring wind and pounding ocean in the background.

'And there's no flooding from the high tide?' Colin asked.

'Not yet. But it's Armageddon out there.' Lee bent over to do one more check of the dressing. 'I'll need to clean it again later. We don't want it to become infected.'

Colin winced, knowing the answer before asking. 'The truth. How does it look?'

'Be thankful it wasn't your face.' He kissed Colin on the lips. 'Whoever did it meant business.'

Colin stretched back and stared at the ceiling. 'Christ!' The image of Lawrence's shattered skull made him want to swim to the mainland. 'We need to get off this island before someone else gets hurt.'

'Listen, I've something to confess.'

This got Colin's immediate attention. 'Go on.'

'I know you need to treat me the same as everyone else, as if I'm a suspect...'

'We're all suspects. Even me.' Colin waited for Lee to speak, dreading the possibilities.

'I know, though it's safe to assume you didn't hit yourself over the head.'

Colin nodded in agreement. 'But *you* can't rule that out as a possibility.'

'Believe me, I've ruled it out,' Lee said. 'Now, and I know this might not be the official police way of doing things, but you need to trust someone.'

Colin stared at Lee. His was not the demeanour of a criminal: patchy eye contact, odd gestures, fidgeting. This was the face of a man who'd looked into his own many times and stated his love. It was an easy call to make. 'If you want to know whether I trust you, yes, I do.'

'*Really* trust me?' he asked.

'I wouldn't say if I didn't.' This was the truth. If he had a sliver of doubt, he'd have lied.

'Because I do have a motive to kill Lawrence.'

Colin shifted uncomfortably, unsure what Lee meant. 'Do I have to prepare myself?'

Lee grabbed hold of his satchel and pulled out an envelope. Removing its contents, he handed a thick document over to Colin. 'My production company is the beneficiary of an insurance pay-out should anything untoward happen to Lawrence Delaney. That's not unusual for a production this size going into the West End. What is unusual is the enormous size of the pay-out when your star is a Hollywood A-lister.' He pointed to a paragraph. 'Look at the amount in brackets.'

'Holy shit! Are you serious?' It was becoming more and more impossible to separate himself – either personally or professionally – from this investigation. 'Lee, in normal circumstances, you do realise this would be my first line of investigation?'

'I know. Don't get me wrong, there were days when I could have happily killed him and for a lot less. Worse days than yesterday.' He took Colin's hand. 'Why would I choose to do it now?' He paused. 'You need to say you believe me.'

Colin thought for a split second before nodding. Sometimes, a risk had to be taken, a leap of faith. Lee wouldn't betray him. He was as certain of that as he could be. 'I believe you.'

Lee smiled. 'Good, because I might have vital information for you.'

'What?' Colin sat upright, eager to hear what Lee had to offer.

'It might be nothing, but then again—'

'Wait! I need to write this down.'

His feet were about to touch the floor when Lee stopped him. 'I'll get that for you.' He ushered Colin back into bed and produced a pad and pen from his satchel.

'Give it here,' Colin said. 'Now, tell me what you know.' He took a note of the date and time and underlined it.

'During the night, I went out to the barn.'

'Why?' Colin, confused, looked up.

'You weren't in bed and I got worried. I know it sounds stupid, but that's what I did. I was still drunk and I thought you might be there.'

'In the barn?' Colin stared at him. 'Why would *I* be in the barn?'

'It made sense at the time, but that's beside the point. If you let me, I'll explain.'

Colin continued scribbling notes. 'Fine.'

'I couldn't find the light switch. So, using the torch, I searched the place, first checking behind the partition. Suffice to say you weren't there.'

'And what time was this?'

Lee shrugged. 'Sometime after 1.30. I vaguely remember looking at the clock in the kitchen. But I can't be sure.'

'And you were drunk?'

'Not rip-roaring drunk, but you wouldn't have wanted me driving you home.'

'I wouldn't want that at the best of times.' He gave Lee a look, before reminding him of the time he drove the wrong way down a motorway ramp.

'Well, I don't drive much. I normally take the tube,' he protested.

'Continue.' Colin went back to writing.

'Put it this way, I was drunk enough to think that lying on the sofa and going to sleep would be a good idea.' Lee let Colin finish what he was writing before continuing. 'I don't know how long I slept. But when I woke it was still dark. But that was the weird thing – I was woken by voices. One of them was definitely Lawrence's. But I couldn't work out what he was saying. Still can't. At first, I assumed you were all playing a joke on me. After that, it got creepy. Lawrence's voice and the others were fragmented, stop-starting like some crazy avant-garde voice piece. Remember that Dutch theatre show I took you to in Greenwich?'

Colin stopped. 'I can't write that down.' He remembered only too well; three hours of hell he'd never get back. 'Keep to the facts. Describe what you heard, what happened, in simple terms.'

Lee took his time, thinking carefully about each part, helping unfold in Colin's mind a clearer sequence of events. 'I called out "Hello", expecting an immediate reply, but no one answered. And as the noises went on, I shouted "Is this some kind of game?" Again, no reply, so I switched on the torch and stormed out from behind the partition, screaming, "I've had enough." Remember, I thought it was all a big joke and that you were going to jump out and scare me.'

'Keep going.'

'The next bit passed so quickly, I'm not sure of the sequence. I mean, even though I had the torch, it was still dark, so someone could have been standing right beside me and I wouldn't have known. But as I ran out from behind the partition, two things happened. A door beside the kitchen flew open – the cold wind must have fully woken me because I sprinted across to the doorway and saw someone running away towards the house.'

'Could you tell who it was?'

'No, they'd a huge cagoule on,' Lee replied, desperately trying to picture the scene. 'Flapping in the wind and bright orange like the one Jim has. But bigger.'

'Was it Jim?' Colin asked.

Lee shrugged his shoulders. 'I don't know. I can't be certain.'

'You didn't see their face?'

'No.'

'Man, woman?'

'I'm not sure. I didn't think about it that much at the time. Just that it was odd. And irritating. But the whole evening had been kind of weird, so I added it to the pile. But today, when I started to remember small things, I thought, what was the person doing in there? I mean, OK, I was there too, but knowing what's happened, it all takes on a whole new meaning.'

Colin wrote down as much detail as he could, circling and underlining key words. 'You said there were two things.'

'Right. At the time I thought it meant nothing, but having thought about it, I'm not so sure. When I first came out from behind the partition, maybe about halfway across the space, my foot kicked something which went spinning off across the floor. To God knows where.'

'Do you know what it was?'

Lee's face took on the guise of someone unconvinced by what he was about to say. 'Well, I've a very basic theory.'

'Honestly, however daft, let me hear it. If needs be, I can dismiss it later.'

'Well, with the crazy, random voices and no one actually being there, at first I thought it might have been my imagination. But there was no way; it was way too real.'

'So, spit it out.'

'I'm now thinking it could have been Lawrence's Dicta-phone I kicked. Or even the cassette from it; that's more likely. It felt light, with a plastic sound.' He paused. 'Is any of this making sense?'

Colin kissed Lee on the lips. 'Oh yes. Perfect sense.'

37

As Peter snoozed, Kath stroked his hair, running it through her fingers, marvelling at how thick and luscious it felt. Gazing as his chest gently rose and fell, seemingly without a care in the world, she burrowed in closer, wrapping her arms around his waist, enjoying the heat radiating from his body. He didn't quite fight her off but grunted and rolled over. Biting her lip, she muttered 'Wanker' so faintly she wondered if she'd even said it at all.

She lay on her back, noticing for the first time the ornate mouldings that decorated each corner of the ceiling, their delicate shapes like icing on a wedding cake. She focused on the central rose, painted a bright white to contrast with the pinks and greys of the rest of the room, deciding it was a colour combination she detested.

'You awake?' she asked, tapping her fingers against his shoulder. She took the complete lack of response to be a yes and ran her fingers along his arm. 'Peter?' She held him closer, burying her nose in his neck. She loved his smell. Even after running, the sweat on his body was sweet, like it had absorbed all the fresh air. It seemed unfair that someone should be so physically blessed.

'Stop it!' He curled into a tight ball and moved to the very edge of the bed. 'Go pester someone else.'

'Which psycho should I choose?'

He raised his head. 'Not funny.'

'We should make a run for it before they start breaking our door down with an axe.'

He turned to her, his face serious. 'I keep thinking I could have prevented it.'

Kath leaned on her elbow. 'How?'

Peter took a breath and glanced at her, turning away, before biting his lip and staring directly at her. 'Last night, after the party…'

'You came up here.' She completed his sentence, her face questioning any other version of events.

'I didn't actually.'

'You were here when I came through.'

'But before that,' he said, 'I went to see Lawrence.'

Kath spread her hands along the bedcovers, smoothing the creases, waiting for him to continue. When he didn't, she looked at him and asked, 'Is that what had upset you?'

'Let's not do this right now.'

'Was he alive? I need to hear you say it. Peter?'

'Bloody hell Kitty. Of course.'

'When you left?'

'Yes. What do you take me for?'

'Then everything's fine.'

'But you have to promise, if anyone asks – if Colin comes poking about – you can't tell them.' He looked at her as though seeing her face for the first time, tilting his head to scrutinise it. 'You know your make-up's all smudged.'

She checked herself in the dressing-room table mirror. 'Just a bit of mascara running.' She dabbed at it with her finger. 'Better?' She couldn't decide whether his obsession with appearance amused or annoyed her. He'd once called her ugly. But that was when they were fifteen, playing teenagers in Brain Friel's play, *Lovers*. He'd scoffed at the idea. 'Us two?' he'd asked. 'No one's going to buy that.' She'd never reminded him of it. Instead, she took comfort that he'd always liked her grey eyes – often complimenting her – especially when she wore her glasses. 'You look hot,' he'd say. Scant return for the praise she heaped on him. Regardless of knowing how deeply shallow it was, she still lapped it up.

'Promise you won't tell?' He offered his pinkie. 'You've got to promise, funny face.'

Not for the first time, she thought how good it would be to knee him in the balls and walk away. 'I promise.' She gripped his pinkie, noticing how sweaty it felt.

'Lawrence was riled. Properly scared.'

'Of what? Who?'

With his thumb, he circled the back of her wrist. 'Me, You.' He flicked a tear from his cheek. 'He said some cruel things.'

'Oh darling, don't. Tell me what he said.'

He wiped his nose against his arm and shook his head. 'I can't. But I should have been there for him. He could have trusted me.' He banged his fist on the mattress, letting out a muted scream.

She'd seen him do the exact same series of gestures in a terrible play at the Edinburgh Fringe. 'But darling, why would he? He barely knew you. Don't torture yourself like this.'

He continued crying in a muffled way and she wondered if he was putting it on. It was a noise she'd heard many actors make – it's what they imagined crying should sound like. But who was she to judge? At times, she'd been as phony as any other young actor when trying to access emotions. Only when her best friend died and she'd stood at the graveside, watching her coffin disappear into the ground, did she experience real grief for the first time. She'd looked over at her friend's mother and saw herself reflected back – how their entire bodies convulsed, the emotion overwhelming.

'You can't tell anyone I went to his room. If the others knew, it might seem suspicious and before you know it, they'll think it was me who killed him.'

She kissed him. 'I've promised, haven't I?'

Satisfied, he wriggled away from her.

'Is that it? You're not going to tell me what Lawrence said?'

But he was undressing, throwing his T-shirt and boxers onto the chair by the window. 'I'm going for a shower.'

'A problem shared?'

He gave her a sideways glance. 'Later.'

'I'm a good listener.'

Grabbing a towel, he tied it round his waist. 'Can I use your shower gel? It smells nicer than mine.'

'Sure. Peter—' Before she could say anything else, he'd disappeared into the bathroom.

THE KNOCK on the bedroom door was so quiet she barely heard it. She dismissed it as Peter messing about in the bathroom, but it came again. Gentle but insistent. She opened the door.

A beleaguered-looking Colin stood in the corridor, his face pale, his eyes puffy, a mass of plasters stuck to the back of his head. 'Is this a good time?'

Kath stepped out into the corridor, closing the door behind her. 'Sorry, Peter's in the shower. I wouldn't want him exposing himself to you.'

'Oh, OK.' Colin stepped back. 'I need to have a proper chat with you about last night.'

'Are you sure you're well enough to do that?' she asked. 'I'm surprised to even see you up and about. Don't you need to rest?'

'I'm fine. I'm going to chat with everyone, not just you. Check if anyone saw anything strange last night. Or today.'

'May I?' She touched his face, moving his head sideways to check the dressing at the back, pressing at it with her fingers. 'It looks nasty.'

He flinched. 'Ouch!'

'Sorry.' She withdrew her hand. 'For the record, after the party, I went straight to bed and slept all night.' She grabbed the door handle. 'You can check with Peter.'

'I will do.'

'And today I was either in the kitchen or here.'

He continued to stare at her. 'I need to do the interview properly. More formally.'

'Oh, so it's an interview rather than a chat?' She looked back at the door, straightening her dress.

He nodded. 'Would now be a good time? The first room upstairs is private.'

She gripped the door handle. 'Sure. I'll let Peter know.'

'The room directly opposite the landing? Fifteen minutes?'

Kath opened the bedroom door. 'Colin?' she called after him.

Behind her, a naked Peter emerged from the bathroom, drying himself without a care in the world. Waving, he shouted over, 'Don't mind me! I'm sure you've seen it all before.'

Kath stepped back out into the corridor, closing the door behind her. 'Actors. Complete exhibitionists.' She beckoned Colin over and pulled him closer.

'Is everything OK?' Colin asked.

She lowered her voice. 'You don't really think it's one of us?'

The door sprang open. Peter appeared in a pair of Roger Rabbit boxer shorts, drying his hair with an oversized towel. 'What am I missing?'

'Nothing,' Kath said. She turned to Colin. 'First door at the top of the stairs?'

'Yes. Fifteen minutes.' Colin walked off down the corridor.

As soon as he was out of earshot, Kath shook her head. 'You're a complete tart, Peter Selby.'

'And what's wrong with that?' he replied. 'Anyway, he was lapping up the floor show. I could tell.' He grabbed her by the waist and kissed her neck, before pulling her back inside the bedroom.

38

Richard's mouth felt as though someone had scrubbed it with a scouring pad. Moving his tongue around, he licked his lips but, devoid of moisture, it only made his mouth drier. Lifting the wine bottle from the bedside table, he shook it and finding it empty, flung it to the other side of the room. As it clattered to the floor unbroken, he threw back the bedclothes.

A sweat had formed on his forehead and his hands were clammy. It felt like the first night of a play: excitement and anxiety racing through his veins as the curtain went up. However, this always sparked a conflict. He didn't know whether he wanted to embrace the entire audience or run from them as fast as possible. The highs and lows, the adrenalin rush – how addictive it was.

He felt wobbly as his feet touched the carpet, but holding onto the bedpost, he managed to stand. Catching his reflection in the mirror, he barely recognised himself; he'd lost so much weight over the last couple of months, he thought he looked positively skeletal. *Better bury me now.* Exhausted by all the promises he'd made to friends, family, colleagues – to himself – he felt like a hollowed-out husk.

He put on his dressing-gown, tying it tight at the waist. Making his way downstairs, he gripped the handrail. If only he could give the appearance of being well, perhaps the others might believe it. For years, he'd managed to pull it off. What was so different now? Not long ago a couple of bottles of wine and some brandy chasers were his way to relax of an evening. How come one bottle of red could now make him feel like he'd been on a month-long bender?

He paused at the bottom of the stair and sat on the step. His breathing was erratic, and his heart felt like it was about to pop. Sweat covered his entire body, making him shiver. He tightened the cord around his dressing-gown further and closed his eyes. He considered having a nap right there on the stairs. No one would mind. Or better still, another drink. A small whisky – that would sort him out.

He knew Kath had confiscated the rest of his stash, but it must be hidden somewhere. And something hidden could always be found. With a nose for locating alcohol, however well concealed, he headed straight to the pantry. Sure enough, a case of champagne sat abandoned in the corner, waiting for a friendly face. He pulled the foil off the nearest bottle, untwisted the wire, and with his teeth, popped the cork. Careful not to lose a single drop, it was at his mouth before the bubbles could rise to the brim. Releasing a long-satisfied sigh, he let out a long burp, before guzzling half the bottle in one go.

Feeling much more himself, he sauntered back out into the hallway in search of some company. 'What the fuck?' He'd not noticed the wall of chairs before, stacked against Lawrence's door and the library. 'Trying to keep the plebs out, are you?' He gulped down the rest of the champagne, then dismantled the obstruction. Instead of neatly placing each chair to the side, he threw them off, shouting at the top of his voice, 'Lawrence, you old fucker, you in there?'

Alerted by the commotion, Lee arrived from upstairs to

see Richard throw the last of the chairs aside, open Lawrence's door, and disappear inside. Breathless, Georgie appeared at his side. 'He's gone in,' Lee explained.

'I can see that,' she snapped. 'Are you just going to stand by and let him?'

'It's a crime scene. I'd contaminate it.'

She pushed past Lee and opened the door, to reveal the room in semi-darkness. Richard stood over Lawrence's body, which had been discreetly covered with a white bedsheet. However, blood had seeped through it, creating a dark rose-shaped stain. The room stank of death. Georgie recoiled and sank into Lee's chest.

'You need to come out,' Lee shouted, offering him his hand as though reaching out towards a man ready to jump.

His eyes large and child-like, Richard mumbled, 'How did I forget?' He stepped towards the bed. 'I need to see his face one last time.'

'You don't.'

'Maybe I'll be able to work out if it was my handiwork after all. Because if I did do the fucker in, for the life of me, I can't remember.'

As Lee was about to plead with him one last time, Richard pulled back the sheet. He stood motionless as Lawrence's body was revealed. Face down, his arms at his side, it appeared like someone had placed a mannequin on the bed as a practical joke. His hair, so silky before, was stiff and matted with blood. The geometry of the huge crater at the back of his head seemed impossible to associate with a human skull.

Richard made the sign of the cross. 'God bless you, Lawrence Frederick Delaney, and may the Lord forgive all your sins.'

'Come on Richard, that's enough,' Lee shouted.

'Please cover him up,' Georgie cried.

'Now!' Lee's command appeared to break whatever spell Richard was under.

Delicately rearranging the sheet across the body, he said, 'I didn't do it!' There was a sobriety in Richard's voice as he returned their gaze. 'I've been terribly disrespectful. I'm so sorry,' he croaked. 'I'd have been happy to do time if I had.' Closing the door behind him, he whispered, 'Was it one of you? Or one of the others?' He waited for their response, but when it became clear he wouldn't receive any, he strode off, muttering to himself, 'Christ, to think there's someone here with a bigger grudge against him than me. Who'd have thought?'

Gliding into the kitchen, he reappeared seconds later with more champagne, and made his way upstairs. 'Do not disturb,' he called back, waving the bottle like he was holding aloft an Olivier.

39

Colin brushed some specks of dust from a pair of velvet barrel chairs and arranged them by the window. Standing back, he decided they were too far apart and moved them closer. It immediately felt better.

When interviewing her, he wanted to study Kath's reactions as well as listen to her version of events. The whole setup had to be perfect. He didn't want to intimidate her: keep to the facts, he told himself, aim for a friendly tone, offer one or two nods of encouragement – that way, people talked, revealing things they'd not intended.

Anyway, when the storm finally did blow over, it would be someone else's problem and he could return to being plain PC Buxton. But the headline – *Hollywood star murdered on remote Hebridean Island* – would never go away. He couldn't help but wonder how this might impact on his career. For now, he banished that thought to the back of his mind.

There was a knock on the door. He counted to ten before moving, taking his time crossing the floor, waiting another five seconds before he opened it. A grinning Kath stood patiently outside, her face glowing. Now wearing a loose white dress with a mustard cardigan on top, she'd scraped her hair back and removed all traces of make-up from her face. Colin was amazed at how young she looked.

She gently closed the door and scanned the room, eyeing the unmade bed and Colin's jumper, which he'd carelessly tossed into a corner. 'Nice room,' she said. 'Richard's thrown a wobbly again.'

'Is he OK?'

'Apparently, he went to confront Lawrence, somehow forgetting he was dead! But Lee's got it under control.'

Colin was keen to go check out the situation, ensure there'd been no interference with the crime scene. But having Kath there, ready to be interviewed, took priority. He knew Lee could cope and would fill him in later. He might not get another chance with Kath.

Picking the chair where Colin had planned to sit, she took in the view of the trees swaying back and forth. 'It's so peaceful up here.'

She was right. Whilst the storm raged outside, and the maelstrom of emotions continued downstairs, the attic felt cut off, cast adrift from the rest of the house. 'Thanks for coming.'

'This won't take long, will it?'

'Ten, fifteen minutes tops.' He readjusted the other chair and sat. Something had changed in her. It wasn't simply her stripped back appearance; gone too were the trivial flirtations, the self-deprecating comments. In less than thirty seconds, by registering the crumpled bedsheets, his jumper, casually mentioning Richard's misbehaviour, choosing exactly where to sit, she was telling him she was in control.

'I'm fascinated by all this – not Lawrence's death of course – Christ, that's so dreadful, but how you work it out. The process. I mean, where do you even start?'

'The perpetrator will slip up at some point. They always do.' He didn't entirely believe it; after all, this was not an Hercule Poirot whodunit, but it was possible someone might. And if so, he needed to be ready to strike.

'You're making me self-conscious. What if I inadvertently look at you the wrong way? Will that make me your prime suspect?' Holding his gaze, she readjusted herself.

For the first time, he noticed her eyes – striking grey, almost silver – set against pale, flawless skin. With one subtle change in the light, she appeared almost invisible. Grabbing some sheets of paper, he positioned them on his lap. 'Full name?'

'Kathryn O'Hare. It's my mother's maiden name. She's Irish.'

'So is that your real name or stage name?'

'Kathryn Keely's my birth name. I didn't like the double K; it sounded too harsh, so I changed it by deed poll when I left drama school.'

'No regrets?'

'None.' She waited patiently for his next question, but he left her to wait on purpose, wanting her to continue talking, to say something she might not otherwise have prepared for. 'Look, I suppose I should know, is this a real interview or not?'

He noticed that both her hands were placed on the armrests, her fingers tapping against the fabric.

'It's good to know these things,' she said.

Colin went back to writing, refusing to make eye contact, despite her wanting him to. He could feel her stare, urging him to look at her. 'I'm not taking an official statement if that's what you're asking,' he said, continuing to scribble away.

'Fine.' She looked at her watch. 'Is that the time?' Her voice was curt, like she'd another meeting to get to.

'Imagine the police knocking at your door following a crime in your area. All I need to know is did you notice or hear anything suspicious? Nothing too intrusive. We can stop at any point.'

The tapping ended and she sat forward. 'OK.' She checked her watch again. 'You can start now.'

The pen was dry. He shook it and tried again. 'Damn!' He opened the drawer of the bedside cabinet but couldn't find another one.

'Here. Give it to me.' She stretched out her arm. 'I can fix it.'

He handed her the pen, watching her rub it between both palms, then with her tongue, lick the nib.

'Try it now.'

He made a wavy scribble on the paper and, sure enough, the ink flowed. 'Thank you.'

'You'll want to know where I was last night.'

He smiled at her. 'You're doing my job for me.'

She no longer seemed nervous. Kath, the actress, had re-emerged, springing into life when summoned. She waved a hand dismissively. 'Well, I was in bed. Boring. But true. As was Peter. But I've already told you this. Next question. Or should I ask it for you?' She smiled, intent on changing the tone of their meeting.

'There was no moment when you left the room? Even to go to the toilet, say?'

'I don't think so.'

'So, you both went to bed at the same time?' Again, he observed the tapping of her fingers against the armrest.

'That's my memory. But we were both very drunk. Well, you saw us. Maybe I went to bed five minutes earlier. Ten. I can't remember.'

'Could it have been ten? Or fifteen?'

'No, I don't think so. I would remember that.'

'What time was it?'

She became aware of her fingers tapping and stopped, flattening her hands on the armrests. 'Now, there's a question.' She stared silently ahead.

'Roughly?'

'I can't say for definite. Sorry. But if I'm pushed, I'd reckon before midnight.'

Colin took his time jotting down some notes, raising his knee to conceal what he was writing.

Kath leaned further forward. 'I'm thinking, maybe I went to bed thirty minutes earlier. You can write that. I was almost asleep when Peter got into bed. I can remember he felt cold, so I'd been in bed longer than fifteen minutes for sure. So yes, put thirty.'

She was now changing her story. Subtly. He'd seen it too many times. But now was not the time to push her. Bide his time, listen to the others first, before comparing. 'And you didn't see or hear anything suspicious?'

'That night? Or since getting here?'

This made Colin smile. 'From when the party dispersed.' As soon as he said it, he got a flashback: him standing by the door with Lawrence, a drunken Peter coming over to speak with them, followed by Kath, then Lawrence leaving. He'd no recollection of Kath being in the kitchen after that. That would mean Lawrence and Kath were very likely together for at least half an hour. And he definitely didn't see Lawrence after that. In fact, he didn't know anyone who had. All except Kath, whom he'd seen leaving Lawrence's room. 'You didn't visit Lawrence's room last night for any reason?'

She laughed, like on the first night when he'd told a dumb joke, and she was the only one who got it. 'Why would I go there?'

'I don't know. That's why I'm asking.'

'Honestly Colin, we were as drunk as farts. Who knew where any of us were? Now, is that us finished?' Before he could reply, she'd stood up.

He allowed her to assume control again. If she felt in charge, her answers to his final questions could be revealing. 'You knew Lawrence before?'

'Barely. Only from that dreadful film. I was on set for three weeks at most. Not enough time to get to know someone.'

The tapping returned, this time her fingers against her right leg.

'But you spent time together?' Both hands rose, flapping, her fingers unconsciously searching for a surface to tap against. 'Did you hang out after filming, for example?'

'I had the tiniest part. Four or five scenes. I was only there that long because technical issues meant they had to reshoot a couple. Most of the time I was hanging around in my tiny trailer doing crosswords.'

'So, your paths never crossed on a personal level?'

'He's a big movie star. I'm no one. And on set, hierarchy matters. A lot.'

'But you spent time with him?'

'Colin,' she said, shaking her head as though she'd told him a thousand times before. 'We did a few scenes together. End of. For Christ's sake! Shoot me.'

'Yet here you are now. You obviously made an impression on him. As far as I'm aware, Lawrence handpicked the cast.'

Her face flushed and she got up. 'There's food downstairs if you fancy eating.' At the door, she paused. 'I was as surprised as anyone to be offered this part. Ask my agent. Ask anyone. Or even better, watch the film. I'm terrible in it. This business is random. My face must have fitted, or he wanted to see it again for whatever reason.' She shrugged her shoulders. 'You'd be better off asking Lee about all that stuff.'

Having decided the interview was over, she opened the door. 'I thought you'd be asking basic things, like my name, address. Nice Colin wouldn't have lied to me. PC Buxton's a different character though, isn't he?'

She'd run out of charm and had resorted to faux chumminess, which rang hollow. 'Can you explain why you were in Lawrence's room last night?' he asked.

Edging the door closed, she stood with her back against it. 'I told you. I wasn't.'

'I saw you leave when I was going to bed.'

'Was that after you'd had a drink or not?'

Quick! But she was right. There was no doubt he'd seen her leave Lawrence's room, but if what he'd witnessed was key, it would be open to question. 'I'm trying to build a picture here.' What she said next mattered. Unless someone came forward to tell him they'd seen Lawrence after Kath left, she'd be the last to have seen him alive. That would make her his prime suspect.

Her expression became softer. 'Oh, I forgot. I needed to ask him about a scene. I was there for a minute at most. It was as people were going to bed.'

He wouldn't press her any further. She'd feel cornered, refuse to speak. Plus, she was partly right. The party had tailed off haphazardly and people had been going to bed when he saw her leave. He couldn't prove it, but he was convinced she'd spent longer than a minute with him.

'Is that me?' She opened the door and stepped into the hallway, making a point of looking directly at him. 'I hope I've been able to help. Even if it's simply to cross me off your list.'

He smiled, trying to reel her back a bit with a blast of *nice Colin*. But she'd already bolted downstairs.

40

'I made all this food hours ago. Do you think anyone will want to eat?' Georgie asked.

'Drink maybe,' Lee replied, pointing at the wine rack. 'No hint intended.'

Jim immediately grabbed a corkscrew and opened a bottle of red. Taking three clean glasses from the draining-board, he poured. 'Tell me when to stop.' He glanced up at them. 'Or not.'

Lee and Georgie both took their brimming glasses and sat at the table. Around them, the empty champagne bottles and bowls of stale nibbles from the previous night's party still haunted the surfaces. Jim joined them, and the three of them stared into space, sipping their wine in silence.

'How did you two meet?' Lee had been eager to know since they'd got there.

Jim and Georgie cut each other off as they started. Georgie placed her hand over Jim's and began. 'Drama school in London. The late 50s. For the first term, I thought he was gay.'

Jim laughed. 'I sort of was. I'd been brought up in the middle of nowhere, so any attention was welcome.'

'Oh Jim, you're a terrible tease! Everyone was after him,

and I've never been the type to compete for people's attention. God knows why I became an actor.'

'We were rehearsing a scene from Pinter.'

'The Birthday Party. Lulu and Stanley. Totally miscast.
There we were, two teenagers, barely knowing which way the
wind blew, grappling with this awful world. But I do
remember looking into his face properly for the first time and
thinking this is the most beautiful boy I've ever met.'

Jim's eyes twinkled and he grinned.

'You wouldn't know it now, but with his razor-sharp
cheekbones and beatnik hair, he was incredibly androgynous.
Kind of lost-looking, vulnerable, unsure of the world. I had to
have him. I mean, I'd been around the block. A whole two
boyfriends.'

'William.'

'Who had the most awful B.O.'

'And Hugh, wasn't it?'

'I called him *Huge*. He had the most enormous cock I've
ever seen. It still gives me nightmares.'

Lee laughed out loud.

'When I saw it for the first time, I said, do you honestly
think that's going in here?'

'And when a handsome knight in shining armour came
riding into the picture, all competitors were swept aside.' Jim
winked at Georgie. 'Well, more like jeans and a Breton T-shirt.
I was a walking cliché.'

'Hugh definitely turned out to be gay and William went
off to do officer training at Sandhurst, so slim pickings.' She
stuck her tongue out at Jim.

'Yet, thirty years later, here we are.'

'Two limpets clinging to a rock.'

Georgie squeezed Jim's hand as she wiped a tear from her
eye. 'Look at me. Silly old cow.'

'Always were. Boom! Boom!'

'And where did Lawrence fit in?' Letting go of each other's

hand, Jim and Georgie both took a gulp of wine. 'Sorry. I didn't mean to pry.'

'Not at all,' Jim said. 'One of the happiest periods of my life. A dream job. We were just out of drama school, looking for a lucky break like every other young actor, and it fell into our laps. *Eros*. Incredible play. Well, you'll know yourself, it's a modern classic – still staged around the world, on the school syllabus too. I ended up teaching it to a group of sixth formers a year or so ago. They didn't believe I'd been the first actor to play the role of Bartholomew. They kept asking. "*Why you in this shithole then? Didn't you make a pile of money?*"'

'Equity minimum,' Georgie added. 'Though it did pay for the down payment on our first flat. Well, with a bit of help from my father.'

'Do you remember the read through?' Jim said. 'The original casting had Lawrence as Bartholomew and me as Harry. What a disaster that would have been. I was meant to be this Lothario with a fuck-off attitude. He was playing the mild-mannered farmer who'd this dream of building a Utopian society in the backwaters of rural Suffolk. Anyway, at Georgie's suggestion, they swapped our roles after the first read through.'

Georgie sat forward. 'Jim stole the show, of course. Lawrence might have won the awards, but he didn't come close to this one.' She stretched over and kissed Jim.

'I was thankful for the job. In those days, awards meant nothing. Nowadays, I'd bite your hand off.'

'Liar!' Georgie slapped his arm.

He smiled. 'Kidding. Awards mean nothing. Like I said, it's all about the work. If the script's good, I'll do it. That's if I'm ever offered anything, of course.'

'We played in the West End, toured Australia and Canada, finally Broadway. It was a sensation.'

'Two years of our lives. The three of us,' Jim said.

'Wow,' Lee cried. 'England's very own *Jules et Jim*.'

'I don't know about that, but during the tour we were inseparable. When it ended in 1963, we went our way, and Lawrence went his,' Jim explained. 'The rest is history. He became the megastar. We muddled on. It's a funny business, eh?'

Kath entered, walked straight to the sink and filled the kettle. Taking a mug from the cupboard, she dropped it in the sink, where it smashed. 'Shit! Shit! Shit!'

'You OK, love?' asked Georgie.

'Do I look like a murderer?' She burst out. 'Me?'

'Who's saying that?' Jim asked.

Kath dried her hands and wiped them against her dress. 'It doesn't matter. Sorry, I'm being stupid. Is there any of that wine left?'

Jim poured her a glass and she snatched it from him, guzzling half of it down.

'Our nerves are frayed, darling. No one thinks you're a murderer.' Georgie pulled Kath towards her and hugged her tightly. 'Silly girl,' she said. 'Come and sit beside me.'

'Colin does.' She finished the rest of her wine and refilled her glass.

'Jim,' said Georgie, 'do you want to open another bottle?'

Lee drummed his fingers against the table. 'And he said that? That he thinks you murdered Lawrence?'

Kath fidgeted with the buttons on her cardigan. 'Not in so many words. He didn't have to. The way he looked at me was enough. And the questions he was asking.'

'For God's sake, it's his job, Kath.' Lee drained the rest of his wine, weighing up Kath's demeanour. Despite sounding aggrieved, her body language was relaxed, unperturbed.

'It sounded like he was snooping, trying to find anything that might give me a motive.'

Lee crossed to the sink. He pushed the broken mug to the side and rinsed his glass. 'I'll catch everyone later.'

'Please don't say anything,' Kath said. 'I know I'm over-reacting. But I'm not used to this. None of us are.'

'I wouldn't take it personally.' He picked up the two halves of the broken mug and placed them in the bin. 'Unless you've something to hide.' He was sure Colin hadn't been as direct.

'What does that mean?' she asked, clutching the edges of the table.

Lee closed the bin lid. 'I'm just saying.' If anyone had an issue with Colin trying to make the best of a dire situation, they'd have to cross him first. '*Someone's* hiding something. Don't you think?'

Kath shrugged.

'Lawrence didn't hit himself over the head, did he?' he continued.

'This isn't helping,' Jim stressed, signalling enough was enough.

'Sorry. I'm tired of all this. I need a lie down.' Lee paused at the door. 'But first Lawrence, then Colin. What you all seem to be forgetting is there's a killer on the loose.'

41

Colin was lying on the bed trying to read *The Murder of Roger Ackroyd* – his favourite Agatha Christie story – when Lee entered. 'What's happening?' He put the book down.

'The peasants are revolting,' he replied. 'Or certainly very tense.'

'Hardly surprising.' He sat upright, eager to hear more.

Lee stood over him. 'I should change your dressing.'

Every part of Colin's body felt like it had been battered, not just his head. And since the chat with Kath, a migraine had been threatening: flashes sparked in his peripheral vision and waves of nausea drifted in and out. Resting with his book for ten minutes had seemed the best solution until he interviewed the next person. He groaned. 'Can't we do it later?'

'Come on. Georgie's organising dinner,' Lee said, 'and we're expected.'

With a couple of feeble oohs and aahs, and some grimacing, he forced himself from the bed.

'No need to milk it, babe,' Lee said, his hands already gripping his head, unpeeling the dressing.

'Christ! You're hurting me,' Colin cried.

'Sit still then. I don't want to pull at the wound.'

Colin flinched again, imagining the worst: a gaping hole, skin flapping, skull exposed. 'How does it look?'

Lee gave nothing away. 'You'll live. How does it feel?'

'Like I've been bashed across the head with a major acting award.' He twisted round to catch Lee roll his eyes. 'I'll shut up and keep taking the painkillers, shall I?'

'Might improve your jokes. Right, I need to clean it.' Lee made his way to the bathroom and returned with a bowl of hot water, cottonwool and the tube of antiseptic ointment he'd used earlier.

'I take it Kath's been spouting off? Ouch!' He recoiled as Lee dabbed at the wound with the cottonwool.

'Got it into her head that you're accusing her.'

'Well, if that's how she wants to interpret it.' His face screwed up as Lee gently applied more cream to the wound.

'Sorry, love. I'll just be a couple more seconds.'

Colin leant against Lee's stomach as the process of applying a fresh dressing began. 'Take all the time in the world.' The assurance of Lee's touch was acting like a balm, relieving the pain and banishing his migraine. 'You should be prescribed on the NHS.'

'Feel good?'

He relaxed further into Lee's body. 'Oh yes.'

'Not wishing you'd gone to Spain?'

'Let's not go there.'

As if on cue, a blast of wind rattled the windows. 'You'd have missed the storm of the century.' Lee gently pressed the dressing, ensuring it was secure.

'Now, that's what I call a good time.'

'Right, all done – you can open your eyes.'

Colin looked over at Lee, tidying away the medical supplies on the bedside table. 'Was she angry?'

'Fuming.' He sat beside Colin. 'You didn't accuse her, did you?'

Colin needed to withhold certain details. Even from Lee. Enough so that things didn't become completely blurred. 'Some people spill their guts as soon as you ask them their name. Others hide their true selves so much they almost believe they're telling the truth when lying to your face. The best criminals are consummate actors.'

'God, that doesn't bode well. We've a house full of brilliant actors and of them all, she may be the best.'

'We'll see.' Colin lay back on the bed and Lee joined him. They snuggled together, listening to the wind outside reel and roar. He allowed himself to further indulge in thoughts of the alternative holiday he could be having. Five o'clock. It wouldn't be long until Happy Hour. Lee read his mind.

'You're wishing you hadn't said yes, aren't you?'

'I'm thinking that two weeks in Majorca as opposed to a surprise murder investigation, might have done the trick.'

'What are your instincts?' He burrowed in closer.

Colin's hand stroked the hairs on Lee's arm – back and forward – making different patterns. The comfort in small pleasures. 'Well, put it this way, I don't think there's been an intruder.'

'So, you've established no one's hiding out in a cave?'

'Pretty much. And Richard is essentially a man down.'

'Ah, but is it all an act? He made such a show of going into Lawrence's room, I did wonder if it was put on – an excuse to mess up the scene. Also, killing Lawrence might well have been the trigger for him to start drinking again.'

'Possibly. Plus, he does have a clear motive. We need to dry him out. I can chat with him later.'

Georgie yelled from downstairs that dinner was ready. Lee crossed to the door, shouting they'd be there in a few minutes, to start without them. He rejoined Colin on the bed. 'I'm not sure I can handle this – trying to pretend things are normal.'

'We're left with the four of them. A tight family unit. They might be covering for each other.'

'What's the motive?'

Colin grabbed a fresh shirt and put it on. 'Well, they've all known Lawrence from before.'

'But years apart. I mean, Jim and Georgie haven't seen him for almost thirty years. What's their beef?'

'True. Which leaves Kath and Peter, who met Lawrence on the set of – what's it called – *Cobalt Dusk*?'

'Dawn. *Cobalt Dawn.*'

'But according to Kath, they barely exchanged a word.'

'There's no way that's true. She filmed exclusively with him for three weeks.'

'So she's lying?' Colin waited for Lee's response. He knew she was but wanted to hear Lee's thoughts.

'Didn't they have some weird exchange last night, towards the end of the evening?' Lee asked. 'I didn't hear what she said, but Lawrence seemed put out.'

'She told him to fuck off.'

'Wow!'

'At the time I assumed she was kidding, but maybe not.'

'Well, if she wasn't, that came from somewhere. You don't tell someone to fuck off you hardly know for no reason.' Lee grabbed the pad and pen. 'Maybe they know each other better than we think.'

'You mean they shagged?'

'Colin Buxton. Language!' Sitting up, legs crossed, Lee wrote down everyone's names, drawing circles and arrows to connect them. 'So, let's imagine they did shag, and he still has a thing for her, but when he gets here, finds out she's now with Peter, he goes ballistic. She tells Lawrence she won't leave Peter, he gets physical with her, she grabs something and hits him over the head with it.' He stopped writing.

Colin shook his head. 'I didn't get a hint of anything romantic between Lawrence and Kath.'

'OK Sherlock,' he said, thrusting the pen and paper at him. 'So, my theory's in its early stages, but at least I've got one. Or one I'm willing to share. Unlike some.' He patted Colin's legs. 'Come on, we need to go and join the Borgias for dinner.'

'Tell them I'm sick.'

'You're not getting out of this!' He forced Colin towards the door. 'You're wearing the invalid look well, Mr Buxton.'

'Straight off the Paris catwalk,' he replied, hobbling towards the door. He stopped. 'Maybe it wasn't an affair. Write that down. Did he ever say anything odd to you? During the casting process, perhaps?'

'Not anything specific that jumps out. I'd seen her in a couple of things, thought she was terrific, but her name hadn't sprung to mind. She's not your typical ingénue. But he insisted we had to have her.'

Colin continued. 'Maybe something *did* happen on the set, it didn't end well, he continued to pursue her and that's why he insisted on casting her.'

'She mentioned an incident. But I don't think it had anything to do with Lawrence. Why say yes if it had been?'

'She needed the job. She's got quite a fuck-it-to-you attitude.'

'Hollywood star, taking advantage? Whatever are you saying about my industry?'

Colin grabbed the pad and wrote something down.

'What have you written?'

'Revenge!'

42

Georgie and Jim were already eating by the time Colin and Lee joined them in the dining room. Several plates of food had been laid out: chicken drumsticks, a bowl full of green leaves, some potato salad, bread, cheeses, as well as a tureen of soup. A couple of bottles of wine had been opened, and Kath was in the middle of pouring herself a glass. 'I know this looks all wrong – disrespectful. But we need to eat.'

Colin hadn't eaten in almost twenty-four hours, and as if on cue, his stomach rumbled. 'Don't be silly,' he said. 'This looks lovely.' To ensure he could see everyone, he chose the chair at the top of the table. 'Thanks for doing this.'

'Sit down, help yourself. It's nothing fancy.' Georgie handed both him and Lee a plate. 'Kath made the soup. Try it. It's yummy.'

The lights quivered. Below them in the basement, the generator whined, as if it were about to expire. 'That's not a good sign,' Jim said, lowering his voice. 'The storm's showing no signs of blowing over; I think we'll be hunkered down for a while.'

'Don't be so negative darling. We've enough to contend with.' She flicked him with her napkin.

Waving a chicken drumstick, Kath asked Colin, 'Was I a terrible witness?'

'You were fine,' he replied, helping himself to some cheese. 'Can you pass the potato salad?'

Lee scooped up the bowl and handed it to Colin. 'Please, no harassing the invalid. He's still recuperating.'

'That's a nasty-looking bump.' Georgie examined Colin's head with forensic interest, gently touching it with her fingers, making considered mutterings about the size and possible strike pattern. Colin wondered if she'd once played the part of a doctor or maybe a pathologist. Whatever, her manner was very convincing.

'Yes, pretty brutal,' Lee said. 'Can I have the red?'

Colin took a drink of water as Georgie sat back down. 'It'll take more than that to get rid of me.'

As they ate, Jim speculated that it might be a series of storms hitting the island rather than a single big one. 'Each seems more ferocious than the last,' he explained. 'As if it's leading to a final crescendo!'

No one responded; instead they concentrated on eating. A branch hit against the window. Then again, repeatedly, as though trying to break in.

'Pass the bread, will you?' Georgie asked, taking it from Kath, who grabbed a piece for herself.

'Peter not joining us?' Lee asked.

'He's taking the whole Lawrence thing badly.' Kath popped a cherry tomato into her mouth.

'Such a sensitive soul,' Georgie added. 'Always has been. Remember when he was small? A stranger would just have to look at him the wrong way and he'd run off crying.' She poured herself a second glass of wine. 'We tried our best to toughen him up. Christ knows why. Look at us. Literally, the embodiment of the feckless bourgeoisie.'

'Did I come across like a criminal, Colin?' Kath refilled her glass and settled back in her chair. She'd been glancing at him while grazing on the food. 'Because I don't think anybody in this house has the capacity to kill someone.'

Colin kicked Lee's foot, their signal to leave as soon as they could. 'People can surprise you.' He looked around the table. Each seemed as innocent as the next. Christ, they were good! Or maybe he was wrong and there was an intruder after all.

'You must have a prime suspect at least.' Kath leaned forward. 'Do you?' He spotted her fingers tapping on the table before she caught herself and stopped. He sensed she was looking for a reaction, enjoying having an audience. As she reached for Georgie's cigarettes, she knocked an empty tumbler over, letting it spin on its side.

'I'm just doing my job.'

Kath lit a cigarette and blew the smoke upwards. 'Are you?'

Lee scowled. 'Kath, can you change the record?'

'I'm doing my best.' Colin sipped more water. 'Now, if we could leave it for a moment so I can finish eating. The food's delicious by the way.' He was lying. The soup had been overly salted, and the salad dressing had a bitter edge to it. One sniff of the wrinkled drumsticks suggested they were past their sell-by date.

'The crime scene's been spoiled,' Kath went on, lighting a cigarette for Georgie and passing it to her.

'Despite my best efforts.' Colin pushed aside his plate. 'I'll be doing more to secure the barn, too. I take it no one's been out there since I was brought back?'

They shook their heads, slowly turning to one another. The fact they needed to check suggested uncertainty.

'You've only spoken to me,' Kath continued. 'When will the others be interviewed?'

'Soon. If you haven't noticed' – he pointed to the back of his head – 'I've been waylaid.'

'But that's it, isn't it? If you've taken a knock to the head, how can you determine anything? If this was the real world, you'd be sent home to recover, barred from going anywhere near a witness.'

The rest of the table kept silent, watching the exchange as if it was the finale of a TV cop-show.

'Once officers get across, a formal investigation will begin. As first responder, I'm simply assessing the evidence. It's my duty – I've no choice.'

'Kath's got a point,' said Georgie, pitching in. 'What about fingerprints? Blood?' She blew smoke in his direction. He coughed, unsure if it was deliberate. 'Won't forensic evidence have been destroyed?'

Suddenly she was a forensics expert, ready to scrutinise and challenge his methods. Her range knew no bounds. What part would she pull out the hat next – Chief of Police?

Colin patted the corner of his mouth with a napkin and laid it over his half-eaten salad. 'You'd be surprised what traces survive. Besides, it's not only physical evidence we search for. There are the events leading up to the crime taking place, as well as individual motives.' He stood. 'Now, if you'll excuse me.'

'Do you honestly believe it's one of us?' Peter was standing in the doorway, his shirttails hanging out of his trousers, like he'd dressed in the dark. He looked around the room. 'Is there a drink somewhere?'

Kath pulled a chair out for him. 'Will red do?' He nodded and she poured him a glass.

Colin made to leave. If things were going to blow up again, he'd rather not play piggy in the middle.

'If you're so sure, you should prove it.' Peter took a drink. 'Otherwise, you should get outside and continue searching for the real criminal. You're not going to get very far sat here stuffing your face.'

Jim blanched. 'Peter, you're out of order.'

'We're scared,' Kath said, appealing to Colin. 'Look at us. Do you think any of us are capable of killing Lawrence?'

'It's my job to investigate,' Colin replied. 'Most victims know their killer – ninety-nine times out of a hundred there's a motive to a murder. It may be obvious, or it may not – as you know, people always have secrets. Do I think one of you might be the murderer? I wouldn't be doing my job if I didn't consider it a possibility.'

Peter shook his head, laughing. 'So, any slip of the tongue and we're an immediate suspect? Is that it?' he sneered. 'It's outrageous!'

Colin wondered if this was a coordinated attempt by Peter, Kath and Georgie to undermine his investigation. The blow he took to the head most certainly was. 'You're all suspects, whether you like it or not. Do you think for one minute I'm enjoying any of this?'

'We didn't say that.' Kath piled more food onto Peter's plate. 'You're jumping to conclusions. As Peter said, there could easily be someone else on the island.'

'A man is dead, and someone attacked me this morning. I've reason to believe the same person committed both crimes.'

'How can you be certain?' asked Kath, picking chicken off a drumstick and cutting it into smaller pieces before putting it on Peter's plate. 'Again, where's your evidence?' She tossed the stripped bone aside. 'You've none.'

'Who knew I was investigating? All of you.'

'What's the point in interviewing us then?' Peter asked, with his mouth full. 'If you've made up your mind?'

Jim cut in, 'Sorry, but I do think they've a point. Are you sure you've searched everywhere?'

Lee's hands gripped the table. 'I've had enough of this bullshit.' His anger startled everyone, including Colin. 'Have you all forgotten who's in charge of this company? Me! And under any normal circumstances, if the police wished to question my company, I would do my level best to make sure they cooperated. How do you imagine this is any different?'

'He's no authority,' Kath snapped. She pointed at Colin, her body swaying from the alcohol. 'These are our lives he's meddling with.'

'Witnesses and suspects obstruct us all the time,' Colin said. 'I don't take it personally.'

'Someone's already tried to hurt you,' said Peter. 'Maybe best to back off?'

His veiled threat was more than Colin could stomach. 'No one wishes to be questioned, I take it?' The four of them sat, stony-faced. 'You can be assured, someone *will* pay the price for what happened to Lawrence.' He turned to Jim. 'And yes, I checked the island thoroughly. There's no evidence to suggest anyone else is here or has been.'

They were all keen to discredit him; that was becoming obvious. The reason less so. Perhaps to do with the beating; maybe they considered it a weakness? Or was it the friendliness he'd shown them since arriving? What they failed to appreciate was how far he was willing to go to identify the culprit. 'And so that we're clear, aside from the murder of Lawrence, the attack on me – a police officer – comes with a heavy sentence too. Someone will be going away for a very long time. Mark my words.'

43

Lee plumped up the pillows. 'Things sure got nasty.'

Far on the horizon white lightning sliced the dark sky, followed by threatening rumbles of thunder. If open hostility was their only weapon, Colin could deal with it. 'Goes with the territory, I'm afraid.'

'For him to turn on you like that?' Lee rearranged the pillows on the bed, glancing around for other things to do. 'He basically threatened you.'

'Maybe I was being too defensive. I don't know. At the end of the day, it's all part of the job.'

'And I thought mine was tough.' Lee threw a log on the fire and sat in the armchair facing Colin. 'So, do you have a plan?'

'Sit it out. Keep the bedroom door locked, don't go wandering the corridors alone.' He crossed the room and locked the door. 'Can you go over what you saw again?'

Lee repeated his story of going out to the barn, falling asleep, waking to the sound of Lawrence's voice.

'You said there were other voices, too. Male? Female?'

Lee shrugged his shoulders. 'It was fast-forwarding and

rewinding so quickly, I couldn't tell. Loads of garbled words, though.'

'And it was completely dark?'

'I'd just woken, so my eyes hadn't adjusted. When I walked across, that's when I kicked something.'

'The Dictaphone?'

'It felt smaller, lighter. *I'd* say it was the cassette. But I can't be sure.'

Colin thought for a moment. 'It's a longshot, but our best hope is that the killer didn't notice anything drop. Whatever it was, it could still be there.' He gazed out at the barn. 'You're sure no one's left the house since I came back?'

'As sure as I can be. I'd have heard the door opening. And believe me, I was listening.'

'Good. Mind, would anyone be stupid enough to go back in there?' He took another look at the wreckage of the barn. 'I'd say it's about to cave in.' Colin crouched in front of the fire, watching sparks fly off the log, tongues of flames rising higher, radiating welcome heat towards him. There was no doubt – hitting him had bought someone time. Who knew what had been covered up whilst he lay unconscious?

'Here's a thought.' Lee's expression was pained. 'Tell me what you think.'

Colin smiled. Lee loved to throw his theories into the mix. 'Go on.'

He lowered his voice. 'This is pure conjecture, but what if they're all involved in some way?' He sensed Colin's scepticism. 'Hear me out. Not at first – I'm not saying it's been planned before we got here – but to help cover up.'

'That's a lot of awkward conversations, a lot of reasoning things out. Killings tend not to happen like that – they're more typically impulsive than planned.'

'Actors improvise, learn things quickly, put on a performance.'

'If that's the case, we've more trouble on our hands than we imagined.'

A barrage of knocks beat against their door.

'What the hell?' They stared at each other before Lee rose to answer.

'Ask who it is,' Colin whispered.

Lee edged closer to the door. 'Who's there?' He strained to hear anything – except for a soft whine. 'Richard? Is that you?'

A low, strangulated *yes* came in reply. Lee unlocked the door and threw it open, catching Richard as he collapsed into the room.

The reek of alcohol was overwhelming, and his eyes were popping, as if about to explode.

Colin rushed over to help. 'What's happened?'

'I'm so ashamed,' he wailed, doubling over, his voice attempting but failing to say more. A series of long sobs followed.

Lee fetched a blanket and wrapped it around him. 'Here, try to calm down. Breathe slowly.'

They sat him beside the fire and watched him rock back and forth, at the same time listening to the house groan under the pressure of the wind.

'He didn't deserve that. Poor bastard. I mean, he was a proper shit, but no one deserves that.' The sky lit up spectacularly and thunder boomed overhead. Richard shivered. 'It's the end of days.'

Lee sat next to him. 'The others have sent us to Coventry.'

'Oh, is that what they're conspiring about? I looked into the dining room and it was like the witches' scene out of *Macbeth*.'

'Did they say anything?'

'Double, double, toil and trouble.' Richard laughed so hard at his own joke that he began to cough. 'You think it was one of them, don't you?' he spluttered.

Was this Richard's tactic? Avoid scrutiny by apportioning

blame? 'Unless there's someone else on the island.' Colin crossed to the bathroom and returned with a glass of water. 'Here.' As helpless as he appeared, out of everyone, Richard had the most obvious motive. To have been sacked so cruelly – who wouldn't want to avenge that?

Richard took a sip. 'Surely it's not impossible that someone could be out there?'

Glancing at Colin before answering, Lee explained how Lawrence was convinced Jackie Adamson had followed him here. But that there might be others too: stalkers, crazed fans. 'He asked Colin to be his bodyguard.'

'I'm sure he did. Nice-looking fella like him.' He winked at Colin. 'Whatever he was paying, I'll double it.'

'I know it lets everybody off the hook, but I'm not convinced by the whole intruder theory,' said Colin. 'There's no evidence.'

'Richard, did you see anything last night?' Lee asked, trying to keep him focused.

'Only my pillow.' He settled into the chair, conscious of an opportunity to spin out his part. 'You know boys, having been around a lot longer than you, I've seen and heard a few things. Some of which might be true; the rest spiteful gossip.' He looked around the room. 'You don't happen to have a teeny bit of vodka?'

'Richard, we need you sober,' Colin said.

'Is that a no?'

'It's a no!'

'Lee, your boyfriend's got such a pretty face, but what a bitch.' Richard's hands shook as he placed his water on the table. 'Aren't you going to take notes?'

Colin grabbed his pen and paper.

'Should I leave?' asked Lee.

'Not on my account.' Richard gripped Lee's hands. 'I'd prefer you to stay.'

'Colin?' Lee asked.

He nodded his approval.

Adjusting himself, Richard sat upright in the chair. 'Well, you know they were in the original production of that fabulous play, *Eros*?'

'Jim, Georgie and—'

'Lawrence. That's right. I saw it half a dozen times. Incredible. All three of them lit up the stage. It was electric. Spellbinding. And my God, they were so beautiful. But Jim – wow. You wouldn't know it now, but he was extraordinary looking – there was something so modern, other-worldly about him. If you look closely and the wind's blowing in the right direction, you can still see it. You do know it was him who was tipped to be the huge star?' His expression glowed, as if transported back in time.

'What happened?' asked Lee.

Richard gave him a look, as if to say, *honey, you might be young, but you weren't born yesterday.*

Colin stopped scribbling. 'Am I missing something?'

Richard cleared his throat. 'Why would someone of Jim's talent, looks and star quality end up working as a supply teacher?'

Again, Lee seemed perplexed. 'Bad luck? Plenty talented people miss out on chances. I've a filing cabinet full of their faces.'

Richard shook his head in dismay. 'Sit tight and listen.' He was now in full stride. 'Rumour has it they were in a ménage à trois, and when I say rumour, I mean I have it on good authority. But Jim put a stop to it once the play ended. Of course, like most things born out of lust, relations soured somewhat. And that's when Lawrence began bad-mouthing Jim at any given opportunity. You know what it's like? You get a little success, it goes to your head – you worry you're not as good as others says you are, so you best get rid of the competition. No?' He canvassed the room quickly before continuing. 'Apparently, Lawrence connived to ensure Jim's career was over before it even started. Got all the right people on side too – including Brendan – God rest his soul. A wonderful man who I loved dearly, but easily swayed by a pretty face. Anyway, Jim was about to be cast in one of Brendan's productions – *Death of a Salesman* – the role of Biff. And that's when Lawrence stuck the boot in, bent Brendan's ear that Jim was unreliable. Of course, Brendan, silly old queen, changed his mind and guess who he cast? Lawrence! The production went on to be another spectacular success: Broadway transfer, winning awards across the board, the works. It was that production which established Lawrence in America. And as a consequence, Jim was never able to capitalise on *Eros*. He was forgotten about, and his career never took off.'

'That gives Jim a motive.' Colin circled what he'd written.

'If they knew, it potentially gives Georgie and Peter a motive too,' Lee added. 'Mild-mannered Jim. Who'd have thought?'

'Can I have that vodka now?'

Colin leafed through his notes. 'Why, after all that, would Lawrence want to cast Jim in the play?'

'He never explained,' Lee said. 'Jim was the first person offered a role. After that, I thought he wanted to make it a family affair by adding Peter and Georgie. And like I said, he said nothing specific about Kath, merely that she was the only actress he'd consider for the role. And she said yes, albeit after a couple of weeks wrangling over money.'

'Did Georgie delay?' Colin asked.

'Yes. She was the last to commit.'

'Now, I'd say that's interesting,' Richard stated, his eyes widening, evidently relishing the role of informant. 'Why delay? Her whole family were going to be involved.'

'She's in demand and actors are forever hedging their bets if they get regular offers. There was a little tussle over her contract, but nothing out of the ordinary. In fact, overall, it was one of the easiest casting processes I've ever had.'

'Why so easy?' asked Colin. 'If you're saying that's unusual.'

'What Lawrence wanted, he usually got. Typically, by offering more money. It's true what they say: everyone has their price.'

Colin shook his head. 'Except now he's lying dead downstairs and one of those lovely people he insisted on casting probably murdered him.'

'I'm assuming I've been discounted?' Richard drained the last of the water. He stared at Colin. 'Well, have I?'

Colin wasn't about to eliminate him entirely, but unless he was playing the helpless drunk to perfection, he wasn't currently at the top of his list. 'That'll be a no. Is there anything else you need to tell us?'

'That's me told,' he quipped. 'Is she like this in the bedroom? The only dilemma I have these days is whether to sleep with the lights on or off.' Sniffing the air, he pushed the blanket away and smelt his armpit. 'Christ, I need a shower.' He kissed Lee on the cheek, tried the same with Colin, who stood awkwardly and ended up kissing Richard smack on the lips. 'My luck seems to be in again,' Richard said, shuffling out the door. 'Now, let's hope it continues while I find me some vodka.'

'Should we be afraid?' Lee asked after he was well out of earshot.

'Well, there're four of them. Five if you include Richard. Six if someone's prowling about outside.' The sky lit up again, filling the room, creating long, tremulous shadows. Colin considered his next move. 'I think we have to assume that all of them are potentially dangerous.'

44

A YEAR AGO

Taking the 5.20 AM train from Victoria was brutal, but Kath wanted to arrive early and settle in before her first day of filming. She ignored the view as the harsh cityscape of south London gave way to suburban uniformity, and finally a lush landscape of green fields. Instead, she clung to her script, marked with her notes from reading and rereading it. The film was a gritty British crime drama, and she'd be playing Rosie, a rookie policewoman, the sidekick of the film's star, played by Hollywood legend, Lawrence Delaney. It would only be a few scenes, as her character was killed early on, but the director had suggested there might be scope for a couple more if she played her cards right, so they'd contracted her for three weeks rather than two. No doubt, there'd be loads of downtime. In preparation, she'd brought two books and a copy of The Times for the cryptic crossword.

The excitement of getting the part had been like winning Best Actress. For two years, she'd tried out for film roles only to be rejected each time. Too plain, too busty, legs too short, didn't connect with the camera – every sexist, badly phrased excuse under the sun. Even theatre parts were becoming thin on the ground. The competition was fierce and getting fiercer.

One more year, she kept telling herself. In a drawer at home, sat applications ready to be sent off to a variety of colleges. The idea of retraining as a social worker, giving something back, was beginning to feel like a real option. Then bingo! She got the call.

Arriving on location, a production assistant, June, earphones wrapped around her neck, clipboard in hand, mumbled a quick welcome. Leading her along a muddy walkway, they arrived at a tiny static caravan. 'Your home for the next three weeks. She's no looker, but there's a toilet, a kettle and a comfy sofa. Most importantly, she's all yours.'

'What? Seriously?' Kath looked round. As a child, she'd been on caravan holidays with fewer amenities. 'This is fantastic.'

'If you need anything, holler.' A tired smile crept across June's face. 'Someone will know where I am.'

'Thanks. It's really kind of you,' said Kath, deciding that the first thing she'd do would be to make a well-deserved cup of tea.

As she was about to leave, June said, 'Oh, Lawrence hasn't arrived yet, but he'll be on set soon, and when he gets here, he'd like a chat with you.'

Kath had first seen Lawrence in the Tony O'Malley films, where he played a downtrodden private eye. A mid-80s box office phenomenon, they weren't her thing. And although the first one was quite good and she'd gone to the cinema to watch it, the second received bad reviews and she'd caught it on video. A third, maybe even a fourth, came and went. But whatever the quality of his films, as an actor, he'd invariably bring something interesting. His first appearance on screen was etched in her mind: him stepping naked from a shower with an impossibly sculpted backside. As the film progressed, his face constantly radiant, he was able to switch emotions as simply as a lightbulb going on and off. A movie star who could truly act.

And here she was. About to play a scene with him at a car-wrecking yard outside Maidstone, where he confesses to her that his drinking's getting out of hand, and he's missed an important clue on the case they're working. A rush of nerves swept through her. Deep breaths, she told herself. What's the worst that could happen?

She sat on the sofa and took the script from her bag. She'd only been given her scenes – all with Lawrence – and she didn't think much of them. The dialogue was clunky and clichéd, her character too passive, and with so little screen-time, zero character development. The fact that at one point Lawrence's character was to kiss her seemed tacked on. With a pen, Kath circled it and wrote, *NEED TO ASK!*

Outside, a multitude of people were scurrying around, full of purpose and intent, setting up cameras and moving scenery. A world within a world. If audiences could see back-stage on productions, they'd be amazed at how the ordinary sat next to the extraordinary; people still ate, peed and gossiped while around them, an illusion was being created. She could have sat there all day and watched as giant mirrors were hoisted into the sky, backdrops flown in, actors sewn into costumes; it was entrancing. But she needed to use her time to rehearse.

Leafing through the scenes, it struck her how little actual dialogue she had, but she knew the craft would be in her reactions. She hadn't a clue how they'd do that. Mid-shots, close-ups, tracking shots. Another thing to get her head around. She'd only had speaking parts on camera twice before: once for an advert, advertising a disgusting boil-in-the bag ready meal where she'd played a tired but smiley, young mum; then a tiny role as a cockney runaway on *Take the High Road*. A long way from the big-time.

A loud rap on the door made her jump. Before she could answer, June had popped her head inside. 'I've someone who'd like a word with you.'

She stood, self-conscious of her handwritten notes on the script. She swiftly closed it over. The audition had been with a casting director, who never mentioned the actor she'd be doing her scenes opposite. A few days earlier, her agent, giddy with excitement, had called to tell her. She took a deep breath as the door swung open.

'Kitty!' a voice shrieked. Only one person in the world called her that. Peter Selby. The last person she was expecting to see. At fifteen, they'd both joined youth theatre before going on to the same drama school. After that, they'd lost touch. She'd always had a massive crush on him, but knew he was way out her league. The last thing she heard he was dating a friend of Kate Moss. With his perfectly coiffed hair, he stood in the doorframe smiling at her, wearing a boiler suit, strategically splattered with grease to create the illusion he'd been working. And if she wasn't wrong, a face caked in make-up. To her, he looked like he was playing dressing up, and she burst out laughing. 'Peter, why are you wearing that ridiculous outfit? And what's wrong with your face?'

'I'm in the film too.' Filling the caravan, he strode over and gave her the biggest hug. 'Wow, isn't this incredible?' He sat. 'Look at the pair of us. Movie stars.'

She didn't have the heart to tell him she was only in four scenes. 'It's crazy, isn't it?'

'I mean, have you been out there yet? It's a proper movie. That actress from the film we saw together – Teri...'

Kath was forced to think. 'Granger?'

'That's it! She's here too. Looking as hot as.'

One Saturday at drama school, after their college panto, they'd gone to see her latest film with about a dozen other student friends. A howler of a movie, trying hard but failing to emulate the success of *An Officer and a Gentleman.* Kath recalled how he'd sat at the furthest end of the aisle from her. 'How can you even remember that?'

'My only talent,' he joked. 'Only need to look at a script once.'

Kath knew this wasn't true. Famous in college for mangling up lines in even the most basic scene, he would compensate by improvising outrageously; frustratingly, this often made the scene better. Born into an acting family – his mum was in a soap opera on TV – he had a star quality which covered a lot of the cracks in his acting ability. Plus, being the stud-muffin of their year, students would flock en masse to work alongside him. A natural light comedian with matinee idol looks, he often grappled with understanding which choices to make, but Kath knew he'd do well. With a good script and kind direction, he'd shine. 'What part do you play?' she asked, realising the answer was staring her in the face.

He pointed to his costume. *'Grease monkey #2*. Background fodder. There're another three of us in this get up. I mean, I've a couple of lines, but it's things like, *"Your car's ready,"* and *"It's out front."* But it's six weeks of paid work and easy money. By the way, spoiler alert, I've worked out who the villain is.'

'They only sent me my own scenes.' She held up her slim script and laughed. 'It could be me for all I know. Or you.'

'Well, it's not. It's the owner of the wrecking yard.'

Unsure why he was even talking to her, Kath felt like she was fifteen again, sitting at the lunch-table, trying to make him notice her.

'Look, I don't know what time you finish.' He bent down to tie his shoelace. 'But we're heading out for drinks tonight back in town.' He sat up, expecting an immediate answer. 'Fancy it?'

'Do you mind if I see how the day goes?'

He prodded at her arm like she was his long-lost mate and gave her that dazzling smile of his. To be that beautiful, to have all his social graces, wrapped up with an unwavering confidence. It didn't seem fair.

'They're a great bunch of guys. Honestly, it's so much fun. And Lawrence might be there too.' His eyes twinkled, as though referring to some God-like being.

She could feign tiredness if need be, so smiled and said yes, enjoying the smell of his aftershave as he kissed her on the cheek.

He jumped up. 'Got to go. I said to myself, it's not, is it? Then June told me it was. Kitty O'Hare. Of all people. It's so good to see you. And you're looking great, by the way. Different. But still great.'

As he opened the door, the flash of his smile made her insides leap. *Christ, no, not again.*

45

As Colin gripped the barn door handle, Lee stood behind, clinging onto his shoulder. It had taken them ten minutes to walk the short distance from the house, through an ever-thickening slurry of mud. Bolts of lightning flashed overhead, and a screeching wind threatened to lift them into the sky.

'We should turn back,' Lee shouted, barely able to see in front of him through the blinding rain. 'It's too dangerous.'

Above the barn, gnarled and grey, an aged Scots pine was threatening to fall – relentless gusts of wind wrenching it back and forth in a macabre dance.

'That's definitely gonna go.' Lee attempted to drag Colin back from the door.

'But we need to find whatever was dropped before someone else does,' Colin insisted.

'There's no point in risking our lives. We tried.'

'Can't we check? It won't take a minute.'

'Okay, but quick!'

Colin wrenched open the door. They both gasped at the damage before them. Gone was the perfect interior, replaced by a cave-like space, littered with leaves and fallen branches, with water cascading through an enormous hole in the roof. Nature had taken over.

'It's unrecognisable.'

Colin didn't listen and stepped inside. Lee followed, staying as close to him as possible.

'I was sleeping over there.' Lee pointed to where the partition had been. Broken furniture, shattered timbers and chunks of plaster were scattered across the floor, as if the barn had been hit by a hurricane.

'And you can't remember what Lawrence was saying? Even a word? It could save us a helluva lot of trouble.'

'I've tried my hardest, imagining myself waking, hearing the voices, thinking there was a party going on, but it sounded like Lawrence was alone.'

Colin took his arm and tugged. 'Maybe you're right. Let's get out of here and head back to the house.'

'There's a phrase he used to say.' Lee seemed stuck to the spot. 'What is it again? I'm sure I heard him say it when I woke up.'

'Come on.'

'Christ! Of course.' Lee's face sparked into life. 'I've remembered.'

There was a momentary lull before a slicing sound cut through the air, as if someone had swung an axe through a last remnant of connecting tissue. An overwhelming sense of movement followed as the tree fell, ripping up roots and earth.

Colin seized Lee by the arm, pulling him from the barn. As he did so, the impact felt like an explosion. The collision of timber on timber was thunderous: smashing, splintering, tearing, followed by rain pouring through the roof, turning the floor into a river.

Outside, as the furthest part of the barn collapsed in on itself, they jumped out of the way, landing on the mud. Turning round, they could see that only the nearest side remained standing. The kitchen walls had all but disappeared, leaving the white cooker exposed, like a gleaming tooth, a branch hammering down on top of it.

'My God,' Colin cried. A second time that day he'd cheated death. First, at the hand of human nature, selfish and capricious. And now Mother Nature, much clearer, with no ambiguity: *I will kill you if you try to mess with me.*

Lee seemed to have read his mind. 'Let's get back to the house.'

46

A YEAR AGO

Lawrence beckoned Peter over and asked who the girl was.

'She's playing your sidekick. Her name's Kitty. I mean, Kath, or if you want her full title, Kathryn O'Hare. I went to drama school with her. In fact, we go back even further – we did youth theatre together when she was plain old Kath Keely.'

Lawrence's interest in Kath confused him. She wasn't your typical actress, yet he had to admit, there was a newfound radiance about her. Her lips seemed fuller, her cheeks more sculpted, and the make-up around her eyes enhanced their sparkle. She smelled good, too. He dipped his hand into the long pocket of his overalls and adjusted his semi-erect penis.

'I've a key scene with her,' Lawrence said, winking at Peter. 'I go to kiss her, but she pulls away. But I think I might get that changed. Her character dies soon after, so it'll provide more pathos for my character if she responds to his advances.'

'She's a brilliant girl. Mega-focused. She'll do a great job.'

Peter marvelled at Lawrence. Nothing seemed to faze him: lines were always perfect, hitting his mark consistently spot on, there on time before anyone else. All around, dozens of people were scurrying about, setting up his next shot, running errands for him, shouting over each other, and yet not once did he bat an eyelid. It was as if he existed in a parallel universe, beamed in specially for each scene, while in between, he was thousands of miles away, relaxing by his pool in the Hollywood Hills.

'The boys are still on for tonight? Gonna hit the town again, paint it red?' Lawrence asked, gazing into the distance.

'We're all up for it. I've told Kitty. Hope that's OK?'

'Any friend of yours is a friend of mine.'

As Lawrence squeezed his arm, Peter's heart skipped a beat. For days, in between takes, Lawrence had been calling him over, asking him to sit, chatting to him like some long-lost friend. Only the other day he'd given him a script, asked him to read it, see if he thought it was any good. Peter had taken it from his hands as though accepting an Oscar. As soon as he got home that night, he'd devoured it.

In theory, Lawrence had asked for his opinion, but he kept checking for any part that might suit him. There was one character – Bobby – a schemer aiming to fleece his wealthy father. He could hardly sleep, thinking up new ways to make Lawrence see how perfect he was for the part, how American accents were his thing. In the end, Lawrence told him he'd passed on it, that the director attached to the script was a loser. But it had made Peter feel special, singled out as someone to watch.

'This Kath, Kitty – she's good?'

'In drama school, she got all the best parts, but she was never showy with it. There was this one girl in our year, zero talent, who used to go around telling people how big she was going to be. I mean, what's that all about? One day, she was doing a scene with Kitty, and she was ballsing it up big time, kept going bigger. People were starting to laugh, wondering what the hell she was thinking, but I remember Kitty whispering something to her. I think it must have been a direction or a suggestion, because this girl, this proper no-talent, turned it around 360 and gave an amazing speech. I mean, pure emotion. She's got a real gift, Kitty.'

'Compassion.' Lawrence uttered the word with the authority of God himself. He held Peter's eye, waiting to be refuted.

'That's it exactly,' Peter enthused. He sat with bated breath, waiting for another pearl of wisdom, then began to worry he'd got overexcited and spoken too long. He couldn't forget that while they might occasionally hang out, Lawrence was the big star. His own character didn't even have a name for God's sake. *Mechanic 2*. Enough said.

Out of the blue, Lawrence clicked his fingers and ordered an espresso. He asked if Peter wanted one, but he shook his head politely, knowing it would send him hyper. Tonight, he would alternate between alcohol and water, make sure he didn't get too drunk and end up saying the wrong thing. Recently, he'd been allowing himself to go too far: picking fights with random guys, shagging the wrong girls, waking up slumped in doorways.

Lawrence was handed an espresso by Miranda, the cutest of the runners. They'd snogged the previous weekend, but she'd been playing it cool ever since. Doubtless had a boyfriend. Who cared? It *was* only a snog. She smiled at him – the first time she'd done so in days – but he'd already decided he wasn't interested, so stared into the distance.

Lawrence, who missed nothing, gave him a look once she turned her back. 'Nice.'

'Not my type.'

'Seemed to be last Saturday.' He smirked as she walked away. 'Pretty little thing.'

Peter felt his face redden. Caught out. It was impossible to keep a secret on set. 'I thought what happens on set stays on set.'

'Oh, it will.' Energised by his caffeine fix, Lawrence picked at his armrest. 'As I was saying, compassion, it's a very rare quality in an actor. In this business, you make lots of friends, but you also meet a lot of competition. Take yourself, handsome boy, decent enough actor who knows instinctively how to handle himself.' Lawrence looked him up and down again, appraising the qualities he was listing.

Self-conscious, Peter focused on an electrician unwinding cables. 'I try to be nice to everyone. That's the way I was brought up.'

'Trust me, there's no point. Quit being such a brown-nose.' Lawrence looked at his watch. 'There's a dozen, two dozen, a thousand others exactly like you.' He gazed over Peter's shoulder, responding to a signal from an assistant. 'You need to stand out, my boy.' He leaned in, whispering into his ear. 'Nice doesn't cut it. My advice: grow a pair.'

'But if I'm rude to people, no one's gonna hire me.'

'No one's asking you to be rude, just don't be nice. It grates.' Lawrence brushed some flecks of dust from his trousers and mouthed 'Two minutes' to the assistant. 'Having talent doesn't always cut it either.' He looked him straight in the eye. 'Take the beginning of my career. I worked with two of the biggest talents ever. Powerhouses. Yet today, complete nobodies. I mean, one's on the telly now and again, but the other… Nada.'

Peter touched his arm. 'The part of Bobby would be ideal for me.'

This caught Lawrence's immediate interest. 'That script? The son?' Again, he looked Peter up and down, though this time, more considerately. 'You've his sensitivity, his eagerness. Yes, I can see that. You'd need to work on being more ruthless: that's at his core. Without it, he's simply a mummy's boy. Directionless.'

It impressed Peter how much detail Lawrence took in. A hawk perched on the highest branch, overseeing everything.

'How can I get an audition?' He waited as Lawrence closed his eyes, his mind ticking over, giving nothing away. Peter wondered what Lawrence dreamt about at night. When you'd achieved so much, what did you desire?

He opened them again. 'Aren't you curious who those actors were?'

'The who?' Peter mistakenly imagined the conversation had moved on to him, to Lawrence organising an audition for him. But no, he was still going on about those two deadbeats from years ago. 'You mean the actors you worked with, whose careers went nowhere? Does it matter?'

Lawrence nodded, and without skipping a beat, said, 'They were your parents.'

47

As Colin and Lee stumbled into the hallway, their bodies shaking with adrenalin, the others rushed towards them; the awkwardness of a few hours before seemingly forgotten. Instead, Kath helped them off with their waterproofs while Georgie and Jim ran off to find towels. Only Peter stood apart, admiring his reflection in a mirror by the stairs, and adjusting his hair.

They'd all heard the noise of the tree falling but had been unable to make anything out in the darkness. They bombarded Colin and Lee with questions: *Has the barn been destroyed? Is the house in danger? What should we do?*

Peter's voice piped up. 'What were you doing out there, anyway?'

'Give us a moment.' Colin stood against the wall, trying to catch his breath.

As Lee patted his hair dry, he recounted what had happened. All but Peter listened. 'I think we're safe enough in the house; any other falling trees would be far enough away.'

'So, unless one's picked up by the wind and dropped on top of us, we should be fine,' Colin added.

'You've not answered my question. What were you pair

doing out there in the first place?' Peter stared at them, demanding an answer.

Colin crouched to unlace his boots. 'I needed to check something. That's all. Nothing sinister, mate.' Without Peter noticing, Colin caught Lee's eye, as if to say, *who is this guy?*

'You're still searching for clues, aren't you? Still trying to nail one of us.' Peter puffed out his chest, his lip trembling as he spoke.

'Look, why don't we all have a cup of tea?' Kath said. 'Today's been hideous – the worst of my life – I'm sure it's the same for all of us. There's no reason we can't sit down together and help each other through this.' All focus turned to Kath – a cheerleader without her pom-poms, willing everyone to muddle on through.

Clapping his hands, Peter announced, 'We could play a game. Anyone up for a bit of fun?'

'There's no reason for sarcasm, son,' Jim said.

Peter scowled. 'Who's being sarcastic? Anything to take our minds off this shit.'

Colin took Lee's waterproof and hung it in the cupboard along with his own. At the back, hung an orange cagoule. There were a few yellow ones, two blue, a distinctive red one. But Lee had said the person running from the barn was wearing an orange cagoule – a huge one he insisted – and the one hanging up appeared tailored. In the dark could he have been mistaken about the colour? And the size? Colin checked inside for any blood stains, but there weren't any. He'd come back later to check more thoroughly.

Standing in his stocking-feet, he felt like a guest who'd arrived late to the party, unprepared for the energy of the room. Peter was still going on about playing a game, trying to enthuse the others. He wanted to shake him, make him understand the severity of the situation. But he didn't have the energy. 'I need a shower,' he said.

'Later, we can all sit by the stove in the kitchen and chat.

Would you two be up for that?' Kath's insistence on chummi-ness bordered on the manic. It felt like if he and Lee refused, there might be consequences.

'We'll see,' Colin said, nudging Lee up the stairs.

'Maybe they're tired,' Jim commented. 'Today's been a nightmare.'

'But it's not even nine,' said Georgie. 'They can't be tired yet. Plus, Colin slept most of the day.'

As Kath revealed a cupboard full of board games, and Peter yelled he hoped they had Twister, the knot of rage in Colin's chest grew tighter and tighter. He felt Lee clasp his hand.

'I know,' Georgie shouted, as though she'd come up with the best idea ever. 'We could get into teams,' she suggested. 'I'll go get some pens and paper.'

As Colin climbed the stairs, an electric spark went off in his head – a firework rushing past at light speed. He imag-ined himself falling back into a void of darkness. Only the chorus of voices shouting, *Watch out!* told him that his body was actually sinking, that the head spin he was experiencing was real. He hit the carpet with a heavy thud.

COLIN CAME to with a row of eyes peering down at him. Immediately, he could tell Lee had been crying and was being propped up by Kath. Georgie was by his side and Jim in front, holding a cup of tea in one hand and a blanket in the other. Richard had appeared and was sitting on the stairs, drink in hand, commenting on how the commotion had woken him and asking whether he could go back to bed. Only Peter, rummaging in the hall cupboard, showed no concern.

'You scared the bejesus out of me,' Lee said.

Colin saw he was in the hallway, sitting on a chair commandeered from the barricade, a steaming cup of tea placed against his lips. How he got there was another thing.

'It's got four sugars in it.' Georgie, playing mother, stroked his hair. 'Lee said you don't like sugar in your tea, so don't be too surprised. But it'll help with the shock.'

'You fell,' Jim explained.

'Well, you fainted, lost your balance. But you seem fine. No bones broken, we think,' Kath continued.

'Jim, give me that blanket, will you?' Georgie asked. 'He feels cold.'

'You didn't take enough rest, babe.' Lee's red eyes were focused on him. 'It all got too much.'

Richard drained his glass. 'You could have bunked up with me. There's plenty of room for two. I'd have looked after you.' He struggled to stand before giving up and slumping against the banister.

Colin tried to stand. 'But I can't rest. There's too much to do.'

'You need to,' said Jim, helping Georgie tuck the blanket around him. 'Your body's telling you. Rest. No exertion. That's an order.'

'I heard you toppled over like one of those trees out there. Smash!' declared Richard, enjoying the sound of the word *smash* on his lips.

Echoing this, Peter dropped a game of Monopoly on the floor.

'Why don't you leave that and go upstairs?' Kath proposed, carefully modulating her voice to appear calm.

'I thought we were playing Twister.' Peter continued searching. 'Everyone's got Twister. It must be here somewhere.'

The sweetened tea was forced against Colin's lips again. He swallowed but could barely keep it down.

'Upstairs!' Georgie snapped.

'Such a lousy idea, Peter.' Kath gave him a dirty look. 'Show some sensitivity for a change.'

In the hubbub of being fussed over, it occurred to Colin

that maybe he was in the ideal position; helpless, he was more able to scrutinise how and why they were interacting. It was like being on the other side of the two-way mirror in an interrogation room. And if they imagined he was too incapacitated to have his wits about him, maybe he'd be able to do his job. It was akin to becoming invisible. To truly observe, you had to remain quiet, drift along with people, politely agree, smile, never force an opinion; in many ways, he preferred to be overlooked. He saw it as a special skill – an escapology of sorts – allowing him to notice more. Once the mask slipped – and it always did – he would reel every fragment in, gather them together, make sense of what he'd gathered.

He rolled his head back, groaned a little, and half-closed his eyes. Jim and Georgie were still playing the part of a doting couple – if anything, the constant eye contact, the smiles to assure each other, had increased. Since Lawrence's death, Kath, whatever her complicity, was playing a blinder. Running from hot to cold, she was either the mastermind behind it all, or had unwittingly stumbled into something she didn't fully understand. Richard was so far gone the entire house could collapse around him and he wouldn't be fazed.

That left Peter. Vacuous, offensive, the embodiment of an egotist. The only one to have shown zero concern.

48

A YEAR AGO

Lined with decorative gold mirrors and glittering wall lights, the corridor back from the toilets led through to the VIP section, where Peter and Lawrence sat in deep discussion. Kath held back from entering, pondering why it was only the three of them. Peter had mumbled something about a last minute change of plan, but after discovering they'd postponed her next scene by a couple of days, and that Lawrence's personal chauffeur would drive them into London, she doubted the story.

At the bar, she ordered a whisky and went to pay. However, the barman, pale-skinned, red-haired and with the most beautiful smile, shook his head and gestured towards Lawrence. 'All paid for.'

'You'd better give me another.'

She'd listened patiently all day as Lawrence made suggestions during filming. Fixated on detail, he took time to explain to her about angles, pick-up shots – all far too technical – she zoned out after five minutes. At one point, he praised her energy, but advised her to tone down certain reactions a smidgeon. 'Don't let them know what you're feeling. Leave them asking questions.' Later in the day, after an hour spent on a close-up, he demanded a complete reshoot. 'When she puts her chin down, didn't you see the shadow fall across her face?' he barked. He moved closer and adjusted her collar. 'Amateurs!'

She'd smiled, thanked him, and stepped aside as Lawrence demonstrated to the crew the full extent of his star power. 'Can no one do their job properly?' he shouted. Though the director was experienced on set, there was no doubting who was the boss.

She threw back the second shot. 'Wish me luck.' Waving goodbye to the barman, she returned to find Lawrence and Peter nose to nose. A complete love-in: Peter basking in the attention, Lawrence in his element, dominating the conversation. She was definitely the third wheel. 'I should head off. It's getting late.'

'Absolutely no way.' Lawrence pointed to the gold Rolex strapped to his wrist. 'It's only eight. Anyone hungry?'

'I live miles away. It'll take me ages to get back.'

'I'm staying in town tonight. My chauffeur will drive you,' he insisted. 'It's decided. Come on. A rose between two thorns.' He patted the seat between them. 'Peter's been telling me how you were the star of your year.'

As if. There were at least four others more talented, far prettier, and more employable than her. Two were currently in the West End, one was about to shoot a film in America and the other had married an award-winning producer. Whatever promise she might have possessed as a bright young thing was evaporating fast.

'You always got the lead roles,' Peter stressed, his expression excited, elbowing her to tell Lawrence more.

'Immediately after drama school, I did my share of small roles,' she replied, squeezing in between them. 'For a year, all I played were waitresses and prostitutes in terrible fringe productions. Oh, and I was cast as a deaf and dumb girl in one, too. That was a hoot. Two hours staring into the audience.'

Lawrence took out a cigarette and Peter jumped up to find a lighter. He was so quick that the contents of his pocket fell out onto the table, including two condoms, a packet of mints, and some loose change.

'It's good to see you're playing safe,' Lawrence laughed, banging the table and calling a waiter over. 'Can you set up a private room? We'd like to eat.'

Kath watched as Peter flicked the lighter twice before it sparked into life. Lawrence leaned across her, positioning the tip of the cigarette within the flame, holding it there for a few seconds too long before releasing. She looked on as Peter swept everything from the table and slipped it back inside his pocket. She began to wonder if there was something more going on between the two of them, if she was simply there as a decoy for any paparazzo.

'I take it we're hungry? The catering's pretty lousy on set. That salad today looked like it had been sitting for days.' He refilled her glass with champagne. 'Kath?'

'Maybe something light.'

'I'm starving.' Peter threw back the rest of his beer.

'Good. The food here's the best in London. And you can have anything you want. You name it, they'll rustle it up.'

'Bangers and mash. Nothing beats it,' Peter burped. 'Sorry.'

'I might join you. It'll make a change from bloody avocado sushi – it's all they fucking eat in California. Or that new Atkins craze. Disgusting.'

Peter and Lawrence clinked glasses, rejoicing in their newfound friendship, before proceeding to talk over her for fifteen minutes until their table was ready.

The touching started almost as soon as they sat down in the private dining room. At first, she thought it was her imagination. But as Peter got drunker, his hand kept brushing against hers under the table. She continued to think it was by accident until his pinkie touched hers and coiled around it. She tried catching his eye, but he avoided looking at her. Instead, he continued to hang on Lawrence's every word, gripping onto her tightly.

Through the haze of whisky and champagne, she tried keeping up with the conversation about films Lawrence had made, which stars he knew, who were bearable and who were bastards. Meanwhile, a hand squeezed her knee. It wasn't Peter's. This time, the gaze from Lawrence made it clear he wanted her to notice. *Fuck!* Was this the plan – some bizarre ménage à trois – or were they totally ignorant of the other's advances? Too busy caught up in their laddish banter, they weren't even talking to her. She'd had enough. 'I need to go.'

'What? The night's just getting interesting.' Lawrence clicked his fingers at a waiter, who scurried towards them as though his life depended on it. All this clicking at waiters was starting to irritate her.

Peter was still refusing to look in her direction. 'I feel really drunk,' was all he muttered.

'Another bottle of Krug and three clean glasses,' Lawrence boomed.

Kath hesitated. Red-faced, Lawrence looked like he might keel over at any second. Then again, so did Peter. She didn't want to be the centre of their pathetic little game. 'I'm bursting for a pee.'

'I'll time you.' His Rolex glinted in the light from the chandelier. 'Go!'

Slipping from the room, she bolted along the corridor, her head pounding. Fidgeting with her blouse, worried she was showing too much cleavage, she paused and stared at her reflection. *I'm not grotesque, but I'm no babe.* Imagining herself thinner, she gripped her excess flesh as though it might magically disappear if squeezed hard enough. It simply bounced back into place. *What are they seeing in me?*

Out in the bar, she sat on a stool and thought about the day's events. Day one, and already she was being pursued by the film's lead actor and by someone she once had a massive crush on. It all felt like an elaborate joke.

She raised her hand, and the cute barman nodded and came over; his body looked way better in his uniform than previously. His smile was even wider than before, too: more eager to please. The blush on his cheeks told her all she needed to know.

'Nightcap?' he asked.

She gawped at him, laughing. 'Seriously?'

'I'm about to finish, and there's a wee bar along the road that does the best cocktails.' His Scottish accent was soft, inviting.

Unbelievable. The shine from a Hollywood star had somehow rubbed onto her. No one had ever come onto her so quickly.

'First one's on me,' he added, winking at her.

She didn't have to think twice. Wild horses wouldn't drag her back into that snake pit. 'Bring me my coat and it's a deal.'

49

J im marvelled at Georgie sitting in the corner of the kitchen, fully immersed in her book, feet curled up on the wingback armchair, taking sips from her glass of wine. He was in awe of her ability to block out the world. Despite being a seasoned actress that the bravura required, she was never happier than reading quietly on her own. How many days of their marriage had been spent in silence? Sometimes they'd even unplug the telephone. As though reading his mind, she looked up from her book and smiled.

He wandered over to the window, watching rivulets of rain run down it. The storm was relentless. If it continued much longer, there was a strong chance of further arguments. Staring at the door handle, he wondered how far he could get. At that moment, the wind howled, a rebuke for considering any thought of escape.

He finished the dregs of his beer. Ambling over to the fridge, he opened the door and pulled out a fresh one. 'Georgie, love.' He waited till she put down her book and lowered her glasses, the ice-cold bottle chilling his hand. 'We should chat.'

She looked him straight in the eye. 'What's wrong?'

Since Lawrence's death, Jim had felt adrift. Wave after wave of clashing thoughts clouded his mind. He needed a moment to sit and think properly. Take things in. Alone in the kitchen with Georgie seemed the right opportunity. 'Checking in, I suppose. See if you're OK.' He opened his bottle of beer and took a large swig.

She uncurled, pushing the loose hair back from her eyes. Jim noticed it remained unbrushed, and she'd not removed any of the make-up applied the night before. 'I'm fine, darling. You?'

He took another mouthful. 'Colin's right.' He waited, hoping for a reaction, but there wasn't any. 'They'll catch whoever did it eventually.' Hoping this might provoke a response, it surprised him to see her curl back into the armchair, take a sip of wine, and return to reading.

'Lawrence was a grade-A shit, darling.' She turned a page without looking at him. 'I know it, you know it, everyone in this house knows it.' She gazed over the top of her book, pulling a quizzical expression, suggesting he must feel the same.

'That's not a defence.' He watched as she turned another page. Returning to the window, he stared into pitch blackness, the torrential rain and the pounding wind laying siege to them. There was no doubt; this was a hurricane. 'Georgie?'

She slammed her book shut and set it aside. 'You won't give up, will you?' Her smudged mascara reminded him of when they were young, rolling home at dawn, falling into bed and having messy sex.

'What did you have against him?' He took another gulp of his beer and sat at the table.

'Jim!' She raised an eyebrow. 'We're not doing this now, are we?'

'We all loved each other once. Now, he's gone. When's a better time?'

'We were in our early twenties! Everyone loves everyone at that age. You've not lived enough to know what hate is.'

At the start, they'd given their very best to each other. An energy sparked between them, fuelling them with an intensity of emotion which shook them and took hours to come down from. They formed a fierce bond that excluded anybody who dared threaten it. Only on one occasion, in rehearsals, had there been a serious disagreement, and that only lasted a few days. Georgie and Lawrence had clashed over a line. To Jim it had seemed inconsequential, but each had defended their position, screeching at the other. Neither would let it go until the director and writer called a meeting, saying they'd decided to toss a coin. Thrown by the randomness, both rallied and backed each other up, the offending line soon fading into memory.

'He seemed a different person, don't you think?' Though she didn't appear to be listening – or even care – he wanted to have his say. 'We should have had a proper conversation together – the three of us.'

Georgie placed her glass of wine on a side table and sighed. 'Lawrence realised from the off that you were the better actor. You possessed depth. He was all show. He didn't want a conversation, not then and not now. Lawrence Delaney wanted to display how much he'd made it. That's all. Rub our noses in his success, his power, his money.'

Jim drained his beer. For him, acting was never a competition, regardless of the vagaries of the business. 'Isn't it sad that the connection we had dwindled to nothing?'

'We'd all changed.'

Jim plucked another beer from the fridge, knocking the cap off using the edge of the kitchen counter. 'We all missed out.'

'Did we?' Her face was fully lit, burning as she stared at him. 'You know the score. It's true of any production. You form a band of brothers, with promises of everlasting kinship.

Sometimes you kiss, sometimes you fuck, but afterwards you go your separate ways. Real life always takes over.'

'I'd like to have understood him more.' Jim placed his beer on the worktop. 'That's all.' Their early careers were so entwined; seeing him again felt like encountering the ghost of a relative who'd died years before: distant, untouchable, disconnected.

'What's to understand?' Georgie asked, narrowing her eyes.

'For all his success, he couldn't see what was in front of him. I'd liked to have known why.' Jim poured himself some water and drank the entire glass.

She sat up. He'd finally got her full attention. 'You asked what I had against him. The simple truth is: nothing. Whatever we experienced together and whatever we shared, it was fleeting. No actual substance. I worked that out a lifetime ago. I thought you did too.' She stood and brushed past him, turning on the tap, splashing her face with water.

Her absolutism perplexed him. 'I don't think you're being honest,' he said. 'There was a spark, a connection between all three of us.'

She lifted her head and shrugged.

In their entire marriage, few moments had made him so angry.

'*Her face looks like death.*'

'What are you gibbering on about now?' she said, searching for a clean towel.

'You wanted the line changed from "*Her face looks like death*" to "*Her face looks gone*".'

'Not that old chestnut! I was right, wasn't I?' She dried herself with the towel. 'Death was far too obvious, too definite. The spirit of someone lingers on. Sometimes brighter than when they were alive. To this day, I stick by it. It was the whole fucking point of the play.'

'But you let Lawrence win the argument.' Jim went to touch her, but she pulled away.

'No.' Georgie headed towards the door. 'I won. By letting it go, he had to say the wrong line every single night for two years. Every performance, knowing I was right. So, no Jim, Lawrence didn't win.'

50

Waking in a panic, Colin was puzzled to find Lee at his bedside, nonchalantly flicking through a copy of *Hello!* with a gloomy looking Princess Diana on the cover. It took several seconds for him to separate the sinking sensation of his dream from his memory of collapsing on the stair, and the pounding sensation in his head from the sounds of the storm raging outside.

Lee tossed the magazine aside. 'How's the invalid?'

'I feel dreadful.' That was an understatement; it was more like he'd died and been dug up. 'I need to interview the rest, continue the investigation.' He tried to get out of bed, but his muscles refused to cooperate.

'No, you don't. You need to rest,' Lee said, gently pressing him back into his pillows. 'You're not going anywhere, and neither are they. The storm's back with a vengeance, so we're all stuck here for the foreseeable.'

Colin let his eyes close again, drifting in and out of sleep, aware of Lee beside him, the chaos outside continuing. Eventually, sensing that Lee had finished reading, he opened his eyes to find him out for the count – head to one side, the magazine trailing against the carpet. Now fully awake, he'd revisited the events of the last twenty-four hours, considering each moment, each clue, and each suspect in turn.

'Oh no! You've that look on your face.' Lee had woken. 'I can tell when you're plotting. Problem shared?'

There was no one quite like Lee. The only person who genuinely understood him. On complex investigations where he had to draw conclusions, establish a theory, his mind would disconnect from the everyday. Any daily punctuation – lunch, dinner, sleep – would be forgotten. It was like a mist falling. He'd always had it. His mother would refer to him on those occasions as "The lost boy, just like your father." The worst insult she could cast.

Colin manoeuvred himself upright, fixing the pillows behind him.

'You don't have to share if you don't want to,' Lee said.

The lump on his head throbbed. 'Could you get me some paracetamol first?'

'I'll do better than that; I've some co-codamol.' Lee went into the bathroom, returning with the pills and a glass of water. 'These are your last for tonight. I can't have you over-dosing on top of everything else.'

Colin swallowed them, hoping the pain might instantly disappear. It didn't. He wasn't sure where to begin, because his conclusions were far from clear, however his instincts were. 'My gut tells me Peter's our man. The mood swings, the open hostility to me, the lack of empathy. I mean. What's all the nonsense with the board games? It's got guilt written all over it.'

'He does seem to have some anger management issues, and he's pretty vain and immature. However, to my knowl-edge, none of those are a crime. Any evidence?'

'None. And no obvious motive.' Colin grinned a little. 'Though when I passed out, he didn't seem to care at all. If anything, he seemed to enjoy seeing me weakened. There must be a reason. And, this is circumstantial, but he's the only one strong enough to have risked tackling me and Lawrence.' Scenarios spun around in his head. None of them added up. He'd need to observe Peter more. Was it him or could he be protecting someone close to him? Whatever, *he* was the key. He felt sure of it.

'Last night, when I was out in the barn and saw the person run off, I mean, Peter, he's what, six two? He's a big guy. Athletic. Even with the waterproof covering them, I reckon the person I saw was smaller.'

'So, what you're saying is my theory's for shit?'

'I'm saying I don't think it was Peter running from the barn. That's all.'

Colin lay back. The painkillers were kicking in. His head had gone woozy and the words coming from his mouth seemed to be slowing down. 'Before the barn collapsed, you said you'd remembered something.'

Lee moved closer. 'Lawrence was always saying "I can do what the fuck I want." We used to joke about it, making it his catchphrase. I remembered hearing that in the barn. It was repeated several times.'

Colin thought for a moment. Lee's pills were working their magic, and the pain in his head was receding. 'Maybe he was speaking to Richard? I mean, he'd just been replaced. The sentiment fits.' As his eyes closed, his mind wandered: the what ifs, the whys, the hows. At one point he became aware of Lee sorting out the sheets. His eyes snapped open. 'What time is it?'

'After 10.30. Hopefully people will head to bed soon, the storm will have passed in the morning, and we can leave here.' Lee kissed him. 'Sleep, babe. You need it.'

'Where are you going?'

'I'll be back soon.' Lee moved about the room – checking outside, turning off the light in the bathroom. 'Need anything from downstairs?'

Colin shook his head and lay back, staring at the ceiling.

His mind was racing. All he could think about was Peter's behaviour and Kath's weird reaction to his questions. She'd definitely lied to him, which meant she was hiding something. Then there was Jim and Georgie, the perfect couple who appeared generally nonplussed by the murder of their onetime friend and supposed lover. And of course, Richard, who seemed the least physically able, but had the clearest motive. What he couldn't get out his head was Lee's insistence that the person running from the barn was smaller than Peter, his prime suspect. But instinct alone wouldn't cut it. He had to consider motive; who else besides Richard had a motive? Lee for one. And Jim and Georgie, by the sounds of it, had history. From what he'd witnessed himself the previous evening, Kath had history too. In fact, while Peter's behaviour since Lawrence's killing was the most suspicious, out of everybody, as far as Colin knew, he had the least reason.

'Be careful,' he mumbled, as the door closed, and the sound of the key turning in the lock chimed with the co-codamol fully kicking in.

51

A YEAR AGO

The following days on set were demanding. Early starts, endless hours waiting around, finishes well past ten at night. Having to travel back home by public transport made the day even longer. By the end of the week, Kath was exhausted. However, no further midweek shenanigans meant she could be as focused and professional as possible.

Her disappearing act was never mentioned. Peter and Lawrence were so drunk, they probably hadn't noticed. And after careful consideration, she felt it best not to bring it up. Thinking it was all forgotten, she was surprised when Lawrence had a dig at her the following week. 'You know you kept two hungry boys waiting.'

She wasn't sure what to make of his remark. Yes, it was true; they hadn't eaten by the time she left, so he may simply have been alluding to that. However, there was something in the manner he said it, pointed, suggestive, that implied otherwise. She recalled both their hands on her, feeling their way up and down her body, suggesting food was the last thing on either of their minds.

Peter, on the other hand, kept away. She could see he was busy shooting an intricate fight-sequence. A stunt-coordinator had been working with all four mechanics whenever they weren't filming. The boys were in their element, the stage fighting taking them right back to the playground. Shrieks and hoots could be heard whenever the cameras weren't rolling. Occasionally, she'd catch Peter's eye and he'd smile back, but he'd quickly turn away, carrying on with a karate chop to the neck of another mechanic or falling to the ground in his death throes. She decided he wasn't being rude, but neither was he going out of his way to be friendly. She supposed she'd have to make it up to him sooner or later.

At lunch, there was a strict pecking-order. In order of importance, the *top talent* went first, with key behind-the-scenes personnel next. Smaller parts, like hers, and any extras followed, and lastly the runners and anyone else not accounted for.

She pointed at the beef stroganoff and felt fingers pinch her waist. Startled, she spun around, ready for a fight, only to find Peter behind her, holding his tray against his body as a shield. 'Was that you?'

'Who? Me?' He held his hands and tray in the air, feigning innocence.

With her own tray, she batted him away. He stepped back, shouting 'Help, she's attacking me.' The people around them smiled politely as she hit him again, harder this time, proclaiming in an American accent, 'Everything's under control. Stand aside, sir. Officer with a casserole coming through.'

They retreated hanging the furthest corner of the marquee, which functioned as a canteen. Both devoured their lunch without talking. She watched him scan the room, smiling at a few people, scrutinising the behaviour of others. Struggling to eavesdrop on a conversation, he whispered to her, 'Those two must be fucking.' He nodded to the left. 'Don't look!'

He grabbed her arm as she instinctively turned round. Too late. Already staring at two of the costume designers, she whispered, 'But he's over fifty and the other one, he's mid-twenties at most.'

'Ah, but true love never lies, does it?' His hand remained on her arm, his thumb gently stroking up and down her skin. At first, she thought to pull back, but he didn't make a thing of it. Rather, he wasn't even looking at her as he did it. Only when someone passed the table did he draw his hand away. 'What happened to you the other night?' He stared right at her and popped a chip into his mouth. 'So rude.'

He hadn't forgotten after all. 'I had a headache. So, I...' She picked up the salt cellar and shook it, but nothing came out.

'Liar.' He threw a chip at her. But she dodged it in time, letting it fly past and land on the floor.

'I'm not! I got the last train and was home by twelve-thirty to be up for five the next morning.'

'You went off with that ginger barman. We saw you.'

'What do you mean? You saw us?' In the end, she hadn't been comfortable with either of their attention that night. It was too confusing, Lawrence especially. Despite his movie star aura, and how kind he'd been, she didn't sense any spark with him. In fact, close up, the perfect tanned skin looked weird and artificial, the product in his hair too liberally applied. Sure, a roll in the hay with a film star would be fun and something she could tell her friends. But she wanted to stay professional. With Peter, it was different. The truth was, she *did* want his attention, just not with Lawrence in the picture. If something were to happen between them, she wanted it to be special.

'You looked so sweet together.'

So, they'd been spying on her. Her face turned scarlet. She got up and a glass of water tumbled to the ground and smashed. The tent was noisy so no one seemed to notice the unfolding drama.

'He was good-looking I suppose. You're young, free and

single, aren't you? Come on, sit back down.' His body language urged her not to make a scene.

She took her seat again. For five, ten minutes they remained in silence, the din of the canteen sounding louder than before. She was embarrassed at being caught out, but she wasn't ashamed. She'd surprised herself that evening. She wouldn't normally pick up random strangers, but part of her needed to prove something to herself. It grated: Lawrence and Peter imagining they could have her whenever they liked, so when the opportunity arose, she took it. 'I need to get back.' She picked up her bag.

He pointed at his watch. 'You've another fifteen minutes.'

'I've lines to learn.'

'Kitty.' He stretched out to touch her arm.

'Get the fuck off me!' This time, others looked over. 'Stop touching me, Peter. You're always touching me – quit it. And stop calling me Kitty. Fuck's sake. My name's Kath. Got it?'

She stumbled out of the tent, imagining Peter behind her, laughing it off, shrugging at the behaviour of the crazy woman. He could handle it. The pinkie wrapped around hers, the thumb stroking her skin; what was he playing at? It was an invasion of her privacy, her personal space; he was playing to rules she didn't understand. Why had she become the butt of some boys' in joke?

'Hold on, hold on! Where are you heading so fast? It's lunchtime.' Lawrence stood in front of her, his body a barrier, preventing her from going any further. For whatever reason – it was a moment she'd go over time and time again – she collapsed crying into his arms. 'There, my darling Kath. Hush. Hush,' she heard him whisper.

LAWRENCE'S TRAILER was at least four times the size of Kath's. While hers resembled the tiny caravan her grandmother kept for many years in Llandudno, his was more akin to a suite in a five-star Mayfair hotel. Trimmed with brocade, a heavy silk blind blocked any daylight from entering through the large window. Cloaked in shadow, the interior was dark and luxurious, concealed lighting accentuating the ostentatious fixtures and fittings. A deep, buttoned settee, upholstered in sleek, ebony coloured leather, snaked around the room's perimeter. Several doors led off from the main space, suggesting the trailer was even bigger than she first imagined. She wouldn't have been surprised to find a swimming pool concealed behind one of them.

'I asked for the bog-standard trailer, but they gave me this. A drink?' He gestured towards an ornate globe suspended within a frame. Gold lacquered, it was studded with blue jewels, the image of a minotaur on the side putting her in mind of a Picasso drawing. He slid back the top half to reveal sparkling bottles of alcohol within.

'I'm fine,' said Kath. 'I've some pickups to do in fifteen minutes, before my big scene.'

'A little one won't do any harm. Here, try this. It's rum, but like you've never tasted. You like rum?'

Why did she feel like a child being summoned to the head teacher's office, only to be tricked into playing hooky? Her mind was focused on her scene that afternoon where she would get shot trying to save Lawrence's character. All she had to do was fall – it would be filmed from behind – and the close-ups filmed later. But however simple, it mattered that she got it right.

'Come on. You can't let me drink alone.'

Outside, lunch was still going on, huge bursts of laughter implying the crew weren't back on set. 'OK,' she said. 'Just a tiny one.'

Watching him pour the clear liquid into crystal tumblers, she noted his precision. The same attention to detail he brought to his job – knowing exactly where to position his body, what inflection of the smallest muscle might reveal a hidden, inner emotion. Spending time with him was a lesson in considered perfection.

Taking the glass, she edged away slightly as he sat next to her. His teeth were sparkling, reminding her not to show her own, stained from too much red wine and coffee.

'Are people treating you well? I know the director's a bit preoccupied most of the time – totally out of his comfort zone – but he's giving you enough direction?'

Truth be told, he hadn't. However, she didn't mind. The part was straightforward, the meagre instructions made sense – so there was no need to ask questions. 'Everything's fine.' She took a sip. The taste of the rum, both sweet and bitter, filled her mouth, like honey dripping down her throat.

'Good, isn't it? I had it flown in. They'd tried to substitute some cheap rubbish, but I was having none of it.' Slapping his thigh, he rose. 'More?'

'You've got to be joking. They'll have to carry me to the set.'

'Well, I'm going to have another.'

A dissatisfied look crossed his face. Otherwise, his charm was effortless – a study in relaxed hosting. She smiled as he took her glass. 'The tiniest amount,' she instructed, keeping an eye on his pouring. 'Stop!' she cried out. 'That's plenty.'

He returned to the settee, and they clinked glasses. 'Bottoms up,' he bellowed, knocking his back, before diving up for a refill. 'Should I cancel today's pickups?' He made his way over to the door and glanced back. 'Fuck them! They can come get us if they dare.' He laughed.

Again, he sat beside her, though this time much nearer. She could feel the heat of him burning into the side of her body, the smell of his aftershave catching the back of her throat, his physicality large and intrusive bumping up beside her. She tried to inch away but found herself wedged in the corner.

He edged closer, his tanned chest glowing through the

whiteness of his linen shirt. The brightness of his eyes staring directly at her was too much, too dazzling. It all seemed out of place in suburban Maidstone.

She scanned the trailer, desperately looking for something to chat about, something that might distract him; anything but return his gaze. 'I've never seen such a glamorous trailer.'

'This was redecorated especially for Michael Caine,' he said. 'Some Michael Winner film, I believe.' Lawrence's fingers ran back and forth across the leather upholstery. 'Are you enjoying filming?' he asked. It seemed more out of politeness than any real interest.

Having already answered that question, she shrugged. Sitting around in a trailer all day was boring and repetitive. There were only so many crosswords to do, so many interrupted chapters of her book she could read and reread. 'Yes. But the technical side doesn't interest me. I mean, I'm happy to be here, and this is wonderful.' She made a nodding gesture to the trailer.

'Baubles.'

'Nice baubles,' she added. A silver fruit bowl caught her eye. A sculpture in itself, she reckoned it must be worth more than her entire fee.

'Very nice baubles,' he replied. 'But meaningless. Michael's one week, mine the next.'

She finished her drink and placed the empty glass on the table. Lawrence refilled it fuller this time. She could see him assessing her attractiveness. Most men did the same. She had begun to understand that while her appearance might be unusual, there was something to celebrate about that. And the less self-conscious she became, the more people responded to her – and not just sexually. Directors would comment on the inscrutability of her face, that it could be two things at once, more if the part was complex and the lighting correct. To her, it was merely her reflection, and though her appeal helped pay the bills, she gave it little thought. Only in situations like this, when its effect caused men to behave oddly, did she worry about it.

'I should get going.' She stood but fell back. Far drunker than she expected, she giggled as Lawrence moved in and kissed her, pinning her to the sofa, while he thrust his tongue down her throat.

As he broke for breath, imagining it would go further, she shoved him off. 'Sorry Lawrence, I need to prepare for this afternoon.'

'I'll cancel it,' he said, still gripping her wrist. 'We could head back into town. Go for some lunch. My hotel has an amazing restaurant.' He twisted her body towards his.

She had to think fast. If she rejected him outright, she sensed it would come back to bite her. On the other hand, let him think it's what she wanted, he would never take no for an answer. 'I'm so sorry if I've given you the wrong impression. I'm flattered of course, but I never mix business with pleasure.' She pulled herself away from him, grabbing a door handle and praying it was the exit. 'Honestly, any other time,' she called back, as the fresh air hit her.

All she could think about as she stumbled from the trailer was the smell of his aftershave clinging to her costume; she needed to scrub it off at once.

52

Expecting Richard to be in bed, Lee was surprised to find him sitting by the window, a blanket over his lap, with a book in one hand and a glass of red wine in the other.

'Is this a good time?' Lee asked, hovering in the doorway.

'Come in, my darling. Always a pleasure. Draw up a chair.'

Lee dragged over the red leather stool from the dressing-table and joined Richard. 'This is cosy.'

'Some vino?'

Lee raised his hand to say no.

Richard grinned as he refilled his glass. 'Don't judge me, dear boy; it's just till all this nonsense blows over. My nerves are wrecked.'

He could have challenged Richard about his drinking but chose not to. That was for another time.

Lee checked the book cover: two masked figures locked in combat. 'Any good?'

Richard turned the book over, as if he'd forgotten what he was reading. 'Oh, it's Baldwin. *Another Country.* Lots of bed-hopping. I love it. You know I met him once?' He left no space for any comment. 'Gorgeous man.' He put the book down, giving Lee his full attention. 'And you've certainly landed on your feet, my love. Or is it your back? That man's a keeper. How is he? Poor doll.'

'Sleeping like a log.'

'Is that wise? With concussion?' Richard pulled a concerned expression.

'He's absolutely fine. Tired and a little bruised, that's all.' If Lee knew Colin, he'd be back on the case in no time; a little head wound wouldn't stop him.

'Keep an eye on him. We don't want a second body before the night's out. Though what a beautiful corpse he'd make.'

Lee shook his head. 'A Richard quote if ever there was one. But I'm not here to talk about my boyfriend.'

Richard took a large mouthful of wine before placing his glass on the table. 'One of those bastards has a lot to answer for. Then again, for all I know,' he continued, 'it could be you. You must have wanted him dead many times.' His eyes sparkled, and in that moment, he became the person Lee knew and admired; full of contradictions, a mysterious mind constantly whirring. 'Tell me, what's Colin's theory? Someone must be the prime suspect.'

'That's what I want to discuss.'

Lee sensed Richard searching his face – trying to work out what he was thinking. 'What other useful knowledge I might have?' He resettled the blanket across his legs.

'You're an encyclopaedia of showbiz scandal – onstage and off. Who's copped off with who, who holds a grudge? Have you any further thoughts – any more insights to share?'

'Beyond the ménage à trois I told you about?' he said, draining his glass and flicking through his mental Rolodex.

'I'm genuinely shocked. Jim and Georgie come across as the type who'd be in bed by ten with a warm cup of cocoa.'

'Ah, the vanity of youth, assuming it's only you who gets to have all the fun. People have lived lives, and people change. You can't tell what slings and arrows of misfortune a person has suffered by looking at them. Remember, one of them became a huge megastar. And although Georgie's career has been good, look at poor Jim.' Richard filled his glass, as though settling down for the night. 'Just saying.'

Lee couldn't see Jim as someone who'd go on a killing spree for some past grudge. Success didn't seem important to him. Georgie was different – he couldn't quite work her out – restless yet resolved. 'What do you know about Kath and Peter?'

Richard brought the glass to his lips and took a sip. Then another. With each one, he seemed to both revive and diminish. 'Well, Kath *is* very special. I remember seeing her graduation show and she blew the others out of the water. Did a stint at the Royal Court straight out of college. Managed to breathe life into some terrible dialogue. A dazzling *Cat on a Hot Tin Roof* in Birmingham, a season at the RSC. I could go on.' Richard was in full flow, sitting forward, flapping his arms. 'At her age, more regular parts might open doors, of course. But very highly thought of. Definitely one to watch. When you first mentioned her name, I almost jumped out of my seat in excitement. There's a feeling amongst us directors that give it five or ten years, she'll have gone stratospheric. You saw the Chekhov she did?'

Lee had. He'd been mesmerised by how, without seeming to do very much, she drew your gaze towards her. When Konstantin handed her the gull in Act Two after he'd shot it, there was a gasp from the audience at her reaction – raw, pure.

'The girl's young, feisty, a wonderful future ahead of her. Why kill some middle-aged has-been?'

True, but hardly conclusive. 'And Peter?'

Richard raised his eyes to the ceiling. 'Christ, you pushed my buttons when you said Lawrence was insisting.'

'Not a fan?' This surprised Lee, who considered Peter a plausible lead actor – great looks, some depth, a little rough round the edges, perhaps. He was sure Richard could have worked with that, help him develop.

'I mean, the role you cast him in?' Richard took a huge gulp of wine and refilled his glass. 'Please!'

'Lawrence cast him in,' Lee stressed.

'It needs sensitivity. So far, I've seen little evidence. Let's leave it at that.' Richard licked his lips and paused to build the tension – a juicy piece of gossip was about to be shared. Lee could always tell, but the extra sparkle suggested something special.

'Apparently, they were fucking.'

'Who?'

'Lawrence and Peter.'

'No!'

'On the film set. Or had fucked. Or were about to. Or, or, or. Whatever, sex was at the heart of that little travesty.'

Despite knowing a fair number of gay men in the theatre who were bisexual or who *passed*, he'd never considered Peter to be anything but straight. 'But he's with Kath. Has been since the film. She told us.'

Richard gagged on his wine. 'You do know *I* was married?'

'You weren't?' Richard constantly surprised him. It was like he'd lived ten lives simultaneously.

'For about four chaotic minutes. To a lovely American woman – Susannah – who miraculously gave birth to my child. Emily. Thirty-three, a lawyer based in New York. I mean, her mother's a lesbian now, but she wasn't at the time. Didn't let me see my daughter until she was sixteen.'

'I'm sorry.' The hurt in Richard's expression was clear – the empty wine glass at his lips told him the rest. 'But Peter? Into men? He literally swerves if there's a chance he might brush past you.'

'Certainly gives him a motive if true. Young, handsome, straight-acting – the fear of being exposed.'

'No, I don't buy it,' Lee said. 'I'd need more evidence.' It didn't add up. This was third-rate gossip. 'And what about Lawrence? Any other enemies you can think of?'

'Outside of his illustrious acting career, he co-founded a production company to help revive the British film industry.'

'I remember the fanfare. Whatever became of that?'

'Sold his share for millions before it sank, leaving his partners with zilch. Any one of them has a motive. Moved into American TV, made even more money as co-producer of this, executive producer of that. Stood on a lot of toes I'm told. During the early 80s, his name was on everything. Every day was pay day. Lately, you might say, he's lost his touch. Flop after flop. That messy two-month marriage to the Hungarian model, who demanded millions, was a publicity disaster. She was silly enough to sign a prenup. So, she must be pretty high on the list. I mean, you could close your eyes and suck his cock if you were sure of getting ten, twenty million at the end of it.'

Lee rose and kissed Richard's forehead. The gossip didn't hold any weight. A Hungarian model hiding out in a cave in this weather? Some media type waiting to exert revenge on an island thousands of miles from the Hollywood Hills? Peter and Lawrence in some bizarre tryst? 'Right, I need to get back, check how the invalid's doing. Night.' He hesitated. 'One final question before I go.'

'You have my full attention,' Richard said, smoothing out his blanket. 'Go on.'

'You weren't in the barn last night? I mean later, after everyone had gone to bed?' Lee could see Richard's mind rattling at full pace, seriously considering whether he might have been.

'Truth is, I can't recall. It's a possibility. But this,' he pointed to the wine, 'is my only interest at the moment. I've not got the headspace to be thinking about doing anyone in.' Richard squeezed Lee's hand. 'I'm certain of one thing though, the key to this horror is somewhere in the past. Tell your handsome man that. But I'm sure he's knows that already. And anything else he needs, I'll be here for the next few hours nursing a rather wonderful Beaujolais.' He let go of his hand. 'I promise I'll put my thinking cap on. Personally, I wouldn't discount someone else being on the island. Our esteemed playwright, little gem that she is, once threw a bottle of champagne at The Times' critic – missed him by inches. Told him to watch his back, that one night, when he least expected it, she'd be there to remind him of how much he disparaged her play. Writers never forget, my love. And Lawrence was vile towards her.' He shivered and pulled the blanket around himself. 'Give me more time though and I might come up with a better theory.'

Before Lee left, he looked back. Richard was uncorking the bottle of wine he'd hidden beneath the table. Caught in the soft lamplight, he was framed beautifully, as if he'd directed the tableau himself.

53

After checking in on Colin, who was sound asleep, Lee left the door ajar and ventured downstairs in search of a cup of peppermint tea. He'd only be a couple of minutes.

In the kitchen, Peter was standing by the Rayburn, staring at a pan of hot milk.

'Seems like we've the same idea,' Lee said.

'Ugh?' Peter grumbled, shuffling aside.

Lee placed the kettle on the hob and sat at the table. The back door, rattling violently in its frame, seemed insufficient protection from the howling wind and driving rain, yet neither of them commented on it. Only when a high-pitched scraping sound began, as if the storm were dragging a dozen steel scythes across the cobbled courtyard, did Lee say something. 'You don't think that's the barn again?'

'Dunno.' Peter shrugged, pouring his milk into a cup.

The sound stopped, replaced by the crash of wood splitting. Neither of them said a thing.

It was as though the bubble they'd found themselves in could never be breached. Within the confines of the house, they'd become cocooned in their own nasty little drama. If it continued much longer, Lee thought, there'd be more than one body being lifted off the island.

The smell of hot, creamy milk wafting towards him was a brief respite. 'Nice.' Lee smiled at Peter, thinking that maybe some gentle love-bombing might soften him, force him to chat like a normal grown-up. However, yet another grunt was emitted as Peter sat at the table and raised the steaming cup to his mouth, a glazed expression on his face.

When the kettle boiled, Lee rose and popped a sachet of peppermint tea into a cup, filled it with hot water and rejoined Peter at the table. They couldn't sit in silence – that would be excruciating. He had to think of something, anything. 'So, work's been good lately?' Actors couldn't resist talking shop. This should be safe territory.

Peter made a so-so sign with his hand, took a sip of milk, and placed his cup on the table. 'The last year's been crazy busy, but this fiasco won't help my prospects.'

Typical actor. Lee had been avoiding considering the consequences, preferring to concentrate on the present: getting safely off the island, discovering who murdered Lawrence. He knew any thoughts of a swift return to normal life were slim; that would all be for later.

'I mean, Lawrence Delaney – a major movie star – is dead. And we're all guilty by association.' Peter's voice shook, trailing off at the end.

Roughly the same age as Colin, he seemed so much younger, totally unprepared for life. But give him his due – he was right to be worried. The media storm they were going to walk into would be far worse than the one currently gripping the island. As soon as news got out, the tabloids would descend, their talons ripping through any available flesh. It would be a literal free-for-all: weeks and months of journalists camped outside their homes, his office, phoning every minute of the day. And when it was over, they'd be left scraping up the debris of their lives. Lee suddenly felt protective. Poor

Peter. He'd no idea what was about to hit him. Yet Colin's words rang in his ears – *I think Peter's our man.* 'But ultimately, not all of us are guilty,' Lee said, taking a sip of tea.

'You don't get it, do you?' Peter said, his tone harsher than before. The boy's face was transformed into that of an angry, dissatisfied man. The lines that would settle later in life revealed themselves on his forehead – crisscrossing tributaries of anxiety and disappointment. 'It's alright for you, Richard, my parents – Kath even. You've all had opportunities, you're all established. This was my big break. But after this fiasco, I'm finished.'

'Not if you're innocent.'

Peter's head sunk, staring at the steam rising from his cup. 'You think anyone will care?' he said, without lifting his head. 'They'll invent things. I mean, there's no evidence, is there?' He finally looked up, his face fierce, unhinged, his eyes wild. 'And your boyfriend's not been much help, has he?' He banged the table with his fist, sending a tremor around the kitchen.

Lee pushed his chair back and crossed to the sink. After washing his cup and setting it on the draining-board, he blew out a candle on the windowsill which had nearly burned out. 'I'm off to bed.' He headed towards the hallway. 'Where's everyone else?'

'How should I know?' Peter snapped, flexing his shoulder muscles. 'Upstairs. Somewhere. No one can sit together for more than five minutes thanks to your other half. Even Kitty can't bear to be in the same room as me.'

Lee looked at the man-child before him, soothing himself with hot milk, concerned his career was over, refusing to believe anyone he knew and loved could be capable of murder. 'You never know. Someone might confess.'

'You're deluded. Like your boyfriend.'

Maybe he should ask him outright. *Did you kill him?* Colin

would – keen to see the reaction, spot any tell-tale signs of lying or a cover-up.

As he was about to cross to the table, sit back down, continue their chat and see what he could elicit, Peter's lip quivered as if about to burst into tears. In a low, threatening voice, he whispered, 'I thought you were fucking off to bed?'

Lee held on tightly to the door handle. One more hostile remark and he'd holler. Despite the co-codamol, Colin would be down in a flash. 'Goodnight,' he said, reaching the safety of the hallway before finally breathing out.

54

A YEAR AGO

Since the incident in the canteen, Peter had mostly been avoiding Kath. On the Friday of that week, he asked if she fancied going out clubbing; but all he got back was a shake of her head. He backtracked, apologising profusely for taking up her time, nearly falling over as he walked away.

Despite her head saying to keep away from him, that he'd crossed a line, every other part was telling her he'd made a mistake. As much as she liked him, in the end she resolved to give him the cold shoulder, refuse to accept any more invitations or laugh at his jokes. He'd soon get the message.

In reality she barely had time to think about him. Filming was boring but arduous: the picking-up of scenes, the reshooting, constant technical issues. Worst of all, Lawrence had taken to watching from behind the camera and congratulating her each time *Cut!* was shouted. 'That's it babe, you nailed it!' he'd yell, like some demented cheerleader.

The unwanted pass in his trailer told her everything she needed to know: he was a chancer. Over the following days, flowers had arrived, tickets for the theatre were left for her, a dinner at one of London's swankiest restaurants was suggested. All to prove what? He could buy her? She found herself making up increasingly elaborate lies: her elderly grandmother had fallen badly; her brother had broken up with his boyfriend and needed a shoulder to cry on. She didn't even have a brother.

At the start of her final week of filming, she'd an extra scene to shoot with Peter. It was simple enough; she was to enter the garage and ask the whereabouts of his boss, and Peter was to reply, 'Out back,' and point her in the right direction. But no matter how often they did it, something would go wrong. Either she'd mix up the words and miss her cue, or the angle of Peter's finger would be wrong. The director, at this point close to a nervous breakdown, shouted they'd try again at the end of the day, that they'd wasted a valuable hour of his time.

It didn't help that on the way back to her trailer, doing her best to hold back tears, she overheard Lawrence make a snide comment about amateurs and how this would be his last British film. 'The talent's all across the pond,' he said to the make-up artist retouching his face. As she passed, he snapped his fingers. 'My trailer? Six,' he yelled.

As well as the social invitations, he'd continued to ask her to his trailer, under the guise of chatting about work. Yet, each time it was the same – a cursory nod to some innocuous work thing, followed by offers of alcohol, which she flatly refused. He'd attempted to kiss her once more, but she'd put her foot down. He took that as a challenge, telling her she'd give in at some point.

She'd no intention of ever going to his trailer again. As she wracked her brain for a new excuse – however implausible – Peter appeared at her window. He pulled a face and silently begged to be allowed in. She laughed at his pathetic mime: sad clown crying, turning a lock with a key, head peering over a wall. He still had that talent for slapstick she remembered from drama school – incongruous she thought, given his looks. She opened the door, positioning herself across it, acting as a clear barrier. And to give him his due, he remained at the bottom of the step, all puppy dog eyes and boyish exuberance.

'Will Madam allow me to enter?'

'Go away,' she shouted, throwing an imaginary bucket of water over him. He continued with the routine, falling backwards in an athletic roll, legs kicking in mid-air, as he wiped excess water from himself.

'Can I come in?' he asked, flat on his back.

Sitting together on the narrow banquette which passed as a sofa, she noticed how long and awkward his legs were. His bum had sunk into the cushion so much that his knees almost touched his chin.

'How bad was I today?' she asked, hoping he'd console her and not take the piss.

'Not as bad as me. All I needed to do was point.' As if to stress the fact, he lifted his hand, pointing his finger in the air, then down at the floor, feigning confusion.

'That was all my fault. I kept looking in the wrong direction – I get mixed up with my left and my right,' she whined, covering her face with embarrassment, and throwing herself back.

'Ah, so *you're* to blame. If I was directing, I'd have marched you off set and kicked your sorry ass.'

'Would you now?' She bashed a cushion against his arm.

'Hey,' he shouted as she continued to hit him, 'that hurts.'

She stopped. The temptation to keep hitting him – to block out that beautiful face – was too great. Like a VIP pass he'd been given at birth, all Peter needed to do was flash it whenever he wanted something.

'Friends?' he asked.

She poured herself a glass of water. 'You don't get off that easy, Peter Selby. What you did was cruel.'

'I know. I'm sorry.' He moved his legs out of the way as she brushed past him.

'Why do it in the first place?' Slamming the glass on the worktop, she startled herself at the loudness of her reaction. 'Do you understand how embarrassed it made me feel?' He was a captive audience, and nothing would stop her from continuing her tirade. 'It was humiliating. Unforgivable.'

'Can I explain?' He tried to stand up straight but banged his head against an overhead locker. 'Ouch!' He sat back down, sinking even further into the upholstery than before.

'In order to make up? Be best buddies? Nah. Not interested.'

'I thought maybe I'd overstepped the line,' he said. 'You know, when…' He trailed off.

'When? How?' She was confused. He seemed to be talking about something else, not the barman. Arms flapping, face puffed up, she shouted, 'Explain, Peter! Come on. Spit it out!'

'Touching you under the table.'

About to slam him once again, she stopped midflow. 'What? I thought you were drunk.'

'I was. I was blootered.'

'You and Lawrence were taking the piss then?'

'What's Lawrence got to do with it?'

She hesitated. Had she been wrong about Lawrence and Peter having an agenda that evening? 'To be clear, you didn't know what you were doing?'

'I knew exactly what I was doing.' He smiled at her, his face glowing with tenderness and a weird, goofy sexiness and all the things she'd swore to avoid. Desiring someone as unavailable as Peter could only ever lead to trouble and disappointment. Yet, having promised herself she'd never go down that road again, here she was, recast as her teenage self.

Somehow, in one go, he'd lifted himself out of the sagging cushion and was beside her, his hands gripping her waist. She was already imagining the sweetness of his kiss.

'Can I?' he asked.

She placed her arms around him, feeling the tightness of

his body, making her immediately conscious about the softness of her own. *Why would he want me?* Gentle, kind, passionate; she felt a thrill as his lips pressed against hers, pleasure as his tongue dug deeper inside her mouth. Everything that was missing from the cold, aggressive and unwanted advances from Lawrence. Even thinking about him made her squirm.

That's it. Tomorrow, I'll tell him if he doesn't back off, stop pestering me, I'm going to make a complaint.

55

Colin woke with a start. The shadow sitting on the edge of his bed made no sense; it definitely wasn't Lee. His dry throat ached, and when he tried to speak, he could only manage a croak. 'Who's there?'

In the darkness, he struggled to fill in the detail as the figure stood, dragged a chair across, and switched on the bedside lamp. He raised his hand to block out the glare. 'Kath?' Her face appeared soft again, kinder than when he'd interviewed her. Then, she'd squirmed, her darting eyes cold. 'You OK?'

Her hand pressed hard against the mattress, she whispered, 'You think Peter killed Lawrence, don't you?' She sat back, waiting for an answer.

'How did you get in here?' he asked. The last thing he remembered was the key turning in the lock.

'The door was unlocked,' she said, holding his gaze. 'I saw the look on your face in the hallway; even when the others were fussing about you, you were watching Peter the whole time. Like you knew something. Or thought you did.'

Christ, he imagined only Lee had noticed. 'Look, I'm tired,' he said, forcing a yawn to emphasise the point. She didn't care. Her stare, intense and unwavering, suggested she would sit there all night if necessary. 'Maybe we could chat downstairs. Give me a minute, I'll get dressed.' He made a move to get out of bed.

She drew closer, the warmth of her breath against his ear discomforting. 'Maybe I can help.'

'How?' He sat on the edge of the bed, unsure what kind of help she meant.

'If you tell me what you know, I promise I'll tell you everything,' she continued.

Laying her cards on the table – yet what did she actually have to offer? 'I can't do

that. Sorry. But if you need to say something, please, I'm listening.'

She drew back, revealing the grit in her expression. 'You don't see, do you? I'm the only person who can help.'

Was she being sincere? Or was this a performance, a game? He recalled her on the first night, time and again wrong-footing everyone at poker, only to reveal a straight flush.

'So?' she asked. 'What's it to be? I can leave if you don't want to hear, but I can tell you right now, I won't be offering again.'

Bargaining seemed the only way to make her talk. But how much to give? He hesitated, unsure where it might lead. 'Full disclosure?'

She nodded, eager for what he had to say.

'I've a theory regarding Peter.'

It wasn't what she wanted to hear. She watched the fire crackle. 'He's innocent. I know that for a fact.'

How could she be so certain? Was this all a diversion to protect him or was she about to confess? The look on her face – composed, meditative – suggested otherwise. 'I've a theory around everyone,' he added.

'Oh?' Her tone didn't change.

He lifted his cable-knit sweater from the floor and put it on. 'From what I've established, Kath, *you* were the last person to see Lawrence alive.'

Only then did she look in his direction. 'Me?' She grinned. 'So, I'm the prime suspect?' The grin developed into a shake of her head – an *if only you knew* expression settling on her face.

It wasn't the reaction he expected. 'Look Kath, you've either come to tell me something or you haven't.' He needed to gamble. 'Why not start with what you and Lawrence were discussing in his room? I know you left in a hurry.'

'It's private.'

'Well, if you haven't come to tell me what went on, you may as well leave.'

She took a breath and held it several seconds before exhaling. She looked behind her, checking that the door was closed. It all felt too mannered, too self-aware. 'During filming a year ago, and for a few months after, Lawrence…' She hesitated, looking straight at him before continuing. 'For want of a better word, he harassed me: phone calls, letters, appearing at my parents' home on one occasion. That sort of shit.' She breathed slowly. 'I made it clear I wasn't interested in him like that. But he didn't get it. He claimed he was being a mentor, that he was looking out for me. But I knew what he really wanted.'

If this was the truth, it provided another piece of the puzzle. 'Why take the job?' he asked.

A smile of recognition; a question she'd no doubt asked herself many times before. 'Because I was an out of work actress working nights in a bar and about to jack it all in. Don't mistake me for Peter; I wasn't born with a silver spoon in my mouth. I've had to work hard for everything, every step of the way. Plus, Lawrence hadn't been in touch for nine months. Foolishly, I thought it was safe, that he'd got over his stupid obsession or whatever it was.' She gazed at him, no doubt hoping he'd say something to reassure her. 'I'm an idiot, aren't I?'

Her emphasis on the word *safe* stood out. To what degree had she felt in danger since arriving on the island? 'So, you were never in a sexual relationship with him?'

She bit her lip and shook her head. 'Last night I went to his room to clear the air. His comments during the evening had annoyed me, and I needed him to know that I wouldn't tolerate them anymore, that if he continued, I'd leave the island. Of course, he thought I was overreacting, blowing things out of proportion, that I didn't know how to accept a compliment. I admit he riled me, and I raised my voice, but when I left that room, Lawrence was very much alive.'

Colin suspected there was more to tell, that she wasn't ready to divulge everything. Not yet. He needed to push her. 'It must have made things awkward. With Peter.' He watched her fingers start to drum against the side of the chair. 'He knows. Right?'

The tapping of her fingers grew more agitated. 'He hasn't a clue.'

Secrets. Even the tiniest could build, growing larger until finally bursting, destroying everything around. 'You're sure about that?'

'You still think it's him, don't you?' She stoked the fire. 'You know, Colin, I thought you were smarter. You don't seriously see Peter as some knight in shining armour, rushing to my defence against Lawrence, do you?'

She traced her fingers against the outline of a vase sitting on the mantelpiece, her face half-hidden in shadow. It felt like she was playing him. 'Do *you* think it was Peter? That maybe he found out, was defending you?' Another gamble, but her reaction might reveal something.

Her face emerged – anguished – any hint of calm suddenly gone. 'He barely notices when I've changed the colour of my hair, never mind what mood I'm in.' This appeared to affect her more than any of the details she was sharing about Lawrence. She moved to the other side of the room and pulled at the curtains, tugging them open to reveal the raging storm outside.

He didn't buy it. Peter could easily have found out about her and Lawrence; he'd been asleep in the library whilst they were having their tête-a-tête. Their voices could have carried, woken him, and if so, he'd have heard every word. 'Think about it, Kath. If Peter had wanted to protect you...'

'Ask yourself one question,' she said. 'Why would Peter kill Lawrence, who he adored? And if you think Peter would sacrifice his career to protect my honour, you haven't a clue.' She stopped, almost as though a new thought had occurred to her. 'It's funny, for a moment last year, I did wonder if they might be lovers, because Peter wouldn't stop talking about him.' She rolled her eyes. 'But nothing that exciting I'm afraid. They were buddies. It was as simple as that. I think Lawrence saw something of his younger self in him – all that vanity – which doesn't bode well for the future.' She pressed her face close to the glass. 'God, look at the state of the barn.'

All Colin could think about was her suggestion about them being lovers. That certainly put a whole new spin on things. What proof did she have they weren't? Someone like Peter would deny any transgression till he was blue in the face.

Unsteady on his feet, he followed her to the window, where she stood, engrossed in the darkness outside. 'If the storm continues, it'll tear the place down. The roof's almost totally gone.'

She drew her hair back to reveal a vague, lost expression. 'Such a beautiful place.' She let go of the curtain. 'I'd better go. You need to sleep.'

'Whoever killed Lawrence left the house last night.' It was a clue he was prepared to disclose if it would elicit a further confession. If Peter did kill Lawrence, maybe she was his accomplice, and it was her out in the barn. Had guilt brought her to his room after all? 'Did you leave the house last night?'

She regained her composure. 'I was tucked up in bed beside Peter. So, there's no way either of us could have done it.' She smiled. 'I need to go.'

He couldn't let her. 'Kath, is that really everything you came to say?' He scrutinised her face for any flicker of doubt. 'You'll feel better. I promise. Did you witness anything else last night? Anything that might help the investigation.'

Her eyes cast down, she shook her head. 'Peter is innocent. That's all I came to tell you.'

56

B it by bit, a timeline was falling into place. Lying back on the bed, Colin went through the sequence of events, testing for any gaps or anomalies.

From nine onwards, all of them had been at the party – drinking, dancing, enjoying each other's company. Despite the scene with Richard earlier in the evening, the atmosphere remained relaxed, jovial.

At around eleven, he remembered Kath bounding over, urging him to dance, being rude to Lawrence. At the time, he'd passed it off as a bit of friendly banter, but if Kath was telling the truth, her comments had clearly been pointed, more loaded.

At some point – 11.15ish – Lawrence and Kath had each left the party, well before the others. He reckoned he was dancing at that point. Whether anyone saw them leave, and whether they left together, he'd need to follow up. But to the best of his knowledge, and excepting the killer, Kath was the last to see Lawrence alive.

After everyone had gone to bed around midnight, he'd tidied away some glasses, popped his head into the library and found Peter asleep on a chair. That placed him next door to the crime scene, and not tucked up in bed, as Kath had suggested.

At midnight, the adjoining door to Lawrence's room was closed. He was certain of that, as he'd specifically checked.

Minutes later, he'd been heading to bed when raised voices from Lawrence's room caught his attention; from the kitchen, he'd observed Kath rush from Lawrence's room. If she'd just killed him, he'd surely have heard cries or a struggle, and she would have had blood on her. What he witnessed suggested Kath was telling the truth when she swore Lawrence was alive at that point.

Between going into the kitchen and waking at 1.15, he didn't see or hear anything out of the ordinary, though the whisky had knocked him out cold. Given the degree of rigor mortis he later observed, he thought it likely Lawrence was dead by then. Peter had left the library and the adjoining door to Lawrence's now lay ajar. Could Peter have gone through to Lawrence's after overhearing the raised voices, found out about Kath's accusations of harassment, confronted Lawrence himself, before killing him? Or might Peter have had another motive, fuelled by something else, something hidden? Such as them being lovers? The attack on Lawrence had been forceful. Out of everybody, Peter was the tallest, the strongest, the one more physically capable of beating a person to death.

At the time, Colin had thought little of the open door. In fact, the house seemed calm; with only the howl of the wind disrupting the silence. Was it feasible that Peter could have woken and gone to bed as *he* had, oblivious to the murder having taken place, only feet away?

The vomiting he'd heard from outside the top floor toilet struck him as odd. No one had replied when he called out to them. Was it someone who'd drunk too much, or the killer, physically reacting to what they'd done? If the latter, it suggested shock – an argument that got out of hand – a murder that hadn't been planned.

Colin shivered. He got up and sat at the dressing-table, writing everything down on a fresh piece of paper; arrows pointing to connections and possible explanations.

From that point, what Lee had seen and heard came into play. Having gone out to the barn and fallen asleep, he'd woken hearing voices. That person, most likely the killer, had both Lawrence's Dictaphone and the murder weapon with them. However, after the attack on him and the damage to the barn, it was doubtful either would be recovered anytime soon, by him or the killer. If Lee was right and he'd kicked the cassette from the Dictaphone, it could be buried under the debris, with any incriminating evidence potentially destroyed.

His mind leaped forward along the timeline to earlier that day. After examining and securing the crime scene as best he could, he'd gone outside at midday to search the rest of the island. Someone else had left the house shortly after and headed for the barn. Had no one witnessed that person leaving? What reasons could they have to go there other than to retrieve the murder weapon and locate the tape if they'd realised it was missing? But they'd mis-timed things, not counting on him being there at that precise moment.

That's when he was attacked. 12.30 PM at the latest. With him incapacitated, his attacker may have had time to retrieve the cassette and smash it to pieces. Would they have risked spending time in the barn to do so? More likely, their priority would be disposing of the murder weapon. And what of the Dictaphone itself? His search hadn't revealed any trace of it.

He had a timeline of sorts but lacked concrete evidence. Shadows, cast by the fire, danced across the ceiling. It was almost 11.15 and the house was quiet again. In the morning, he would interview the others, do another search, try to fill in more of the blanks. It was inevitable that, like Kath, someone would reveal something, slip up even, give him a morsel of info he could develop a definite theory from.

Lee entered, headed straight to Colin and nudged him to move over. 'I'm glad you're awake. There are a few things I need to tell you.'

'Me too,' Colin said. 'Like you know you left the door unlocked?'

'Shit, sorry. I didn't mean to take so long.' He seemed genuinely alarmed.

'Apology accepted. But more importantly, there's been a development.' Colin recounted the new information Kath had told him, crucially her possible motive for killing Lawrence. 'Right, what have *you* got for me?'

Lee spoke about Richard's suspicion that Peter was sexually involved with Lawrence.

'Kath had her own suspicions around that, too.'

'I get why Richard might think it, but I wasn't convinced.'

'Me neither. The guy's a classic jock, very awkward around us. I mean, there's some sort of self-loathing going on, but I wouldn't say it's to do with his sexuality.'

'You don't mind?' Lee grabbed the paper from Colin and added to his notes.

'But he *was* definitely closer to Lawrence than I'd assumed,' Colin continued, checking that Lee wasn't tampering with his own ideas. 'Kath emphasised that, so we can't rule it out.' He looked over as Lee scanned the sheet. 'What's bothering you?'

Lee took his time, the words uncharacteristically stilted. 'I see you've highlighted Peter's name and no one else's. I've been chatting with him in the kitchen. I mean, the guy's a dickhead in lots of respects, but I don't think he's got the wherewithal to cover up a murder. And I get the sense he's genuinely upset.' He put the paper down. 'I don't think he's our man.'

'You don't think that could be guilt? Kath came here specifically to provide an alibi for Peter, but I know she's not telling me the whole truth.'

'The thing he seemed most concerned about is the impact on his career. The guy's self-absorbed, not a killer,' Lee said. 'There's something else going on, something we're missing. You've written that he was asleep in the library and that he could have overheard Lawrence and Kath arguing. He's impulsive; would he not have gone in immediately? Or spoken to Kath? Plus, I'm now one hundred percent sure it wasn't him running from the barn, so even if he did kill Lawrence, he didn't do it on his own.'

There were points in an investigation when, after powering along, convinced you were heading in the right direction, you looked around and realised it was a dead-end. Perhaps Lee's assessment was right and his instincts around Peter were wrong. 'Tell me, what age is Peter?'

'In theory, the same as you – twenty-four or twenty-five – but he's pretty immature. Why?'

'If the ménage à trois around the original production of *Eros* is true, and not theatre tittle-tattle, could Georgie and Lawrence have carried on with something after Jim put an end to it? Who knows, Peter could be the result. That would explain why he's so upset.'

'Or, what about a totally new slant and Jim knew about Lawrence and his son having a bit of a ding-dong? All got a bit messed up. That gives *him* a motive.'

'Or, Peter found out about the affair between his parents and Lawrence, it messed him up, giving *him* a clear motive. Remember, I saw Georgie banging on Lawrence's door last night. So, if she had an affair and gave birth to Lawrence's son, she could have a motive. A woman scorned?' Colin scribbled it down.

'What a family!' Lee said.

'We're maybe getting carried away – these theories are a bit melodramatic – but they all have one thing in common.' Colin circled and underlined a word.

Sex.

57

A YEAR AGO

One of the producers, Melanie, agreed to meet Kath
early, before filming began. Despite it being her last
day on set, there would still be studio work to complete,
scheduled for the following month, but Kath couldn't wait.
There were things she needed to say now.

Melanie's office was tucked away at the back of the scrap-
yard, in a caravan even smaller than hers. To get there, she
had to step over streams of cables, dodge eager runners
rushing from one errand to the next and avoid her costume
getting splashed with mud. Miraculously splatter free, she
arrived and knocked on the door. A voice yelled 'Enter!'

Melanie, mid-30s, perfect hair and skin, sat behind a
tiny, makeshift desk. Distracted, she was scribbling in a
notepad and didn't even stir as Kath entered. To one side,
a mountain of paper teetered – probably just her morning's work. The woman was a legend on set – an adminis-
trative machine – arriving before everyone else and
leaving when the last light went out. The five minutes
Kath had been allotted were probably her only free ones
that day.

'You said to come at eight,' Kath said.

Melanie continued to stab at the notepad. 'Come in. Find somewhere to sit.' Her face barely moved a muscle.

Kath lifted some folders off a plastic seat. As she sat, she took care not to crease her shirt and trousers; costume would go crazy if she ruined them.

Melanie looked up for a brief second. 'Dump those on the floor.'

Kath placed the folders on a grubby rug, noticing her own headshot peeking out, her eyes wide and sparkling, trying too hard to impress. 'Here OK?'

She nodded. 'Can you hand me your file? It's near the top.'

At the final audition, Kath remembered how considerate Melanie had been, insisting that another actor, rather than an assistant, should read the lines with her. She'd also let Kath redo a scene that she wasn't happy with. Afterwards, she'd shaken her hand warmly, informing her that her agent would be notified in the next hour. When Kath had arrived home two hours later, an answerphone message from her agent confirmed she'd booked the job.

In front of her however, was a different version of Melanie: unsmiling, business-like, terrifying. 'Thanks for seeing me,' Kath said, conscious of her fingers tapping nervously against her thigh. Once, at an audition, a casting director had berated her, shouting at her to *quit that fucking tapping.* 'I need to make a complaint.'

Melanie's full attention was now on her. Until that moment, she'd not been sure she'd been listening. All it took was the single word – *complaint* – for her demeanour to change from lack of interest to one of pure concern. She put down her pen. 'Are you OK?'

No, Kath was not OK. She was about to make a complaint against the lead actor on a major film, a man so powerful his very presence made people cower. If he wanted something, however extravagant, he got it. No questions asked. Ever. 'It's complicated.'

'Well, take your time. When are you called for?'

'Nine.'

'Would you like me to push the scene back?'

Kath let out a sigh of relief – the old Melanie was back in the room – she'd deal with it. 'It's fine. I'll be quick.'

'I don't want you to feel pressured. Would you like your union rep here?'

Suddenly, Kath felt stupid and naïve. What if she was making a mountain out of a molehill, or worse, wasn't believed and nothing happened as a result? Her career was on the line, and maybe she was about to blow it. 'I hadn't thought. Do you think I should have one?'

'I don't know. If your complaint's about the catering, we should be fine.' She smiled. 'But it's not, is it?'

Kath shook her head, remaining focused on Melanie's kind expression.

'Let's hear what you have to say.'

'It's about Lawrence,' she blurted out. There, she'd said it. There was no going back. 'I want to make a complaint against him.'

As if following some unspoken industry protocol, Melanie rose, lowered the blind, then returned to her seat behind the tiny desk. She opened her notepad at a new page, and in a gentle voice, said, 'Go ahead.'

'He keeps pestering me. And I've made it clear I'm not interested. I don't know how many mores times I can tell him to leave me alone without coming across as rude, but I need it to stop.' It had taken her two weeks to fully understand how uncomfortable his advances made her feel. The last straw was his assumption she'd go to an industry event with him. When she declined, he stomped off, shouting and swearing, calling her a bitch.

Melanie remained silent. Instead, head down, she continued writing in her notepad as Kath went through the details: she had done nothing to warrant his attention – she was adamant about that. Yes, she'd socialised outside of work with him once and been alone with him in his trailer several times – which she knew was a mistake – but what else could she do? He was her boss, an executive producer on the film, and he was using work as an excuse to harass her. And it was getting worse. Even after she'd asked him to stop, he continued his pursuit, pressuring her at every opportunity.

While telling her story, Melanie didn't meet Kath's eyes or ask her a question. It was as if part of her had left the room and run off to warn Lawrence. The averted eyes, the dropped head and the silence told Kath everything she needed to know: noted, but nothing of consequence would come of it.

However, Melanie continued scribbling. A couple of minutes later she finally looked her in the eye. 'Is there anything specific you'd like me to do?'

In that instant, Kath wanted to grab all the words she'd said and push them back inside her mouth. Why did she imagine Melanie, or anyone else for that matter, could do something about Lawrence's behaviour?

She watched as Melanie ripped a sheet from her notepad and placed it on the desk in front of her.

Kath glanced at it. Key words and phrases had been underlined – *alleged … no witnesses … continued having drinks with him.*

'Don't get me wrong, I believe you. But if I go to anyone with this, your name will be mud. The film industry in this country's tiny, and word gets around. Fast. Without corroboration, it's his word against yours. For what it's worth, my advice would be this: finish your scene today, complete the week's work next month in the studio, and be done with him. In my experience, pursuing this won't be in your best interest. You'll be seen as a troublemaker. And trust me, he'll get bored soon enough. His attention will turn to someone else.' She said all this in a hushed tone, as though someone were skulking outside the caravan, listening. Or maybe she was being recorded. She'd heard Lawrence liked to do that,

Kath contained the sting of tears at her eyes. 'I didn't tell you; he phoned my mum. How did he get my number? Because I certainly didn't give it to him,' Kath stated. 'That's not right, is it?'

Melanie pushed the sheet of paper further towards her. 'You've got talent, Kath; protect that at all cost. Don't let the bastard win. Take this. Rip it up. Walk away. Ensure you're never in his company alone.'

Heart racing, Kath stumbled out of the caravan, holding the sheet in her hand. She scrunched it up and threw it in the first bin she came to. *Your word against his*. Of course, that's what it boiled down to. Why'd she been so stupid to think otherwise?

It was almost her call-time, so she headed back to her trailer to try and calm down. In the distance, she spotted Lawrence with Peter. He was obviously telling Peter a joke, his arm around his shoulders. At the punchline, both their bodies moved in unison, erupting into laughter. Lawrence wandered off, shouting at someone for not warning him how late it was.

As she stepped into her trailer, she heard her name being called. It was Peter. He'd run over to catch her. Breathless, his face was red with joy and exuberance. 'Just to let you know, I can't make the movie tonight. Me and the boys are heading out with Lawrence. We can catch it next week. That OK?'

Of course, it wasn't, but she nodded in agreement as she closed the trailer door behind her.

58

Kath had little time. Colin and Lee were still awake, chatting. She could hear their hushed voices as she paused outside the bedroom door, no doubt dissecting what she'd said. With Peter asleep, and Georgie and Jim in their bedroom, the coast was clear. No need to worry about Richard; after a day's drinking, he'd be incapable of putting one foot in front of the other.

Last night's impromptu party flashed before her: the dancing, the singing, the laughing. Despite *his* presence, it had been joyous. For the first time, with Peter by her side, and his parents so supportive, their relationship finally felt right. So, when Lawrence grabbed her arm, her first instinct had been to tell him to get lost. But after a moment's reflection, she'd waited till no one was watching, before approaching him. 'We need to chat.'

'My room?' he'd suggested, walking ahead of her down the hallway. When she didn't follow, he turned around, urging her, 'Come on, Kitty O'Hare. I've not got all night.'

Before arriving on the island, she'd built him into this fearful character – an all-powerful presence. But seeing him up close again, it felt like Toto pulling back the curtain in *The*

Wizard of Oz, to reveal nothing more than a vain, ineffectual middle-aged man; his constant finger-clicking for attention tolerated rather than taken seriously. The nonsense with his bed was a case in point. Who in their right mind would demand others rally around and organise such a thing on your behalf?

That was all in the past now. Grabbing a torch from the kitchen, she went to the hall cupboard and pulled on one of the waterproofs. She checked the coast was clear. This had been her first mistake: being seen by Colin leaving Lawrence's room; her second being caught by him in the barn. Though she regretted having to hit him, there'd been no alternative. She still felt queasy at the sight of him slumping into the mud, blood oozing from his head. In that moment, she knew a life of crime was beyond her; she was too honest, too caring. But where had that got her? Taking matters into her own hands was the only way out of this mess. Throwing the award into the sea afterwards felt like a release – washing away the proof. She still had loose ends to tie up – not least the clothes soaked in Lawrence's blood she'd stashed in the toolshed.

From the hints Colin had dropped about what he knew or suspected, it felt like he was closing in, that time was running out; keeping him onside was a priority. She had tried throwing him titbits, but nothing that might point him towards anyone in particular. By telling half-truths, she hoped to divert him, confuse the situation. And with someone in need of her protection, she'd do whatever it took, regardless of the cost.

She gripped the front door, using all her strength to ensure it didn't fly open, or come crashing back and wake the others. As she stepped outside, the full force of the wind and rain buffeted her. One more barrier to overcome. Closing the door behind her, the latch snapped securely into place with a definite click. Her entire body trembled from cold, fear, nerves;

reaching the barn was now her only goal. Battling against the raging storm, and sticking to the shadows, she made her way round – each step an effort of will – a reminder of how she'd got to this point.

MELANIE HAD AVOIDED her for the rest of that day on location, but also in the studio the following month. Her advice had been pretty clear: *don't rock the boat.* Initially, part of her wanted to walk away from the job, leave with no explanation. But that, she knew, would have done her no favours, and only aggravated the situation. Like Melanie said, *be done with him.* So, she'd fulfilled her contract and slipped away, hoping for that to be the end.

However, in the weeks after filming ended, Lawrence's inappropriate behaviour continued. He would phone her multiple times a day, demanding she meet him. Even after he returned to the States, he'd subjected her to a two-hour monologue about how he loved her, and how she should drop everything to join him in LA; that there was a part just right for her in a pilot he was producing. He'd pay for it all: the flight, an apartment. All she had to do was say yes. 'I've got commitments, a life here. You can't expect me to drop everything.'

'I can do what the fuck I want,' he shouted down the phone, continuing to rant on about women bleeding him dry, how he'd be better off without them. 'It's never about me,' he cried. As he continued, her fear had faded and she became perplexed more than anything. None of it felt real – or even about her.

Peter suggested keeping their relationship under wraps during the shoot. Though doubtful, she was relieved they'd done so, and continued to keep it secret afterwards, agreeing it was for the best. That way, Lawrence would never find out about them, and could never use it against Peter, who was developing a friendship with him. After the film wrapped, both men continued to exchange calls, promising to meet when Lawrence was next in town. Throughout that period, Kath didn't mention a thing to Peter about Lawrence's behaviour. As she listened to Peter go on about what a cool life Lawrence led, how much influence he had, she wanted to slap him out of his daydream. And then, as quickly as they'd begun, Lawrence's calls to her stopped. Thinking that was an end to it all, she got on with her life.

WITH EACH STEP towards the barn, Kath worried she'd be spotted. If anybody did see her, she'd no idea what she'd say. "Going for a stroll" wouldn't wash.

Tripping on a rock, she almost fell over. *Fuck this island,* she muttered under her breath, cursing the play, Lawrence, anything and anyone she could blame for ending up there.

Peter had got the call first. Kath was getting ready to leave his flat and was searching for one of her shoes when his agent rang, so she was only half-listening. With Peter's flat such a mess, the search for the shoe took priority. She remembered the coolness of his voice on the phone as she got on her knees to look under the sofa. He kept repeating 'Yes' over and over, giving nothing away. Realising it was something important, she tried to listen in.

As soon as he got off the phone, he jumped on the sofa, screaming at the top of his voice, 'I got the part! I got the part!' Grabbing her by the waist, he spun her around, saying, 'This is my big break. I knew Lawrence would look after me.'

'Congratulations.' She tried to sound enthusiastic. 'That's amazing,' she said as he filled her in with the details.

As he fantasised about what it might mean, how he'd try America for sure, maybe give it two years out there, she listened without saying a word. 'Kath, this is it,' he screamed, hugging her tight.

'It's one play.' She pulled free and grabbed the rest of her clothes, stuffing them into her bag. 'Not a win on the pools.'

'It's way better.' He picked up the phone and dialled his friend, Matt. 'After the play, we can go out to America, mate. The two of us. The place won't know what's hit it,' he shouted down the phone.

Insisting she could be late for her shift this once, Peter had run to the shops to buy some champagne when the second call came. Only her agent knew to find her at Peter's. But as she listened to her describe the "exciting" offer, Kath simply said she'd think about it. Putting the phone down, she stared at the wall. For ten minutes, she went through in her head what she'd tell Peter. *I'm not doing the part, the guy's a creep, he makes me uncomfortable, he's manipulative. Here's a list of the abusive behaviour I've been subjected to.* In the end, she thought it better to avoid telling him altogether, discreetly decline the offer and get on with other things; let him go off and play happy families with Lawrence.

Red-faced and breathless, Peter popped the bottle of champagne as he entered the flat, lapping up the excess bubbles pouring down the side. Instantly, she knew saying nothing wasn't an option. Unable to look in his direction, she was zipping up her holdall when she mentioned the call. 'But the part doesn't sound right for me,' she said, before asking him where her umbrella was.

'Don't you need to read the play before making a decision like that?'

She couldn't answer. Instead, she took one sip of the champagne and set it aside. 'I don't know, you're probably right. I'll think about it,' she replied.

'A play in the West End with Lawrence fucking Delaney. Think of who'll come to see it. Doors will open for both of us.'

'Will they?' she said, throwing on her coat. 'Anyway, I've that second audition for a rep season in Bristol. The jobs would clash.'

'Are you mad? Anyone in their right mind would choose London, right part or not. And it means we'll be able to spend time together,' he said, taking the holdall from her and tossing it back onto the sofa. 'Please, Kitty, think about it. We might not get many more chances to act together. I want this to work.' Cuddling her, he rocked her gently, whispering how great an actress she was, how much he needed her, how he couldn't do it without her.

That's what convinced her. Them. Together. That stupid moment of romantic tenderness sealed their fates in ways neither could conceive.

It didn't take long for her to settle on a strategy; accept the job, and if Lawrence started his nonsense again, she would rub his nose in it, ensure he squirmed as she told him every little detail of her and Peter's affair. Watch *him* suffer. Maybe then he'd leave her alone. As Peter held her, promising he'd be the best co-star she ever had, all she could think of was how much she wanted to hurt Lawrence. And if that meant Peter waking up to the reality of who he was, so be it.

CASTING the torch around the barn, the damage was clear. From the doorway, Kath could see the enormous rafters had been ripped in two, their jagged ends pointing towards her. One half of the roof had been lifted off completely, and a river of rainwater flowed through the furthest end of the barn. Bizarrely, the part containing the kitchen was largely intact. She could still see the sink where she'd tried desperately to wash the blood from Lawrence's award.

Last night, after they'd snuck away from the party, the conversation with him had not gone well.

'You don't mind if I turn on my Dictaphone for this conversation, do you?' Those were his opening words. As he searched his leather suitcase, she remembered him brandishing it on set, making a hullabaloo about pressing the record switch. He took it out and placed it between them. 'Now, Kath, what can I do for you?'

'I want to clear the air. I need you to promise you'll leave me alone. As I've spelt out, I'm with Peter now.'

His lips became thin, and his eyes bore into hers. 'And yet here you are. With me.'

'Sorry?' There was something in the way he looked at her that made her instantly realise this was all a mistake – taking the part, coming to the island, asking to speak with him. As he moved towards her, she clenched her fists.

'Tell me, does he know about us?' he asked.

'There *is* no us,' she shouted, feeling a tightening in her chest.

'All those phone calls. Those intimate conversations. What would Peter say if he found out?'

'There's nothing to find out. There was no intimacy – well, not from me.' Peter would believe her. She had to trust that. Having gone over it in her head so many times, she was convinced that after telling him the details of Lawrence's harassment, he'd side with her. But why hesitate till now?

'What about all the times you came to my trailer for drinks? How would that appear to Peter?'

'I'd no choice. That was for work,' she stressed, her tone weakening, realising how Lawrence might twist things 'That was it. End of.'

'What work? To go over your five lines? Explain how to avoid looking directly into the camera? Tell me, what other actor on set was I having private meetings with?' He shook his head. 'Kitty O'Hare, what will I do with you?'

Before she knew what was happening, he'd grabbed her waist and thrust his body against hers.

'Come on, Kitty,' he whispered into her ear. 'You can't keep this up forever.'

Pushing him away, his hands kept bouncing back, gripping her tighter. 'Get off me!' she said, her voice echoing round the room.

That's when he forced his hand against her mouth and pulled at her dress. If she hadn't reacted quickly, he'd have overpowered her. With one shove, she unbalanced him, sending him toppling onto the floor.

Sat on his backside, his arm outstretched, waiting for her to lift him, he said, 'You're forgetting who's paying your wages.' The way he laughed at her was the final insult. 'Come on, pull me up. No offence taken.'

At that moment, she knew exactly what she needed to do. He was never going to leave her alone, never going to respect her. Her mind was made up. He needed to suffer as she had.

59

1963

The first time Georgie met Lawrence was at the read-through of *Eros*. Breezing in alone, having decided that Jim should go on ahead, in case it appeared too weird them arriving together, she'd complained about the weather and delays on the tube, whilst fussing with her scarf.

She scanned the room. 'You haven't started without me?' Sitting at the long, rectangular table were Jim, the director Terry, his assistant Kevin, the writer John Wightman – a close friend of her and Jim – and several other production staff. They politely shook their heads no, said hi, then returned to their scripts, the words on the page of more interest to them than an actual conversation.

Only Lawrence, sitting at the far end of the table, got up, walked the full length of it and shook her hand. 'Georgie, isn't it? It's lovely to meet you.'

His hands were soft, and although only average height, with his piercing gaze he had a commanding presence. Part of her felt like she'd met him before, but she couldn't have. She'd asked around and discovered he'd studied, not in London, but at the Bristol Old Vic.

'What?' she asked, feigning mock horror, 'I've to play against these two gorgeous men and still be noticed?' She winked at Jim, and the room burst into laughter.

'Can we start?' Terry said, glancing at his watch.

Georgie pulled the script from her bag. 'Right, I know I'm playing *The Girl*. No name?' John explained his reasoning, that he wanted her character to symbolise aspects of the change from one society to the next. He offered a working name, but Georgie declined, saying if it was good enough for Brecht, it was good enough for her. 'I know Jim is Samuel, *The Fiancé*.' She peered over at Lawrence. 'So, you must be Bartholomew, *The Farmer*?'

He nodded.

'Shall we?' interrupted the director.

Jim and Lawrence read the first scene, a random meeting on the outskirts of a village at sunset. As they spoke their lines, stumbling as they searched for the emotions, she gazed at them; suited and clean-shaven, they could be mistaken for brothers. Same height, similar bone structure, but while Lawrence had dark hair and those trance-like green eyes, Jim was fairer and blue-eyed. Lawrence was also more athletic looking, whereas Jim had a lithe body, currently twisted away from everyone. She wanted to untwist him, tell him to sit up straight. But she remembered: whilst doing the job, any relationship niggles came second.

As the scene progressed, something didn't feel right. The reading sounded stilted. Visually, it seemed wrong too. She slammed down her script. 'You should switch.' The room stopped and stared in her direction. 'Jim ought to be the farmer.' The character needed to be awkward, restless; Jim was perfect casting. 'And Lawrence, you should be the fiancé.' Assured, striking, he was born to play the part. There was a look of shock from the others, but interest too. 'Could we at least try it?'

Terry, the director, tried to speak but was interrupted.

'She's right,' Lawrence said, his sculpted lips moving sensually, revealing a row of perfect teeth. 'Here, where the farmer talks about his body, how he wasn't born to be a farmer, that his soul was made to think, to dream. I mean, look at us.'

They all listened as Lawrence continued for five more minutes, apologising for taking up time, but referring to at least four other points in the script where him playing the fiancé and Jim playing the farmer made more sense.

John applauded first. Georgie had never experienced anything like it. It was only her third job, and the other two had been short runs where she'd been expected to make tea as well as play minor characters. But now, all around her, an entire production team was applauding actors for expressing their opinion. All except the director, who sat scribbling notes, only looking up when the writer spoke.

'Terry, I know you wanted to cast against type, but it's how I always saw them,' John said, his eyes filling with tears.

Throughout the rest of the reading, a spark took hold, lighting up all three of them, igniting the room; like making love and truly experiencing pleasure, Georgie felt. No awkward, fumbling hands trying to force enjoyment, but instead, something natural, carnal, unstoppable. As the read-through continued, lines that seemed flat on the page came to life, nuances of words suddenly made sense. Entire scenes she'd forgotten revealed meanings and clues that opened up the world of the play, unveiling something magical and revolutionary: this was a play about sex and love and how it can either destroy or liberate you.

She tried to catch Jim's eye, but he didn't notice; he was far too busy gazing at Lawrence. She smiled, recognising the adulation Jim gave those he admired. Such a silly, complex, loving man. Sometimes when they were together, his expression would change like the shifting sky, and she'd wonder, who is this person I sleep next to, fuck, laugh, cry with? From humble working-class beginnings, and without much of an education, he was the most intelligent and creative person she'd ever met; his thirst for knowledge of literature, art, music was endless. Such a mystery wrapped up in someone so unassuming.

At the end of that first day, the three of them had sat in a corner of the room, chain-smoking, scripts in hand, tossing lines back and forth, asking questions and underlining words.

'Why does she ask them what they've been doing?' Georgie asked. 'Wouldn't she keep quiet about her suspicions?'

'Why wouldn't she ask?' Lawrence looked up from his script, smiling knowingly at her. 'She wants them to know that *she* knows.' Though expensively dressed, his shirt hadn't been properly pressed. It sounded stupid, but all she wanted to do was take it off him and iron it. This shook her, as she'd never ironed a man's shirt in her life and berated her own brother for expecting their mother to do his. Who was this man?

'I suppose she's expected life to be one thing,' Jim said. 'The society she was brought up in, the way she's been taught to think, it's all so staid and distorted. Suddenly, she's seeing things, being curious. She needs to ask questions.'

'Are there any circumstances in which she could have walked away without asking them?' Lawrence asked.

Georgie considered the question. 'No. She's bound to both of them by what she's witnessed. A secret they share.'

'Sadly, she pays a price for what she's seen,' Jim added. 'Protects them both by pointing the finger at herself, destroying her reputation at the same time.'

Lawrence took her hand. 'A trailblazer.' He turned to Jim and took his too. It felt magical – three bonded spirits. If the roof had opened and they'd glided upwards on a cloud, she wouldn't have been surprised.

Snubbing out her cigarette, she closed her script. She stood, pulled them up by their hands and announced, 'I'm going out to get pissed. Anyone want to join me?'

60

C olin's body clock was out of sync. Wide awake now, he'd left Lee asleep in bed. His observation that they were missing something – that *he* was missing something – felt right. There was work to do and it was pointless leaving it to the morning.

He crept downstairs and opened the first of the hall cupboards. In his initial sweep of the house, when looking for signs of an intruder, he'd taken a cursory glance through it. He was now wondering if Peter's focus on the board games inside, earlier in the day, might have been a pretext to hide or remove evidence. He scanned each shelf, pushing boxes aside. The cupboard was shallow, with nothing suspicious that he could see.

He moved on to the larger walk-in cupboard, closer to the front door, which functioned as a boot room. The door creaked as he opened it. He inspected the orange cagoule again – there was no way it could be described as huge and there were definitely no signs of blood. Shoving boots and wellingtons aside, he stepped further into the cupboard, pushing through the layers of cagoules and coats to the very back of the cupboard, desperately searching for the huge orange one. It was potentially a key piece of evidence but was nowhere to be seen. He fell to his knees and felt along the skirting of the back wall; his hand grasped a waterproof which had fallen to the floor. *Thank God!* But pulling it out into the light, he could see that it had a camouflage pattern. As he hung it back with the others, he noticed its white lining had reddish-brown smears across it. Stepping out into the hall, he opened it up – could they be bloodstains? It certainly looked so.

Voices sounded from above. Pulling the door to, he hid inside the cupboard. Jim was saying something about toast and Georgie replied, 'Hot chocolate for me please.' Through the crack in the door, he watched Jim pass down the bottom of the stairs and cross to the kitchen.

Carefully folding the camouflage waterproof, he took a black bin bag from the shelf in front of him and placed it inside. With Jim occupied in the kitchen, he returned upstairs, gently putting the black bin bag behind his and Lee's door before heading down the corridor; now was as good a time as any to speak to Georgie on her own. He needed to test if there was any truth to Richard's stories about her and Jim's previous relationship with Lawrence.

Though she didn't say a lot, he'd noticed the consideration she'd shown to both Richard and Kath, but also what a strong presence she had. With the smallest look, she could put an end to Jim and Peter's bickering. He had the impression that she was definitely the matriarch of the family: what she said went. He was also curious about Lee's comment on how she'd played hardball on the contract, unwilling to take the role immediately. Why? He wanted to observe her reaction when asked.

Arriving at the slipway on the mainland two days ago, Georgie's had been the only face he'd recognised. When he was a child, she'd been a part in a Sunday night drama on TV, a wartime story about GIs stationed in rural Surrey. She'd played one of the main characters, a housewife who was having an affair with an American officer. Complete fluff, and he probably never watched an entire episode, it being more his mum's thing. But although it was years ago, he still remembered the steeliness of her character, which didn't seem so far removed from the real Georgie.

Since getting together with Lee, he'd met other well-known faces from the telly. There was invariably something unexpected about them: their hairstyle or height, usually their accent. How incredible it must be to become another person, subsume them, express their thoughts and desires, but never actually be them. He knew, of course, that at the end of the day, the costume and make-up were taken off, and actors went back to their own lives. But it fascinated him all the same – the parallels to police work – having to see things from another's point of view.

He knocked on the door. Within seconds, it opened. Georgie stood before him; a silk dressing-gown wrapped round her tiny frame. 'You!'

'Can we chat?'

He'd anticipated an immediate rebuff, but instead she opened the door wider. 'I was wondering how long it would take. You'd better come in.'

For a moment he felt like the American officer she had the affair with on the programme, as she led him into her bedroom and offered him a seat. Although petite, she had a dancer's strength and poise about her. Earlier in the day, holding onto him, he'd noticed the defined muscles of her arms. Strong enough to hit and kill a man?

He felt her sharp gaze assessing him. 'Jim will be back in a minute.'

'Good. I'd like to chat with him, too.'

'The truth is Colin, as I've already made clear, I'm not sure how I can help. I was in bed after the party. Ask Jim. Asleep by twelve. Both of us. Very boring.'

No point going down that line of inquiry if Jim was merely going to confirm it. He now had two couples, each offering an alibi for their respective partners. But someone was lying. If Lee was right about the figure in the orange cagoule, with his discovery of the bloodstained waterproof, it seemed likely that at least two people were involved in Lawrence's murder. He decided on a different tack. 'You knew Lawrence well?' Like Kath, she was a twiddler. The gold band on her wedding finger was being twisted and turned as she considered his question. 'You started your careers together, didn't you?'

For the briefest second, an emotion he couldn't identify, flickered across her face. But, suddenly composed, she looked him straight in the eye. 'Yes, Lawrence was an old friend of ours. We first met over thirty years ago – 1961 – when we did a play together. It's common knowledge.' She was twirling the ring around her finger so quickly he thought it might spinoff. 'But we haven't been close for a long, long time.'

Maybe it was the truth. But her body language suggested otherwise. It was stiff, as if she'd rehearsed her lines. 'Lee said you didn't accept the role immediately.'

She bristled. 'So, I am being questioned?'

'Just trying to get to the bottom of all this mess.'

She took out a cigarette and lit it. 'I'm in the fortunate position to be able to turn down work. I don't take everything I'm offered. The truth is, I thought my character was under-written.' She grabbed an ashtray and flicked ash into it, tapping once, twice. 'She only appears in the first act, and although she sets up a key strand of the story, her own wasn't resolved. Fortunately, the writer agreed to make changes. That's when I accepted.' Stubbing out the barely smoked cigarette, she released a puff of smoke from her mouth. 'Remind me, this isn't an official interview?'

He shook his head. None of the conversation could be used as evidence. She could confess she'd murdered

Lawrence and he wouldn't be able to prove a thing. His word against hers. But he needed to understand their relationship: their connection then and now. The supposed sexual tryst between them was foremost in his mind, but he couldn't lead with that.

He liked to imagine each interviewee as a family member or a close friend. How would he chat with them? He'd witnessed plenty seasoned officers getting nowhere by being blunt and unsympathetic. Without asking the direct killer question, was there another way to the truth with Georgie?

'Lawrence seemed to rub people up the wrong way. Was that always the case?' he asked.

She stifled a yawn, letting go of the gold band around her finger. 'The person I used to know was different.'

'In what way?'

Her expression suggested that while she resented his line of enquiry, she'd nonetheless committed to answering. She settled into her chair, as though about to embark on a bedtime story, albeit cautionary. 'He couldn't have been further from the image of a Hollywood star in those days. I mean, yes, he had that sparkle. But he was sensitive, caring, a player for sure, but it was all about the work.'

'You think he'd lost interest? He seemed pretty focused to me.'

'Successful actors like Lawrence can easily fall into the trap of believing their own hype. Don't get me wrong, the play we were about to do is great – it has emotional depth, magnificent speeches. It's ironic, but had he still been serious about the work, he'd have taken Jim's part, the less showy one' She paused, and the twisting of her ring began again. 'The friendship we had together, what we created in that play all those years ago, I wanted to hold onto that memory, not ruin it. That's another reason I didn't accept right away, I suppose.'

This didn't sound like the truth. Georgie didn't strike him

as the sentimental type. 'You never saw Lawrence again after that first production?' He couldn't resist asking, to check if she would bite.

She laughed. 'Oh, we saw each other. There was a time when I saw more of him than I did my own husband. Parties, award ceremonies, that sort of thing. But we didn't *see* each other; we weren't friends. He had ceased to be Larry, the man I first met in 1961. He'd become Lawrence Delaney – a movie star, my dear. That most precious of things: loved and adored by everyone around him. Probably despised and deplored in equal measure, too. Who knows? Our paths diverged. You have to appreciate that Lawrence needed to be the most important person in the room. Well, you saw it for yourself, didn't you? He had to come up with the best idea, ensure others knew he was smarter, more engaged. Even back then, when we were too young and naïve to obsess over people's little foibles, it showed. Owning little moments as though he'd come up with them, mythologising himself. Quite a talent. Perhaps there were a few little niggles that were never ironed out, but nothing that ever festered.' She lit another cigarette, delighting as she inhaled. 'Now, is that all? It's what, after midnight, well past my bedtime. Jim's downstairs making some hot drinks and he'll be back soon.'

There it was again: that Home Counties steeliness.

'So, no resentments whatsoever?' Colin wanted the question to seem like an afterthought. He even put away his pen to suggest it was off the record.

But as she was about to answer, the door burst open. Peter rushed in, distraught. Georgie immediately went to him, trying to calm him. 'What's wrong, darling?'

'It's Kath – I can't find her anywhere. The last time I saw her was hours ago.'

Colin noted the tears on his cheeks. 'Did she say anything?' he asked, anticipating a hostile response. 'Anything that might indicate where she'd go?'

Peter dried his eyes and looked over at Colin. 'No, nothing. Sorry, I didn't see you there.'

'Have you searched the whole house?'

At that moment, Jim walked in, carrying a tray, having heard the last part of the conversation. 'What's going on now?'

'Kath's missing,' Georgie explained.

'We'd better go look for her then, hadn't we?'

Colin watched them hurry out the room, two generations of a family in apparent disarray. But he'd no doubt – it wasn't just Kath who was lying.

61

Using the torch to light her way, it had taken Kath at least twenty minutes to identify a route through the pile of debris on the barn floor. It wasn't easy. Sliding her body through an opening, she was careful not to disturb anything. An earthy smell rose up, immediately filling her nostrils, heightening her feeling of claustrophobia. The fallen timber and sheets of roofing had created a dark, dank cavern which she would be able to navigate on her hands and knees; and though the floor was thick with mud, she hoped that despite the limited light, she might locate what she'd come to find.

Having left Lawrence flat on his back like the cockroach he was, she'd escaped to a spare room on a top floor bedroom to clear her head and consider what to do. First, she would tell Peter what had been going on, then she'd make an official complaint to Lee. She rubbed her wrist; the area where Lawrence had grabbed her was already starting to bruise. If Lee sidetracked her, like Melanie had, she'd leave the production, get off the island and go to her union. He wouldn't get away with it again.

She waited several minutes to allow her breathing to calm

and her heartbeat to settle before returning downstairs. Opening his bedroom door, she found Peter on his stomach, spreadeagled across his bed, crying into a pillow in long drawn-out sobs.

'Peter.' The thought flew through her head that Lawrence had already told him. 'What's wrong?'

He barely reacted as she sat beside him and ran her fingers through his hair. Instead, his body convulsed, as though he were having a fit. Through the tears, she thought she heard him say Lawrence's name. If he'd already spoken to Peter, given his twisted version of events, she'd have no chance.

Kath retreated to a chair, going over what she needed to tell him: the manipulation, the attempts at coercion, the emotional blackmail. She watched from the other side of the room as his body shuddered, eventually lying still. 'You awake?' she whispered. But he didn't reply. 'I need to tell you my side. Can you sit up and listen? It's important,' she said. He didn't stir. 'Please?' She rested a hand on his shoulder, but he was asleep. What she had to tell him would have to wait till morning.

Heading out to the corridor, scenarios played out in her head. *What if Peter won't listen to reason? What if no one believes me?* With Lawrence bankrolling the production, and his name above the title, too much was at stake for people to take notice of her. As she rested on the stairs, her mind turning, her body exhausted, a blast of wind, like an exhalation, shook the house. The door to Lawrence's room slowly swung open to reveal an object glinting on the floor. His award. Strange; it hadn't been there when she left. But moving closer, she couldn't quite comprehend what she was staring at – the award, so prominently positioned on the mantelpiece, displayed so that everyone could see and comment on it admiringly – appeared to be covered in blood. She crossed the threshold into his room. *What the…?*

· · ·

IN THE SPACE of fifteen minutes, Kath's life had been turned upside down.

Having stumbled across a scene of unmitigated horror, she was presented with the worst choice of her life: tell the truth about Lawrence's death or lie to protect a killer; someone she cared for deeply. Quickly making her choice, she began to take action.

Matters upstairs resolved for the time being, she returned to the hallway, tripping over the hem of the enormous cagoule she was wearing. She removed her shoes and closed Lawrence's door. Despite it being her second sighting of his body, witnessing the shroud of blood draped across him was just as horrific. Should she check for a pulse, just in case? She placed her fingers on his neck. He was dead. There was a grapefruit-sized crater where the back of his head should have been, and pulpy bits of skull and tissue lay scattered across his shoulder. On the bedcover, a single green eye stared up accusingly. Of course, he was dead.

She now had to think quickly, as any incriminating evidence needed to be destroyed. She picked up the award, but was there anything else she needed to think about? Luckily, there weren't any bloody footprints, or none that she could see, so cleaning the floor wasn't a priority. If she'd had limitless resources at her disposal, she would've done things differently: picked up his body, dragged it outside, dumped it in the sea, cleaned the room from top to bottom – made it seem like he'd disappeared of his own accord. That, however, was not an option. Lawrence's body would inevitably be found in the morning, but she reminded herself, all of them had been in and out of his room since they'd arrived, each of them leaving fingerprints. She had to believe that without the murder weapon, tracing it back to anyone specific would prove impossible.

As Kath was leaving, she spotted the Dictaphone on his bedside table – she'd watched Lawrence place it there earlier.

Picking it up, she saw it was still recording. *Fuck!* She switched it off and shoved it into the pocket of the cagoule and headed out to the barn.

All the way there, she kept telling herself: *it's your duty to sort this.*

The first thing to do was clean the award, ensure no fingerprints were left, and place it back on the mantelpiece. Vowing not to look at his body again, she turned on the tap in the barn kitchen, and scrubbed vigorously. With her other hand, she switched on the Dictaphone and tried to rewind it to the start, hoping to erase everything. But she couldn't work out how to operate it. Without warning, her own voice blasted out, odd bits of conversation between her and Lawrence from earlier that evening, followed by Peter's. She fast forwarded by mistake – each click sparking a line or two – sometimes from Peter, other times from Lawrence. Voices were raised at points, but she couldn't work out what they were talking about: *Hollywood, his Malibu home, where Peter could have stayed if he wasn't such a disappointment.* Nothing made any sense. Then, out of the darkness, came Lee's voice – not on the tape – but there in the barn.

Without time to think, she left the half-washed statuette in the sink, pulled up her hood, and rushed from the kitchen, dropping the Dictaphone in the process. Bending down, she fumbled to retrieve it; but as she grabbed it, she inadvertently pressed the eject button and the cassette slid out. Patting her hands along the floor, she knew there was no time to search for it. Everything had happened so quickly, and she could hear Lee moving behind the partition. Fearing he was about to turn the corner and catch her, she knew she needed to get out as fast as she could.

KATH SCRABBLED through the mud and rubble, scanning the floor for any sign of the cassette; the gritty floor ripped at her knees and palms, but she could cope with the pain. In the darkness, with the wind howling outside however, finding anything seemed an impossible task. At the back of her mind, it occurred to her that all of this effort might be futile, that Colin could have already discovered it. But she had to try.

Moving inch by inch across the floor, telling herself if it took all night, so be it, she heard someone call her name outside. Not once, but several times. She froze. Knowing she couldn't get caught, her priority was still to find the cassette. As the wind rose again, the creaking around her grew louder. So much wreckage. One wrong move, and the whole barn could come tumbling down. Whatever was on the tape needed to be destroyed. Otherwise, the consequences would be devastating; that's why she was risking her life, that's why she'd thumped Colin over the head.

The torchlight picked up something glistening ahead – a transparent corner of plastic, nestled behind some fallen timber. She daren't risk moving it to get to the cassette, but she reasoned that she could squeeze her hand through the final gap. She had to at least try.

The wind outside surged – a warning roar – louder than ever. A chorus of voices continued to call her name as she stretched between the broken beams, her fingers straining for the tiny object up ahead. One more inch and her fingertips touched it, dragging it back into her clasp. 'Got you!' she whispered.

At that moment, a sudden crash descended, like nothing she'd experienced before. An implosion that seemed to swallow her up, along with everything around her. The last thing she heard was Peter's voice, desperately calling her name.

62

OCTOBER 1966

Georgie sat in the snug of a bar off Piccadilly Circus, waiting for Lawrence. It was after five-thirty, and the place was beginning to fill with office workers; already, the mood was changing from one of sophisticated afternoon cocktails to something much louder and leerier. She considered suggesting a walk in St James's Park. But it was October, freezing outside, and the purple hew of sunset was descending into soft drizzly sleet, smearing the window where she sat. She supposed she could bear it a little longer.

As soon as Lawrence entered, smiling to himself in that knowing way, she regretted agreeing to meet. As he looked around for her, she thought about slipping out the side door, but before she knew it, he was beside her, leaning over, kissing her on the lips. 'Lawrence! Behave,' she scolded, checking that no one had noticed.

'What do you fancy?' he asked, stroking her arm. 'Though I see you've started without me.' He was referring to the empty glass she was clutching onto.

She didn't want another drink, but to be polite, she said, 'Another sherry?'

'Lush!' He pecked her on the cheek. 'I'll only be a minute – don't go anywhere.'

And he was off, his expensive aftershave lingering in the air, his tailored jacket discarded beside her; as if their meeting was a common occurrence.

She watched him at the bar, waving his wallet, catching the attention of the barman, chatting to him as though they were best buddies, whilst others waited in vain to get served. Always at the head of the queue, his needs invariably met before anyone else's. Nothing ever changed.

On his return, they clinked glasses. She took one sip of the sherry and set it aside. After that, she told herself, she wouldn't drink any more. She needed her wits about her, because she knew Lawrence had contacted her for one reason only.

'How's Jim?' he asked, lighting up. 'Done any work recently?'

Why start with that? He knew well enough how Jim struggled, unlike her and Lawrence, who'd had it easy after *Eros*. Jim was a victim of his own success – majestic as his performance was, it seemed to stay too long in people's minds. That was her analysis. Perhaps there was a more mundane reason, but whatever it was, the man she loved had been working in a bakery for the past eighteen months whilst she'd been busy doing stage and radio work, even some TV. Lawrence, on the other hand, had starred in another Broadway show, been nominated for yet more awards, and was about to make his first film in Hollywood. 'Don't be a bastard.' She grabbed his packet of cigarettes and lit one for herself.

'You'd find it odd if I didn't ask.'

He was right. Lawrence and Jim were like brothers – but the type who never spoke to each other. After Jim ended the ménage à trois – proclaiming that he felt the arrangement had run its course, explaining his desired monogamy – both men had retreated from each other. Shame? Embarrassment?

Resentment? Who knew? Jim didn't speak about it much – he'd once mentioned the aspects of those days he missed, but never specified which parts.

'You look incredible.' Lawrence's gaze was fixed on her breasts, which she'd deliberately covered up. 'Pity you're dressed like a middle-aged hausfrau.'

'Oh, shut up and drink your whisky.'

They skirted around things for the best part of an hour. But after discussing recent projects, the latest theatre gossip, and downing two more rounds, they found themselves staring at each other in the same famished way they always did.

She hated herself for finding him attractive. Beyond an initial acknowledgement, she typically lay little store by looks. But Lawrence was different. Despite having had sex with him countless times, she still fantasised about him. And it wasn't something she could discuss with Jim – not that he'd be jealous, but he would be hurt. So, occasionally, she allowed herself the memory of his body: its weight and his controlled and insistent thrusts, his eyes locking on hers as she orgasmed.

'I'd like to spend the night with you. There. I've said it. My cards are on the table. And I've something special for you. A friend of mine dropped off a little present today. You still use, I take it?'

She gathered her bag and coat and stood. Despite meeting up half a dozen times in secret over the past three years, she'd made it clear she was done with it. 'No Lawrence ... don't... I can't do this anymore.'

'Oh, sit down and stop being a prude.' He gestured to the barman to bring another round of drinks. 'What has suburban life done to you?'

'We're in Fulham, for God's sake.'

'Exactly. The burbs. Fucking grim.'

She refused to argue with him when he was like this. 'I'm expected home.'

'I don't know by whom.' He grabbed another cigarette and lit it. 'Jim's at an audition in Leeds, isn't he? He's staying overnight before heading to Bristol for another one in the morning, so by my reckoning he'll not be back home until tomorrow evening.'

'How did you…?' She sat back, grabbed the packet of cigarettes away from him, and lit one for herself.

He tapped his nose. 'I've spies everywhere. Plus, I called him last week. Didn't he say?'

Jim hadn't. '*You* organised both those auditions, didn't you?'

'What else are friends for?'

She blew smoke in his face. His self-satisfied look was one she'd grown to hate. 'Stay away from us, Lawrence.'

He shook his head, his gaze firmly fixed on her. 'No can do.'

'He's my husband. Remember? Whom I love very much. And you, Lawrence Delaney, with your flashy smile and your bags full of money, don't hold a candle to him.'

'Oh, I know that.' He knocked back the whisky the barman had brought over.

Once again, she picked up her bag and coat, readying herself to go. This time, however, he took hold of her wrist. Running his fingers up and down her arm, he lingered over the track marks beneath her blouse. He hummed a tune they'd sung together during rehearsals. A baritone, his voice was rich and pure. 'Sing along.'

'Why me, Lawrence? When you can have any woman you want?'

He shrugged. 'Habit?' He pulled softly at her hand, trying to coax her back. 'We both have one of those, don't we?' he said, before quickly adding, 'only teasing.'

She took out her purse and laid money on the table. 'For my drinks.'

'He'll never know. For old time's sake? What do you say? That little present's got your name all over it.'

She hadn't used in over nine months. A secret code – a small circle marked in her diary – was pencilled in each day at the top left-hand corner. *Today's a new day,* she'd tell herself.

Picking up her sherry, she gulped the whole of it down. 'I'm sad it's come to this.'

'Is that a yes?' he asked, collecting her coins and stuffing them in his pocket.

She met his eyes, hungry and dissatisfied. One last time and after that, she wouldn't have to see him again. She knew he was moving to America, where there'd be other distractions. Soon, he'd barely remember her. 'Never again – you need to promise.'

'Suits me.' He threw his jacket on. 'I've a room booked at the usual place.'

63

A s he emerged blinking from their bedroom, Lee seized Colin's arm. 'I think I've pieced something together.'

'Throw on some clothes and come with me. Kath's missing.' Colin said, following the others downstairs.

Outside, the wind was fiercer than it had been all day. Ferocious waves boomed against the shore, echoing in the darkness, as all around, branches were cracking and falling as if the island was being torn to pieces.

'I can't remember when I last saw her,' Peter was shouting, struggling to run ahead. 'It's been hours.'

Georgie held onto him. 'Don't worry, we'll find her.' She was trying to calm him, but it wasn't working. She shouted to Colin, who was pointing the way with a torch. 'Why the barn? She could be anywhere.'

'I doubt it,' he cried.

Lee caught up with Colin. 'I've worked something out – you need to listen.'

'Tell me.' He was keeping as close to the others as he could. With tensions high, he didn't want to miss any of the conversation, any possible slip-ups or clues.

'It was Lawrence and Peter who were arguing on the tape,'

Lee whispered. 'That's what confused me. It sounded like Lawrence was arguing with himself. But after my conversation with Peter in the kitchen, it occurred to me how similar they sound. Not their accents exactly, but the tone of their voices.'

Colin took in the information, but there were more important things to deal with first.

Jim arrived at the barn first. Waving his torch across the ground, he said, 'Look, there's fresh footprints by the door.'

Georgie and Peter shouted Kath's name, but the wind carried their voices off in the other direction.

'This is hopeless.' The rain lashing against him, Colin pushed past to join Jim at the barn door. 'I'm going in.'

'No way – it's not safe.' Lee grabbed hold of Colin. 'It's too dangerous. Please.'

Colin felt Lee's entire body press into his. But if he didn't go in, who would? 'Jim, give me your torch. It's more powerful.'

Inside the collapsing barn, it was worse than he'd anticipated. The torch beam revealed a maze of splintered wood – a wreck of horizontals and verticals – all piled on top of each other, creating angled, jagged structures that appeared impenetrable. There was no sign of Kath.

He called her name, hoping for some response and a possible direction he could steer towards. But with the rain beating down and the wind howling, it was impossible to discern any reply. Dropping to his knees, he shone the torch across the ground, and the beam illuminated a muddy handprint under the debris.

Clenching the torch between his teeth, his belly flat on the ground, he propelled himself forward inch by inch, using his elbows. The floor was a mushy pulp of earth and splintered wood, but there was a route of sorts through the void, created by the fallen roof. His spirits sank though, as the space narrowed, and an enormous sheet of metal blocked the way ahead. He paused to catch his breath, taking in the suffocating aroma of the mud, feeling the grit sticking to the back of his throat.

If Kath was under this, she couldn't survive; no one could. This was a recovery, not a rescue. Outside, there were people who loved her – waiting, hoping – and so he needed to keep going, give it all he had, but it felt futile.

Reversing, Colin attempted a different route. He hoped he was still heading towards the kitchen, which was the one part of the barn that had previously seemed intact. Or rather, where he imagined it had once been. If his theory was right, Kath had returned for one reason only: to retrieve the cassette. And if she had, there was little doubt she'd already tried to find it. It all fitted: Kath was the person in the orange cagoule who Lee had seen running from the barn after trying to clean the murder weapon; and it was Kath who'd gone back to the barn and hit him over the head when their paths crossed.

But certain things still didn't fit. If Kath had murdered Lawrence, why was there a second bloodstained waterproof, and why, as Lee suggested, had Peter been on the tape arguing with Lawrence? Was she Peter's accomplice?

Colin had lost his bearings. With the torch battery failing and visibility almost at zero, he realised he could be crawling around in circles. There was a lull in the wind. Outside, he could hear the others calling Kath's name. He called out too but was met with an eerie silence.

If Peter had killed Lawrence, he must have confessed to Kath. Therefore, it made sense she would try to protect him. An argument suggested it had happened in the heat of the moment; Peter was immature, impulsive, in that respect your typical killer. But what could have driven him to smash Lawrence over the head? Not once, but several times, to ensure the life was sucked out of him. Maybe Richard was correct, and it was a crime of passion after all.

Despite the cold, a sweat had formed on his forehead. He stopped to take stock of the situation, but he was overwhelmed by a sense of claustrophobia. Crawling around under tonnes of fragile rubble, he was essentially on a death mission. One wrong move, and his life would be snuffed out in the blink of an eye. He felt the panic rise and get inside his head. Even if he found Kath alive, how would he get her out?

In the pitch black, Lee's face flashed before him: what they had together, what they meant to each other. He couldn't lose that. He'd find a way back to Lee whatever the cost.

Ahead, as he was about to give up hope, turn around, find a way back through the rubble, the torch beam lit a bright triangle of yellow, and a hand, clenched and muddied.

At last, a glimmer of hope.

64

SIX MONTHS AGO

'He's my son, isn't he?'

Lawrence sat across from her at a table laid for dinner; his face improbably youthful, as though the last twenty-five years had never happened. But for Georgie, they had. In those years directly after the play, recovery from addiction had become a lifetime's commitment, despite Lawrence's attempts to derail her with his unwanted appearances, waving a bag of goodies in front of her. She'd hated him for it – the manipulation, the implication he held power over her because of her illness. Pathetic. But hating him had been useless. Only she had the power to get herself clean. And she had. That night in Piccadilly, over twenty-five years ago, was the final time she'd used.

No surreptitious assignation in a West End pub now. This time, they were meeting in Lawrence's penthouse suite overlooking Green Park. She caught her reflection in the mirror and noted the flattering lighting. There was no doubt she was a woman in her fifties; a few more wrinkles around the eyes than she might want, but her cheekbones were still intact. Looking over at Lawrence however, she wondered how time could tell its story on her face and not his. All without a hint of plastic surgery – just good, clean, expensive living. And yet, at the same time, it was blank – an absence of being – as though he hadn't lived at all.

'When I said I didn't want to see you again, I meant it.'

'And yet here we are again.' He reached out for her hand, but she quickly withdrew it. 'So, Peter?'

It was meaningless to her whether he was Peter's father or not. Beyond a certain point, the details of that night were hazy. Yes, she admitted to sleeping with him, but as far as she was concerned, it was in the past and could stay there. The fact that Peter was born nine months later was of no relevance. Jim was his father, and that was that. He'd raised him, taught him values, kept their family together through all its ups and downs. How dare Lawrence try to interfere!

'I won't discuss Peter.'

He leaned towards her, his eyes catching fire in the candlelight. 'I want a paternity test.'

'No way.' Outside, far below on the street, a heavy truck passed, causing the mirror to shudder. Her reflection trembled for a second before settling.

'For the first few weeks I'd no idea. On set, he seemed like any other eager to please young actor. My producer Melanie happened to mention who his parents were – that's when the penny began to drop. And the more time I spent with him, the more suspicious I became. A quick look at his CV told me the rest. From his date of birth, it didn't take an idiot to work out the lie. Besides, anyone can see I'm his father. Christ, he has all my features.'

His body was stiff, alert, imagining he held all the best cards – but for an actor, he made a lousy poker player. The sanctimonious tone annoyed her, but maybe he'd a right to be angry. Ultimately though, she didn't care. Like everything else in Lawrence's life, fatherhood would have been cast aside as soon he became bored with it. Through the tabloids, she'd seen how he lived his life: the countless photos with an ever-changing parade of supermodels, his constant, aching smile set against a backdrop of red carpets. She regretted nothing.

'How happy are you, Lawrence?'

He narrowed his gaze, his mouth curling into a snarl. Swirling his whisky and ice three times, he took a sip and glowered. 'Very.'

'Then carry on as you are. It was what, one lousy fuck a quarter of a century ago?'

'He's *my* son,' he insisted. 'And you deliberately kept him from me. What sort of person does that?' He sat back, his expression darkening. 'I deserve that boy – I deserve *my son* – in my life.' His hand trembled as he lay down his glass.

'Is this about me?' Once again, he swirled his glass three times before sipping, the shine fading from his eyes, leaving nothing behind but emptiness. 'It is, isn't it? Christ, Lawrence!'

There was a knock at the door, and his personal assistant appeared from the adjoining room. 'Your entrées are here, Mr Delaney. Shall I get the waiter to bring them in?'

'If I wanted my entrée now, I would have said, don't you think? Now fuck off and don't dare disturb me again.' Avoiding Georgie's eyes, Lawrence swirled and sipped again. 'This is not about you at all, Georgie. The world no longer revolves around you like it used to.' Sweat had formed on his forehead. He wiped it with a napkin.

She stared at him, waiting ten, fifteen, twenty seconds before he finally looked at her. 'But this *is* about me, isn't it? Peter's just the excuse.'

He threw back the rest of his drink, banging the glass on the table. Crossing to the sideboard, he poured another large whisky from the decanter and added fresh ice, before returning to the table. 'Here's my proposal.' The light was back in his eyes and suddenly, she saw the young man she'd met all those years ago – full of energy, full of optimism. 'Come and live with me.' He grabbed her hands, forcing his sweaty fingers between hers. 'I promise you'll want for nothing,' he continued, tightening his grip. 'If you do that, I'll never mention Peter's paternity again.'

Faced with his delusions, Georgie averted her gaze. Whatever difficulties there'd been in her marriage, it was filled with care and devotion. It had taken her years to fully appreciate those qualities. Now, she couldn't imagine life without them; they'd been too hard-earned. 'I'm sorry Lawrence. I really am. I love Jim. You know that. You've always known that.' She wrestled her fingers free.

As he lifted the glass to his mouth, some whisky spilled down his shirt. 'Shit!'

Georgie cackled. 'Look at the state of you, you old lush. Here, take my napkin.'

'It's these fucking tumblers,' he snapped, dabbing at the stains.

She searched again for the young man in his face, but he was gone. How innocent they'd been: with all the energy of youth and endless dreams. She took out a cigarette. 'Is it OK to...?'

'I'll join you.' He grabbed a cigarette and placed it in his mouth. Lighting it from the candle, his eyes flickered. 'He hates Jim,' he said, exhaling smoke from his nostrils.

She wasn't expecting this. 'What makes you say that?'

'He told me himself. Said they weren't on the same wavelength.'

'At a certain stage, all sons say that about their fathers,' she replied, not rising to his bait. It was true they didn't see eye to eye on many things. Growing up, Peter was wild, reckless, unwilling to recognise the parameters Jim and Georgie set. But while he never took it out on her, Jim had increasingly become his punch bag, unable to do anything right. And when Peter became an actor, his father's apparent failure in the business became a further rod to beat him with.

'*I'm* his father.' Lawrence banged his hand against the table and held his forehead, as though attempting to keep this thought in place. 'I want him to know me for who I am. Is that too much to ask?'

'No Lawrence, you want what Jim has. First, you took his career. Then you tried to take me. Fucking me on the sly and trying to keep me addicted was your way of achieving that. This is my life you're playing with. And it's got to stop. You don't control the narrative on this one. Am I clear? For too long, you've got away telling others the story of your life, letting others believe every idea or success was all down to you. A myth of your own making. But give it a good hard blow and it evaporates.' She stubbed out her cigarette, waiting for him to disagree. But he didn't. Instead, he leaned back in his chair, closing his eyes, as though wishing she would vanish. Momentarily, she recalled the tenderness the three of them once shared: the fun, the laughter, the lovemaking. All gone. 'Lawrence?'

With his hand, he waved her away, like some old king dismissing a barren queen who no longer served any purpose. 'Go!'

'Tell me you won't repeat any of this. Not to Peter, not to Jim, not to anyone? Please.' She moved to the seat beside him, but he drew away, his eyes firmly shut. 'Raking over the past,' she said, 'you know that no good can come of it. Jim didn't deserve what we did to him, but we've moved on. I'm not the same person, and I don't think you are either.'

After gathering her things to leave, she crossed the room and paused at the door. 'Peter's a young man who needs the right kind of guidance. He has the potential to make a good life for himself, to make the right choices. Slowly, he's getting there. If you say anything about this to him, I won't be responsible for my actions.' She stood, waiting for him to open his eyes, rise from the chair, hug her, weep for their missed years together; do something, anything that might end all the bitterness. But he didn't. Instead, he remained in repose, his face displaying no more expression than a death-mask.

65

Colin struggled through the labyrinth of broken branches and splintered beams, dragging Kath's body alongside him. The last section proved impossible to manoeuvre and he had to leave her lying in the muddy ground, barely breathing. Crawling to the barn entrance, a hand reached in and pulled him free of the wreckage.

He lay on his back, gasping for air, incapable of speaking, unable to open his eyes, which were filled with grit. Though the rain and wind thrashed around him, he felt safe. Voices bombarded him with questions: *Where's Kath? Is she in there? Should I go in?* He tried to respond, but he'd no energy.

'Breathe,' Lee was saying. Not for the first time, he was there by his side, holding his hand, calming him. What would he do without him? 'Take your time.'

Colin blinked, and the blurred outlines of the others appeared as he wiped the mud from his eyes. 'I need, I need...' His body felt like he'd been stripped naked and thrown out into the cold. 'Help,' he continued. 'Kath's hurt.'

A coat was placed around him. Hands helped him to his feet. His legs wobbled as he struggled to stay upright.

'Steady,' Lee said. The comfort of his voice. The care. It overwhelmed him.

'Thank you,' he croaked. 'But I'm fine.' Feet firmly on the ground, he stood up straight.

Peter's voice emerged from the darkness. Shining a torch directly into Colin's face, he asked, 'What do you mean hurt?'

'She's out cold; but she's breathing,' he explained, fearful that the truth was far graver.

'Why'd you come out without her?' Peter queried, slipping in the mud as he stepped closer.

'Steady!' Grasping his shoulder, Jim averted Peter's fall. 'Give Colin a chance to speak.'

When Colin had discovered her, he felt sure she was dead. At first, he couldn't detect a pulse. When he finally found one, it was very weak; she was barely alive. 'I need to go back in. But I need one of you to help me.'

Peter immediately stepped forward. 'I'll do it.'

Georgie grabbed hold of him. 'Darling, I'm begging you, don't.'

'But she's *my* girlfriend.'

'There must be another way,' Georgie pleaded.

'I'll go,' Jim said. 'You stay here, look after your mum.'

'It's my responsibility.'

'Son, let me do this for you.'

Peter eventually conceded, stepping back to be beside his mother.

'Decided?' asked Colin.

'Decided,' Jim said.

Colin instructed Jim to enter the barn, lie sideways on the ground and keep the torch beam focused on him. 'It'll be dark. Muddy too. I'll be ahead of you but hold onto my belt and when I say "Pull", pull with all your might. It'll take both our strength to get her out of there.'

Behind Peter and Georgie, Richard appeared, ghost-like, standing soaked in his dressing-gown.

'So, this is where the fun's at?' Colin heard him say. 'What's all the fuss?'

'I need the rest of you to stand well back,' shouted Colin. 'The front of this could go at any second.' From the corner of his eye, he saw Lee look away as he re-entered the barn.

There was little time. Kath lay only feet from the entrance, but he'd need to wrench her body around a narrow gap created by the fallen pine. Jim held onto his belt, his grip firm and reliable. 'Whatever you do, don't let go.'

'I won't.'

Using a broken slate as a shovel, he attempted to make more room by digging downwards: every extra millimetre would help. Extending his arms, he grabbed hold of Kath's shoulders and gripped under her arms. 'I've got her,' he called to Jim. 'Now, pull!'

Kath's limp body was a dead weight, and his hands slipped from beneath her. 'Let me try again,' he yelled, wrapping both arms around her chest and locking his fingers together. 'Pull!' he shouted again.

'She's moving,' Jim cried.

'Thank God!' Colin yelled back, relieved to be past the first hurdle.

The next part, getting her past the tree trunk, was going to be more difficult. If he could get her head through first, he hoped the rest of her body would follow.

His worst fears were realised. It was no good; her shoulder immediately got stuck. He needed to devise another way of getting her out. 'This isn't working, Jim. I need you to be where I am, while I crawl through and push. We'll manoeuvre her together. Can you do that?'

'Yes.'

'I need all your strength. But don't touch anything. Not even for leverage. We don't want the whole barn coming down on top of us.'

Pushing Kath's shoulder back, he wriggled through the

gap to the other side. Though she was still breathing, her skin felt horribly cold. There was no time to waste. 'If this doesn't work, I don't know what else will,' he told Jim. 'See where the gap's slightly higher here?' Carefully, he dragged Kath towards it. 'Can you take hold? While I push, I need you to pull her. But we need to twist at the same time. Does that make sense?'

'Yes. No problem,' Jim replied.

Oblivious to everything else, they concentrated, easing Kath through the tiny gap inch by inch to safety. Despite Colin's concerns, their efforts – slow and steady – proved successful. At the final stage, Colin scrambled over her, helping Jim to drag her outside.

Face down, he collapsed, his sweat mingling with the rain and the mud. 'We did it,' he said.

'She's still alive.' Jim squeezed his hand. 'Well done.'

IN SILENCE, the six of them carried Kath back to the house, their faces glowing in the darkness, the storm unable to put them off their stride. Colin wondered what they were each thinking? That Kath was the murderer? Or that she knew the identity of the killer? At the very least, they must have wondered why she'd put her life in danger.

Entering the house, they lay her gently on the chaise in the hallway. A cacophony of voices spoke over one another before Richard's rose above them all. 'Blankets, towels, first-aid kit. This girl might not last the night. Quick!' he shouted, as the others scattered to search. Carefully removing her wet clothes, he used the towel Lee passed to him to dry her. 'She's definitely suffered a head injury. How she fares will depend on how much trauma there's been. If it's a fracture, she could be up and about by morning. But if there's internal bleeding, there might be nothing we can do. And by the time someone gets here, it could be too late.'

'How do you know all this?' Colin asked.

'Three years of medicine darling, before falling prey to Mistress Theatre. My parents, God rest their souls, never forgave me.'

'Will she survive?' Georgie asked, handing Richard a blanket.

'Let's get her more stable before we think about that.' As he tucked the blanket around Kath, Peter and Jim returned with a first-aid kit and bandages. 'Thanks.' At that moment, the lights flickered and hissed. 'Please God, not now!' Richard groaned. Seemingly in response, they burst back to full brightness. 'We'll keep her here for now while I try and determine just how bad she is.'

Peter, who'd said nothing since Kath's rescue, slumped heavily into a chair.

'Are you OK?' Lee asked.

He shook his head and opened his mouth to speak, but no words came out. Both Georgie and Jim huddled around him, whispering not to worry, that everything would be fine.

Colin signalled to Lee he needed to chat in private. He led him into the dining room and closed the door. From his pocket, he produced a small plastic object: the cassette. 'You and I need to search this place while they're all distracted. There's a Dictaphone to find.' He checked the hallway was clear. 'We should start upstairs.'

66

K ath's bedroom was somewhat at odds with her personality: the bed was made, the sheets were sharply tucked in on all sides, and a suitcase lay squarely on a chair, its contents neatly folded. A pair of tights draped across the door handle and a pair of shoes placed beside the chest of drawers, were the only indications she'd used the room at all.

'She could easily have thrown the Dictaphone and Lawrence's award into the sea,' Lee said. 'That's what I'd have done.'

Colin scanned the room, working out where to begin. 'We still need to search the place. I'll start here – you start over by the window.'

Together, they methodically worked around the room, looking under the mattress, inside drawers, the lining of the suitcase, the wardrobe. Colin thought it unlikely she'd stash evidence in her own room, but he had to be sure. She'd been careful all along, not quite a full step ahead of him, more like half. Enough to give her the advantage. Disposing of evidence had clearly been top of her list.

Finding her lying unconscious in the barn, her arm outstretched, her fist clenched around the small cassette, he understood the danger she'd placed herself in. To take such a risk suggested its importance.

'I can't find anything. I'll try the bathroom,' Lee whispered, creeping across the carpet, terrified those downstairs might hear.

'Check the cistern.' Colin looked around the door to ensure Lee was doing a thorough search. He needn't have worried. The lid was already off, and he was fiddling about inside with his hands.

Lee came back out. 'There's nothing here.'

'We need to check the other rooms.'

'Shouldn't we call it quits, wait till morning? No one else knows we have the cassette.'

'We need to keep searching,' Colin said, giving the room a final once-over. If there was evidence on the tape, it could lead to a confession. Finding the Dictaphone, being able to play it back, might enable him to wrap things up before the big guns arrived. And if Kath was working with a second person, what's to say they weren't trying to destroy evidence too. He couldn't take any more chances.

'You're the boss.' Lee cracked open the door to check the corridor was clear. 'They're still downstairs. For now.'

'Then we'll need to be quick, won't we?' Colin pointed to Peter's room.

'Why would she take the chance and hide evidence in someone else's room?' Lee asked.

'Why would she do any of this?'

Lee stood with his back to the door. 'Do you think she's that devious?'

'I wouldn't be surprised if she'd tiptoed into our room and stashed it there. Come on, we're wasting time.'

Careful not to make a sound, they crossed to Peter's room.

'You stay outside and knock on the door if you think someone's coming. Maybe try and distract them, lead them back downstairs. OK?'

Lee nodded.

Colin surveyed Peter's bedroom. Unlike Kath's, the place was a mess: the bed unmade; clothes, shoes and towels scattered across the floor; drawers pulled halfway out. He'd seen tidier crime scenes.

He'd always admired the old-school officers at the Met, with their mantra to *leave no stone unturned*. They knew how to read a room: an art form he'd been keen to master. There were tell-tale signs: angles of furniture that didn't seem quite right; dents in a carpet where a chair had been moved; or the imprint left on a dusty shelf where an object had been taken. If you knew where and how to look, you could track a person's movements through a space.

Adrenalin pumping, Colin focused on the search. Feeling his way along curtain fabric, under the base of the bed, the mattress, the pillows, all were examined meticulously, but to no avail. If the Dictaphone or the award were there, they'd been carefully hidden. Even in the bathroom, which was as much of a bombsite as the bedroom, nothing ultimately appeared out of place. The room was clean. Well, nothing a good vacuum couldn't fix.

He slipped out to the corridor to find Lee waiting at the top of the stairs. Colin nodded towards Jim and Georgie's room. Lee mouthed, 'Are you sure?' But Colin already had the door open.

Inside, both bedside lights were switched on. The fire crackled in the background, and the covers on the bed were turned down, waiting patiently for its occupants; the room felt cosy, welcoming. Colin caught his reflection in the mirror above the fireplace. Soiled with dirt, his face looked grubby and anxious.

After checking the wardrobe, he moved over to a large chest of drawers. Starting at the top, he pulled out each drawer, sifting through its contents, feeling around the sides. The bottom drawer was stuck; with a brisk tug, he yanked it free, only to find it empty. As he placed it back on its side, his fingers felt something. He flipped it over. Bingo! A brown A5 envelope had been taped underneath, Lawrence's name and address clearly printed on the front. Folding it in half, he stuffed it down the back of his jeans.

A quick knock at the door was followed seconds later by the sound of voices coming up the stairs. Colin shoved the drawer back in place and dashed out into the corridor, closing the door behind him.

67

W ith a pained expression, Lee muttered 'Sorry' to Colin.

Arriving at the top of the stairs, Georgie caught him as he emerged from her room. 'What the hell do you think you're doing?' she demanded.

'My job,' Colin quickly replied, his outward calm belying the adrenalin rushing through his body.

'While Kath's lying down there, barely alive, you decide to go sneaking around?' she shouted. 'My son was right all along.'

Conscious of the envelope stuffed down his jeans, he was in no mood to enter into a debate with her.

Thankfully, Lee stepped in. 'If you want to blame someone, blame me. I said it was fine. Technically, this is still a place of work and I'm in charge.'

Peter came bounding up the stairs, with Jim close behind. 'Am I hearing right?' His voice was unsteady, on edge. 'Explain what you were doing,' he yelled, squaring up to Colin.

Colin stood resolute. 'You seem to be forgetting that someone's been murdered.'

'We're not forgetting,' Jim said, 'but why the focus on us? For all we know, you had a motive to kill Lawrence. Lee too.'

'And not to mention Jackie Adamson,' Georgie added.

Colin decided to gamble. Taking the cassette from his pocket, he asked, 'Then why was Kath searching for this?'

'What the hell's that?' Jim stepped closer to inspect.

'Lawrence had a habit of recording his conversations,' Colin explained. 'Whether for protection, security, who knows? The fact is, Kath risked her life trying to retrieve this.'

Georgie wasn't convinced. 'Why go snooping in my room?' she asked.

'Lee saw someone, who had been in possession of the Dictaphone, running from the barn to the house on the night of Lawrence's murder. I believe that person was Kath. Surprised by Lee, she panicked and dropped the cassette, but potentially still had the Dictaphone with her. If she did, it's reasonable to imagine she hid it somewhere in the house. It's not in her room, so that's why I need to search yours.'

'You think Kath's responsible?' Peter laughed. 'How? Or even why? It's absurd.'

There was no going back. Colin needed to reveal what he knew. 'Lawrence had been sexually harassing Kath for months.' Peter let out a gasp, as if he'd been punched in the gut. 'It started during the film you made together.'

'Bullshit!' he cried, pushing past his mother. 'Think she wouldn't have told me?'

'She said this to you?' Georgie asked, her expression changing from anger to concern, as though a mask had been lifted.

'Yes,' Colin said. 'A few hours ago.'

'How did she seem?' Jim asked. Like Georgie, his body language had softened.

'Preoccupied. Distressed.' He wasn't going to sugar-coat her state of mind. It was the truth after all.

Peter scowled. 'And you just let her go? What a fuckwit!' Georgie grabbed hold of him, doing her best to rein him in.

'I'd no idea she'd go to the barn,' Colin continued. 'If I had, I wouldn't have let her.'

Georgie stared through the tall staircase window, out into the darkness. Gripping the balustrade, she said, 'How do we know you're telling the truth?'

'When she wakes, she can tell you herself – that Lawrence pursued her aggressively for several months, that she tried her best to put him off, and then he stopped. Only it seems he hadn't.'

'Nah, this doesn't sound right.' Peter broke free from Georgie. 'He's making this up. He's trying to mess with us. Lawrence wouldn't do that.'

'Lee's company will benefit from Lawrence's death, won't they?' Georgie held onto her arms, her fingers digging into her flesh. 'Jim, you know about all that legal stuff. What I'm saying is right, isn't it?'

'I don't see the relevance.' Colin sensed Lee beside him, his hackles rising.

'Georgie does have a point,' Jim said. 'That's a clear motive.

'Colin knows this,' snapped Lee. 'And like everything else, it'll be investigated by the proper authorities; I've nothing to hide.'

'We're all in the same boat,' Georgie stated, fixing her eyes on both of them.

Colin pointed out the window. 'Well, it looks like it might be answered for us sooner than we thought. The storm's dying down.'

As the clouds parted, the noise from the storm abated: the sound of the rain reduced to a pitter-patter, the growl of the wind now a mere whisper.

'All I ask is that you all remain in the house,' Colin said.

'We'll pick things up again in the morning – work out the best way to get word to the mainland. But my best advice is to get some sleep. Things might look different in the morning.'

68

Colin dragged Lee into their bedroom, locking the door behind them. From the back of his jeans, he pulled out the envelope. 'This may be the smoking gun.' He held it up. 'Look, addressed to Lawrence. Hidden in Jim and Georgie's room.'

'Seriously?' Lee angled himself to get a better look.

The envelope had already been ripped open. 'I need to see what's inside,' Colin whispered, aware there may be eavesdroppers. 'Pass me that pair of gloves.'

'There you go.' Lee handed him a pair of calfskin gloves he'd given to him as a birthday present. 'Now, take a second. Breathe. Think.'

'I don't need to think. I can feel it,' he said. 'This could change everything.'

'I hope you're right.'

'Peter's our man. You saw how he was. The guy's on a knife edge – I can see the signs. One wrong move back there and it could have turned violent.'

'But it didn't,' Lee reminded him. 'Don't jump to conclusions. It could easily be he's upset about Kath.'

Colin's hands were trembling; he couldn't wait any longer.

'Here goes.' He drew out a sheet of crisp white paper, unfolded it and read through the details. He scanned it a couple of times, ensuring he understood. 'It's the results of a paternity test.'

'Let's see.' Lee read through the contents. 'Wow! So is this why that old bastard had me arrange a medical for Peter weeks after he'd already signed his contract?'

69

Colin waited until everyone had gone to bed before knocking gently on Richard's door. He prised it open a few inches and a pool of light fell across the floor of the corridor. Though it was after three, Richard was still awake. 'Is the coast clear?'

'No need to be so respectful,' Richard bellowed. 'Are you coming in or not?'

The door swung open to reveal him relaxed, book perched in hand, sitting by the window.

'What a lovely surprise. I thought the grim reaper had finally come calling.'

'Sorry, I hoped you'd still be awake.' Colin closed the door behind him and looked over at Kath lying in the bed. She seemed settled, peaceful. 'I see they got her safely upstairs. How is she?'

'Her temperature's down, but she still hasn't woken. I said I'd sit with her overnight,' Richard replied.

Standing in the centre of the room, Colin suddenly felt like an ingénue waiting to audition before the maestro. From what Lee had told him, people feared and respected Richard in equal measure. In his silk pyjamas, propped up with cushions in the leather armchair, the glow from the open fire gave him a regal air. He even looked healthier than earlier. Not exactly bright-eyed and bushy-tailed, but his eyes were alive. 'I need your permission to do something,' Colin confessed.

'That would be a first. Come, sit down.' He pulled one of the many cushions from behind him and threw it on the adjoining armchair. 'I promise I don't bite.'

Despite Richard having barricaded himself inside the room most of the previous day with a crateful of alcohol, the room smelt fresh. The window was open, and a light breeze flowed through it. 'How are you doing?' He sunk back into the chair.

'If you're asking if I've had a drink, the answer is no. The last time alcohol touched these lips was...' He looked at his watch. 'Well, a few hours ago at least.'

'Well done.' Colin smiled.

'Ask me in an hour and it might be a whole different ball game. We'll see. One step at a time, that's what they say. Anyway, what can I do for you?'

'I need to search your room to check whether Lawrence's Dictaphone or his award are here.' Though he'd not eliminated Richard entirely as a suspect, the odds against him being the killer had lengthened with the discovery of Lawrence's letter.

'Of course. Please be my guest. But to my knowledge, Kath was only in here once prior to tonight.'

Under Richard's watchful gaze, Colin checked the room, being as delicate and careful as he could. Each drawer was scrutinised inside and out for anything suspicious. The wardrobe was similarly inspected, but there was only one shirt hanging in it. He noticed Richard hadn't fully unpacked. 'May I?' He indicated the larger of Richard's suitcases, which sat half-open in a corner of the room.

'Of course.' Richard seemed embarrassed. 'Blame my years of touring – one night here, one night there.'

Colin pulled the suitcase into the middle of the room and unfolded it. Packed precisely, clothes had been rolled into little balls and stuffed beside each other, like multi-coloured pebbles on a beach.

'It's my special technique,' Richard said, 'taught to me years ago by the prettiest trolley-dolly.'

Unrolling each item carefully, Colin placed them back exactly as he'd found them.

'There's no need to be so considerate. Honestly, just stuff them in.'

'It's no trouble.' After completing one side of the suitcase, Colin unzipped the other. This was not as neat. Pulling out three jumpers, his attention was drawn to a toilet-bag, which appeared to have been stuffed underneath. He glanced through to Richard's en suite. 'Did you unpack your toiletries?'

'Now, that I did do. There's nothing worse than scrambling around looking for your toothbrush first thing in the morning.'

Colin held up the toilet-bag. 'What about this? It seems to be full.'

Richard peered over. 'That's strange. I could swear I'd put that in the bathroom. I remember emptying it. See for yourself – everything's on the shelf over the sink.'

Colin carefully unzipped the bag.

'Have you found something?' Richard joined him, peering over his shoulder.

Inside was filled with tissues. 'Did you do this, by any chance?'

Richard shook his head. 'I can't say one hundred percent, but I've no memory of doing it.'

Colin unfurled the tissues. Hidden within the folds was what he'd been searching for. He lifted it out, pieces of plastic falling to the carpet as he did so: Lawrence's Dictaphone, smashed.

'Not what you hoped to find?'

Colin returned the broken pieces and the tissues into the bag. 'Sorry Richard, I'll have to take this as evidence.'

'No worries, my dear. It's only some faux leather thing from Boots.'

'You said Kath had been in the room yesterday?'

Richard lowered his voice. 'I woke and there she was, sitting at the bottom of my bed. Could have been there for hours. I was out cold.'

Holding onto the toilet-bag, Colin asked, 'Can I take a plastic bag to put this in?'

Richard nodded.

'Thanks.'

'Don't tell me you think our delightful young Kath killed Lawrence?' Richard eyed him as if Colin himself was under suspicion.

Discussing her as she lay injured didn't seem right. 'I need to put this somewhere safe.'

As Colin went to leave, Richard asked, 'Colin, I know I'm an old drunk – put me on a witness stand and I'd buckle – but there's something I think I should tell you.'

'Go ahead. Honestly, anything might be helpful, even if it makes no sense.'

'Well, in that case I've two things which may or may not. 'You see, I've wondered why Kath took this job. On the film she made with Lawrence, they didn't get on. I only know this because I'm a friend of the producer. Lovely woman but would have defended Goebbels if he was investing in one of her projects. Got a loose tongue too, so when I told her I was going to be working with them both, she was surprised to say the least.'

'This woman – would she verify this?'

'She knew what Lawrence was like and will talk if pushed. Deep down, she's a good person; it just takes a bit of digging.'

'You said there was a second thing.'

'Oh, it's more of an apology. The night of the murder – I mean I was dead to the world – and God knows how much I drank. But it was only this morning I remembered I'd got up during the night.'

'Did you see something?'

Richard's face went scarlet. 'It's a bit embarrassing because it involves you.'

'Me?'

'For some reason, rather than use my own, I'd thought it a good idea to go wandering about the house looking for a bathroom. I recall going to the top floor, opening a door and there you were, legs akimbo, having a pee. I mean, how were you to know that some old perv would be roaming about, spying on you?'

Colin laughed. He'd forgotten hearing a sound behind him. 'I accept your apology wholeheartedly.'

'That's not all. And this *is* probably nothing. Quickly realising my mistake, I closed the door. But as I did, a door at the far end of the corridor was thrown wide open and out popped Georgie. I mean, she looked a wreck, didn't even notice me at all, and went straight downstairs. But much to my surprise, Kath appeared – a vision in orange – and followed her down. I mean, girls go to the toilet together all the time, don't they? But the odd thing is – and this is where I'm doubting myself – but I could swear that Georgie was dressed in camouflage gear, you know, like in the army? I mean, it was so incongruous, I thought I was hallucinating.'

Day 3

70

'What's he playing at?' Colin cried.

'What's ... who? What are you talking about?' Lee muttered from the bed.

'Bloody Jim. After I told everyone to remain inside, I've just watched him traipse across the garden and take the path down to the shore.'

'What time is it?'

'After eight. It's looking much brighter; the storm's definitely passed.'

'Have you slept?'

'Not really. I dozed in the chair.'

Lee patted the mattress. 'Come back to bed, babes.'

'No, I should go after him. I'll not be long.'

COLIN PICKED his way over the lawn, which had transformed into a muddy quagmire, and entered the woods. All around, roots had been ripped from the earth and trees had toppled, becoming entangled with their neighbours. Elsewhere, branches had been torn from trunks, while saplings lay scattered on the forest floor. It would take years to recover, he thought.

He spotted Jim beyond the treeline, staring out at the dark sea. Though the storm had passed, leaving only the faintest drizzle behind, the waves still frothed furiously. He wondered if it was still too rough for a boat to cross.

As Colin walked towards him, he raised his hand. 'It's calmer. No?'

'Past the worst for sure,' Jim called back.

'Any sign of a boat?'

Jim shook his head.

Colin clambered up to join Jim on the rocks. The first thing he observed were the odd socks Jim was wearing – one yellow, the other black – as though he'd dressed in a hurry. 'I'd like to hear your thoughts on a couple of pieces of evidence I found last night.'

Jim squinted at Colin. 'Yes?'

Colin sat beside him. 'I found Lawrence's Dictaphone.'

'Where?'

'Richard's room. But I'm pretty sure Kath hid it there.' Colin noticed Jim flinch at the mention of her name. 'It all fits.'

Jim blinked. 'You know that girl's far too good for Peter. I mean, *way* too good for him.'

'She's quite something. The fact she almost died trying to retrieve the cassette speaks volumes. Whether to protect herself, or someone else, I'd like to know.'

Jim sighed and turned to face the breeze, letting his greying hair blow free. 'A misguided sense of loyalty?'

'Yes.' Little spots of rain fell, pathetic, compared to what they'd been subjected to the day before, but it was still cold. Colin blew on his hands and shoved them in his coat pockets. He saw that underneath his own jacket, Jim was wearing only a thin t-shirt. 'The Dictaphone's been smashed to pieces, so I can't listen to the cassette. And Lawrence's award is still missing. Until Kath regains consciousness, I'm back to square one.'

'You never interviewed me yesterday. Nor Peter. Why not?' It didn't look as if Jim had slept; his eyes were red and puffy.

The fact was, Jim had not been at the top of his list; Peter was more slippery. 'Things got in the way. But we're talking now, aren't we?'

Jim's gaze returned to the horizon. 'Do you know who attacked you?'

'I'm certain it was Kath.' He noticed Jim flinch again before picking up a stone and attempting to skim it across the water. The surface was too rough, and it bounced once before disappearing.

'You said you had two pieces of evidence to discuss,' said Jim.

'The other evidence, I found in your room.'

Still no eye contact. 'Really? Can I ask what?'

'It begs some questions.'

Getting up from the rock, Jim patted Colin on the shoulder. 'The results of the paternity test by any chance?'

'*You* hid them?'

Jim hung his head and took a deep breath. Crossing his wrists, he presented them to Colin. 'No handcuffs?'

A confession or a theatrical gesture? Colin wasn't sure. 'Why would I need handcuffs?'

'I did it. I killed Lawrence. So, please arrest me. That's what you do, isn't it?' He stood looking at him, arms held out, his expression resigned.

'On what grounds?'

'That I, James Selby, murdered Lawrence Delaney in cold blood by beating him across the head. Then, without attempting to help him, I left the scene of the crime. I'm your man. If you'd come to me earlier, I'd have probably confessed.

And maybe Kath wouldn't be lying half-dead back in that house.'

'Are you sure this is what you want to do? You're not trying to protect someone? Peter? Georgie?'

Jim shook his head. 'Both were fast asleep.' He grabbed Colin's hands. 'Now, arrest me.'

Colin tried to break loose, but Jim's grip was vice-like.

'I'd like to speak with my wife and son, explain what happened. Will you give me that?' His entire body collapsed into Colin's, as if suddenly sucked of all its strength. 'Five minutes,' Jim pleaded. 'That's all I'm asking.'

'You do not have to say anything…' As Colin continued to read Jim his rights, he still couldn't work out why Kath would take such a risk to protect him. She barely knew the man. And although he was Peter's father, was that enough to risk her own life?

71

THE NIGHT BEFORE

At the best of times, Jim could never sleep after drinking alcohol, but all the dancing had left him more over-stimulated than usual. A cup of camomile and a bit of light reading might do the trick. Georgie's snoring wasn't helping either. As soon as they'd entered their room, she had collapsed on the bed fully clothed and within seconds was asleep. Careful not to wake her, Jim pulled a dressing gown over his pyjamas.

He crept downstairs and noticed that the light was on in the kitchen. Through the sliver of the open door, he saw Colin slumped across the table, a bottle of whisky beside him. Tempting as it was to wake him and share a toddy, he decided against it; sitting up half the night chatting wouldn't do him any good. If the new director made it over tomorrow, he needed to be ready for what might be thrown his way. The door to the library lay open. Perfect. Fifteen minutes of reading, and he'd be ready for bed.

Though the fire was in its final stages, the room still glowed with warmth. With the roar of the wind outside and the pelting of the rain against the window, he felt at home. Browsing the shelves, he selected a book on the birdlife of the

Outer Hebrides, full of colourful close-ups – nesting, in flight – along with some detailed descriptions of their life cycles. He stretched out on the leather sofa and pulled a rug over his knees.

At first, the sounds were muffled, and he assumed they were coming from outside. But as he attempted to read, they became more intrusive. He looked around, straining to listen.

Lawrence's voice.

He'd felt sorry for him standing alone by the kitchen door whilst the others danced. It struck him as sad how detached he seemed, how changed. He was practically unrecognisable as the young man he'd once loved: the young man who created excitement every time he walked into a room, every time he stepped onto a stage. How had success turned him into someone so disagreeable, so resentful?

He carried on reading, becoming absorbed in the story of the spoonbill, a bird which had been sighted occasionally in the Hebrides. Absurd looking, with its elegant white body and comical splayed bill, he felt an instant kinship for it. Browsing through more illustrations, the voices from Lawrence's room grew louder.

He put the book to one side and pressed his ear to the adjoining door. At first, he thought Lawrence was alone rehearsing his lines, but, after a few seconds, he realised there was a second male voice. He panicked that it might be Richard, confronting Lawrence about his sacking, but as he listened more carefully, it became clear who the other voice belonged to – Peter. That wasn't so surprising; after all, he and Lawrence had become close on the film-set the previous year. What surprised him was Peter's tone.

He drew closer. Peter's voice was strained, and he was stuttering – something he'd not done since he was a child. He was clearly upset. Jim placed his hand on the door handle, ready to intervene. He then heard Lawrence saying, *Get the fuck out. We're finished.*

Footsteps – presumably Peter's – could be heard disappearing upstairs. A door slammed shut. Silence followed.

Entering the connecting box room, Jim knocked on Lawrence's door, edging it open to find him standing by his bed in a silk kimono, his face red with fury.

'Not you too. What is it with you and your bloody family?'

Jim stepped further into the room. 'What's going on? Was that Peter I heard?'

Ignoring Jim's question, Lawrence pulled clothes from his suitcase and threw them onto

the floor, muttering to himself. He searched under the bed next, then returned to another of his bags.

'Have you lost something?'

Lawrence stopped what he was doing and smiled. 'I've something I want to give you.'

'Me?'

'I just need to find the damned thing.' Without warning, Lawrence picked up the first suitcase and threw it to the other side of the room. 'You know what I'm sick of? Lies. Lies upon lies. Well, no more.' His kimono had become undone, revealing his naked body: a smooth, athletic torso, rich tan head to toe. Jim remembered what it was like to touch his skin, how thrilling and dangerous and unexpected it felt.

But he also recalled the rages Lawrence would fly into. Usually about insignificant things – the temperature of the rehearsal room, someone in the audience coughing – things that he and Georgie managed to ignore. But she'd no time for his tantrums, so it was left to Jim to find the words, talk him down from the edge – but that was thirty years ago. They'd a special bond then – tight – like brothers. 'It *was* Peter's voice I heard?'

Lawrence groaned and faced the wall, his arms outstretched as though trying to push through. 'It's crazy to think I once looked up to you.' He turned, his eyes dazzling in the soft light of the bedside lamp.

Jim didn't take the bait. Whatever he was going through, it would soon pass.

Lawrence tightened the cord of his kimono, double knotting it.

'Maybe I should go. We can do this tomorrow.'

Lawrence's gaze was now fixed on Jim, as though *he* were searching for the young man he once knew. Having examined him, he spoke. 'I'd like you to stay. We should chat.' His words sounded hollow: scripted, rehearsed. 'We should have chatted years ago.'

'I'm not sure this is the...'

'It can't wait any longer.' He was smiling, teeth bared, specks of saliva on his lips.

The subdued light made it difficult to read Lawrence's face – humility or arrogance, Jim couldn't tell. Perhaps that's why the camera loved him. So much ambiguity. 'I'm going to leave.'

'I had a test done.' A shadow flickered across Lawrence's face, before he found his light again. 'At last!' Lawrence yelled, pulling an envelope from a leather folder. 'This is what I was looking for.'

'Sorry. You've lost me. A test?' He retreated to the door, suspicious of Lawrence's intentions. 'Look, I'm sure this can wait till morning.'

Lawrence followed him, was now inches from his face. There was no ambiguity to his expression – self-satisfied, sneering. 'I've had Peter's blood genetically tested against mine. *I'm* his real father, not you.' He handed Jim the envelope. 'Take a look.'

He'd imagined this moment many times, but never like this. Not with Lawrence breathing over him, reeking of wine. The silent understanding between him and Georgie had survived intact for years: decades. He'd known an affair of some description had continued between Georgie and Lawrence after the tour ended in 1963. And he'd known Peter might be a result of that. But it hadn't mattered. Georgie had chosen him. And if he never questioned it, then Peter was *his* son, no one else's.

'But you're welcome to him, he's a lost cause. The boy means nothing to me.' Spittle from Lawrence's words landed on Jim's face. 'I was about to offer him everything, open every door. But he fucked me over. That pathetic relationship with Kath was the last straw.' The performance had come to an end. A middle-aged man, his face full of hate, was all that stood before him.

'What exactly did you say to my son?' asked Jim, folding the envelope and shoving it in his pocket.

'Daddy to the rescue, is it? Now that's what I call a joke. You do know the boy can't stand you?' With the full force of his body, he shoved Jim against the door. 'Like I told *him*, get the fuck out of my room.' He took Jim's throat in both hands and snarled, 'What a waste. Look at the state of you – a sad, old hippy. A fucking loser with no idea how the real world works.'

Jim wrenched Lawrence's wrists away. 'Bringing us here had nothing to do with the play, did it?'

'By Jove, he's got it!' Lawrence said, patting Jim's cheeks.

Jim struggled to push him away.

'You didn't seriously imagine you got this job on merit?' Lawrence laughed. 'Some sixties' has-been whose last job was doing panto in Crewe? Have you any idea how much you disgust me? I actually can't bear to look at you,' he hissed. Without missing a beat, Lawrence struck Jim hard across the face and pushed him to the floor. Turning his back, he tidied the piles of paper strewn across his bed, all the time spewing bile. 'It's Georgie who people feel sorry for, lumbered with a joke of a husband, and it's you they blame for all her past problems. Did you know that? She could have made way better choices for herself. But no, she always stood by sad, old Jim – the embodiment of unrealised potential, dragging her down. Though what does that say about her?' He looked back over his shoulder. 'Christ, you're not still here, are you? Have some self-respect and piss off.'

Dazed, Jim clambered to his feet.

'Fuck me,' Lawrence muttered. 'I'll bet its Georgie who's been going through my things. That bitch needs to learn who's boss around here.'

Jim wasn't sure how the award got into his hands. All he could feel was the weight of it in his grip.

'Oh no, you don't.' Lawrence sneered. 'You're welcome to the boy, but that's mine.'

The dull thud of the smack came from nowhere: a full stop to their conversation. Jim dropped the award, the sound of Lawrence's laughter ringing in his ears; a thin line of blood dripping slowly from his forehead, creating a red rosette on the ivory bedspread.

Jim staggered along the hallway, wrenched open the front door, and ran out into darkness. Despite the storm and the icy cold biting at his skin, he kept running across the lawn, through the trees and towards the sea. He wanted to lose himself; disappear in the dark and never return.

72

Securing Jim to an old chair using cable ties he'd found on a shelf, was easy enough. Seeing someone who, until moments before, had seemed the epitome of kindness, shackled in a dusty basement, sat less well with him.

'He supplied Georgie with heroin,' Jim blurted out, as Colin checked the ties around his wrists. 'Lured her into his bed, knowing how sick she was.'

'This is only until the police arrive.' Colin checked the ties one last time.

'Like he was taking my rejection of him out on her,' Jim continued, 'but that wasn't the case. I just loved Georgie more.'

Colin smiled and nodded. People, after they confessed, often chatted aimlessly, sharing any random thought in their head. 'I'll check in on you regularly, but for now you can't leave the basement. And I promise I'll give you a moment with Georgie and Peter.'

'I should have come to you straight away. It was cowardly to say nothing. I couldn't believe I was someone who could do that.'

Colin stood back, considering the heap of a man before him. Was this really the same person who'd rushed to help him with Kath's rescue? 'But why?' Colin asked. 'You've so much to lose. Why, after all this time?'

He shrugged. 'It wasn't him trying to humiliate me; people in the industry have told me for years how he badmouthed me. Sure, the idea he could still disrespect Georgie troubled me greatly. No, it was his attitude to Peter. Cruel. Unnecessary. Unforgivable.'

Colin paused outside the door of Lawrence's room. Entombed inside was a lifetime of secrets and betrayals. Dismantling the stacked barrier of chairs, he opened the door. The same dreadful smell greeted him. In the movies or on TV, crime scenes often appeared staged, grizzly tableaux arranged for maximum impact. This was no different, it just happened to feature one of the most famous actors in the world.

What they didn't show on TV – what the cameras didn't linger on – were the details. The complex patterns of blood spatter, the nuances of the damage a person could inflict on flesh and bones. And what it failed to communicate was the stench of death. There was no doubt the body was beginning to decompose. A scent was developing: putrid, heavy, all-encompassing.

Standing in the centre of the room, absorbing as much detail as possible, he was satisfied he'd made a note of everything important. There was nothing more to add.

Lifting the sheet, he studied Lawrence's body once again. The evidence of violence never ceased to shock: the gaping head wound, the vast amount of dark, sticky blood, the lumps of brain and skull scattered on the bedcover. There was no doubt. The attack had been brutal.

He reflected on Jim's explanation of how he'd entered the room; the spot he was standing when talking to Lawrence, where and how he'd hit him, the level of force, how he'd fallen back. Staring at the crushed skull, he knew for certain – none of it added up.

73

Colin knocked once and listened as a chair was scraped across the floor and the key turned. The door cracked open, and Lee's anxious face appeared. Colin hurried inside and closed the door behind them.

'What's going on?' Lee asked.

'There's a boat crossing. I saw it from downstairs. I reckon it should be here in about fifteen minutes.'

'We should pack.' Lee threw a suitcase on the bed. 'Give me a hand.'

'Listen, that can wait. I need you to do something first.' If Colin's instinct were correct, Lee could now be fully trusted. 'Stand outside the basement. Make sure no one enters or leaves.'

'Any particular reason?'

'I'm holding Jim down there.' He could see Lee's face registering the meaning of his words. 'There's more I need to figure out. I'll be ten minutes tops.'

'Will you be safe?' Lee took his hand.

Colin kissed him on the lips. 'As ever.'

. . .

GEORGIE WAS SITTING with her feet up on a sofa in the bay window when he entered. A couple of suitcases, already packed, sat on the bed. 'I see there's a boat's coming.' She pointed out to sea, as though she'd radioed it in herself.

Colin scanned the room.

'Is everything OK?' Her tone seemed genuinely concerned.

'May I?'

'Of course.' She drew her legs back to allow him to sit at the other end of the sofa.

They both stared out the window. Directly above Lawrence's, the room had a perfect view of the garden and the sea beyond. A shaft of sunlight cut through the clouds, making the waves shimmer and the small grey dot heading towards them sparkle.

'Not long now.' Colin observed her as she smoothed out the wrinkles from her silk skirt, adjusting her legs. The light caught its blue and green peacock feather pattern. Dazzling.

'This has been a terrible ordeal for my family.'

Colin sensed her draw breath. 'I'm glad I caught you alone.' He lowered his voice, as if he'd a secret to share. 'I need to tell you something. Is that alright?'

'That depends on what it is.'

He felt about in his pocket, first pulling out the little quartz pebble he'd picked up from the beach when Lee arrived, before finding his pen. He opened his notebook. 'Some details about the case.' Scanning through his notes, he was aware of her watching him. 'It won't take long. You sure you don't mind?' he asked. 'Five minutes.'

Georgie switched her focus to the boat making its way towards them. 'Is that wise? To be sharing details about the case with me?'

'Just a few thoughts I have.'

'Involving me?' Her attention returned to him. At that

moment, the sun disappeared and the room fell dark, the furniture and the walls growing heavy and morose.

'Yes.'

'Did you ever check the rest of the island?' she asked. 'Someone could so easily have arrived before us, hidden themselves, planned all of it.'

'No one has been here but us.' As if to emphasise this, he drew a box around what he'd previously written: FOCUS ON THE FAMILY.

She seemed irritated by his statement. 'Your little investigation hasn't gone well though, has it, Colin? Surely, it'll need to start again.'

'I'll pass on the evidence. But yes, the local force will start from scratch.'

She rose, offered him a cigarette – which he declined – before lighting one herself. Cracking open one of the sash windows, she blew a stream of smoke outside.

'I'm confident that what I've discovered will get them off to a good start.'

She glared at him, stubbed out her cigarette impatiently and closed the window. 'The boat will be here soon.' She gestured towards her suitcases.

It was the politest *get lost* he'd ever received. 'One more minute?'

'Your investigation's dead in the water. In five minutes, you'll no longer be in charge.' She crossed the room and opened the door. 'I'll follow you downstairs shortly.'

'I have the results of the paternity test.' He unfolded the envelope he'd tucked in the last page of his notebook.

She quickly closed the door back over. 'That's a family matter. Private.'

'Except that Lawrence, who's Peter's biological father, is dead.' He approached her. 'It's the first thing the police will investigate. Surely you see how incriminating it is? Me finding Lawrence's test hidden in your room?'

She clearly hadn't known: no amount of acting could disguise the shock of him revealing this fact.

'Can you give me my cigarettes?' She sat on the edge of the bed and lit another cigarette. She took several draws before looking at him. 'You understand what love is, don't you? I can see you do. Your face lights up whenever Lee steps into a room. But you've been together, what, a year?'

'Not even that. Seven months since we met.'

'I met Jim thirty-odd years ago and fell in love with him almost immediately – well, give or take a few stops and starts. My face might not light up every time he walks into a room, but I still love him with every fibre of my body. I'm not sure he even believes that. But it's the truth. He's honest, good, caring, all you'd want in a person.'

'Yet?' The mask hadn't fully slipped. But layers were peeling away. Her expression had become softer, her face more relaxed, as though she was taking a breath between acts.

'For a time, Lawrence was an issue. I can't say there wasn't a connection, but I didn't love him. Not like I loved Jim.' The pain in her eyes was now clear. She'd made a mistake and had carried the consequences all those years. 'Jim was never supposed to know.'

'Georgie.' Colin sat beside her. 'He did know. Lawrence taunted him about it, there was a scuffle, and he hit him over the head. Your husband has confessed to murdering him.'

As the words spilled from his mouth, Georgie's body fell forward, her face staring at the floor, her arms hugging her body. A cry grew from deep inside her, rising to a shriek. 'No!'

'I've detained him in the basement. The case is closed. Unless there's something you need to tell me. Is there? Georgie?'

Her entire body was now shaking. She grabbed Colin's hand, gripping him so tightly it felt like her rings could pierce his skin. 'It wasn't Jim. How could my beautiful husband ever do something like that?' A final breath was taken, the delivery of the line considered and decided upon. 'It was me,' she said. 'But you already know that, don't you?'

74

_____

THE NIGHT BEFORE

Georgie had woken to find herself alone in the room. Still fully clothed, she knew she couldn't have been asleep that long. Even so, it was unusual for Jim to get up during the night without telling her. If he was going to the bathroom, he'd whisper, *I'm just going for a pee*, waking her in the process.

She went to the bathroom and took a long drink of water from the cold tap; her mouth was bone-dry, and her head throbbed from too much champagne. Refreshed, she crept downstairs, hoping not to disturb anyone. She fully expected to find Jim in the kitchen: enjoying a nightcap or chatting away to someone, continuing the party. Now she was up, joining in seemed like a good option.

Passing Lawrence's door, she noticed it was shut; hopefully asleep and not causing further mayhem. In the kitchen, she found Colin sprawled across the table asleep, a bottle of whisky by his hand, soft classical music playing from the radio. He came across as a sweet boy, not intimidated in the least by so many extroverts. But what must he think of them? She was interested to discover. But that could wait till tomorrow. They'd plenty time. She closed the door and left him to sleep.

Jim often liked to read late into the night. She'd check the library. As she approached, sounds coming from Lawrence's room distracted her. Drawing closer, familiar voices emerged.

She'd rarely heard Jim raise his voice. Even when they argued, he'd stay calm, his voice low and measured, never reacting to provocation. It drove her mad, made her scream even louder, more determined to get a reaction from him. But he always retained his composure. Yet there he was, in Lawrence's room, one o'clock in the morning, having a heated argument.

Her blood ran cold. After their meeting in London, discovering the test results in his room, she knew Lawrence had brought them together for one reason only. She'd done everything in her power to avoid taking the part. But once both Jim and Peter had signed contracts, she felt compelled to be there. She had no choice. If she knew one thing about Lawrence – and she knew far too much – it was that he couldn't be trusted. She pressed her ear against the door, hoping against hope she was wrong.

The night of Peter's conception, as she'd surrendered to the drugs, engulfed by their warm embrace, he'd whispered, 'Close your eyes – I'll take care of you.' In that moment, as his grip tightened around her body, a sense of relief overwhelmed her. She'd decided she could live without the type of care he offered. Though she'd vowed it many times before, she knew this was the last time. She no longer needed him. Nor the drugs. 'You make me a better man,' were the last words she remembered him saying. And, as she drifted from reality, she thought *that's the stupidest thing I've ever heard.*

As footsteps came careering towards the door, she'd enough time to dive into the library without being seen. From there, she saw Jim run out the front door, cross the lawn and disappear into the darkness, his dressing gown flapping in the wind like a ragged bird about to take flight.

Lawrence was pushing himself up off the bed when she entered. A thin line of blood rolling down his forehead, he smirked. 'Not you too. Come to finish me off?'

'What the hell have you said to Jim?'

'A few home truths. Someone had to.'

'About Peter?'

He smirked.

'Why are you doing this?'

'I'm Lawrence Delaney. I can do what the fuck I want.'

'Are you even thinking about Peter? Do you care about him at all?'

Lawrence shrugged, 'I'm in no hurry to claim him as my own. The boy's a bore. His mother on the other hand, she could teach him a thing or two.' As he removed his dressing-gown, expecting her to perform as she'd done in the past, he boasted about a night out In London with Kath and Peter – how a threesome was on the cards. 'It didn't happen that time, but it might happen yet. Now, that might really fuck him up; give him some character.'

As soon as he turned his back, Georgie grabbed the blood-stained award that lay on the floor and swung it at his head. Not once, or twice, but three times.

THE NEXT THING SHE KNEW, Kath was gripping her wrist.

'Georgie, listen to me.' She gently steered her towards the door. 'I'm going to handle things, but you need to do exactly what I say. Do you understand?'

She remembered nodding, but what happened next was a confusing blur: sitting in the tiniest of bathrooms with Kath rubbing her hands under the tap, blood running down the plughole; standing in her bedroom as Kath helped her out of an old army waterproof, her bloodstained clothes being taken away; Kath picking up Jim's new cagoule, saying she needed to replace the one she was wearing, that things would be better in the morning.

She did everything as instructed. The consummate performer.

75

Lee ran up the stairs, shouting Colin's name.

'I'm in here,' he called back. 'With Georgie.'

Lee barged into the bedroom. 'Jim's broken out of the basement – he's making a run for it. I couldn't stop him.'

'What?' Georgie cried, rushing to her feet.

Colin grabbed her arm. 'Stay here.' Turning to Lee, he asked, 'Where did he go?'

'He was heading for the cliffs.'

'I have to speak to him,' Georgie insisted, wriggling free from Colin's grip.

'No way.' He scanned the room, considering how best to restrain her. 'Follow me.' He guided her towards the bathroom. 'Do not move from here.'

'You don't understand,' Georgie yelled, 'he'll only listen to me.'

'You're the last person he needs right now. Jim still thinks he killed Lawrence, so he's capable of anything. Do you want that on your conscience, too?' He slammed the door shut.

'What the hell's going on?' Lee's face was a mixture of anxiety and confusion. 'I thought Jim had killed Lawrence.'

Colin shook his head. 'Georgie's confessed; I've no time to

explain. Don't let her out – under any circumstances. Not even if she screams the place down. Not even if the building's on fire. Am I clear?'

OUTSIDE, the sun was now breaking through the clouds. However, the sea still churned with a memory of the storm, surging waves giving way to deep swells. Despite this, the boat had managed to moor. A different skipper, older, with a kinder face, listened as Colin quickly explained the situation and what was required. Without hesitation, he radioed the information in.

'We were worried when we couldn't get through on the phone, so I set off as soon as it was safe,' the skipper explained, holding his handset, waiting for a reply. 'We knew the storm would be bad, but no one was prepared for what hit – it's ripped a path through the coast north and south of here – it's absolute chaos.'

Colin nodded at the radio. 'What are they saying?' he asked.

'They've scrambled a helicopter; it'll be with us in thirty minutes tops.'

COLIN RAN along the beach and climbed over the jagged rocks. He'd made mistakes and couldn't make any more. He'd been right about Kath protecting someone but had jumped to the most obvious of conclusions; in doing so, he'd misunderstood her. The ferocity of the attack had also led him to imagine that only someone young and fit like Peter could inflict such injuries. The fact that someone so lacking in empathy was not the killer still seemed hard to believe. That the blows had been dealt by Georgie proved how far ordinary people could go when pushed to the extreme. The tiny cassette in his pocket, containing Lawrence's conversations, would surely testify to that.

Scaling the rocks, he stopped to take breath. The next section looked even more precarious, but in the distance below, he could see waves breaking around a lone figure. Jim. He was staring out at the ocean, apparently oblivious to the danger he was in. Colin shouted his name, but there was no response.

To reach him, he had to continue upwards across razor sharp rocks. He winced in pain as a thousand tiny daggers cut his palms. Jim was now diagonally below him – perched on rocks – facing the full force of the sea. How he'd got there without breaking his neck, Colin couldn't fathom. He watched him take a step forward.

'No!'

Surprised, Jim looked round.

Even with his boots on, climbing down the rocks was high risk. Each step needed to be considered, taken slowly. Colin kept his eyes on the sea thirty feet below; if he fell, he'd be dashed against the rocks for certain. As he drew level with Jim, a huge wave pounded the rock-shelf which separated them. Crossing directly to him would be impossible, but he could tell from Jim's body language that time was of the essence.

'It wasn't you,' he shouted, as the sea retreated, providing a moment of calm.

Jim's face didn't change expression.

Having made his choice, Colin knew he had seconds, minutes at most, to convince him otherwise. 'Look at me, Jim.' Blood oozed from the cuts to his hands as he clung to the rocks. 'Give me a minute to explain.'

'I could almost live with the guilt of killing Lawrence, but after seeing Kath…' Jim's attention drifted back out to sea, the crash of waves carrying his words away.

Colin edged around the back of the rock-ledge. 'You hit

Lawrence *once*. But he was killed by multiple blows to the head – his skull was smashed in.' Around them the ocean boomed, intent on drowning out his words. 'I can prove you didn't kill Lawrence.' He prayed Jim had heard this.

There was a moment of respite, as the wind and the sea once more receded.

Jim stepped closer to the edge, where waves licked the tip of a rock. 'If it wasn't me, then who was it?'

Closing in, Colin remembered the first evening playing poker with Jim and Georgie. How in tune they seemed – obviously in love, but without the need to make a display of it. At the time, he wondered if that would be him and Lee in thirty years. 'This can be sorted.' He jumped down off the rock-face and was now within touching distance of Jim.

'How?' Jim shouted. 'You've the cassette. Like you said, everything's on it. No one should have to take the blame for me. Whatever happened, I struck the first blow.'

'Georgie killed him.' Colin stepped closer, unsure if it was the right thing to say. 'She's going to need your help.' The harsh sound of a helicopter passing overheard cut through the clamour surrounding them, forcing them both to look up. 'That's for Kath. She's going to be well looked after. Come on Jim, this isn't the right solution.'

Jim took several quick steps away from Colin. He was now teetering on the very edge of the cliff. 'Georgie's character in *Eros* is destroyed by this damaged youth. The violence is all played off stage. We only hear about it; how he lures her with promises, only to turn on her when she least expects it. Her only crime is trying to protect others. No one else could have played that part. Only someone who cared, understood deeply.' Jim took a breath and stared down into the abyss.

Colin fumbled in his pocket, producing the cassette. 'Jim, no one will ever know without this. If I make it disappear, there's no evidence it was Georgie.'

Jim stared at Colin's hand. His mind was considering all the possibilities. But Colin knew he was running out of time. 'You'd do that?'

Nodding, Colin held up the cassette, his bloodied hand gripping on tightly. 'Step back. If you do, I'll throw this away. It'll be gone forever.'

Jim studied Colin's face. 'Throw it away first. Then, I'll decide.'

'I can't do that. Not till you promise to step back.'

'If you protect Georgie, I'll promise anything.'

Colin launched it into the air. They both watched it ascend, glinting in the sun, before disappearing below the surf. 'There. Now, will you step back?'

76

When Colin arrived back at the house, Jim securely in his grip, the ambulance crew were carefully placing Kath – laid out on a stretcher – into the helicopter. Overseeing the operation was Richard in a beret, sunglasses, and scarf, looking every part the West End director. He called to Colin, 'She woke and asked me to stay with her. I assume I'm allowed?'

Colin glanced over at the ambulance crew, who nodded.

Richard eyed Jim, whose head was bowed. 'Is everything OK?'

Colin walked over to join him. 'It will be.' Kath's eyes flickered open, searching for something tangible to hold onto. 'It's good to have you back,' Colin whispered.

Fearful, her eyes attempted to connect with his, but were unfocused, disconnected. Struggling to reach out, she grazed the tip of her fingers against his arm. 'Sorry.' The word was distant, shallow, only meant for him. He'd no time to respond as the crew informed him to step aside and started to organise themselves for take off.

Buckling himself in, Richard blew Colin a kiss. 'See you on the other side.'

. . .

HAVING SECURED Jim in the basement for the second time, there was one last thing Colin needed to do. From the hallway, he called out, 'Peter?' No reply. He checked the downstairs rooms, but they were empty. Heading upstairs, he bounded up two steps at a time. All was quiet on the top landing. He looked in on Lee. 'Anything I need to know?'

Lee approached him. 'They've taken Kath in the helicopter. Did you see?'

'Briefly. And she's awake, thank God.'

'Georgie's not said a word,' Lee whispered, pointing at the bathroom door. 'Should we let her out?'

'Not yet.'

He now had two confessions. Hopefully, there wouldn't be a third. On the way back to the house, it occurred to him that Peter might be responsible after all – that both parents, in desperation – could very well be attempting to take the blame.

'What's going on?' Lee asked. 'Or is it still developing?'

Colin kissed him. 'Give me five minutes. I should know everything by then.'

He walked along the corridor, throwing open each door, scanning inside. The rooms were empty, but he hadn't yet reached Peter's at the end. 'Peter?' he called again. Sounds of scraping, heavy breathing, were coming from his room.

Could he have been right all along?

The door was closed, but there was definite movement within. He edged the door open, half-expecting the noise to stop, but it continued. The door swung wide.

Peter stood in front of him, a huge suitcase in each hand. 'You know I asked Kath to marry me?' A crazed grin was stretched across his face.

Colin entered the room, checking for any potential

surprises. 'What did she say?' he asked, half-looking at him, half not.

'That's when the ambulance crew arrived, so I'll have to wait for my answer. But she smiled. I think that's a good sign, wouldn't you say?'

Phew! No need to fake congratulations! 'It was good to see her eyes open.'

Peter stepped into the corridor. 'By the way, where is everyone?' His mood seemed bright, as though all his problems had been lifted. Perhaps this was his normal state, rather than the petulant child he'd been playing since arriving.

'Who've you spoken to?' Colin asked.

'Just Richard. But he's gone with Kath. First time in a helicopter. Like a little kid, so he was.' Peter checked the room to ensure he'd missed nothing. 'And I've packed Kath's stuff, too.' He looked at him. 'So, are we leaving?'

'Soon.'

'Good. Where are mum and dad?' he asked.

The sound of a second helicopter could be heard approaching. 'They're around,' Colin replied, still searching Peter's face for clues. He watched him stroll over to the stair window and gaze out to sea.

'They're finally coming to rescue us. Amazing, isn't it? Then they can work out who killed Lawrence. They'll find out, won't they?'

After all that, Lee was right, the guy hadn't a clue. 'Why don't you go outside? I'll follow in a minute or two.' Someone else could explain to him. For now, he was done.

THE POLICE HELICOPTER came into full view as he was about to head downstairs, descending on the lawn like a second storm. He rushed outside as it touched down, the force of the updraught chilling him. He could see three officers inside – one CSI, a detective and a PC.

As the blades stopped, the detective, early forties, slight paunch, stepped from the helicopter, meeting Colin halfway; the PC, half the detective's age, more hawk-like, right behind. After exchanging pleasantries, he filled them in on the details of Lawrence's death, Kath's injury, and the two confessions. The CSI stood to the side, listening attentively.

'So, there's one body downstairs and another with head injuries being flown to the mainland?' the detective asked, as the PC, precise, keen, jotted down notes. 'Looks like you've taken a battering, too.'

'I'm fine. It's Lawrence Delaney – yes, the Hollywood actor – who's dead, and Kathryn O'Hare was badly injured when the barn collapsed. I believe she's an accessory to the murder.'

'You mentioned there'd been a confession.'

'Two, in fact.'

Colin continued with the details – explaining about Jim's mental state, the camouflaged waterproof with blood on it he had in his room – when first Peter, then Georgie appeared, accompanied by Lee. Trailing a suitcase behind her, she seemed calm and collected, as though heading home after an exhausting tour. Colin recognised the look, however. Head held slightly too high, unable to make eye contact, just holding it together. How long she'd stay in denial was anyone's guess. She said nothing, hardly acknowledged their presence. Placing her suitcase on the ground, she perched on top, taking in the view.

'You'll go in the helicopter,' the detective explained to her, glancing over at Colin, who shrugged at her lack of response.

'Mum?' Peter said. 'Did you hear? They're flying you back to the mainland.'

Georgie finally shook her head. 'I need to see your father.' She got up, gazing around, before Lee helped her sit back down.

Peter knelt in front of her, taking her hands in his. Unable to get her to look directly at him, he appealed to the others.

'Will someone tell me what's going on? It's like she's been drugged.'

The PC, face full of purpose, emerged from the house with Jim, whose head hung low. Escorting him across the lawn, everyone focused on their slow, steady steps. Only Peter, suddenly alert to what might be happening, scrambled about, trying to elicit answers. 'Why's he handcuffed my dad? Mum? Mum?'

'Georgie?' Jim said, as he got closer. 'Everything will be fine. I promise.'

'Dad?' Peter asked, beginning to understand what might be unfolding. 'You didn't, did you?' He tried to grab onto his father, but the PC intervened and belted Jim securely into a seat on the helicopter.

'If I can ask you to come with me?' the detective said to Georgie, nodding towards the helicopter.

She ignored the instruction and remained seated.

'Georgie,' Colin said. 'You need to go with him.'

As the detective guided her into the helicopter, she turned to Colin and whispered, 'I need you to tell my son the truth – that Lawrence is his father. And that what I did, I did for him; to keep him safe. He won't understand at first, but it was the right thing to do.'

C olin sat at the prow of the boat, watching it cut through the dark waves. The sun broke through the clouds, turning the sea a clear, emerald green. For the briefest moment, he could have sworn he spotted Lawrence's award gleaming on the seabed, but the boat carried on, the opportunity lost.

On the horizon, any hint of blue sky had been replaced by grey, where another storm was gathering. PC McIntosh was accompanying Lee, Peter and him back to the mainland. From there, they would be driven north to Inverness to join Jim and Georgie at the police headquarters for questioning. As they prepared to leave the island, another helicopter arrived, this time with more forensics, who fell on the house like seagulls after a picnic. They'd have their work cut out Colin had thought. It was galling that, within seconds, one appeared holding a huge orange cagoule wrapped around a bloodied dress. 'I found it in a tool shed,' he heard him say.

With Peter deep in conversation with Lee, Colin took a moment for himself. The preceding forty-eight hours had been a nightmare. Georgie's final words were playing on his mind. What jury would see it from her point of view? And

Jim: was he really so naïve to imagine everything would be fine? As for Kath, she'd face charges for certain, all for trying her best to protect Georgie. It didn't seem right.

The water became choppier as they reached the open sea, but the skipper shouted to hold on tight and not to lean over the side. PC McIntosh, his face a sickly green, clung to his seat, desperate to avoid hurtling or hurling overboard, whichever came first.

Like an old seadog, Lee stepped confidently down the centre of the boat and sat beside Colin. He gave him a peck on the cheek, asking, 'You OK, babe?'

He nodded. Placing his hand in his pocket, he felt the familiar shape of the cassette. When Jim threatened to jump, Colin's fingers had found the pebble in his pocket. About the same size as the cassette, Jim hadn't noticed him swap it. So, when he'd thrown the pebble into the water, an assumption was made, and Jim hadn't jumped.

With the evidence on the tape, justice could be done. 'Here, I've something for you,' he called over to PC McIntosh, who staggered over to check what Colin was holding. 'This will help your enquiries.'

Peter, caught up in his own thoughts, barely blinked. Instead, he remained staring in the direction of the mainland.

'You'll never guess what boy wonder over there was asking me.' Lee gripped his arm, keeping his voice low.

'You'll have to tell me,' Colin laughed. 'I've had my fill of guessing games for a while.'

'He was wanting my opinion on Lawrence's estate – whether I knew if there'd be any other claims on it – from relatives. Can you believe that?'

'He's full of surprises that one. Barely blinked when I told him Lawrence was his father. He might not be a murderer, but you wouldn't bet against him becoming one.'

'So, Jim and Georgie – both of them are guilty?' Lee edged closer.

'Kind of.'

He lowered his voice even further. 'Did they plan it?'

'I'll fill you in later,' Colin replied, snuggling into Lee's arms, catching PC McIntosh's curious look. 'Jim thought he'd killed him. Georgie struck the fatal blows.'

'All to protect Peter?'

Colin shook his head. 'Not exactly: each other as much as anything. Misguided, though. A lifetime spent together. Sharing, loving. Yet in the end, they let their secrets destroy them.'

'But where does Kath fit in?'

'She simply got it into her head she could help.' He smelt the freshness of Lee's hair and the sea spray blending with its aroma. 'Come here, Mr Murphy.'

Lee wrapped his arms around Colin. 'You know the police officer's looking?'

Colin nodded. 'Oh, I know. Clocked us as soon as we got on the boat. But don't worry, he'll get over it.'

COMING SOON

The Look of Death, **Book 2** in the **Colin Buxton Series**, is available for pre-order ahead of publication in **2023**.

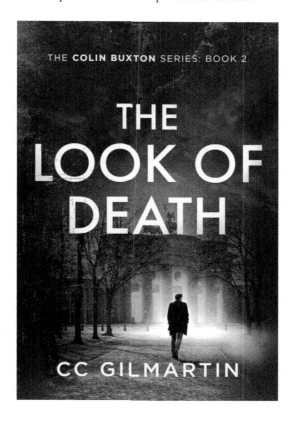

ABOUT CC GILMARTIN

We're Chris Deans and Colin Thomas Begg, and together we write as CC Gilmartin.

If you'd like to know more about our books, please visit www.ccgilmartin.com and join the **CC Gilmartin Readers' Club** for **FREE**. As a member, you'll receive your **FREE** digital copy of *In the Stillness*, the **Colin Buxton Series Prequel**, plus regular updates on the progress of the series, as well as our other projects.

We love to hear from our readers. To contact us directly, email: contact@ccgilmartin.com

You can also follow us on social media:

facebook.com / CCGilmartin

twitter.com / CC_Gilmartin

instagram.com / CCGilmartin

ACKNOWLEDGMENTS

A huge thanks to the following people for their expertise and input: copy editor Shelley Routledge; proof reader Mary Torjussen at Jericho Writers; designer Stuart Bache at Books Uncovered; and website designer Stuart Grant at Digital Authors Toolkit.

Special thanks to the **CC Gilmartin Readers' Club** for their support - especially our ARC Team - and to Heather Deans, Hellen Gillies and Michele Deans for their feedback.

Printed in Great Britain
by Amazon

14507786R00236